KU-295-253

DEATH IN WHITE PYJAMAS

&

DEATH KNOWS NO CALENDAR

JOHN BUDE

with an introduction by
MARTIN EDWARDS

This edition published 2020 by
The British Library
96 Euston Road
London NW1 2DB

Death Knows No Calendar and *Death in White Pyjamas* were originally
published in 1942 and 1944 respectively by Cassell & Co. Ltd, London.

Introduction copyright © Martin Edwards, 2020
Death Knows No Calendar copyright © 1942 The Estate of John Bude
Death in White Pyjamas copyright © 1944 The Estate of John Bude

Cataloguing in Publication Data
A catalogue record for this book is available from the British Library

ISBN 978 0 7123 5316 8
eISBN 978 0 7123 6741 7

Front cover image © NRM / Pictorial Collection /
Science & Society Picture Library

Typeset by Tetragon, London
Printed in England by TJ International, Padstow, Cornwall

CONTENTS

INTRODUCTION

John Bude is a once-forgotten author whose crime fiction has enjoyed a remarkable revival thanks to its reappearance under the imprint of the British Library Crime Classics. He returns again to the series by popular demand. This volume comprises two of his rarest books, the original editions of which have proved almost impossible for twenty-first century collectors to obtain, other than very occasionally, at sky-high prices.

Both of these novels were written during the Second World War and in each of them Bude's tone was conspicuously light-hearted. One of his strengths was a willingness to be a writer who adjusted his style from time to time. His early crime novels drew much of their appeal from attractive and nicely evoked regional settings (Cornwall, the Lake District, the Sussex Downs, Cheltenham) and in the post-war era he added a little glamour by venturing across the channel in books such as *Murder in Montparnasse*, *Death on the Riviera*, and *A Telegram from Le Touquet*. He tackled various different kinds of story, including tales about amateur detection, police procedurals and even a serial killer mystery, *A Twist of the Rope*, his penultimate novel. During the 1940s, his main priority was to keep up the spirits of readers seeking a little comfort and relaxation during the hardest of times.

Death in White Pyjamas was first published in 1944 in an era of rationing and austerity. Bude's enthusiasm for the theatre shines through. He satirizes the theatrical world, but in a gently amused and affectionate way. In real life, he indulged his taste for amateur dramatics while teaching in Letchworth, and during the 1920s he worked as stage manager with the Lena Ashwell Players. Ashwell, a colourful and dynamic figure who had once been a suffragette, was an actor, theatre manager and producer and the troupe performed at venues around the country. Before and after his marriage in 1933, Bude was a keen participant in local dramatic groups. After becoming a full-time author he continued to produce plays on behalf of charities in his spare time.

The novel also offers a country house mystery of the type so often associated with traditional British detective fiction. The country house in question belongs to the wealthy Sam Richardson, and a group of actors have gathered together with their producer Basil Barnes and a playwright whose star is rising on the drama scene. There is rivalry between three of the female performers, Clara, Angela and Deirdre, and matters come to a head when Deirdre is found murdered in the grounds of the house. Mysteriously, she is wearing white pyjamas...

Death Knows no Calendar originally appeared in 1942. It's a non-series novel, and here the principal detective work is conducted by an amateur sleuth, Major Tom Boddy. At the start of the book, he is one of a number of people in Beckwood to receive an invitation to attend an event organized by John and Lydia Arundel. Major Boddy is one of a number of Lydia's male admirers in the neighbourhood. Rich, glamorous and outspoken, she is a successful artist. She and her husband, who spends a lot of time researching a novel but never seems to get much writing done, "had much in common – an easy morality, quick wits, imagination..." Soon it becomes clear that Lydia is one of those characters so familiar to whodunit fans – someone whom several people might have good reason to murder.

Lydia does indeed die – but in circumstances which at first seem to indicate suicide. Presented with a classic "locked-room scenario", the police are unable to see *how* she could have been killed by a third party. Boddy, however, includes among his passions a love of detective fiction: "he had saturated himself in this bastard form of literature and probably retained in his head more ingenious murder methods than any living man." With the aid of his trusty sidekick, Syd Gammon, he conducts an extensive investigation, and it is that interest in the ingenious modus operandi. which ultimately enables him to solve the puzzle.

The most attractive feature of this novel is the inclusion of not one but two cunningly contrived versions of the "impossible" mystery. Bude did not specialize in this type of mystery in the manner of, say, Anthony Wynne or John Dickson Carr, two other writers whose work has been republished in the Crime Classics series; indeed his only other foray into the "locked room" sub-genre was in *Death on Paper* (1940). The key puzzle here concerns the shooting of Lydia in a locked studio. If it was indeed murder, how was it committed? The solution is technical and elaborate, and calls for the inclusion in the final chapter of a helpful explanatory diagram of the kind sometimes also employed by Freeman Wills Crofts and Miles Burton, two other authors represented in the British Library series. The second and subordinate riddle deals with the disappearance of a car from a stretch of fenced road with no apparent exits. The premise is reminiscent of that in "The Phantom Motor Car", a short story by the American Jacques Futrelle and featuring his formidable Great Detective "The Thinking Machine", but Bude's solution is different.

John Bude was a pen-name. It concealed the identity of Ernest Carpenter Elmore (1901–1957), who was born in Maidstone, Kent, and died suddenly in Sussex a few years after helping to secure the foundation and early growth of the Crime Writers' Association. The CWA thrives to this day, an organization with an international reach and an ever-expanding membership which owes a debt of gratitude to pioneers such as Elmore, who together with the CWA's founder, John Creasey, recognized the need for a professional members' association for crime writers.

MARTIN EDWARDS
www.martinedwardsbooks.com

DEATH IN
WHITE PYJAMAS

To
JOAN
at
Merriehills

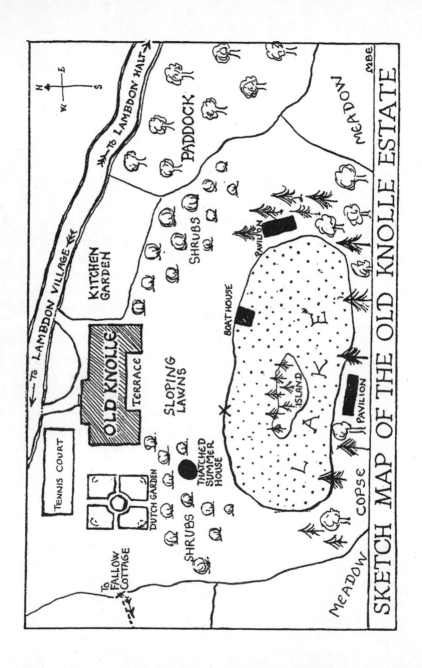

SKETCH MAP OF THE OLD KNOLLE ESTATE

CHAPTER I

Basil Buys a Cottage

I

MANY PEOPLE WHO HAVE A GENUINE LIKING FOR THE MORE INTEL-lectual type of play will doubtless recall Sam Richardson's efforts to provide such plays for them at a price suited to their pocket. It is, of course, a notorious fact that intelligent theatre-goers have no money and moneyed theatre-goers have no intelligence. So a stall at the Beaumont Theatre cost no more than three-and-sixpence, tax included, and the seats were suitably hard.

The Beaumont was not a West End theatre. It was tucked away between a third-rate café and a second-hand shop in Bowman's Place, which is somewhere between the groves of Ladbroke and Westbourne. From the outside it looked like a chapel on to which had been grafted the foyer of an un-prosperous cinema. This was a little deceptive, for inside it really was a theatre, with excellent acoustics, ample seating-room and a licensed bar. But for these facts, Sam Richardson wouldn't have put his money into it.

Like all progressive concerns it had started off in a blaze of publicity, pretty nearly dropped dead after the novelty had worn off, and had provided a devil of a headache for the management. Then it had not run true to type. Sam Richardson not only had money—he had faith. He *knew* there was a public for his theatre; shy, perhaps, but there to be harvested if one had patience and tenacity. Sam had both, and half-way through the first winter season, the pilgrims began to roll up. His faith had not let him down, and when the season came to an end in April he had not only put the Beaumont on the theatrical map, but shown a credit balance in the box-office.

Sam, like so many promoters of stage entertainment, knew absolutely nothing about the theatre. He knew a lot about biscuits because he'd spent a lifetime making a cool million out of them. But one day he had suddenly sickened of Petit Beurre, Butter Fingers and Thin Lunch, and turned his back on them for ever. He'd sold his factory and looked around for fresh stamping-grounds.

Then at somebody's party in Tite Street he met Basil Barnes, and his cultural aspirations were given direction.

2

They were poles apart: in looks, character, ideas, ambitions, everything. Where Sam was short, fat, bald and benign, Basil was tall, slender, sleek-haired and slightly sinister. Sam, apart from business in all its aspects, was a child. His simple faith in everybody was delightful, if expensive; for he could never listen to a hard-up story without putting his hand in his pocket. If Basil put his hand in his pocket you expected him to produce a revolver. Actually, he produced plays.

This was the immediate link between them. Sam, at that moment, was itching to get at least one foot into the artistic life of London, and Basil was itching to get at least two hands on some of Sam's money. They paired off perfectly. There and then Basil suggested that the financier should come and "have one" at his flat in Byron Crescent, off Sloane Square.

"The fact of the matter is, Mr. Richardson, I think we could do with each other. You've never had any experience of play promoting?"

"Never."

"Well, that's all to the good. You'll start without any prejudices."

And in the Byron Crescent flat Basil Barnes more or less talked Sam Richardson into the Beaumont Theatre.

"Producing is really a matter of personality," he explained. "It's a power to electrify, to stimulate and inspire. Take it like this. In your biscuit factory, for example, you're handed the raw material of biscuits. Say, flour and water." Mr. Richardson shuddered. "But you, with your genius, take that raw material, breathe on it and transform it into something unique. Well, it's the same in the theatre. Raw material—play, actors, lights, scenery. You breathe on 'em and hey presto! there's the 'Talk of the Town', a recordbreaker, a show that will run for six hundred performances and put thousands of pounds into the pocket of the promoter. Yes, there's a lot of money to be made in the theatre, Mr. Richardson, if you know how to set about it."

"But I don't want to make money," protested Sam. (It was Mr. Barnes's turn to shudder.) "Especially out of the theatre. I've always believed that the theatre should combine entertainment with education. Now, if it were possible for people to see the very finest plays for very little money—well, I might be interested in your scheme. Mind you," he added quickly, "I'm not a philanthropist. I should want such a project to be run on correct business lines. I should expect it to pay its way, even if it didn't make a profit."

"Naturally. Naturally. That's only common sense. And let me say here and now, Mr. Richardson, that even if I've had to produce—er—pot-boilers, my real interest has always been in, what one might call, the classical theatre. I'm glad we see eye-to-eye over this. Now, suppose we get down to a more detailed discussion of our scheme…"

3

In the ensuing months Sam bought the Beaumont lock, stock and barrel, from an ex-colonel and his wife, who had been trying to run the place as a cinema. He called in an architect and made a lot of interior alterations.

The exterior and the seating Sam left strictly untouched.

"There's a psychological aspect to consider," he explained to Basil, who urged an ultra-modern foyer and pneumatic stalls. "The intelligent theatre, as far as I can gather, has always been associated with dilapidation and discomfort. We mustn't frighten away our intellectuals with the refinements of a super-cinema. Make the actors as comfortable as you like. But not the audience. Hard seats mean alert minds. Luxury breeds lethargy."

"All right," said Basil. "Now, what about the company?"

"Oh, I leave that to you."

Basil was well satisfied with this division of labour, and suggested that a stock company should be engaged to form, what he called, "the hard core of our acting talent".

"Then if we get a long cast with small parts and walk-ons, we can engage our extras as we need them."

Sam was content. From purely business reasons he had made one or two discreet inquiries about Basil Barnes's standing in the theatre. It was undeniably good. Whatever his shortcomings as a man, as a producer Basil was worth his weight in gold. In the theatre he not only knew what he wanted but he knew how to get it. Sam felt very happy about the future of his new project.

4

Basil made two scoops when engaging the original company. He landed that grand old character actor, Willy Farnham, at a salary which wouldn't kill the venture before it was afoot. And he "discovered" a brilliant young *ingénue* from the provinces, called Angela Walsh. For the rest, the company was well served by actors with whom Basil had often worked in the past. There was, in fact, always a family-party atmosphere about rehearsals at the Beaumont.

But gradually, as the second winter season progressed, the atmosphere underwent a change. Eccentricities previously amusing became irritating; small jealousies sprang up, particularly among the women; there was a lot of intrigue and scrambling for the fattest parts. Further complications were induced by humanity's time-old habit of falling in and out of love at the slightest provocation; a habit which the emotional life in the theatre was inclined to foster. The more elderly actresses, with a predatory eye on Sam's cool million, vied with each other in wangling weekends at his country house in Sussex. The younger females, with reputations still in the shell of the egg, fell over each other in their efforts to be agreeable to Basil. But promoter and producer, though for totally different reasons, remained unmoved. Sam, the congenital bachelor, was shy and ill at ease in the presence of large women with vivid personalities. Basil, the congenital philanderer, was bored and sickened by the adulation of unrisen stars. Sam was pleasant to everybody. Basil was condescending. He always looked on actors and actresses, as he had explained to Mr. Richardson, as so much raw material, only some of it was rawer than the rest. For all that he got the best out of his casts, and his bitterest calumniator had to admit that he knew his job inside out. Rehearsals were alive and efficient. His touch was sure. His ability to weld the individual members of his company into a perfectly balanced team was unfailing. A great deal of the success which came to the Beaumont was due to his energy and inspiration. In the theatre, everybody declared that he could be relied on. Outside it, they were not so sure.

5

At the end of the second season, when the future of the Beaumont seemed assured and Basil, on a part-percentage basis, was earning quite a lot of money, Sam Richardson persuaded him to buy a country cottage.

"A quiet little place not far from my own at Lambdon. Going for a song, dear chap. It will need a little modernizing, but worth it, well worth it! These places always are, even as an investment."

"Beams, inglenooks, roses round the door—that sort of thing, eh?" asked Basil.

Sam nodded. "But it will give you the chance to read new plays and work on your prompt-copies in peace. No traffic. Nobody to drop in at awkward moments. As a week-end and summer place only, of course. Not as a permanent residence."

"It's an idea," said Basil.

"It's an inspiration," asserted Sam.

One day when Basil was spending a week-end with Sam at Old Knolle, they walked over the fields to Fallow Cottage and inspected the place. It lay on the outskirts of the village of Lambdon, in a small hollow at the end of a sunken lane. Much to Basil's astonishment, despite its isolation, it was quite civilized, with main water and an electric supply from the grid. Admittedly it was uncomfortably quaint inside, and inclined to be gloomy when the sun went in, but Basil, with a practised eye for a good setting, was quick to sense the possibilities.

"What about the drains?" he asked. "You must always inspect the drains of these medieval gems, otherwise you'll get something more pungent than a purely Tudor atmosphere foisted on to you."

Sam suggested they should inspect the drains, and though they knew next to nothing about sanitation, they were so averse to displaying their ignorance that they O.K.'d them on the spot. After that they looked for mildew, dry-rot and death-watch beetle. Then they took a turn round the overgrown garden and discovered a well-established asparagus-bed. That tipped the scales.

"I've always been inordinately fond of asparagus with butter sauce," said Basil.

Three weeks later he bought the place and became Sam's fellow parishioner in Lambdon. During the early part of that summer, when the Beaumont company were scattered about their lawful occasions, Basil spent his time on the road between London and Lambdon, with odd bits of furniture roped to the back seat of his M.G. sports. He engaged a Mrs. Ewing to come in and tidy the place up. He began to mow the lawns, dig the garden, and read horticultural books by the dozen. He bought a couple of tweed suits of amazing hairiness, and a shooting-hat, and tried to emulate the genteel untidiness of the parish élite. But even with a white-and-tan spaniel at his heels, he never looked more than an actor from Byron Crescent about to air his dog in Kensington Gardens. And, somehow, the rooms in his cottage wouldn't go quite right. No matter where he placed his various "pieces" the effect was either that of a Chelsea antique shop or the sets in a rural melodrama.

Sam drifted over to see how he was getting along.

"Not too well," admitted Basil. "I can't get the place to look as if it has been lived in for three hundred years. There's something wrong somewhere. Do you like that pair of Stafford dogs on the mantelpiece?"

"I thought they were calves," said Sam. He glanced round with a gentle but critical eye. "I quite agree. There's a lack of something. A flavour. Or perhaps it's just the patina of age."

Basil gave a doleful nod.

"Any suggestions, Sam?" He had long ago given up the formality of "Mr. Richardson".

"What about Deirdre? She might step in and help. She can stay over at Old Knolle."

"Deirdre!" Basil slapped his thigh. "Why the deuce haven't I thought of her before? She's the answer to the whole thing!"

6

Deirdre Lehaye was another of Basil's "finds". He'd come across her in the studio of a friend, up near Hampstead Heath. She was tall, dark, icy and so dead sure of herself that the majority of men were scared to approach her. Not so Basil. The enigma of her slanting eyes, Gioconda smile and faultless diction intrigued him at once. No sooner had their glances crossed, like two slender rapiers, above the heads of the other guests, than Basil felt he must know more about her. And with Basil this meant everything about her.

He handed her a plate of olives and introduced himself. She pulled him down beside her and assured him that he was probably the one man she still wanted to meet in London. And now she had. But Basil, profoundly aware of those ice-green eyes, knew that her reason for this was not the one which came automatically into his mind. She was not flirting. She was manœuvring herself into an advantageous position, so that in due course she could pounce and make her kill.

Was she an actress in search of a job? He doubted it. An estate agent anxious to rent him the perfect studio? Never! Then what? He tried the old shop-soiled gambit of, "Look here, I've seen you before somewhere. Was it at Teddy Brassington's?"

She granted him a faint smile which miraculously combined the utterly dissimilar emotions of pity and disappointment.

"Please—surely you can do better than that? You *know* we've never met. You had to cross the room and introduce yourself. If we had met before you'd never have forgotten me. I should have been something so vivid in your life that the moment you entered the studio, you'd have recoiled a step, clapped your hand to your mouth, and said under your breath, 'My God! There's Deirdre Lehaye—after all these months!'"

"Deirdre Lehaye. That, of course, is not your real name?"

"It's the one I prefer to be known by. It's funny, but I always imagined you with a moustache."

"So you've even troubled to imagine what I looked like? I'm flattered." Basil stretched his legs like a self-satisfied cat and offered a cigarette.

"I knew you produced the Beaumont shows for Sam Richardson. That's all. This is purely a business talk."

"Good Lord!" thought Basil. "She *is* an out-of-work actress."

"Business?" He smiled down at her as if to suggest that a butterfly's sole job in life was to be beautiful. "What's your line?"

"*Décor*. I'm a designer of stage sets. Now you can see why I was anxious to meet you."

"*Décor*? Then why haven't we met before?"

"Because I've been busy with the De Sulemann's Ballet in Paris for the last three seasons. This winter they went into liquidation, and I went on the dole. I'm on the labour market again. I've been meaning to ring you up."

"De Sulemann's!" Basil was excited. He knew at once that Deirdre was at the top of the ladder. She was not angling for a job. She was magnanimously offering him the chance to snap her up in the face of every other envious manager in London.

"Come down to-morrow and meet Sam Richardson at the Beaumont. This is one of my lucky days."

Deirdre smiled one of her brilliantly artificial smiles and allowed a smoke ring to emerge from the perfect O of her full and carmine lips. Her eyes searched his meaningly.

"I wonder," she said simply.

7

But the culminating success of that second winter season was in no small part due to her. Show after show went on with the same unvarying

excellence of setting. Heavy realism; faultless period; delicious fantasy—
all seemed to gain by being projected on to the stage through the lens
of Deirdre's sparkling imagination. She was as much an institution in
Bowman's Place as Sam Richardson or Bert Whiffle, the commissionaire.
She began to darken quite a large portion of Basil's existence, with her
irritating detachment and her inhuman flair for knocking every attempted
intimacy bang on the head at the exact psychological moment. If Basil
took one step towards her she took two steps backwards. If, to consolidate
her, he pretended to take one step back, she, with devilish teasing, took
two steps forward. For once he had met his match and, before the season
was out, he was ready to acknowledge his defeat.

They were friendly, even a mutual admiration society where work
was concerned, but for some reason Basil could never throw off the idea
that Deirdre was playing with him. She was holding her hand the better
to make her kill.

For all that, Sam's suggestion about Fallow Cottage was a good one.
That same night Basil rang her up. She promised to come down in a few
days' time and cast a professional eye over what she called his *lares et
penates*. Yet somehow, the moment he had expressed his gratitude and
rung off, Basil wondered if he had done the right thing. Why? He couldn't
say. Was it possible he *had* seen her before? Yes—in the earlier days of his
career when he *had* worn a moustache.

CHAPTER II

Characters Off-stage

I

OLD KNOLLE, SAM RICHARDSON'S PLACE IN LAMBDON, WAS LARGE, impressive and crenellated. It looked like a castle. It was built, unlike most of the houses in the neighbourhood, of grey stone—Kentish ragstone, in fact—and there was no doubt that the mid-Victorian architect who had designed it for a new peer had been influenced by Balmoral. It had one or two useless towers stuck on the corners, like saucy P.S.'s to a highly respectable letter. Originally, since there were ample springs in the district, the architect had planned to circle the place with a moat. At this the peer had put his foot down. He was a riotous old boy, very popular in local society, and he found it quite difficult enough to re-enter his castle after a convivial evening without having to negotiate such a hazard as a moat full of water.

However, the water was there to be used and an artificial lake was designed as a compromise. It was at a sensible distance from the house, on the south side, at the foot of several long-sloping lawns and shrubberies. Sam had it stocked with trout. In the earlier days he was often to be seen squatting reflectively in a punt moored in the middle of the lake inventing new and more appetizing forms of Shortcake, Garibaldi and Custard Creams.

Since his interest in the Beaumont, new forms of life had circulated in the veins of the place. Bell-voiced blondes and languid youths with golden torsos bathed in the lake or sunned themselves behind the shrubberies. Fruity character actors extended their old limbs on *chaises longues* and dreamed of past glories. Generous-hearted actresses, who had once played simpering heroines in the plays of Pinero and Henry Arthur Jones, loosened their corsage, so to speak, and lolled about on the terraces of

Old Knolle regardless of their "public". Throughout the months of early summer, in fact, Sam threw open the doors of his castle as a kind of theatrical rest-house for his company. They came and went as they pleased. They stayed as long as they liked. They could smoke in the bedrooms; play poker in the conservatory; sing in their baths—everything, in fact, as long as they didn't shock Mrs. Dreed, Sam's ancient and formidable housekeeper.

Many of the company, at one time or another during the blank months, availed themselves of Sam's hospitality. The winter season ended in April. May, June and July left them free to accept short-term engagements or take a holiday, according to their whims and finances. In August, preliminary rehearsals were held of the new plays for the next winter season, which began on the first of October. Often these first rehearsals were held at Old Knolle, in a house-party sort of atmosphere. After resting, strained nerves were relaxed. Old feuds were forgotten. Fresh verve and inspiration welled up in the company. Basil got through a great deal of hard mechanical work in a very short time at Knolle.

2

When Deirdre came down to Lambdon that particular July to help Basil over at Fallow Cottage, she found one or two other familiar faces at Old Knolle. Willy Farnham was there, with his nutcracker face, his cravat and silken voice, tip-tapping down the parquet corridors like a ballet-master. Willy was a bit of a dandy, and aped a kind of Louis Quinze daintiness, which deceived people into believing him a nice mild-mannered old gentleman. Deirdre and the rest of the Beaumont company knew better. When he was roused, thwarted or offended Willy Farnham was a fiend, a whirlwind, a whip-lash. Even Basil had a deep respect for his temperament, which came unstuck at least once during every dress-rehearsal. On these occasions the old boy literally danced with rage, hopping up and down like a child in a temper, tearing his handkerchief to shreds, kicking at chair, table, or human legs as the fancy moved him. Basil swore that when these fits possessed him he was really insane. For five or ten minutes

Willy allowed himself the glorious luxury of abandoning all control; then he blinked, cleared his throat, dashed a tear from his eye and proceeded to rehearse as if nothing untoward had occurred.

He loved gambling. He'd gamble on anything—cards, billiards, horses, weather, bluebottles or cockroaches. He'd lay nightly odds as to the amount of money in the "house". He'd bet on the number of dried peas in a pound. He'd wager ten bob that there were more windows visible on the left of Bowman's Place than on the right. Stroll with him through the Park and he'd have to lay even money that you'd pass a white-bearded man, or an invalid, or a nurse in uniform, before you came out at Marble Arch.

Deirdre annoyed him by employing all manner of little tricks to outwit him in his passion. She'd count the number of capital Es on a printed page in his absence, then later, casually pick up the book, open it at the place marked and light-heartedly take a pound off him. Or it might be the number of repeated patterns on a chintz cushion, or roses on a bush. After a time Willy grew suspicious, but he could never resist the lure of an invitation which began: "I bet you that…" He'd nearly broken his leg that summer after wagering Angela Walsh that he could jump a tennis-net, which shows what a grip this passion had on him, for he was over sixty then, and abnormally short in the leg. Angela had sailed over the net like a thoroughbred.

Angela, Deirdre had long ago decided, *was* a thoroughbred. She hated her because Angela's charm and good manners were absolutely natural. So was her complexion. So was her figure. Her popularity was general. Basil said that her parents knew what they were about when they christened her Angela. Sam said that if he'd fallen in love and married and had a daughter, then he'd have been satisfied with a daughter just like Angela. Even the older actresses mothered her and heaped on her the wealth of their professional and amorous experiences. This helped Deirdre to hate her even more.

Yet, to see them together that summer on the lawns of Old Knolle, you would have thought them soul-mates. Angela was too good-natured to believe that anybody could hate her, and Deirdre was too clever to let her realize that she was wrong. They had met after lunch by the summerhouse, two days after Deirdre's arrival.

"Hullo—where are you off to?" asked Angela cheerfully. "You look energetic."

"I have to be to preserve my *svelte* outline," replied Deirdre tartly. "If you want to know, I'm off to Fallow Cottage to supervise the soft furnishings for our Mr. Barnes. Would you care to come?"

"Yes, I'd love to. Basil's always talking about the place, but so far I haven't had the courage to beard him in his den alone."

"Oh, it's all right. He's promised to behave himself down here. Sam told me."

Angela flushed. "Don't be idiotic. I didn't mean that. I didn't want to break into his privacy—that's all."

"You're awfully considerate."

"Well, he works himself to a shadow during the season. He deserves to put his feet up."

"His feet up!" Deirdre laughed. "My dear, have you seen him? He's gone absolutely agricultural. He's never worked so hard in his life. He goes about swearing that his forbears were yeoman farmers or something, and that he's only just come into his rightful heritage!"

"He's very quaint sometimes, isn't he?" said Angela kindly. "When he 'descends', if you know what I mean?"

"Oh, perfectly. Basil simply adores to act the High Hat who has put aside the sterner side of life to play games with the children. The general off parade, my dear. Has he ever patted you on the head and called you 'My dear young lady' after a particularly fierce rehearsal?"

"Well—yes, he has," said Angela rather defiantly. "But I think he's not half the ogre *you* make him out to be. I've never found him patronizing, Deirdre, even if you have."

"You wouldn't realize, darling. As for me, I wouldn't tolerate it—not for an instant! I'm one of those people Basil has to be nice to whether he wants to or not. There's always Levinsky in the background. He's been tempting me with almost terrifyingly generous offers. And, naturally, I've informed Mr. Barnes."

"But you wouldn't desert the dear old Beaumont?" cried Angela, who was still innocent enough to hitch her star to an ideal. "We're the only theatre in Town that puts on a consistently decent play."

"Oh, wouldn't I? I've no sentiments where the Beaumont's concerned. I merely continue to employ my talents there because the classic play gives me the healthiest chance of self-development. The moment London is fully aware of my genius, I shall snap my fingers at the Beaumont and go to Hollywood with a four-figure reputation."

Angela sighed. "You make it all sound so horribly mercenary."

"Well, isn't it? When you've had to fight every inch of your way up to the top, my dear, you get your values straight. But you wouldn't understand that. Basil was saying that you didn't take up acting as a career, but a pastime. Oh, you're probably quite good," added Deirdre hastily, "but you're not exactly a professional, are you? Not in the strictest sense of the word."

For the first time one of Deirdre's barbed arrows went home.

"Oh, really? I don't see why not. I didn't get on to the stage through influence, whatever you may think! I started with 'walk-ons' in a third-rate rep company just like anybody else. Then I went on the usual touring circuits, with the usual dreary re-hashes of West End successes, playing small parts just like anybody else. And I know *all* about Sunday travelling and Crewe, and good addresses and stingy landladies just like anybody else. So there!"

Angela was quite flushed and breathless by the time she had put her case. Deirdre smiled lazily. She loved discovering the chinks in other people's armour and shooting her pretty feathered darts through the cracks. But Angela was easy, so very easy. It was much more fun drawing a bead on Basil because his armour, forged of a colossal self-conceit, was of a far tighter fit. In fact she often wondered if he appreciated her attempts to wound him.

3

Basil, with his heels dug in, was cautiously easing an enormous roller down the slope of his neglected lawn when Deirdre and Angela came through the wicket-gate. He wore a pale blue silk sleeveless vest, which clung to him like a second skin. His shorts were too small and his sandals too big. He looked like a little boy dressed for a romp on the sands at Margate. Angela wondered, with a little pang of disappointment, how it was possible for a man of such outstanding intelligence to look so incredibly stupid.

He might control a tricky cast at the end of an eight-hour rehearsal, but he couldn't control that roller from the start. It had mastered him completely before he was half-way down the slope. It began, despite Basil's efforts to lay himself practically flat on his back, to gather impetus. It continued to gather impetus.

"Look out, Basil, else you won't be able to stop it!" called Deirdre warningly.

"Confound you!" he shouted back, "I *can't* stop it! Look out! Keep clear of the porch. Nothing but a miracle can prevent me from hitting it."

The miracle, as anticipated, didn't occur, and the roller flattened out the antique trellis arch as if it had been a worm-cast, and clanged up against the front wall of the cottage. Two panes of glass fell out and tinkled on to the flagstones.

"Why the devil you must turn up and distract my attention at such a moment, God only knows. I'd got the thing perfectly in hand until I saw you out of the corner of my eye."

"I'm sorry," said Angela, trying to straighten up the shattered porch and tangled clematis.

"I'm not," said Deirdre. "For once Angela has been able to see you at a disadvantage. A little more of this kind of horseplay, Basil, and she'll begin to think you're merely human. Can we go in? I want to finish arranging the furniture in the sitting-room."

"All right—but mind your head," said Basil with an ungracious scowl.

The others ducked under the low lintel of the door and went into the minute hall. Basil followed and, forgetting to take his own advice, met the length of solid and well-seasoned oak with a gruesome thud. He wondered if Sam Richardson had been right about Fallow Cottage.

They began to set out the furniture, Basil now hunching his shoulders and boring about with his head down like a Bowery Boy on the look-out for trouble. Deirdre sat on a coffin-stool in the centre of the room and issued orders. Basil and Angela struggled here and there with pieces of furniture in order to try them out in various places. He got more and more exasperated, and even Angela felt that the temperature of the room had risen out of all proportion to any meteorological change that might have occurred outside.

"See here," said Basil at length. "I don't know anything about permutations and combinations. I did at school, but I don't now. But I've an idea that eight simple pieces of furniture can be arranged in something like three hundred and fifty thousand different ways. I'm prepared to stay here the rest of my life shoving the stuff around, but I really can't expect Angela to distress herself any further on my account. For heaven's sake, my girl, make up your mind. Is the gate-legged table or the Q.A. bureau to go upstage centre under the window? Which?"

"Neither. I've already decided it's the only possible place for the sea-chest. Do you mind?"

"I do—definitely."

"Well, it's your cottage."

"I'm not thinking of myself. It's Angela. She's not built on the right lines for a furniture remover. Are you, my child?" He patted her fondly on the head. Angela blushed. Deirdre smiled maliciously and threw a quick glance in her direction. Basil, noting it, wondered what the devil Deirdre was up to now and what sinister form of feminine conspiracy lay behind that glance.

They moved the table, the bureau, the Welsh dresser, the high-backed settle and, in less than half an hour, Deirdre declared herself satisfied.

"I don't think we can better the composition. The colouring's not all it should be. I wanted that Bayeux effect—modulated greens and browns with a touch of *vieux rose*. But you'll have to be content, Basil darling. It's the best I can do with the material you've given me."

He slipped an arm round her waist and gave it a gentle squeeze. Angela gazed out of the window at two sparrows ruffling their feathers in the bird-bath. Off-stage, any variation of love-making embarrassed her considerably.

"Now that only leaves the spare bedroom and the sun-parlour," said Deirdre. "I'll come over and tie up the loose ends to-morrow."

"Thanks." Basil turned to Angela. "You haven't been round the place yet, have you?"

"No."

"Care to?"

"Very much."

She followed him around and dutifully praised all the old-world features—the narrow staircase, the cambered ceilings, the lack of cupboard space, the uneven floors. They went into the kitchen. Deirdre was there brewing tea with a studied awkwardness, intended to suggest that she was helpless when it came to domestic matters, however simple. Basil looked at her with a sardonic smirk.

"Charming. You've just dropped your cigarette ash into the milk jug." He turned to Angela. "And now for the bathroom."

He pointed to what appeared to be a huge oak chest pushed against the inner wall of the kitchen. Lifting the heavy lid of the chest, which fastened back against the wall, he disclosed a commodious enamel bath complete with chromium fittings.

"Neat, isn't it? An ingenious conservation of space combined with an æsthetic exterior. I borrowed the idea from a luxury flat in Mayfair. You must come over and have a bath some time."

"Basil! You do say the most dreadful things."

"Ah, well, as long as I only *say* them, my dear young lady."

And before she could dodge aside, he patted her on the head again. Deirdre's smile was more malicious than ever.

They carried the tea-tray into the garden and sat under the mulberry tree. Basil, having recuperated somewhat from the roller fiasco, lounged back in his hammock-chair and drowsed. The soft chatter of the girls' voices came pleasantly through the fog of his receding consciousness. Deirdre was a lovely provocation—irritating but highly desirable. Angela was a sweet young creature. Very naïve and simple, but refreshing after Deirdre's acid detachment. If only, by the exercise of some mystic alchemy, he could have melted down their two entities and refashioned a single woman from the molten residue…

He felt strange stirrings of tenderness for both of them that afternoon. They had been very helpful. They were decorative and stimulating. He began, rather forlornly, to visualize a perfect *ménage à trois*, in which life at Fallow Cottage was not far short of a profane and rustic idyll. It was a pity that Angela and Deirdre seemed to brush each other the wrong way. It was Deirdre's fault. She was a confounded mischief maker. She had a flair for intrigue that was only equalled by the mistress of a French Cabinet Minister. There were times, he thought, when she needed spanking—yes, good and proper!

CHAPTER III

Pigs in Porcelain

I

D EIRDRE HAD BROUGHT OVER AN INVITATION FROM SAM FOR BASIL
to dine at Old Knolle that evening. It was an unnecessary formality, because Basil knew he had *carte blanche* where Sam's hospitality was
concerned. He'd had it from the start and he intended to preserve this
privilege undimmed to the end. Basil was a *bon viveur*. He enjoyed good
food and good wines, expensive appointments and faultless service. He
had never been able to afford these for himself, but he refused to see that
that was any reason for snubbing Sam's generosity. Sam, who was dyspep-
tic, loved to see other people taking pleasure in their meals, and it would
have been rank unkindness to have deprived Sam of his enjoyment. Once
having argued himself into this noble state of mind, Basil was ready to
sponge on Sam to the limit. He was not only ready—he almost fell over
himself to get off the mark.

But Sam's invitation that evening had a special significance. Rudolph
Millar, a nephew of Clara Maddison (the company's most tried and trying
actress), was to read his first play to them in the music-room after dinner.
Clara had worked hard to bring this about, for she had already come to
a very satisfactory business arrangement with young Rudolph—namely,
ten per cent. on all royalties if the play were accepted. She had shadowed
poor Sam with such persistence that more than once he had awakened
during the night from a horrible dream that he was married. In the relief
at finding that he wasn't, he promised Clara that he would consider her
nephew's masterpiece.

During dinner Rudolph was obviously shy and apprehensive. He had
spoken of this as his first play. Actually, it was his seventh. Six of them,

after a round of the managers, had found their way, dog's-eared and bedraggled, into his old school tuck-box. He came to the conclusion that theatrical managers, as a class, ought to pay more attention to personal hygiene. That at least one of them had considered his new MS. over breakfast was certain, as two pages of dialogue in Act I had been stuck together with marmalade and there was an egg stain on the penultimate page of Act III (which to a C.I.D. man would suggest that the criminal had the curious habit of eating his breakfast backwards).

"What is this epic called, young fellah?" asked Willy Farnham, over the fish. "Or haven't you titled it yet?"

"Just a working title. You may not like it, of course. But at the moment it's called…"

"Well?"

"*Pigs in Porcelain.*"

"*Pigs in Porcelain*, eh?" Willy screwed in his monocle and eyed Rudolph with an expression he had used a great deal when playing the name part in *Beau Brummel*. "But, damme, d'you think that's quite nice? I mean pigs. I'm not at all sure if our refined clientele will want to come along and see a play with pigs in the title."

"But there aren't any in the play," explained Rudolph, reddening a little. "It all takes place in Cheltenham."

"But half a minute—tut-tut!—I can't make head or tail of this. In Cheltenham, my dear young fellah? But I thought you said they were in Porcelain?"

Rudolph stammered charmingly. "That's symbolic, too. It doesn't mean that they're really in porcelain."

"Well, well—really, really—dear me!" bumbled Willy, returning with a slow shake of his silver mane to the fish. "So the pigs aren't really pigs and even if they were they wouldn't be in porcelain. My dear boy, it's beyond me. I may be a trifle *fin de siècle*, but when Wilde called his masterpiece *Lady Windermere's Fan* he made quite sure that there was a fan *and* a Lady Windermere in the piece. Henry Arthur Jones—as you may or may not recall—wrote a play called *The Case of Rebellious Susan*, and with masterly logic his heroine was actually called Susan and she rebelled charmingly for three solid acts. Of course, I may be splitting hairs, but…"

Clara Maddison, who was being roguish with Sam, now glanced down the table and came to her nephew's rescue.

"Don't take any notice of him, Rudie. It's his lunatic idea of a joke. Shut up, Willy, and behave yourself!"

"Well, I think it's a lovely title," said Angela warmly. "It arouses one's interest. Don't you agree, Mr. Richardson?"

Sam hadn't heard what they were talking about, but he agreed on principle. It upset his digestion to disagree with anybody during a meal. He returned to his charcoal biscuits, the secret formula of which he had evolved some fifteen years before, and for fifteen years had never ceased to bless his inspiration.

Rudolph looked across at Angela and appraised her in detail for the first time. He approved of the clear-cut oval of her face, her trim red mouth, her expressive blue eyes. Their glances meeting, they smiled at one another and looked down at the same time, crumbling their bread with sudden embarrassment.

"Hullo," thought Basil. "They've clicked, have they?" He scowled to himself because, since that afternoon at Fallow Cottage, he had begun to take a decided interest in Angela. He couldn't have an unacted, unpublished nincompoop of a playwright making cow-eyes at the girl. He decided to damn the play from the start. It would never do to have the fellow hanging about the Beaumont during rehearsals.

2

They sat in a semicircle facing the unhappy Rudolph, who was fumbling with his script. This was his great chance and he felt that he was going to muff it. The faces confronting him seemed to embody all that was meanest in man—cynicism, boredom, intolerance and mockery. Even Sam Richardson, the mildest and most apologetic of critics, owing to certain post-prandial disorders, appeared to have his features twisted into a smile of contempt. His Aunt Clara looked like a broody hen who has been detailed to hatch out a time-bomb. Then for the second time he caught Angela's warm and encouraging glance, her gentle smile, her expression of eager anticipation. He cleared his throat, braced himself in his chair, threw a defiant look round the half-circle, and began to read.

"*Pigs in Porcelain*." This with a stern look at Willy. "The cast is as follows…"

After the first scene even Deirdre ceased trying to look intelligent. With her mouth slacked and parted, she was listening with breathless interest to the rise and fall of young Rudolph's extremely agreeable voice. Sam was no longer aware of those abdominal gurgles which always caused him such distress and apprehension at social gatherings. Willy had let his monocle fall unnoticed from his left eye. Aunt Clara had now obviously come to the conclusion that she was no longer sitting on a time-bomb but a lovely brown-shelled double-yolker that might well hatch out into a handsome ten per cent. Angela was in a mild state of rapture, her shining eyes (as Basil was quick to notice) fixed admiringly on the playwright.

Basil alone presented a hard and critical front to this attack upon his emotions. The first act might be all fine and dandy. So might the second. But what of that graveyard of so many literary aspirations—the third? With the air of a man who is accustomed to producing Shakespeare, Sheridan and Shaw, he curled his arm over the back of the chair, canted himself sideways and yawned like a hippopotamus.

The murder came in the second act. The play was like a Greek tragedy as it progressed towards a series of fateful climaxes. One could smell the aspidistras and the red plush and the carraway seeds in that gloomy Victorian room. The desiccated old ladies moved through the imagination with a jingle of jet and cornelians, with the *frou-frou* of *moiré* skirts with a faint yet unmistakable creaking of stays. The atmosphere was rich with repressions and ugly thoughts, relieved every now and then by the unctuous humour of the seafaring brother who had come home to cast anchor in this seedy backwater of respectability.

"And now for the third act," thought Basil darkly. "Now for the graveyard, my pocket Pinero."

But when the third act came to a triumphant conclusion Basil knew he was going to have a devil of a job to prevent Sam Richardson from producing *Pigs in Porcelain*. It reeked of success. It was one of those morbid pathological little pleasantries which send the audiences home thanking

God that they have managed to preserve their own health and sanity. The critics would swallow it hook, line and sinker. After the customary three weeks' run at the Beaumont, it would probably be revived in the West End and pack the house for at least two years. What the deuce, thought Basil, was he to say?

"Ah, bravo! Bravo!" Willy was piping above the general hubbub of congratulation. "Damme! but I must say you've surprised me. Quite Strindbergian in its treatment. Stark as a blasted oak, young fellah. I've a notion that the part of Moldoney would fit me like a glove. Tut-tut! you might have modelled the part on my distinctive and unique style of acting."

"Oh, *do* shut up, Willy," broke in Clara. "Rudie's never seen you act and I'm quite sure that he never wants to—do you, Rudie darling? And you're far too skinny for the part of Moldoney. It calls for a *man* in the rôle, not a mummy."

Willy Farnham, goggling with amazement at his tormentor, began to dance up and down like an angry parrot on a perch. Noting the danger light, Deirdre said hastily: "I can visualize the setting so perfectly, Mr. Millar. A kind of subaqueous Victorian twilight with a bead curtain over the door which clicks and clicks at every entry and nearly drives everybody mad with its brittle repetition. Can't *you* see it, Basil darling. Why, what's the matter? Don't you like Mr. Millar's play?"

"I think it's thin and trite and artificial," croaked Basil. "You'll excuse me, Mr. Millar, but I believe in straight speech."

A shocked silence descended. Deirdre appealed with a kind of hopeless gesture to Mr. Richardson.

"Sam, please!"

Sam, aware that all eyes were now fixed on him, fiddled with an ashtray. As a mere Philistine he hated having to voice an opinion on anything less materialistic than biscuits. It wasn't fair of Deirdre to place him in this predicament. If he agreed with Basil, young Millar would be offended. If he praised young Millar, Basil would get temperamental and threaten to walk out. It was no fun being a promoter. What on earth was he to say? The majority seemed in favour of the play. Why was Basil so violent in his criticism? But at the last moment the business man came uppermost, and he saw his way out.

"My dear young lady, it has always been my habit to postpone any important decision for at least twenty-four hours. I like to sleep on it. I found your play interesting, Mr. Millar, very interesting, indeed; but whether we can consider it as a business proposition—ah, that's another matter, isn't it? You appreciate my vagueness. To the artistic temperament the very word money is anathema." Here Rudolph managed to direct a very discrediting glance at his Aunt Clara. "But, unfortunately, as the sole box-office representative in this room…" Sam elevated and depressed his arms like the flippers of a seal and turned away to hide his humility. "I'm sorry to be so mercenary." Then, brightening considerably, "I am now going to ring for drinks."

The party broke up into small groups. Angela made a beeline for Basil. He was standing in the open French window, staring down at the moonlit lake with the sulky expression of a man who toys with the idea of murder.

"Basil?"

"Well?" He didn't even turn to look at her.

She laid a hand on his sleeve. "Don't be so grumpy. What's the matter?"

"As far as I am aware, nothing is the matter."

"But you didn't like Mr. Millar's play?"

"Did you?"

"I thought it was wonderful! He's awfully clever."

Basil winced. "And I thought you had intelligence."

"But what's wrong with the play?"

"Everything! Everything! It's a hotch-potch of plagiarism. *Night Must Fall*, *Gaslight* and *The Wild Duck* all rolled into three acts of uncooked, indigestible dough. Its construction is gimcrack. Its dialogue walks about on stilts. Its characterization is rotten all through. It's morbid, unimaginative and deadly dull! I wouldn't touch it with a barge-pole." He caught her by the wrist and dragged her out on to the terrace. He pointed dramatically at the silver shimmer of the lake. "Look!—doesn't that remind you of *The Seagull*? Ah! there *is* a play. What masterly technique, what suspense, what subtlety. You can tell your Master Rudolph to go away and study the great dramatists for ten years and then come back to me with another play. By then, I think he might be able to turn out a passable second-rate thriller with a twist in its tail! Until then… nothing doing, my dear young lady. At least, if my opinion counts for anything with Sam Richardson."

"I think you're horrid!" cried Angela. "Horrid! Horrid! Horrid!"

Basil looked down at her and adopted a three-quarter upstage stance which he much favoured in the production of his love-scenes.

"That's a pity, my dear. A great pity. Because I've come to think you rather adorable. May I kiss you?"

For a moment Angela hesitated. That a god should step down from Olympus and plead with her for a kiss seemed utterly incredible. Basil, of all people, wanting to kiss her! Did she dare offend him by a refusal? If she refused him now, perhaps he would never ask her again, and that would result in an irretrievable loss of experience. There were not many young actresses of promise who could say that they had been helped along the road to success by allowing themselves to be kissed by Basil Barnes. After all, she must never lose sight of her career, no matter what happened to her modesty.

"Oh, I don't think it's safe," she whispered fearfully. "I'm sure that Willy's prying at us from behind the curtains."

"Damn Willy!" said Basil with a ringing, rounded note in his voice. He had never felt so masterful, so generous and protective as he took Angela in his arms. For once he was not showing somebody else how to kiss with conviction. He was performing simply and solely for an audience of one… himself! Oh, and Angela, of course. He was forgetting her!

CHAPTER IV

Red Reddington

I

IT WAS PAST MIDNIGHT WHEN THE LAST OF SAM'S GUESTS RETIRED TO bed. Basil's bombshell had somewhat blunted the edge of the party's sociability. Even alcohol was incapable of restoring the light-hearted good-fellowship which had presided over the dinner-table. Rudolph looked utterly depressed. His Aunt Clara was in a sulk. Willy, tethered to the whisky decanter by a stout yet invisible chain, was simmering and silent. He had not yet forgiven Clara the insult she had levelled against his talents. Deirdre narrowed her slanting eyes and let them rove slightingly over the crowd. She had not failed to register the double exit on to the terrace, and the moment Angela reappeared she guessed that Basil had kissed her. And when, some few minutes later, Basil casually followed her in with an expression of utter boredom on his face, the guess became a conviction. No man could have registered such beautiful disinterest unless inspired by the fact that he had something of great interest to conceal. As for Angela, she looked pink and crumpled and more modest than a nun.

So he was up to his little tricks again, was he? Unable to make headway with her, Deirdre, he was picking up a little easy money on the side by turning the head of this untutored nincompoop. Then when the little silly, at the dictates of a hopeless infatuation, had thrown aside the last grains of her self-respect and reason, Basil would abruptly throw off the mask and reveal himself as the taskmaster, the producer, the near genius, who really hadn't a moment to spare for such a frivolity as love. Deirdre lifted her white and softly rounded shoulders, which emerged from her black evening frock, half provocation and half promise. Oh, well—it was Angela's tea-party. If she had taken it into her head to abandon every maidenly modesty and cleave only unto Basil, there was nobody on earth who could prevent her from making a fool of herself. Basil was a practised stoker of erotic fires. He knew the exact psychological moment at which to add fresh fuel to the flames, and, when the time came, nobody could more blithely shoulder his shovel and walk away to leave his victim to flake away in ashes. Damn his beastly self-assurance! If only *he* could fall in love and know what it meant to be burnt away in a hopeless cause. If only she, Deirdre, could teach him that one big, utterly necessary lesson—of course, she only had to lift her little finger, but no—she really couldn't be troubled. She had never liked babies, particularly great big spoilt babies like the magnificent Basil.

As Basil was about to leave on his solitary walk across the fields to Fallow Cottage, Sam lured him into the study for a night-cap.

"Sure I can't persuade you to stay over for the night, my dear chap?" asked Sam warmly. "I don't like the idea of turning you out after midnight. We've plenty of room. Say when."

"When!" Basil accepted the tumbler and, waiting until Sam had charged his own glass, lifted his to the level of his eyes. "To the season, Sam—may it be a record-breaker!"

"That's kind of you. Very kind. But with you at the helm of the ship I've no qualms about the future. Now we're alone—tell me frankly—what did you really think of young Millar's play?"

"Well, frankly, Sam, I didn't like it."

"I thought it was... rather good," said Sam tentatively; adding with immediate humility, "but of course I'm not a sound judge of a work of art. I know what I like, but I'm ready to admit that what I like often turns out to be pretty indifferent art. It's difficult, very difficult to understand these things. You've had the experience. There's a lifetime of knowledge behind your appreciation, and naturally I'll abide by your opinion. I've always promised not to poke my nose over the wrong side of the footlights."

"You mean the right side. Shall I tell you why I don't like that play?"

"Please do."

"Because it has no moral, Sam. It's waste of time. It glorifies the worst aspects of human sadism."

"Er... like *Macbeth*?"

The question was so pertinent that Basil was taken aback by Sam's perspicacity. It was disconcerting to find the unintelligent always placing their finger unerringly on the truth, apparently without effort and without thinking. Sam was right. *Macbeth* was an *epic* of thwarted ambition and cruelty. But it would never do to let Sam see that he had scored a point; otherwise his own infallibility as a critic might be seriously undermined.

"Ah, but Shakespeare, Sam! Shakespeare! Have a heart. You surely don't suggest that *Pigs in Porcelain* soared to the heights of sublime tragedy? Macbeth is a three-dimensional colossus. Millar's old ladies are nothing but cardboard silhouettes. A couple of nasty mean old backbiters with a leaning to homicide. We've got to think of the *tone* of our plays. Entertainment value isn't enough."

"Then you think we ought to turn it down, my dear chap? Unconditionally?"

"Yes, Sam—I do—most definitely."

"Very well," sighed Sam. "If you say so…"

2

In her large, airy bedroom overlooking the lake, Angela slowly undressed. The experiences which had come to her that evening were not to be measured by any ordinary application of the mind. All the events, small yet great in their implication, needed going over carefully and at length. That morning she had risen a contented, uncomplicated young woman, without a real worry in the world. She was going to bed in a whirl of battling emotions, older, wiser and burdened with novel responsibilities. It was not only Basil. It was not only Rudolph. It was a combination of them both—a kind of synthetic hero compounded of their mutual talents and attractions.

She had known Basil for a long time now, ever since she had joined the Beaumont company at its inauguration. And yet she realized, during that long and hardworking spell of triumphs and disappointments, she had *never* known Basil. She had known only a cold, calculating piece of mechanism called the Producer; and to-night, for the first time, she had been granted a glimpse of the man behind the machine. A warm, impetuous man, with a careless charm and a playfully masterful manner!

"I've come to think you rather adorable…"

Had he actually said that? It seemed impossible, thought Angela, as she stepped daintily out of her scanties and gazed at her slender rosy image in the pier-glass. And did he mean it? But would he have followed up the compliment with a kiss if it were nothing but empty flattery? For all her theatrical experience, Angela was a lamb of innocence in her private life. Men, to her, meant actors, with whom one performed various and intimate acts of love-making in the glare of a hundred lamps and a thousand eyes. Off-stage those romantic gyrations meant little or nothing. Beyond a few hastily snatched kisses in the wings before a first night, her tremendous innocence had armoured her against the wiles of the philanderers. To her contemporaries she was always a "good sort"; to her elders a "child".

And now, gazing at her faultless reflection, she seemed to note a new maturity of figure, something studied and sophisticated in the way she posed, a perfume of provocation which her image distilled. If Basil could have seen her then—oh, dear!—she buried her face in her hands and turned away, blushing.

"What dreadful things I think of," she whispered. "What wickedly awful ideas I get into my head!"

Perhaps, if she put on her nightie…

"He looks so keen and fine and idealistic."

But this time it was the image of Rudolph Millar that looked over her shoulder into the mirror and smiled. A shy, quizzical, rather crooked smile; the smile of a young man who was not quite sure of himself; who needed a companion to lend him assurance and encouragement. From the moment their eyes had met across the dinner-table, Angela felt that she had known Rudolph for a long time. Even longer than she had known Basil. Yet she had met him for the first time only a few hours back, when Sam had proudly ushered him into the circle as if he had been a strange and precious novelty that had chanced to catch his eye. (Dear Sam—he was so good to everybody.) And ever since Rudolph had started to read his play her interest in him had quickened and quickened, until she felt it was running away with her. Then Basil had kissed her and she felt like running away with him.

Oh, it was all so devastatingly difficult! There were tangles in the molten gold of her hair, but they were more easily straightened out than the kinks and knots in her emotions.

The image of Rudolph looking into the mirror over her shoulder grew sharper. There was the faint creak of a floorboard behind her. She turned, startled. And there, with a bewildered and apologetic look upon his lean features, was not the image of Rudolph, but Rudolph himself! She jumped up with a clatter of the fallen hair-brush.

"Mr. Millar—you!"

He was in pyjamas, over which he had clumsily knotted a worn and threadbare Jaeger dressing-gown. He looked very young and gauche.

"I say, I'm fearfully sorry. I thought this was my room. I was thinking of something else, and it wasn't until I saw you like a vision of better things at the dressing-table that I realized my mistake. I'm fearfully sorry. I am, really. Fearfully sorry."

"Oh, it's all right," said Angela, very matter-of-fact, determined to put him at his ease by pretending that the drift of casual men into her bedroom was a nightly occurrence. "I must look an awful freak with my hair all fluffed out like this. You'll have to excuse me." She pointed to a silver cigarette-box on a nearby table. "Would you like a cigarette?"

"Yes, I would rather. That is if you don't mind. I mean—can I stop and have a word with you? I've wanted to get you alone ever since the reading."

"I thought the play was wonderful!" said Angela enthusiastically. "We simply must, must put it on at the Beaumont during the coming season. I know I couldn't do justice to her, but I should adore to play Christabel."

"I'm sure you're the only person to make a success of the part," declared Rudolph, lighting his cigarette. "But it's about its chances of production that I wanted to see you."

"Me?" Angela was suddenly aware that she was standing between Rudolph and the wall brackets in a chiffon nightie. She blushed to the roots of her hair. What *must* he think of her? "Excuse me—I hadn't realized… it's a little chilly. Do you mind if I fetch my dressing-gown?"

He sprang up and dashed politely to the bed in an attempt to anticipate her, with the result that they collided with enough force to undermine Angela's balance. He caught her in his arms before she fell and closed his eyes with the sudden rapture of his sensations. Then, no less embarrassed than she, he disentangled himself from this lucky embrace and apologized.

"I say, I'm fearfully sorry. I am really. Fearfully sorry."

It was apparent that Rudolph Millar had two distinct ways of expressing himself. In his plays he was fluent, masterly, imaginative. In conversation he was like a gramophone needle that has caught in a broken thread.

"Oh, it's all right," smiled Angela. "I caught my foot in my nightie." He helped her on with her wrap, noting with an artist's appreciation the delicate hair tendrils at the nape of her neck. He wanted to blow on them, playfully. Instead, he returned to his chair, whilst Angela sat herself primly on the edge of the bed. "Now please tell me why you wanted to see *me* about your play."

"It's just that I don't think they're going to do it," he blurted out miserably. "Mr. Richardson might, but you heard what Mr. Barnes said. 'Thin, trite and artificial.' And as he's the producer…"

"I think Basil was frightfully mean about it. I can't understand why he was so critical."

"The point is, he's sure to influence Mr. Richardson," said Rudolph. "Aunt Clara says that when it comes to policy Mr. Barnes *is* the Beaumont."

"He *thinks* he is," corrected Angela tartly, wondering how she could be so rude about somebody who had kissed her only a short time back and for whom she was already experiencing a very tender affection. "But I don't see how they can refuse a play like *Pigs in Porcelain*. Willy was awfully taken with it. I could see that. So was your aunt and dear Sam. Even the superior Deirdre had a kind word for it. Basil can't stand out against all of us."

"That's what I mean." Rudolph fiddled with the tassel of his dressing-gown, whirling it round and round like a little propeller. "I say—don't think this awful cheek, will you, but do you think you could use *your* influence to persuade him to take a more rosy view of the play?"

"My influence?"

"Well, yes. This evening—I'm fearfully sorry—out on the terrace—I happened to be taking a glass of sherry to my aunt—and—"

"I see," said Angela quietly. "You mean you happened to be passing when—"

"Yes—at the precise moment. I'm fearfully sorry."

"Oh, that's all right," said Angela magnanimously. "But please don't think that I'm in the habit of— What I mean to say is, I doubt if I've got much influence over Basil—er—yet."

"But in the near future perhaps?" Rudolph looked anxious, yet hopeful.

"Well, I'll do what I can."

"That's awfully decent of you."

"But I can't promise to change his views."

"But you'll try?"

Angela, her feelings now all at sixes and sevens, nodded. What on earth did all this strange talk signify? That she was to allow Basil to make love to her in order to further the production of Rudolph's play. Really! It was all very bewildering. Emotional experiences had been tardy in coming to her, and now, in the short compass of one never-to-be-forgotten evening, they were flocking in like vultures to a kill. The future seemed to be strewn with difficulties.

3

On his lone and moonlit stroll across the fields to Fallow Cottage, Basil was in a reflective mood. He felt curiously exasperated with himself for having been so childish about young Millar's play, for he realized, better than any of them, that *Pigs in Porcelain* was just the kind of sombre intellectual macabre that the Beaumont audiences would jump at. Why, then, had he been so whole-hearted in his hostility, not only to young Millar's play, but to young Millar himself? He'd never clapped eyes on the boy before, and yet from the instant he had intercepted that sympathetic glance between Rudolph and Angela at dinner, he had detested everything about him.

Basil allowed himself a superior smirk. Of course there was one explanation—which in the case of any ordinary man would doubtless prove to be the right one—Angela! But was he, with his long and profound experience of the fair sex, his hard-headed assessment of their virtues, his knowledge of their vices, the victim of an adolescent jealousy? The smirk broadened to a smile of derision. Ridiculous! Why should he record any emotional reaction if these two infants made sheep's eyes at one another? Angela was a pretty and intelligent little creature, and it was quite amusing to gratify the romantic streak in her with a stolen kiss on a moonlit terrace, but to let his judgment go all cockeyed on her account... never! Though he doubtless meant a lot to Angela, Angela was nothing to him. Then why had he been so crushing about that damned play? Why had he advised Sam to turn it down?

Now, if he had been in love with Angela...

Basil missed a step and braced himself against the onrush of a new and shocking idea. Was that really a possibility? Unrealized by him, had some ferment been working under the crust of his self-respect so that his self-respect was now ready to cave in like an empty egg-shell? Had he, by the stealthy influence of this girl, been reduced at one foul stroke from an aloof and sensible man of the world to a gibbering, unreliable, emotion tossed schoolboy? *Was* he in love with Angela?

No, of course he wasn't! He, who had culled the finest of hothouse blooms on his priapic journey through life, was not the sort of man to stoop and pick a simple little daisy. A man retained a standard in such matters. He owed it to himself, his position, his career. These adoring juveniles were ten a penny in the theatre and Angela, though quite charming, had nothing that a score of other young aspirants hadn't got. That kiss on the terrace was merely symptomatic of an old principle—that if one wanted to get the best out of an actress it was as well to make occasional love to her. It was simply a part of his general theory concerning dramatic art.

Somewhat reassured, after a nasty jolt, Basil climbed the stile into the next meadow and continued on his way to the cottage. It was not until then that he was aware of a figure preceding him along the path. The man, for Basil could clearly see trousers, was not more than twenty-five yards ahead, and the manner of his progress made quite certain who it was. That tip-tapping, ballet-master's trot was unmistakable. It was Willy Farnham!

Basil was about to hail him when he thought better of it. His curiosity was aroused. Why the devil was old Willy prancing round the country-side at this time of night? He decided to shadow him and see what transpired.

At the end of another five minutes Willy arrived at the second stile giving access to the sunken lane which linked Fallow Cottage with the main road. He flipped over it like a salmon, and by the time Basil came to the lane he could hear Willy pit-patting away in the direction of the village. He followed cautiously, keeping to the grass verge to avoid any tell-tale scrunching. Then, at the point where the lane debouched into the end of Lambdon Main Street, a second shape detached itself from the shadows. There was a warning hiss. Willy stopped dead. So did Basil. From an animated picture the layout was turned into a tableau. Everything seemed to freeze up in suspense.

But so quiet was the night that Basil could hear every word of the conversation that followed.

"Is that you?"

"I imagine so, otherwise you wouldn't be accosting me."

"You're late, Mr. Farnham. I said 'midnight', didn't I?"

"Quite. But owing to unforeseen circumstances, to whit a play-reading, I was unable to leave the house a minute earlier. It's lucky that I'm here at all. You must give me my due."

"Lucky for you, maybe, Mr. Farnham." The voice was thick and punchy. It jabbed on to the silence in a most disagreeable manner. "Tell me—have you brought the dough?"

"No."

"No?" There was a soft whistle, a long pause, and finally the unknown voice saying, "I see. So you're not going to pay? Well, you needn't say I haven't warned you. Sir Walter's been fair enough. Can't deny that. But time's time and it's also money. This was the zero line, wasn't it? And as I'm acting for Sir Walter…"

"But, damme! I think you would do as well to listen to me. Yes, really— I mean it." In the moonlight Basil caught the glitter of Willy's monocle which he always upped in his moments of emotion. "We must have this quite straight between us, my dear fellah."

"Not so matey," growled the voice. "If it's all the same to you. I'm here on business. We don't want any fancy talk. Jim Reddington to you. *Red* Reddington."

"But look here, Mr. Red Reddington, you really must allow me to make my—ah—points. I've every intention of honouring my obligations to Sir Walter. It's just a matter of a little extra time."

"You said that before—when he wrote."

"Yes, I grant that. I was under an illusion."

"How come?"

"I beg your pardon?"

"What d'you mean you was under?"

"An illusion. I entertained a false premise as to the ease with which I could procure the necessary money, which has naturally, Mr. Reddington, rather unsettled the time element. Sir Walter—yes, damme!—Sir Walter must have a little patience."

"He won't like it."

"Like what?"

"Me going back to him with empty hands. This *was* the zero line, y'know." Then, with a grudging and surly addendum: "How much longer d'you want?"

"Might I suggest a week?"

"There's no harm in suggesting it. But it's for Sir Walter to give the O.K. You've got that?"

"Then unless I hear to the contrary, my dear Mr. Reddington…"

"Unless you hear to the contrary, you'll meet me here midnight one week from now. But with this difference."

"Yes?"

"Next time you'll tote the dough, see? I warn you, Sir Walter's rattled. If I'm any judge of hooman nature, it'll be your last chance."

"Tut-tut! If you could only appreciate the technical difficulties—"

"Cut that! I'm off. I've hung about here long enough."

"Oh, very well, Mr. Reddington. I'll bid you good night."

"S'long. And don't *forget*."

The three-part tableau broke into action. The Voice sidled off down the main road. Willy came pit-patting rather miserably back up the lane.

Basil dived into the shadow of a nearby bush and stayed there until Willy
had mounted the stile and set off across the meadows back to Old Knolle.

As he proceeded, flustered and perplexed, towards Fallow Cottage,
Basil could not help thinking that Willy Farnham had never put up a more
convincing show. To an outsider he might have sounded measured and
nonchalant, but to Basil, who knew every intonation of that precise reedy
voice, since it was one of the many instruments he played upon, there
was no deception. The instrument had sounded a note that was not to
be mistaken—a note of fear. For some reason the old actor had allowed
himself to drift into a very nasty situation, in which a certain hard-hearted
skinflint called Sir Walter was dunning him for money. That much was
obvious. The puzzling factor in the cross-talk had been Willy's sanguine
belief that in a week's time he would be able to honour his debt. This,
Basil knew, was ridiculous, and for a very simple reason. Only the day
before Willy had borrowed twenty-five pounds on account of salary, which
would not be due to him until rehearsals started in a fortnight's time. Sam
Richardson, like all self-made millionaires, refused to lend a penny-piece
to anybody who appeared on his pay-roll. Beggars, casual acquaintances,
old friends, poor relations—yes. Employees—never.

So how the devil did Willy expect to meet Sir Walter's demands within
one week from that very day?

Back in the cottage, Basil took two aspirins, which he washed down
with rum in black coffee, and slipped wearily into bed. He'd had a very,
very trying and disturbing evening, take it all round.

CHAPTER V

Clay Feet

I

MRS. DREED WAS NOT A HOUSEKEEPER; SHE WAS AN ATMOSPHERE. She was a chill wind blowing down a corridor. A draught under the door. A silence descending on a cocktail party. A shadow on the grass. Mrs. Dreed was always present before she was actually noticed. A premonitory shiver went down the spine, a turn of the head, and there she was—tall, gaunt and usually disapproving. Her dresses were severe and tubular. She wore them with the air of a prison wardress. If Sam's theatrical guests, in a general sense, be looked upon as Royalists, then Mrs. Dreed was without question the Roundhead in their midst.

She had not really approved of the Big Men in the biscuit world when they had arrived in their luxury cars with their luxury wives, and dropped cigar-ash and doubtful anecdotes all over the house. But they were respectable, high-minded citizens when set beside her employer's theatrical friends. Towards them Mrs. Dreed displayed a frozen solicitude which was ten times more deadly than the most pernicious insult. She subdued them all with her piercing eye, even Basil, and was never happier than when the winter season started and they all returned to Town.

Angela was the only one who had wheedled a smile from her. It was a rusty smile that squeaked on its hinges, but it put Angela in a class of her own. Mrs. Dreed claimed to recognize quality when she encountered it. Was there the slightest nip in the air, Angela always had a hot-bottle in her bed and a towel warming for her in the airing cupboard.

Unfortunately there had been a very slight nip in the air the previous night, and Mrs. Dreed, portering a belated hot-bottle to her favourite, had seen Rudolph enter Angela's bedroom. Now there was a frost in her heart, for she had hovered in the passage for over twenty minutes and the young man had not reappeared!

She was in a dour mood when Deirdre came on her after breakfast in the music-room. She was arranging the flowers.

"Good morning, Mrs. Dreed. Isn't it scrumptious weather? You look worried."

"And not without cause," sniffed Mrs. Dreed, jamming a spray or two of gladioli into a large pot. "There are certain things…"

She hung up the receiver, as it were, and ripped a cluster of faded roses from a bowl on the grand piano. Deirdre waited. Mrs. Dreed was mute. This was obviously a dramatic pause in the dialogue. Deirdre fed her the appropriate cue.

"You were saying…"

"That there are certain things I cannot tolerate in this house, Miss Lehaye. Mr. Richardson having no lady, I am responsible for the moral tone of his household. And I do not consider it moral for young men to sneak into young ladies' bedrooms—no matter what their profession."

Deirdre looked shocked. "You don't mean to tell me, Mrs. Dreed…?"

"Yes, I do!" snapped the housekeeper, tidying up a spray of phlox with repressed anger. "And I think you should know, Miss Lehaye. I'm not pretending that you're any better than the others, but you're old enough to take care of yourself. Miss Walsh isn't. It's your duty to warn her before things go too far."

"Angela! Oh, my dear Mrs. Dreed, you must be mistaken. How naughty! Who, in heaven's name, was the bold bad gentleman?"

"He was no gentleman," retorted Mrs. Dreed, gathering up the withered blooms and stuffing them into her raffia basket. "It was that new arrival—Mr.—Mr. Millar. Twenty minutes at least he was there. Twenty minutes! It doesn't bear thinking about."

"Oh, doesn't it," thought Deirdre happily, as Mrs. Dreed stalked out like an offended prelate. "I simply can't keep this to myself. It's too delicious. Oh, the sly little puss! Basil will nearly die of laughter when I tell him. Or won't he? I wonder…?"

2

Basil rose in a foul temper about half-past ten. Mrs. Ewing had been rattling about in the kitchen for hours in a subtle effort to suggest that, even though he could drowse his life away in bed, *some* people had to work for a living. As a matter of fact, the aspirins had not done their duty. He had slept fitfully and had suffered from the most awesome nightmares. The garden roller turned up in all of them, usually running away down a slope that ended in a cliff edge, or a stone quarry, or the lake at Old Knolle. Three times the roller plunged into the lake, and three times Basil, with a back-breaking effort, manhandled the confounded thing up on the the bank and hauled it once more to the top of the slope. To make matters worse, Deirdre stood watching his useless performance, tugging at an imaginary moustache and twirling an imaginary cane. It was curious how this moustache *motif* had reappeared in his dream. Once—many, many years ago, it seemed—he had made several brief appearances in a vaudeville act. He had favoured tails, an opera hat and an ebony cane. He was a masher with a toothbrush moustache. It was a period of his existence that he preferred to forget.

After a thin breakfast he went, with a complete lack of logic, to cool his wrath in the rising heat of that perfect July morning. He began to mow the lawns with a kind of vicious energy. Confound young Millar and his play! If it hadn't been for *Pigs in Porcelain* he would never have come to Old Knolle and made eyes at Angela. No, by heaven! he wouldn't stand for any silly nonsense where Angela was concerned! He wasn't in love with her, of course, but he was interested in her, deeply interested. He had to admit that she wasn't just like any other *ingénue* as he had first suspected. There was something fey about her, a certain *je ne sais quoi* which got under a fellow's skin. But he wasn't in love with her.

He pushed the mower with such blind vigour that he crashed into the mulberry tree and nearly winded himself. He had a sudden belief that unless he pushed the mower as hard as he could for as long as he was able, he'd fall in love with Angela. If he stopped being energetic for a moment, if he paused to reflect, he'd be done for! "Head over heels, a forked one," as Shakespeare so blithely said. The vision of himself in love was so ridiculous that he shut his inward eye against it and shivered. At Millar's age one wrote sonnets about girls like Angela. At *his* age girls like Angela wrote triolets about men like him. That was the crux of the matter. It would be *infra dig* to fall in love. He must mow and mow and mow, and sweat this queer fever out of his pores.

But at the end of an hour there was no more grass to mow and the moment of inaction could no longer be denied. He bundled the mower into the garden shed and sat on the handle of the barrow, mopping his brow. He wanted a beer but he was too exhausted to go indoors and get it. His eye travelled over the lawns and he suffered a paralysing shock. Yesterday afternoon, when the girls had come over from Old Knolle, what had he been doing? Rolling the lawns, hadn't he? And why had he been rolling the lawns? Because he had just mown them. One never rolled first and mowed afterwards, because the grass would be flattened and the blades wouldn't catch it properly. And this morning, what had he done? Walked out of the cottage and mown the damned lawn all over again!

Basil gasped at the enormity of his realization. He *was* in love. *He was in love with Angela!* He'd never felt so utterly depressed in his life. He was like a man injected, as he thinks, against smallpox, who looks down and finds himself coming out in unmistakable spots. He felt ready to kick himself for being such a careless fool!

4

Into the middle of this mood walked Deirdre, with her story about Rudolph's visit to Angela's bedroom. If anything were needed to brush the final layer of shadow on to Basil's gloom, this was it. His hackles rose. He felt furious. The knowledge that Deirdre's mocking glance was upon him in his hour of tribulation, drove all thought of caution out of his head.

"Damn him! Damn him!" he blurted out. "What the deuce does he think he's up to? Who the devil does he think he is? What right has he to make this pass at Angela? My God, Deirdre, I'm not going to stand for this. It's incredible. The confounded cheek of it!"

Deirdre's cool glance travelled over him as if he were a spoilt child in a tantrum.

"My, my, my! What a pother. Basil, darling, you're not in love, surely?"

"Love?" It sounded as if Basil had never heard of the word. "No, of course not. I just won't have Angela worried at the start of a hard season's work. When's that—er—youth leaving for Town?"

"To-day. After lunch."

"Good."

"Sam was telling me that you've decided to give his play the cold shoulder."

"We have."

"You astonish me. I thought it was a fine piece of work. So did Willy. So did Angela."

"But as I happen to be responsible for the general policy of the Beaumont, mine is the only opinion that really counts," said Basil with a malevolent look. "I should be grateful if you'd kindly keep to your side of the fence. When I want your advice, my dear Deirdre, I'll ask for it."

Deirdre was quite unruffled. It was by the exercise of this inhuman detachment that she gained her ascendancy over people like Basil.

"Poor Angela will be dreadfully disappointed. She was dying to play Christabel."

Basil ignored this, though it hurt him. "Why was that young man in her bedroom?"

"My dear Basil, don't be obtuse. Why would *you* visit a young lady's bedroom?"

"I wouldn't!" snapped Basil.

"You mean that you'd expect the young lady to visit yours? What a loathsome Casanova you are, dear Basil."

"Don't be coarse. And you still haven't answered my question."

"Why not ask young Rudolph? Or Angela? I can only suppose that he went to Angela's bedroom because she had asked him to."

"Balderdash! He was foisting himself on her."

"Foisting?"

Basil turned away and strode back into the cottage. Over his shoulder he concluded: "It's lucky that the young whippersnapper is leaving after lunch—otherwise I wouldn't answer for the consequences. I won't have Angela distressed in this way. It's damnable!"

5

Seated in the train which was taking him back to Town, Rudolph also reached a new low level of depression. Sam, with charming apologies, of course, had broken the news to him about the play. The Beaumont didn't want it. All the high hopes which he and his Aunt Clara had placed upon this visit had shrivelled to ashes. He was a failure.

When he had told her of Sam's decision, Angela had been nice to him, fearfully nice. Nobody could have been more sympathetic, but even that hadn't done much to yank him out of his black mood.

"It's Basil," she had declared. "It's Basil at the back of all this. I shall never forgive the wretch."

Rudolph, on his part, could have joyfully murdered the fellow. It was not only that the play had been turned down. It meant that his vision of Angela in the part of Christabel was now doomed to remain a vision for ever. Those intimate rehearsals, those *tête-à-tête* over the subtleties of the character, the culminating thrill of the first night… unrealizable dreams. Rudolph groaned. Some day, somehow, he would get even with that rotter, Barnes.

Perhaps he could get a job as a dramatic critic and slang his productions right and left. He could visualize the opening sentences:

The superb acting of Miss Angela Walsh alone saved this deplorable production from being classed as London's greatest theatrical fiasco. Mr. Basil Barnes should employ his energies in producing one-act plays for Women's Institutes and then work his way upwards. That is if he can face the trials and tribulations of a very, very long ascent.

Or, better still, suppose he could persuade some other management to produce the play and the thing turned out to be a howling success? Where would Mr. Basil Barnes be then, eh? Mr. Richardson would not take so kindly to a man whose ill-judgment had persuaded him to refuse a gold-mine. Yes, thought Rudie, his energy rising, that was his immediate job—to hawk *Pigs in Porcelain* round to every manager in London. Then his mood once more tobogganed down a steep slope into the valley of depression. Even if it were produced Angela would not be playing Christabel. She was tied up with the fortunes of the Beaumont. Though a success would mean a lot to him as a dramatist, as a young man on the verge of a violent passion it would mean nothing if this success were not to be shared with Angela. She was wonderful! She was unique! She was heaven-sent and heavenly! And just because one man had decided to exercise his lack of intelligence and damn the play, Angela was to be whisked out of his orbit only a few hours after she had so miraculously entered it.

He had her London address; that was some comfort. And Aunt Clara would always provide a stout, a very stout link between them. She could, so to speak, spread protective wings over her and invite them both to tea in Sundays. Moreover, Angela had promised that when she returned to Town for serious rehearsals she would ring him up and fix a date for lunch. Take it all in all, his depression seemed unnecessarily profound.

But Rudolph, though young, had few illusions about men like Basil. He knew well enough that if Basil decided to make a set at Angela, she would find it very difficult to resist the lure of his synthetic charm. There was something between them even now. And he, with the blind ambitions of an artist, had actually urged Angela to make herself agreeable to Basil to further the chances of his play! Really, last night in her bedroom, he must have been out of his senses. Perhaps the shock of coming on her in that flimsy-whimsy nightdress had temporarily unhinged his reason. He recalled the electric second or two when she had fallen into his arms. His heart quickened to keep time with the beat of the wheels as the train rattled through the suburbs.

There was, of course, another reason why he had spoken to her so stupidly. When, by a lovely error, he had burst in on her privacy he had not been in love with Angela; just warm with an undeclared friendliness. When, about a quarter of an hour later, he had left her bedroom and returned to his own, he was no longer in doubt. The change had been sudden, but complete. Before falling asleep, a vision of her had hovered under the dark ceiling—with an idiotic gesture, which in broad daylight he blushed to recall, he had reached up with his arms and taken that vision into his embrace. He was still embracing it—yes, even there in the train, with a man opposite in a bowler hat and a small boy lolling against his side sucking a toffee-apple. Heavy realism, like many waters, could not quench love, and there was no doubt now that Angela was the one and only woman in his life!

6

At that precise moment Basil, hatless, breathless, impatient, was pounding along the woodland path which fringed the lake at Old Knolle. He had learnt from a gardener that Angela had only just gone in that direction. Never had he felt so fleet of foot, so light in the head, such a complete and utter ass. With a jaundiced eye he saw himself as a twentieth-century Pan pursuing his one and only dryad down a sylvan glade. The terrible part about it all was that he couldn't help himself! He knew he was making himself ridiculous, lowering his dignity, throwing himself open to an almighty snub, but he had to go on with it. Angela, like the irresistible flux of the Severn Bore, had swept him off his feet. He tried to analyse the reasons for this overnight flowering of a bud which he had always considered desiccated. But there was no logical explanation.

He came on her in a small sunlit glen on the far side of the lake. She was gazing reflectively into the water and shattering her own tremulous image with a handful of little stones. His approach was deadened by the rank moss. She uttered a little cry.

"Basil! What's the matter?"

"Why should anything be the matter?"

"You look so hot and bothered. Have you been running?"

"No, of course not! I just happened to be taking a stroll round the lake."

"Well, I'm not stopping you."

"Good Lord! are you piqued or something?"

Angela nodded and threw her little stones more violently into the water.

"I suppose it's about that damned play?" Basil went on. "Well, I'm sorry if you've accepted my criticism as a personal slight. But you wouldn't have me be false to my inner artistic convictions? I can't help being guided by the integrity of my good taste. If I thought young Millar's play was a masterpiece I should have said so without hesitation." He paused to gauge the effect of his argument. Angela remained silent. "Good heavens! You surely don't think I turned down Millar's play because of any personal prejudice?"

"No, of course you didn't."

"No, of course I didn't," said Basil hastily. "The considered policy of the Beaumont must come first. I could see at once that you'd have been a dreadful flop in the part of Christabel."

"Rudie didn't."

"Rudie?"

"Mr. Millar."

Angela returned to her pebble-throwing. Basil braced himself for the real business in hand. So far the whole of the opening scene had gone off the rails. The setting was perfect, but the dialogue was hopeless.

"Angela!" He tried the low, vibrant register of his voice, which was so effective in creating an atmosphere pregnant (as the saying goes) with emotion. She turned in surprise. The strange distortion of his face frightened her considerably. She wondered if overwork had unsettled his mind and if he now contemplated hurling her into the lake. He went on, "Why, in heaven's name, did you let young Millar into your bedroom?"

"Into my bedroom?" Angela flushed and then looked furious. "Ooo! how could you believe such a libel? I didn't let him in. Who said I let him in? Oh, how beastly!"

"Then he gate-crashed, did he?"

"No, he didn't! It was all a mistake. He thought my room was his room, and when he saw *me* there he realized it wasn't. Basil, you don't honestly believe—?"

"I tried not to, naturally—but when I heard the bare facts of the incident—well, it was very difficult to keep faith in—your—that is to say—in you." He put a lovely tortured edge on his voice and posed himself in an attitude of contrite misery. "And the thought of any other man…"

"Basil, what on earth are you saying?"

"Don't you realize? Good heavens, Angela—last night on the terrace—you don't mean to say you thought I was philandering?"

"I wasn't sure. I did—and then I didn't."

"Well, I wasn't. When I kissed you I was obeying an irresistible impulse. I couldn't help myself. My feelings were too strong for me. They are now. I'm half out of my mind—no, don't interrupt!—if I don't tell you now I'll never have the courage to again." Basil grabbed her hands and pulled her round to face him. It was a neat move, and Angela, who had been directed in this sort of scene many times before, fell naturally into the right position. Arms extended, left foot advanced, head thrown up. If only, thought Basil, the dialogue had reached the same high level of excellence as the mechanics of the scene. He went on, studding his speech liberally with dramatic hiatus: "If only you realized what you've—done to me. My peace of mind—broken into. Feel like a tongue-tied schoolboy. I can't reason myself out of this, my dear. I've tried and—I've failed. Failed—hopelessly! Don't you see? Can't you see?" Basil stopped short in alarm. He was dropping unconsciously into a slice of dialogue from last season's production of *Golden Harvest*. He prayed to heaven that Angela, who had played the juvenile lead, hadn't tumbled to the plagiarism. But Angela was gazing up at him with unbelievable admiration—nay more!—with a shy and veiled tenderness. Encouraged, he went on with redoubled ardour: "My dear child, it's no good beating about the bush. I'm in love with you. I couldn't believe it was true. I tried to make an impersonal analysis of my emotions. Hopeless! Quite hopeless! I had to face up to it. I *was* in love. With *you*, Angela, my poor dear child. I was in love with *you*."

"But, Basil—" Rudolph Millar seemed a thousand miles away.

"There are no 'buts'." He took her into his arms with a precise pincers movement which he much favoured as a climax to his love scenes. "From now on there are no buts. To every cue there is only one answer—yes, yes, yes! You understand, my darling Angela? This is something tremendous, unique, unforgettable in your life. It is, isn't it? You *know* it is."

"Yes, Basil—unforgettable."

He sighed with profound relief as he kissed her. Well, that was over, thank God! He had managed to declare himself without really impairing his self-respect. There had been no snub. From now on things should progress smoothly and pleasantly, even excitingly. There was a great deal he didn't know about her, a great deal; and the element of discovery is one of the most potent delights which Dan Cupid showers on his henchmen. Basil felt more sure of himself, more pleased with himself, more devoted to himself than ever before. The future was a broad sunlit plain spread out before him...

CHAPTER VI

Deirdre Walks at Night

I

IT MUST NOT BE THOUGHT THAT THE MEMBERS OF SAM'S HOUSE-PARTY were always idle. July was ending, and soon the first plays would go into rehearsal. The first three, in fact, had already been cast, and the various scripts handed out to the selected members of the company. Angela, Clara and Willy were often to be seen in some private corner of the house or gardens, lips moving, eyes vacant, brows corrugated. A layman wandering into the place would have concluded that Old Knolle was one of those expensive mental homes where the Best People smuggle their slightly abnormal relatives, and thereafter speak of them as staying incognito in the South of France. But, of course, these were only actors and actresses learning their words. Of all the hard work which is to be associated with the theatre, this is probably the toughest. If anybody still harbours the illusion that the stage is all glamour and cocktail parties, let them take up one of the fatter Shakespearian rôles (say, Falstaff), shut themselves up in a room and commit to memory about a thousand lines of non-rhyming verse. It *can* be done, but not without devilish hard work.

Deirdre was not weighted down with this particular labour. She was not concerned with the audible side of the show, but the visual. Her job was to surround Angela, Clara, Willy and the rest of them with suitable and atmospheric settings. But even she did not escape drudgery. If, in her private life, she had no scruples whatsoever, in her work she was highly conscientious. It took a great deal more to satisfy her than it did Sam Richardson, who had to foot the bill if she made mistakes. Deirdre might see the general layout of the scene in a single inspired flash, but thereafter she worked out the details as if she were designing, not a stage set, but a precision instrument. Sketch followed sketch; one colour scheme gave way to another; a line was altered here; an angle there; a new balance struck by the introduction of different planes; a high-light modified; a low-light built up—it was all planning, reconsidering, substituting and scrapping. Sometimes she felt tired and depressed. She suffered for days on end with splitting headaches. She could not sleep.

Insomnia was Deirdre's most persistent nightmare. No sooner did she long to stop thinking, than Nature saw to it that she had several more waking hours in which to think. She tried everything—hot milk, aspirins, hop-pillows, crossword puzzles, detective fiction, bromides. Only the bromides had any effect, and these left her more depressed than ever. In consequence it was nothing unusual to glimpse a spectral figure in a gold mediæval house-coat passing in silence down the corridors of Old Knolle or along the moonlit paths of the garden. Nobody took any notice of it. It was merely Deirdre having one of her "sleepless turns" again.

Nobody took any notice of it until some three days after Rudolph's departure, when Deirdre, now well into her stride, started off on one of her lonely nocturnal prowls. She descended the grand staircase, soft-footed like the cat she was, her feet encased in embroidered moccasins. She crossed the hall and moved off down the east wing, where there was a door giving on to the Dutch garden. And then, half-way along this corridor, she stopped dead and held her breath. A vivid rectangle of moonlight lay across the passage opposite the open door of Sam's study. The fact that the door *was* open was, in itself, curious, for Mrs. Dreed's final act of grace was to stalk round the lower part of the house closing the doors in case they should slam during the night.

But more curious and much more intriguing was the soft scuffling, rustling sound which proceeded from the study. Deirdre edged along the wall, just like a cat, and rubbed her nose round the door-frame. She did not exactly purr with delight, but she drew in a quick breath and care-fully exhaled. For a single glance had convinced Deirdre that the person in the room was up to no good, and if there was anything which gave her real honest pleasure it was the sight of somebody committing a sin. Particularly when they didn't know they were being overlooked. She

savoured her excellent strategic position, gave a little mew of amusement and went in.

Willy Farnham, seated in Sam's desk-chair, slammed home the drawer
which he had been rifling and sprang up. Deirdre could hear his feet tip-
tapping with violent agitation on the floor.

"Hullo! Having a nice little burglary all on your little own, Willy
darling? Bless his little heart—how he does get around!"

"Damme! what do *you* want? It's preposterous creeping about the
place and frightening people out of their wits. It's those soft slippers—
horrible, sneaky things! What do you want?"

"To be taken into the arms of Morpheus, Willy darling. I can't sleep."

Willy, a slender silhouette against the moonlit window, gave a shrill
little laugh.

"Well, well, well, and here am I perambulating round the house for
precisely the same reason. Now that rehearsals are imminent, we're all too
nervy. I wanted a smoke and then… damme!… I found I was out of tobacco.
I felt sure Sam wouldn't mind if I borrowed a pipeful. Such a generous
fellow always—eh, my dear?" Then in sudden alarm: "No—don't do that!"

Deirdre had switched on the light and was now appraising Willy with
the sort of scrutiny he was least capable of sustaining. He placed a hand
over his eyes as if to shield himself from the glare.

"Why, Willy darling, what *is* the matter? You look like a small boy
caught stealing jam in the pantry. Did you find your tobacco?"

"No—unfortunately."

"Perhaps it was difficult to find it in the dark. Why not have another
look?"

"Quite unnecessary."

"I can't understand why you didn't turn on the light."

"Heavens above!" Willy made an extravagant gesture of irritation. "I
had no desire to disturb the whole household."

"Perhaps Sam doesn't keep his tobacco in the desk," persisted Deirdre,
her eyes never leaving Willy's nutcracker face. "What made you think
he did?"

"Damme! it's the usual place, isn't it?" Willy was now frankly agitated
by the trend of the dialogue. He had the impression that he was playing

in a scene which was destined to end in a sudden *dénouement*. "I think I'll go back to my room."

Deirdre's expression altered in a flash. She was no longer lazy and smiling. She had played with her mouse long enough and it was now time to gobble him up.

"I'm sorry, Willy—I just don't believe you. Your acting talents aren't equal to the occasion."

"Confound it, young lady, what do you mean?"

"It's no good dancing like that. I'm not in the least terrified by your tantrums." She made a swift dive at his pocket and snatched out a fat bundle of notes secured with a rubber band. "This is a new brand of tobacco, isn't it, Willy? Smoked only in the Best Circles, I presume. What a fool you are, aren't you?"

"I should deem it a favour if you'd kindly return those notes."

"Don't be so damn stilted! I've caught you red-handed, Willy, and the most polished speeches aren't going to get you out of this nasty corner. What an old fool you are! What a fool, Willy!"

"Damme! but you don't really imagine that I filched that money from Sam's desk, do you? Tut-tut! you're suffering from overstrain. This lack of sleep has distorted your powers of reasoning."

Deirdre found an odd moment to smile again, but it wasn't a pleasant smile.

"Curiously enough, Willy, insomnia has a sharpening effect on the mind. It increases one's powers of perception. You ask any doctor, and see if I'm not right. I suppose gambling is at the root of this sorry exhibition?" Willy said nothing, but he was beginning to dance with ever-increasing wrath. Deirdre's smile went out like a snuffed candle. "This looks like a long professional 'rest' for you, Willy. Sam won't like this one little bit."

"God in heaven! you wouldn't tell Sam anything about this?" Willy's voice rose to a choking treble and he made an ineffectual snatch at the notes. "I'll not answer for the consequences if you breathe a word to anybody about to-night. I'm dangerous when I'm angry. Very dangerous. I go half out of my mind. Damme! I wouldn't stop at murder. I warn you, young lady, don't let me work myself up, because I might do things to you that I should feel sorry about later."

"Stuff and nonsense! These little displays of yours are just part of your stock-in-trade, Willy. I realized that long ago. You may fool the others, but you've never fooled me. Stop that infantile prancing and listen to me." She lowered her voice and went closer to Willy, now trembling and deflated. She pushed him down roughly into Sam's chair and stood over him, a groomed and sophisticated Hecate. "I'm not going to make you put that money back, even if you want to. Sam's so wealthy he may not miss these notes, and your need is obviously greater than his, otherwise you wouldn't have descended to this sort of thing. Well, I'm going to keep quiet and let you get away with it. It *is* a gambling debt, isn't it?" Willy nodded. "How much?"

"A hundred and fifty—that's all. A paltry one hundred and fifty."

"How much is there here?" Deirdre held up the bundle of notes.

"I don't know."

"Very well, Willy—we'll find out."

She split the bundle and began to count. There were two hundred and twenty-five one-pound notes. Deirdre set aside one hundred and fifty and handed them to Willy. The other seventy-five she slipped into the pocket of her house coat. Willy nodded.

"I see," he said.

"Then you're not quite such an old fool as I thought you, Willy darling. And if there *is* a rumpus and you want a alibi—well, we'll waive the conventions and say you were in my bedroom discussing art. Nobody will think anything of it—not even Basil. You're too senile to be classed as dangerous—even at night."

"You're very bitter, young woman."

"I'm very logical," concluded Deirdre.

2

Basil in love, apart from a noticeable change in attitude to Angela, was not very different from Basil out of love. He still saw the world about him as a tragi-comedy in which he played the only worthwhile rôle. Other people were merely so many "feeds" in the act. His most valued acquaintances were still those who could benefit him most. Even in love, Basil hadn't lost his touch. He could still sit on his throne and demand lip-service and genuflexions as a species of divine right. It was natural, therefore, that although one side of him was in a whirl, he did not forget that Willy Farnham had a date.

He intended to be there when Sir Walter's foxy agent collected the "dough". Like Deirdre, he enjoyed watching people squiggle on the rack, and, in this case, Willy had only himself to blame for running into debt.

So, a few minutes before midnight, exactly one week after the first meeting, the three-part tableau again posed itself against the moon-laved landscape. Willy was early. So was Basil. Mr. Red Reddington, piqued by having to wait on the last occasion, obviously intended this time to make Willy do the waiting. The latter, still hoppity after the cataclysm of the previous night, pirouetted and dipped in the road like some spectral Nijinsky. His nerves were unreliable. He felt ripe for homicide. He had made a belated vow never to gamble again.

Suddenly, without the lightest sound, Red Reddington material-ized again. His thick voice came out of the shadows like the croak of a bull-frog.

"So you've made it O.K.? No hokey-pokey about it this time, eh, Mr. Farnham? You got the dough?"

"I have been fortunate enough, Mr. Reddington, to—er—lay my hands on the necessary amount." Basil saw the little package pass into Red's outstretched palm. "I think you will find that all in order."

"Huh! I'm taking no chances. You stay alongside while I count it."

The husky voice began the count—a pair of agile hands flickering in the moonlight with the attached body still smothered in the shadows. Willy tip-toed round and about. He was anxious to have done with the whole fantastic business and get back to bed. The fact that Red Reddington doubted his word hurt him considerably. The voice ceased its sibilant litany.

"O.K. It's right—just. One hundred and fifty of the best."

"And now," said Willy, "may I trouble you for the I.O.U. I gave Sir Walter?"

"You may."

Willy struck a match, shielded it with his cupped hands, while Red brought the slip of paper into the light. Willy examined it closely. Then he blew out the match, took the paper and tore it into small pieces.

"Well," he observed. "That brings down the curtain on the final act of this particular farce. I trust Sir Walter will be satisfied."

"Don't you worry, Mr. Farnham. He'll fling his arms round my neck and kiss me when I show up with this. Here! I almost forgot. He sent a message."

"Oh?"

"Yes, he said that if by any chance you find yourself round about Golden Square drop in again at the Club. You're always welcome, he said. Oh, and I was to tell you that the password's been changed again. Case of necessity. It's Eggs and Bacon. Don't forget. Eggs and Bacon. S'long."

And Mr. Red Reddington, slapping the notes into his pocket, melted back into the gloom from which he had so silently emerged.

"So this pug-faced Ariel returns to his unscrupulous Prospero," thought Willy sadly, as he began to execute his *pas seul* back up the lane. "Damme! what was the new password? Ah, of course, Eggs and Bacon. Faugh! how unforgivably plebeian. Not that I shall have need of it. Tut-tut! Of course not. But for a friend, perhaps—yes, yes—one never knows—"

"Now I wonder how the devil," thought Basil, "the old boy managed to raise the wind?"

Perhaps Deirdre had fallen for his Louis Quinze charm and lent him the cash at five per cent. Clara would have loaned it for ten per cent., no doubt, but Clara was always short of money because she had to keep her husband who ran a hardware store in Streatham at a handsome annual loss.

3

Basil, in tune with Deirdre, had an unhealthy interest in other people's lapses. He wasn't at all interested in his own, but the sort of *impasse* into which poor old Willy Farnham had wandered roused the latent explorer in him. He wanted to see the whole affair projected before him like a film "short", and, at the moment, there was one sequence missing. Between

Willy's promise to pay the hundred and fifty pounds and his ability to do so was a blank strip of film. Since the only possible person who might have helped Willy to clear his debt was Deirdre, Basil decided to have a talk with her.

When, the next morning, he arrived over at Old Knolle, he drew Deirdre aside into the summer-house.

"I want a word with you."

"Professional?"

"No, private. I want to warn you."

"Me? You're very solicitous. I've always felt if I were about to walk over a precipice, Basil darling, you'd let me get on with it just to see what a fool I looked falling through the air."

Basil pretended to a huff. "Oh, all right, if you want to throw good money after bad."

"Money?" Deirdre's expression changed instantly. "Ah! that's different. That's nothing to joke about, Basil."

"Of course it isn't. But if Willy spins another hard-luck story, don't respond. That is, unless you want to turn a loan into a gift. Even the hundred and fifty you've already advanced him—"

"Me? Lend hard-earned money to Willy? Basil darling, it must be the sun. I've never lent Willy a sou. What on earth put that idea into your head?"

Basil glanced round and lowered his voice. He liked being impressive.

"Just this. Willy's managed to raise one hundred and fifty pounds during this last week. He'd already drawn twenty-five in advance on his salary, so I know he's broke. What I want to know is, how the devil did he do it?"

Deirdre looked through her curving lashes and said with a matter-of-fact chuckle: "Oh, he stole it, my sweet."

"Don't be funny!"

"No, he did, really. He filched it from Sam's desk the other night. I walked in on him and spoilt the party. Poor Willy. He's so naïve in his naughtiness."

"But, good God! What's Sam going to say?"

"So far, he's said nothing. These millionaires are pretty casual about their small change." Deirdre glanced up as a shadow fell across the path in front of the summer-house. "Hullo, who's this?"

It was Angela—radiant, bright-eyed, enhaloed in love. In an instant Basil had forgotten Willy, Sir Walter, Red Reddington, Deirdre, everybody—everybody save this slip of *ingénue* young womanhood. His whole being metaphorically flung itself at the feet of this vision, this goddess in a light summer frock, bandeau and tennis shoes. He sprang up, knocked over a wicker-table, and went forward with his hands outstretched.

"Angela! I was just going to hunt you out."

"Oh?"

The monosyllable struck him like a bullet. He recoiled. His arms fell to his sides. There was a look in Angela's eyes that had not been there two seconds earlier; it was a hurt, accusing, slightly angry look.

"I say, is there anything wrong?"

"No, of course not."

Deirdre observed maliciously, "Of course there's something wrong! At this moment Angela is saying to herself, 'If he's in love with me, as he says he is, then why has he sneaked away into the summer-house with that awful Deirdre girl?' I can see the words printed on her frock."

Angela protested, "Don't be so hateful, Deirdre! The thought never entered my head." She wondered how the wretched woman could be so accurate and penetrating. "I was just going to ask Basil to hear my words."

"I'd love to—of course. Let's take a punt and pole out to the island. We shan't be disturbed there. What a morning! What a really grand morning! Aaaah!"

Basil rubbed his hands together and inhaled a gigantic pocket of air. Deirdre looked over him with an amused and contemptuous expression. Was this actually the great Byronic Basil speaking? In all the time that she had known him never once had he offered to hear anybody's lines. He might wax sarcastic if they fluffed at rehearsal, but he never offered to help them with the learning of a part, however long and difficult. Such hackwork was far, far beneath him.

"So this," thought Deirdre, "*is* love! Poor little Angela." Aloud she said, "Well, don't let me detain you from the good work, my children. So this is where you pat me on the head, Basil dear, and walk out of my life for ever. I'm heartbroken. My, my, my—what starry-eyed felicity! Does it really feel so marvellous to be in love?"

Basil, always suspicious when Deirdre sounded meek and inquiring, knew that the question was purely rhetorical.

"Don't sound so damned bitter! What's the matter?"

"I don't think she quite likes the idea of us being fond of each other," said Angela simply. "The sight of other people's happiness seems to annoy her. There *are* wretches like that, you know."

"But, good heavens, you don't really mind, do you, Deirdre?" Basil felt all of a glow because she really did seem to be rather cut up. "After all, Angela and I just couldn't help ourselves. Could we, my child?"

"Go on—pat her on the head," put in Deirdre swiftly. Just in time, Basil desisted. He glared at Deirdre with honest surprise.

"Good God! I never thought you cared a rap for me. It just goes to show how women in love dissemble. If it's been a nasty knock, I apologize. But I thought you guessed which way the wind was blowing."

For a moment, caught on the wrong foot, Deirdre was speechless. She was siphoned clean of all repartee. Then, with an expression of derisive mockery, she lunged at the tough bladder of his self-conceit.

"My dear Basil, how sweetly thoughtful of you to apologize. So unusual. So unexpected. And may I congratulate you on your conquest." She smiled prettily on Angela. "And you, too, my dear. But, if you take my advice, you won't let him out of your sight more than is absolutely necessary."

"Oh, and why not?"

"Because he's under the illusion that the habits of a lifetime can be broken in a night. Some men make love as easily and successfully as others make money."

Basil advanced on her with an attempt to suggest menace and outrage. He looked like a petulant bull-frog. "That's damned rude and damned libellous!"

"Is it? Do you recall the Palladian at Manchester, about fifteen years ago?"

The bull-frog collapsed. This time the bladder of conceit *was* pricked. Basil was suddenly uneasy and unsure of himself.

"And if I do?"

"Oh, it's only that I seem to remember—" began Deirdre in a silken voice. "Yes—I seem to remember—"

"All right—forget it! I know what you're going to say. I've always suspected."

"What?"

"That you—"

"Well?"

"Never mind! Damn it! I'm just not interested. Nor is Angela. Are you, my darling?"

"Of course not, Basil."

Deirdre stood looking at them, laughing in a shivery sort of way. The impossible had happened and Providence had dealt her a Royal Flush. If Basil were to take this love affair really seriously for the first time in his life, well, well, well—

As they strolled down the lawn towards the lake, Angela clinging to Basil's arm, she asked with a delicious *moue*, "What did she mean, Basil? I'm not really interested, of course. But what did she *mean*?"

"I haven't the faintest notion," said Basil shortly. "And I don't see why we should spoil this perfect summer's morning by discussing it. Deirdre's a very unappetizing young woman. I dare say you've noticed that!"

Despite the cloudless sky, Angela had the illusion that a big leaden shadow hung over the lake. A cold wind seemed to sweep up at her from the unruffled water. She clung tighter to Basil's arm, as if in an effort to recapture the mood that had sent her dancing out of the house in search of him. He hated Deirdre. Of course he did! He admired her work. She admired his. Otherwise…

Angela smiled to herself. The cold wind dropped. The shadow moved off the lake, and the man beside her was suddenly as god-like as she had always imagined him to be!

4

But Deirdre, though very penetrating about people of her own kind, knew next to nothing about millionaires. Sam Richardson was the first of the species she had met, and she had not really had time enough to study her subject. When she told Willy, and later Basil, that Sam wouldn't notice the loss from his desk, she was ignoring that prime precept which is the foundation of most large fortunes—"Look after the pence and the pounds will look after themselves." A shop-soiled maxim, maybe, but one which Sam had hugged to his heart from the very earliest days. Like most millionaires, he was prepared to walk half a mile up the Edgware Road on a boiling August day to save a penny bus fare, and equally ready to hail a taxi in Piccadilly for a casual journey to Southampton. If Sam were an open book in his attitude to most things, in money matters he was unpredictable. He had been known to scribble business letters on the backs of his Christmas cards, so that he could tuck in the envelope flaps and cheat the Inland Revenue of a few odd shillings. He had been known to buy three hundred thousand pounds' worth of Government stock in a telephone conversation lasting fifty-five seconds. He would buy a cabinet of choice cigars at seven-and-six apiece, and haggle with a street vendor over the price of a packet of pipe-cleaners.

So the unexpected happened. A few minutes after Angela and Basil stepped out of the punt on to the island, Sam stepped into his study and settled down to the weekly task of making up the pay packets of his employees at Old Knolle. It was a task he enjoyed, because it reminded him of early days in the biscuit factory, when he had personally paid out his men through a little pigeon-hole and known a flush of pride at his growing importance. The weekly wage bill was not inconsiderable, for Sam employed half a dozen gardeners, two chauffeurs, a number of maids, several odd-job men, and Mrs. Dreed. For this reason he always carried a fat bundle of notes in his desk and several bags of silver. When he had made up the pay packets, he deducted the total amount from the amount of cash in hand and made a weekly note of the balance. It was this methodical side of Sam that Willy and Deirdre had overlooked. Willy knew the money was in the desk because he had crossed by the terrace window and seen Sam handling the stuff. The nonchalant manner in which he did it deceived Willy utterly. Willy thought it was due to the natural carelessness of a millionaire when dealing with small change, when actually it was due to a life-long practice in handling notes and silver in bulk.

Thirty seconds after seating himself at his desk, Sam was ringing for Mrs. Dreed. Thirty seconds after ringing, Mrs. Dreed was silently and unaccountably at his elbow.

"Mrs. Dreed, something highly unpleasant has occurred."

"I know, sir."

Sam stared at her in astonishment. "You know? Then why didn't you report the matter to me at once?"

"I'm sorry, sir. I realize now that it was very remiss of me. But as I happened to know that the young man was leaving the following day, I thought it unnecessary to worry you."

"Then you know who was responsible for this outrage?"

"Outrage?" Mrs. Dreed reddened unbecomingly. Her nose seemed to quiver with repressed disapproval. "But really, Mr. Richardson, I had no idea that—I know the *worst* interpretation could have been—But how was I to know. I only saw him go into her bedroom. As to what might or might not have occurred *inside* the room…"

Sam's astonishment was now tinged with alarm. He had often wondered if Mrs. Dreed's Puritanism might not, in the long run, prove too great a strain on her natural instincts and unsettle her mind. He knew from the daily papers that clergymen, after long periods of self-denial, often balanced up the account with sudden orgiastic outbursts of naughtiness.

"Bedroom? My dear Mrs. Dreed, what on earth are you talking about? I never keep money in my bedroom. The two hundred and twenty-five pounds was taken from this desk some time since last Friday. That is to say, when I last made up the wages."

"Oh, dear me! I thought you were referring to something quite different, Mr. Richardson." The red flushes on her pinched cheeks deepened. "You must excuse me."

"Then you knew nothing about this?"

"Nothing, sir."

"Well, I don't intend to let the matter rest. I won't put it into the hands of the police at once. I'll make a few tactful inquiries among my guests. You will do the same where the domestic staff are concerned. We don't want a scandal."

"Quite so. But I've always held that you ought to lock the drawers of your desk. You're far too trusting, Mr. Richardson."

"I prefer it that way, Mrs. Dreed. Too many bolts and bars mean a sad deficiency of faith."

Mrs. Dreed drew herself up to her full height and delivered herself of a final pontifical remark. "Bolts and bars, Mr. Richardson, are the strongest barriers against the devil and temptation."

She was thinking then, no doubt, not of Sam's desk, but of Angela's bedroom door.

CHAPTER VII

Trouble in Ambush

I

S AM MANIPULATED HIS CROSS-QUESTIONING AFTER LUNCH THAT SAME day. It was beautifully done. The subject was wafted on to the conversation like a piece of thistledown, as his guests lounged over coffee in the music-room. But Sam had the advantage of most people who are considered dull—he could air his acumen behind his wall of good-natured stupidity without anybody troubling to suspect it was there. He had found this little bit of dissimulation very useful in a business deal. It was equally useful in his present rôle of amateur detective.

Somebody chanced to mention that, meeting Mrs. Dreed in the hall before lunch, she had looked more than usually severe. Sam saw his opening.

"Not without good reason. The poor soul is greatly upset because our routine has had a serious relapse. Friday, since time immemorial, has always been pay day—and to-day we've had to break this traditional rule for the first time in—now, let me see—yes, it must be nearly fifteen years."

Basil chuckled. "Don't tell us that you've gone into liquidation, Sam. If so, we're all in Queer Street."

"No, it's not exactly that," replied Sam; "but some unprincipled scoundrel has had the temerity to rifle my desk and make off with two hundred and twenty-five pounds."

There was a sudden hush. Sam was now the sole centre of interest. Even Basil swivelled his eyes away from Angela and fixed them stonily on Sam. Willy froze in his arm-chair. Deirdre switched a quick glance from Willy to Basil, then back again to Willy, and finally over to Sam. Angela came forward immediately with her unflagging sympathy.

"I say, Mr. Richardson—what rotten luck! Have you any idea who could have done such a beastly thing?"

"No, none at all. It's all rather mysterious. I suppose you haven't noticed anybody suspicious hanging about near my study?"

Deirdre said, with a snobbish upward curl of the lip: "You mean one of the servants? I mean, it can't very well be anybody else, can it?"

Sam gave her a level look, conspicuously lacking in friendliness. This young woman had a nasty flair for saying the wrong thing at the right time. He felt irritated by her matter-of-fact presumption.

"I've absolutely no cause for suspecting any of my domestic staff. They've all been with me for years, and I flatter myself that their wages are, and always have been, more than adequate. No, no! I think that's quite out of the question."

"Then you suggest that we—one of *us*—has had a hand in the job, Mr. Richardson?" Deirdre made ready to enjoy his embarrassment. Poor Sam was such an easy-going old bear to bait! Besides, this was a double-barrelled slam, with the second charge plugged at point-blank range into Willy's sensibilities. "Well, I suppose in a general sense we're all capable of theft. They say there's latent criminality in every adult, only in some of us it's less latent than in others."

"My dear young lady!" Sam was shocked to the core. "You know very well that I—"

"Now you just keep quiet, Deirdre," broke in Clara, her husky contralto seeping richly on to the air. "Mr. Richardson's had quite enough trouble without you rubbing salt into the wound. I know just what he means. Have we, or have we not, seen anybody suspicious dodging around the house. Well, *have* we?"

"I haven't," said Basil, with the suggestion that if *he* hadn't then nobody else could possibly have done. Taking his cue from Deirdre, he was determined, at the moment, to keep mum about Willy.

"Nor I," said Angela.

Clara declared stoutly, "I haven't seen a stranger about the place since that vacuum-cleaner salesman with the expressive eyes called last week and mistook me for the cook! Mind you, Mr. Richardson, I'm not in a position to be helpful. I've been closeted for days on end in the small conservatory struggling with my part in *The Red Ant*. As far as I'm concerned *anybody* might have slunk along the terrace and hopped into the study."

"And what about you, Willy?" asked Deirdre, in a voice as soft and harmless as a down pillow. "You look terribly repressed."

"Me?" Willy jerked himself upright, like a marionette that has suddenly been yanked out of its passivity. "Dear me—tut-tut! I know nothing. Emphatically—nothing!" He flicked a bit of gallows-humour at Sam. "Damme! Perhaps you stuffed the notes into the waste-paper basket. I know what you millionaires are!"

"Good show," thought Basil, unable to suppress his professional admiration.

Deirdre chuckled. "You really are delicious, Willy—so rare and remote from the tawdry sins of the *hoi polloi*." Then brightly, after a general glance round, "Well, *somebody* must have taken it."

"Exactly," said Sam. "I don't want a scandal, but I'm determined to call in the police if we can't get anywhere without them. It's the principle of the thing. That's what it is, y'know—the principle of the thing."

"Yes, damme!" croaked Willy, with an approving nod of his benign and silvery head. "You're right there, Sam. It *is* the principle of the thing."

More than ever Basil was of the opinion that Willy was putting up a superb show. He looked across at Deirdre who, catching his sly glance, dropped one lazy lid in a wink. Basil, with extreme caution, returned the signal.

2

They met, as if by common consent, about half an hour later in Deirdre's bedroom.

"What about the Dreed?" asked Basil.

"She can't *think* worse than I can *do*," observed Deirdre. "We must have an uninterrupted talk, and the only place where one can be really private in Old Knolle, my darling, is in one's bedroom." Adding musingly: "Though that, of course, isn't strictly true, is it?"

"More salt into open wounds, is that it?"

"Sorry. I couldn't help it. You've grown so beautifully vulnerable. At the slightest allusion to Angela you look so *tortured*. But we haven't forgathered in my bedroom to discuss Angela, have we?"

"No, we haven't."

"Wasn't he wonderful?"

"Willy?"

"Yes."

"By God, the old boy can act, you know. He's so dead sure, so—so reliable. Tell me—"

"Well?"

"Are you going to hand the old boy over to Sam?"

"Oh, don't be beastly, you wretch! Do you want to wreck next season's programme? Character actors like Mr. William Farnham don't grow on gooseberry trees."

"So we're to become accomplices after the fact?"

"We are." Deirdre moved away to the window-seat, plumped up a galaxy of fat cushions and arranged herself provokingly among them. "But with certain reservations, my dear—certain essential reservations…"

Basil, lifting her elegant legs, made room for himself on the edge of the window-seat. By the tone of her voice, he guessed that this was an occasion for soft conversation and a metaphorical laying together of heads. Sculduggery was afoot. The perfume of it mingled on the air with Deirdre's Nuit d'Amour.

"You needn't circle round the point. Coming from you, the most vile scheme wouldn't shock me."

Deirdre was amused.

"It *is* rather vile. I don't know *how* I came to think of it. But you must realize, Basil, that life's never been generous to me. I've had to fight tooth and nail for everything I've wanted, and now that I've rounded into the straight I'm going dead ahead at full stretch. Morals won't stand in my way. I'm ready to knock down every principle *en route* to success. I'll use anybody and everything to get my own back on life. This is a terrible confession to come from the unsullied lips of a girl like me, isn't it? But, for once, I'm serious. I believe, if the necessity arose, I'd commit a

murder. A *safe* murder, of course. I may be ambitious, but I'm not wearing blinkers. Remember that, Basil darling, if ever you feel inclined to
double-cross me!"

"Don't be so damned dramatic. Come to the point."

"It's this," said Deirdre. "What sort of salary does Willy get? In confidence, of course."

"I shouldn't tell you, but I will. Twenty quid a week." Deirdre
attempted a whistle which was more like the hissing of a surprised
serpent.

"So much for so little! But that's all to the good. Willy's tastes, apart
from whisky and gambling, are really very simple. You know, Basil darling,
I don't think Willy's going to find it very unaccommodating to rub along
on fifteen pounds a week."

Basil stared at her with grudging admiration. "So that's it, you little
hell-cat. Blackmail?"

"Don't be gross, my dear. If Willy is prepared to give up whisky,
gambling or both, he won't feel even the gentle breeze."

"So your silence is going to cost him a fiver a week until further
notice?"

Deirdre nodded. "Aren't I dreadful? I think up the most awful ideas,
don't I? Oh, and here's another—this concerns you."

Basil looked down on her, specifying her mature curves in his mind's
eye. She still had the power to disturb his physical equilibrium.

"Me?"

"Yes. On second thoughts, I swear I was mistaken the other night. I
said Willy was messing about at that desk. But now I come to think of
it, I believe—no frankly, Basil—I *believe* it was Rudolph Millar." Deirdre
sighed. "Human nature is really rather moth-eaten, isn't it? I suppose it
was his idea of getting his own back on Sam for turning down his play."

Basil shuddered. "By heaven, you're horrible! Uncanny! You think
of everything."

"I try to," said Deirdre meekly. "It occurred to me that if I were going
to let you into this little business arrangement pending between Willy and
myself, you'd naturally want a rake-off. I'm offering you Rudolph. When
I tell Sam my story, with reluctance and embarrassment, of course, I'm

sure I can be convincing. Even if the actual proof of Rudolph's guilt isn't forthcoming, Angela will realize what a lucky escape she's had."

"She no longer cares a rap for the boy," pointed out Basil with a haughty eye. "She's head over heels, one hundred per cent. in love with me."

"Quite. But she gave him her London address and promised to make a luncheon date."

"The little twister! I mean young Millar. I expect he wore her down. She had to say 'Yes' to get rid of him."

"Quite—with a long, lingering hand-clasp and a lovely melting look. I was in the hall alcove. The poor sweetings thought they were alone." Deirdre paused, and then asked politely, "Will you accept the offer while it remains open?"

"Yes—confound it!—I will. But I warn you, his Aunt Clara's going to fly off the handle. She'll cut you dead after this."

"That, my darling, will be her loss and my gain. Don't you worry about little me. All I want you to do is to forget what I told you about Willie. I made a mistake. That's all." She raised her arms with a languorous gesture, and cooed, "Now kiss me and seal the bargain. Come on—be your age!"

Basil sighed. It was curious how Deirdre had slipped aside from his advances during those tantalizing months when he had longed to kiss her, and now, when it was a matter of complete indifference to him, she *demanded* to be kissed.

"Oh, all right," he said sulkily. "Sit up. I'm not a contortionist."

For all that, the kiss was far from amateurish. When two experts meet on a tennis court, even for the fun of the game, the match is usually prolonged and exciting. The same principle applied here.

3

It was all in keeping with the general deterioration of circumstances at Old Knolle that Deirdre's bedroom should have been at the extreme end of one wing and Clara Maddison's at the extreme end of the other. These two wings formed the two arms of a U on the south side, and acted as wind-shields to the terrace. After lunch Clara, as usual, had taken her library book up to her bedroom, pushed the ottoman under her wide-open window and prepared herself for a siesta. Her novel was merely an aperitif to the greater relaxation of an hour's solid sleep. It was the nicest, most treasured part of her day.

That afternoon, however, Clara had no sooner laid aside her book than her eye was arrested by the double portrait in the window opposite. Even an overwhelming desire to close her eyes gave way before her determination to keep them open. She recognized Deirdre and Basil at once. Their proximity suggested the shape of things to come, and Clara was not disappointed. She registered that kiss with perverse delight, since it had presented her with an opportunity to make things uncomfortable for both the participants. She had never liked Deirdre, and Basil, of course, was now damned in her sight for turning down her nephew's play. Rumours had already reached her about Basil and Angela, and since she was passionately devoted to Angela she gave up her forty winks without a sigh and went to search her out.

She was sun-bathing in the Dutch garden—emerald sunsuit and orange-brown limbs casually arranged on a li-lo. Clara came to the point without delay.

"I don't want to disturb you, my dear, but I'm sure you ought to know. Now don't be upset. Take things calmly. Men are all the same, given the opportunity and the leisure to take advantage of it."

"What *are* you babbling about?" inquired Angela.

"I've just seen Basil kissing Deirdre in her bedroom."

Angela sat up with a jerk. "Basil? Oh, no, I'm sure you've made a mistake. Basil can't stick her apart from her work. As for making love to her—" Angela's little laugh was not very convincing. She had not fully recovered from the summer-house episode of that morning. It seemed that no sooner was her back turned before Basil went sneaking off to Deirdre, like a dog after a buried bone. But she refused to let Clara see that she was hurt. "In any case, Clara, I don't see that it's any concern of mine."

"Don't you? I thought Basil was rather sweet on you. A little bird seems to have told me so. He's looked terribly devoted these last few days. Of course, if there's nothing in it…"

"We're just good friends," said Angela.

"Oh, in that case it doesn't matter if Basil kisses her all over the house, does it? Well, here he comes, anyway. I'll slip off and leave you to your good companion. But remember—if ever you want any advice I've always more on hand than I can do with, my dear. I've not had thirty years on the boards for nothing!"

"Thanks. You're an angel."

"I'm a charitable institution," concluded Clara as she waved a quick hand and vanished up one of the many yew-lined alleys.

"Oh, hullo!" called Basil as he entered the far end of the Dutch garden. "I wondered where you'd got to. Sunbathing, eh?"

"I was."

"Who was that?"

"Clara."

"Boring you to tears, no doubt."

"Far from it. I was deeply interested."

Basil flung himself down in the grass beside her and ran a finger up her golden bare arm. Angela gently escaped from his disturbing touch. This time there must be no weakening. She must preserve her indifference and sustain her sulks until Basil had been taught, once for all, the kind of lesson he would best remember.

"She's a good soul," said Basil generously, "but she has all the drawbacks of her type. Kind-hearted, motherly women are infernally dull. Don't you agree? They mean well, but they're insensitive. A kind heart can only function inside a thick skin. That's my opinion."

Angela said with pathos, "I could do with a thicker skin, Basil. I'm too easily hurt."

"Good God! has somebody been getting at you? I won't have that."

"Perhaps I'm *over*-sensitive."

"Who is it? Come on! don't beat about the bush. I'll wring his neck!"

"You couldn't."

"Why not?"

"Because I've always understood it's a physical impossibility to wring one's own neck."

"Me? Me?" Basil was incredulous. "But I've done nothing to hurt you, have I?"

"That's for you to judge. I may be silly, but I don't really enjoy the thought of your making love to Deirdre—particularly in her bedroom window."

"But look here—"

"You kissed her, didn't you?"

"No, confound it, I didn't! She kissed me."

"It's the same thing."

"Oh, no, it isn't. I was negative throughout. I told her I didn't want to kiss her. I just had to—to keep her quiet."

Angela levelled on him a steady and discrediting glance. "I've always found," she said primly, "that if I have no desire to be kissed I am *not* kissed. So there!"

"Yes, but look here, my darling Angela, it's different for a man. You can't be rude. You can't leave a girl in midair, so to speak, and just turn on your, heel and exit up centre. There are certain obligations."

"I thought, perhaps, you owed those obligations to me."

"But it didn't *mean* anything."

"It might have done to Deirdre."

"Why should we worry about that?"

"But I do worry, Basil. She warned me not to let you out of my sight. Now she's been able to prove herself right. Don't you see how she'll crow over this? I'm sure it was deliberate. She just wanted to see if you were really in love with me, and now—now—" Angela's voice began to quiver with approximating sobs. "Now she knows you're *not*! So do I. After all you've said—"

Basil was dumbfounded. Never in the whole of his career had he come across this particular argument. Ordinarily he wouldn't have been moved by it, but this time he really was in love and, to his profound dismay, he realized that Angela actually had a point of view. For a mere kiss he had never experienced remorse. Now he did. He felt ready to tear himself in pieces and scatter the remnants at Angela's feet in atonement. Confound Deirdre and her casual sense of morality! Didn't she know that when a man was in love he was, to all other women, *verboten*? Didn't she realize that a kiss *was* a kiss, no matter how carefully it was arranged? She had taken advantage of his ignorance concerning the correct behaviour of a man in love. Angela was young, very young, but she was wise. Deirdre had played this foul trick on him deliberately; no doubt having spotted Clara Maddison in the window opposite.

"Oh, for the love of Mike, Angela, must we quarrel all over again? This is the second time to-day."

Angela had already collected her impedimenta. She now uncorked the li-lo and sat on it to expel the air. In a few seconds it was as limp and deflated as Basil himself.

"But, Basil, it's all your fault. You make it so difficult. I hate having to quarrel quite as much as you do."

"Then, damn it! I'll say I'm sorry. Will that meet the case?"

"No—it's got to go deeper than that. When you apologize you sound as if you're offering me a cigarette."

She took the bundle of oddments into her arms. Basil threw a nostalgic glance at the embraced li-lo and envied it. How long would it be before he was in a similar position? Angela this time was not to be bought off with a few explanatory words and a smile. She was more independent than he had first surmised.

"Here," he said, gallant even in his defeat, "let me carry your things."

"Thank you," concluded Angela as she turned away towards the house. "I'd rather you didn't bother."

Fifteen seconds later Basil was alone in the Dutch garden.

4

Sam was unhappy as he sat half dozing in his study. The amiable atmosphere which had enveloped his house-party during the earlier weeks of the summer recess had been dissipated. Freed from the onus of the season's work, they had drifted down to Old Knolle in a holiday mood. Everybody had been exceptionally pleasant to everybody else, and they had all gone out of their way to overlook those petty differences which had divided them at the Beaumont. Now, thought Sam, the charm of release was wearing thin. Old Knolle was slowly being transformed from a holiday camp into a home for nervous wrecks. Ominous flickers of hostility and ill-humour were daily becoming more apparent. Soon there might arrive a sudden conflagration and his house-party would go up in smoke and flame.

In Sam's opinion the one hope of pulling his guests together lay in the approach of new rehearsals. Once more at work, their individualities, over-developed by so many weeks of leisure, would be welded again into an harmonious team. It would no longer be Willy, Clara, Basil, Deirdre, Angela under his roof, but the flower of the Beaumont Repertory Company about their job. Over the latter he had some control; over the former he had a headache.

This unanticipated relationship between Angela and Basil disturbed him. So had Mrs. Dreed's misplaced report about young Millar's visit to the child's bedroom. Above all, he was worried about the theft of that two hundred and twenty-five pounds. Unfortunately he hadn't troubled to list the serial numbers of the notes, for precisely the same reason that he refused to lock the drawers of his desk. It would have advertised a miserable lack of faith. But somebody had fallen below the average standards of decency and walked off with the cash. It couldn't have been a member of the company. It certainly wasn't Mrs. Dreed. Then perhaps some weak-minded creature on his domestic staff? Any of the maids or gardeners would know the money was kept in his desk because, on every normal Friday afternoon, they filed into his study for their wages. It hurt him to think that somebody he trusted had let him down. But of course—Sam brightened at the thought—it *might* have been an outside job; a proper professional job; a job carried out by an individual who had long ago been conditioned to ignore the ordinary principles of *meum* and *tuum*. In which case he'd never recover his money, but his faith in human nature, which he treasured beyond all wealth, would be restored.

Yes, Sam felt decidedly better for this reflective period in his arm-chair.

Then Deirdre came in, willowy and persuasive, with a big black portfolio under her arm.

"Turn me out if I'm a nuisance. But I've got to see you about these sets. It's the Toulippski play. Basil's O.K'd them. It's now only a matter of costs."

"*Only* a matter of costs!" chided Sam. "You creative artists are all tarred with the same brush. Money's the least of it, eh? You make me feel thoroughly ashamed of myself for having devoted the best years of my life to amassing a million. You and Willy and Clara—there you are!—wedded to your art. Not caring a tinker's curse about money. And here am I, my dear young lady, fretting over the loss of a couple of hundred pounds."

"Mr. Richardson!" Deirdre had now thrown aside the portfolio and was gazing at Sam with a shamefaced expression.

"Well?"

"I wasn't quite honest with you after lunch. It was utterly wrong of me not to speak up, but—but somehow—with everybody in the room—"

Sam found her embarrassment not only unsettling, but charming. He took her hand as if to reassure her.

"My dear young woman, please don't allow my troubles to trouble you. If you know of something about which you'd rather not speak—"

"But I must. Out of fairness to everybody in the house. I know you're far too much of a dear to suspect any of us, the servants included, but you must wonder who took that money."

"Naturally."

"Well, on Thursday night—that is the night before last—I couldn't sleep. So I came down with the idea of strolling down to the lake. Your study door was open and as I went by I—I saw—"

She dropped her glance in confusion and began to peck at her handkerchief with nervous finger-tips. Sam projected a sudden wave of tenderness towards her, admiring her reluctance to "tell tales out of school". He felt he had rather misjudged her, in thinking her hard and unprincipled. But his curiosity easily overrode his sympathy and he egged her on with:

"You say you saw—?"

"Please understand this, Mr. Richardson—when I say 'I saw', I mean 'I *think* I saw.' Any misapprehension would be too ghastly, wouldn't it? If I were the cause of anybody being wrongly suspected, I could never forgive myself."

"I appreciate that," said Sam gently, "very much. But if you care to tell me in confidence, my dear young lady, I'm prepared to shoulder all responsibility for any actions I may or may not have to take in the matter."

"That's awfully good of you. It makes things so much easier, because the person I *thought* I saw at your desk was not one of the domestics."

"Really?" Sam's heart sank. He braced himself against the disillusionment which he guessed was coming his way. "It was somebody you—er—knew and recognized, eh?"

"I'm afraid so, Mr. Richardson. I'm not prepared to swear to it in a court of law, but I think—oh, I hate having to say this! but I *think* it was Mr. Millar."

"Millar? Young Rudolph Millar? Impossible!"

"That's just what went through my own mind at the time."

"But he'd returned to London."

"I know. But if it was Mr. Millar, then I suppose he must have sneaked back."

"What time was this?"

"Just after two o'clock."

"You actually spoke to him?"

"No. As I went in, I called out to him, but before I could turn on the light he had slipped out through the French windows on to the terrace."

"Young Millar," repeated Sam quietly, with a sad shake of his head. "But why should he want to do a thing like that? He struck me as being a very honest and intelligent young man. Even in the face of Basil's expert opinion, I still like that play of his, y'know. I'm sorry to hear of this. More sorry than I can say. It's always distressing to find one's judgment at fault. You're quite sure you weren't mistaken?"

"I *may* have been," admitted Deirdre. "That's why I said nothing to you before. Of course I know he's rather hard up, and I expect he was banking on the acceptance of his play to help him out with his finances—but even then I just can't believe he'd sink to the level of out-and-out robbery."

"But if he can prove he didn't leave Town that night?" suggested Sam with a gleam of hope.

"Oh, I agree. He may have a perfect alibi. In which case the poor boy will be cleared at once, won't he? As I said before, Mr. Richardson, I hate the thought of maligning him without good cause."

"Perhaps I ought to have a private word with Miss Maddison. She's his aunt. She might be in a position to assure us that he *was* in London."

"But you won't mention my name?"

"I wouldn't dream of it. I'll just say that 'it has come to my notice', or something to that effect. We don't want any misunderstandings."

"You're very thoughtful."

"Not at all. The whole affair has depressed me. I'm only anxious to clear the matter up and forget it." Sam patted her arm and added paternally: "Don't take it to heart, my dear. You're only doing what's right, and I must say I admire your moral courage. Now to business! Let's take a look at those sketches. Here! I'll clear a space on the desk while you sit in this chair and tell me the tale. How's that?"

5

Sam, like the village blacksmith, believed in striking the iron while it was hot. Now that he was obsessed by this question of the theft, he was determined to push it through to its logical solution without waste of time. It was an unsavoury matter and Sam couldn't regain his usual good-natured frame of mind until it was neatly tidied up. Deirdre had dropped a hint. He hoped Clara Maddison would go further and provide him with a few concrete facts.

After tea on the terrace, therefore, he ushered her into a hammock-chair in the shade of the blue cedar. He touched in the general outlines of the picture with the hand of an impressionist. His aim was to suggest rather than state. Somebody—he wouldn't mention names, of course—was in the study rifling the drawers of his desk. Somehow, to the Somebody who looked into the study, the Somebody in the study seemed familiar. And so on.

But Clara, although maternal in figure and motherly by tendency, was not quite the dullard Basil claimed her to be. She hacked through Sam's tenuous innuendo with her direct mind, like a strong-armed explorer through tropical undergrowth. She burst through, as it were, into the full glare of the sun.

"You're trying to tell me, Mr. Richardson, that this eavesdropper—if you'll allow me that outmoded word—thought that the figure at the desk was my nephew?"

"Yes, that is the—er—suggestion."

"What time was he seen in the room?"

"Just after two a.m."

"Then may I ask, my dear Mr. Richardson, what this eavesdropper was doing wandering about the house at two a.m.? It looks highly fishy."

Sam was flummoxed. The fact that Clara might ask a few pertinent questions on her own account had never occurred to him. If he told the truth, Clara would immediately suspect Deirdre, since she had a monopoly of insomnia at Old Knolle. He looked foolish and remained obstinately dumb. Clara smiled.

"It wasn't Deirdre, by any chance, on one of her nocturnal promenades, was it?"

Sam looked at his boots, reddened, cleared his throat and remained obstinately dumb. Deirdre should have anticipated the possibility of this quandary. But for all her "infernal dullness", Clara drew the answer, like a practised conjuror, from the empty silence.

"So it *was* Deirdre! Really, Mr. Richardson, you amaze me! You've also wounded me cruelly. You were so ready to believe that it was poor dear Rudie! You were ready to accept Deirdre's infamous opinion instead of your own honest judgment. In your heart of hearts—now, do be frank!— you don't really think my nephew stole that money?"

"No," said Sam with enormous relief. "I don't and I didn't. I felt all along that Miss Lehaye had made an unfortunate mistake."

"Unfortunate!" The full bosom swelled with indignation. The rich contralto voice was vibrant with scorn and anger. "Unfortunate! What a lamb of innocence you are, Mr. Richardson. It was a deliberate mistake! She put up this story to shield herself. A few minutes ago I didn't know who stole that money, but now I've a very shrewd idea. So have you, but, like the gentleman you are, you're too damned polite to say so. Oh, the nasty, unprincipled creature! I could—I could tear her hair out by the roots! To try and lay the blame on my poor Rudie! I never heard of such two-faced behaviour! It's disgusting, Mr. Richardson. There's no other word for it! Disgusting! I'll never speak to the vile woman again. I'll tell everybody what she said. I'll—I'll—"

Sam, aware of Clara's ability to sustain and build up a really dramatic passage, had already scrambled to his feet. In another minute the doors and windows of the house would open and everybody would come scurrying across the lawn to see what it was all about. It was a *contretemps* he dared not contemplate. Already he had been a positive bonehead in rousing Clara's very natural ire, without sufficient proof to back up his deadly accusation. No aunt, however good-natured, likes to hear her nephew called a thief. Somehow he must calm her down, and at once!

"Now, now, now, my dear Miss Maddison. Please, please, please. I see just how you feel, of course—but not *quite* so articulate. I mean, we don't want everybody to know about this disagreeable error. It was just a case of mistaken identity."

"It's a case of unmistakable libel!" cried Clara with robust conviction. "She's not going to get away with this. All the soft words in the world aren't going to turn away *my* wrath! I'll cry her rottenness from the house-tops, Mr. Richardson. I will really. I'm just in the mood for it. I'll tell Basil. I'll tell Willy. I'll tell Angela. I'll tell them all—yes, even Mrs. Dreed. That Deirdre creature's a serpent in our midst. Yes, and even if she is clever at her job, you ought to sack her. I should. I should sack her on the spot!"

Sam cast an anxious eye at the house. He recalled Clara's performance in Ibsen's *Lady Ingar* and how the clarity of her diction had been particularly commented upon by the back row of the pit.

"No, no, no! Don't let's be hasty. Miss Lehaye acted in good faith. She was most anxious that her name shouldn't be mentioned in connection with this unappetizing business."

"You're telling me!" snorted Clara with invigorating vulgarity.

Sam ignored the interpolation. "I'm sure it's quite unnecessary for us to pursue the matter any further. I can't see why I allowed myself to be persuaded against my better judgment."

"That, Mr. Richardson, is what Adam said in the Garden of Eden." Clara rose, a stately monument to outraged aunthood. Her mind was made up. "Either that young woman apologizes to Rudie and me, Mr. Richardson, or I won't answer for the consequences. My nephew is not the type to lie down under such an insult. He's difficult. I've got absolutely no control over him once his temper's roused!"

CHAPTER VIII

Russian Gloom

I

W HEN, IN ABOUT TEN DAYS' TIME, THE REST OF THE COMPANY
playing in *The Red Ant* arrived at Old Knolle for preliminary
rehearsals, they were aware of several strange phenomena. They noticed
that Clara Maddison was not speaking to Deirdre Lehaye, and that
Deirdre was acting as if Clara's too-solid flesh had already melted in the
August heat. They noticed that Willy shied away at the mere mention of
a bet, and that he, too, never addressed himself to Deirdre unless it was
unavoidable. They noticed that Basil, for the first time in his life, was at
the mercy of a feminine frown and smile; and that the particular frown
and smile, which respectively plunged him into the depths or raised him
to the heights, belonged to Angela Walsh. They noticed that Angela and
Deirdre, though still on speaking terms, were far, far too polite to each
other to be considered friendly. They noticed that Basil seemed to lose
half his colossal self-assurance in Deirdre's presence, and that Deirdre
seemed to be making a set at him, where previously she had done her
utmost to freeze him up. They noticed that Sam Richardson's geniality
was a trifle forced, that he seemed on tenterhooks, as if, at any minute,
trouble in ambush would open fire on him. They noticed that Mrs. Dreed
was more starchy, more severe and less prepossessing than ever. The two
adjectives they would have chosen to describe the tension at Old Knolle
were, undoubtedly, "electric" and "ominous". It was lucky they were
opening the season with Toulippski's *The Red Ant*, because they found
the atmosphere of the play ready-made and waiting for them.

Whether, in the light of what eventually happened, Igor Toulippski
was in part to blame, it is impossible to say. Certainly the stark and

primitive flavour of his play slopped over into the private lives of the
players. It is impossible, with a piece as sincere and masterly as *The Red
Ant*, to step out of its setting and forget all about it over a cigarette. It
was the kind of play that haunted one's idle moments and tinged one's
dreams with the red glow of its realism. His characters, far larger than
life, demanded the last ounce of talent and imagination from the actors.
Their smallest action was symbolic. Their lightest word charged with an
undercurrent of tragedy.

How could Willy Farnham, as the frustrated, hare-brained Petrovka,
sink himself into the rôle and avoid seeing himself through Petrovka's
eyes? If Willy were frustrated in the play, outside it he felt as if he were
being pulverized by an unrelenting Fate with the face and figure of
Deirdre Lehaye. In the play, Clara was the brooding, sulky-mouthed Olga
Dennikin, and off-stage it was difficult to believe that she had ceased to
act. Even Angela, as the blithe and pretty Natasha, whose love-life flaked
away to ashes in the third act, was in private ridden with a premonition.
Was there not something of Basil in the heartless Ivanovitch? And Basil,
whose duty it was to interpret every character in turn, was overloaded
with such a burden of indigestible emotion that everything at Old Knolle
seemed to be twisted out of shape. Once or twice, when making dark
love to a passion-starved Angela, he called her "little mother", and found
nothing odd about it. There was no denying it, the whole of the Beaumont
company had been badly bitten by *The Red Ant*.

And Nature, not to be outdone by Igor Toulippski, lent further
atmosphere to those first rehearsals. The cast moved about the lawns
against a towering background of stormy sky. Thunder muttered and
rolled around the castle. Lightning stabbed the hushed and gloomy air.
Fingers tingled. Hair stood on end. Nerves were stretched. The parched
ground waited for the cooling rain, but the rain did not come. To the
accompaniment of this celestial tympani the play began to take shape.
Old Knolle seemed to hump its roofs under the shadow of the general
Russian gloom.

Deirdre, and Deirdre alone, seemed unaffected by these ominous
trimmings. Perched on the terrace balustrade, eternal cigarette between
infernal lips, she watched Basil directing the harassed cast. Her ice-green

eyes were untroubled. Her smile was not that of the young lady of Riga,
but of the tiger who took the young lady for a ride.

2

In the midst of all this Angela and Basil suddenly announced their
engagement. After their quarrel in the Dutch garden, Angela had kept
Basil at arms' length for three days and then graciously relented. He had
gambolled back to her, wagging his tail. He was like a puppy ostracized
on the mat who suddenly finds the front door has been opened to him
again. He no longer kept one eye on his dignity. He fixed them both
on his adored Angela. This, he claimed, was the primitive passion of a
Toulippski *moujik*. To gain his ends, Basil, for the first time in his life,
was ready to go down on his knees and thank heaven, fasting, for a good
woman's love. Turn by turn he was considerate, watchful, jealous and
ecstatic. It has been said that love, like mumps, is far more virulent when
contracted latish in life.

Certainly, the Basil who was prepared to engage himself to the object
of his affections was a new Basil. Marriage, he had often declared, was
the last resort of the unimaginative. It was so damned unoriginal. And
here he was, slipping an expensive ring on the third finger of Angela's left
hand as a preliminary to the more solid joys of matrimony!

He accepted the congratulations of the company with pride and self-
satisfaction. He was quite convinced that no man had ever wooed and won
such a nubile prize as Angela. They announced that the marriage would
take place at St. George's, Hanover Square, three weeks before Christmas.
Everybody was astounded, and not a little awed, by the change in Basil.

Although he spent most of his time over at Old Knolle rehearsing,
every night he returned to sleep at Fallow Cottage. Angela would see
him home across the meadows to the cottage and then he would see her
home across the meadows to Old Knolle. From the corner of her unreliable eye Deirdre watched the couple with a scheming look. She was torn
in two by the engagement. One half of her was offended and wounded
by Basil's indifference to her recent advances. The other saw in Basil's

desire to legalize his devotion a heaven-sent chance to make mischief. She awaited her opportunity and, one night after Basil had seen Angela home for the second time, she pounced on him from behind a blackberry bush.

"Good God! What d'you think you're doing?"

"Oh, did I frighten you, Basil darling? I'm sorry. Can I see you home?"

"No, you can't!"

"Thanks. I will."

Basil stood squarely in her path. She did not bat an eyelid.

"Look here!" he thundered. "This may seem all very damn funny to you, popping out at me from behind bushes, waylaying me at night, kissing me in windows—that sort of thing. But, once for all, my girl, I'm not interested. Twice already you've got me into hot water with Angela, and I'm not going to let you scupper me again. If you think I'm ready to play games with you now I'm engaged to Angela, you're damn well mistaken. Once I was moron enough to think you pretty wonderful. Now I think you're an interfering, trouble-making, double-crossing witch! And that goes from now on. Good night."

He turned on his heel and made ready to disappear dramatically into the night. Deirdre clung to his coat-tails.

"A minute, my dear Basil." Her voice was like the caress of a velvet paw; the paw of a cat that conceals sharpened talons. He shivered at the sound of it and stopped dead. A sudden wave of anxiety and frustration overwhelmed him. "You and I are going to have a little pow-wow," went on Deirdre. "Suppose we walk on to Fallow Cottage and you brew me some coffee."

"Never! If we've *got* to talk, we talk here in the middle of an open field. I'm taking no chances. Where should I be with Angela if she got to know that you'd visited me at night over at the cottage?"

"That's easy. With your previous reputation, Basil darling, you'd be in the soup."

"Then we talk here. Understand?"

"Oh, no, I think not. What I have to say may take some time. I prefer to be comfortable. I've always believed in indulging my body when there's no need to do otherwise."

"Well, you won't indulge it with me!"

"Don't be coarse. You know what I want to see you about, don't you?"

"I've a very shrewd idea."

"Then suppose we start walking."

"But—"

"This round is all with me, Basil darling. It's no good wriggling."

"Damn you!"

"Allow me to return the compliment."

Side by side, in silence, they began to walk towards Fallow Cottage.

3

With great subtlety, Deirdre and Basil were dropping here a hint and there a hint concerning Rudolph and the missing money. Neither spoke directly of the matter to Angela, though it was for her sole benefit that they were putting up this underhand performance. Deirdre, because she wanted to side-track all suspicion from the scrawny pigeon she was plucking in the guise of Willy Farnham; Basil, because he was anxious to discredit Rudolph, once for all, in the blue eyes of Angela. It was Mrs. Dreed who first let the cat fully out of the bag.

"I'm sure you're as upset about this horrible theft as I am," she sniffed. "Really, Miss Walsh, I never suspected that one of *our* guests would be capable of—" She broke off and added with a watchful eye, "You've *heard*, of course?"

Angela was nonplussed. "Heard? No, nothing. Has Mr. Richardson discovered who did it, Mrs. Dreed?"

"Well, he hasn't actually told me—but they say that Mr. Millar was seen in the house that night—"

"Rudolph?" broke in Angela. Then in a tremulous echo, "Rudolph?"

"So I've *heard*," reiterated Mrs. Dreed. "But I've no intention of speaking out of place, Miss Walsh. It's not for me to air my opinion of some of Mr. Richardson's theatrical friends. But in view of your apparent interest in the young gentleman, I felt you should know."

"I just don't believe it's true!" declared Angela hotly. "He would never, never, never dream of such a thing!"

"It was my duty to inform you of these rumours, nevertheless," retorted Mrs. Dreed, as she sniffed for the second time and haughtily withdrew.

Angela was thinking of the eloquent tempestuous letters which had followed up Rudolph's departure from Old Knolle. He had written nearly every day. He had written charmingly, intimately, almost passionately. He pleaded with her to return as soon as possible to Town. Life was empty and intolerable without somebody really understanding to talk to. He was depressed. He had been depressed from the moment he had said "Good-bye" to her. She alone possessed that virtue which would re-establish his inspiration. He had attempted to rough-out the plot of a new play, but it had crumbled between his hands like a clod of dried earth. He was a well gone dry. He was a riderless horse. He was a vacuum.

And, in spite of the fact that she was now head-over-heels in love with Basil, Angela could not help feeling pleased and flattered by Rudolph's postal attentions. She sent in return one cautious little note, preparing him for the announcement of her engagement to Basil, which, at the time, was still under discussion. She was determined to retain a cool friendliness towards him, without letting him expect for an instant more than she could possibly give. But his letters continued to pour in—impulsive, tempestuous and charming as ever. Whatever his failings, Rudolph had pertinacity.

But was it credible that he could have written to her with such ardent frankness if he had stolen that money? He might wring the last ounce of self-pity from his melancholia, but he certainly didn't sound like a man who had anything criminal to conceal. Angela's pretty jaw stiffened. This was probably Deirdre's doing. She had noticed at once that Deirdre and Clara were no longer on speaking terms. She made up her mind to have it out with Sam.

Sam drenched her with apologies. "My dear child, please think nothing more about it. It's all a miserable mix-up, a clear case of mistaken identity. No doubt about it. No doubt at all. That young man is incapable of a mean act. At least, that's my impression."

"But do you know yet who took the money?"

"No," admitted Sam. "Not yet. No."

"Then Mr. Millar still isn't cleared of suspicion?"

"His aunt is seeing to that. After all, my dear, if Mr. Millar just writes and explains *where* he was that evening, we've no need to trouble our heads any longer. That does away with the final breath of suspicion, doesn't it?"

It would have done, naturally, if Mr. Millar that evening hadn't acted on one of his mad impulses and caught a late train from Victoria to Lambdon. He had then been away from Angela for about forty-eight hours and an imperious desire to see her again had driven him half-crazy. He made no plans. He had a vague idea of creeping up to the castle and throwing gravel against her bedroom window. He had a vision of her in that flimsy-whimsy slip of a nightdress looking down at him from the balcony. He avoided thinking of Romeo and Juliet because it was so obvious as to be inartistic. But, sitting in the acrid atmosphere of his third-class carriage, his courage had evaporated. What the devil was he doing hareing off to Old Knolle in the dead of night in order to throw gravel at the bedroom window of a girl he barely knew? What would be her most plausible reaction? (*a*) She might rouse the household and make him the laughing stock of the whole crowd. (*b*) She might hand him his *congé* with a jugful of cold water. (*c*) She might, with justifiable common sense, tell him quietly but firmly to go away and behave himself. In consequence, by the time he stepped out on to the platform at Lambdon Halt, Rudolph knew well enough that he had no intention of visiting the house at all. All he desired to do was to take the next train back to Town and get a proper grip on himself.

He inquired of the station master, who recognized him as the young gentleman he had seen two days earlier with one of the chauffeurs from Old Knolle portering his case. Always anxious to oblige any friend of Mr. Richardson's, who never failed to tip him at Christmas, the station master was sorry to inform Rudolph that there was *no* train back to London that night. The next up train from Lambdon Halt was the 5.25 a.m. milk "special". It was slow, but there was always one passenger coach attached. He refrained from asking the young gentleman why, having just stepped off a train *from* Victoria, he was now anxious to step back on to one *going* to Victoria.

"Maybe you could rouse them at the Cassel, sir." (Old Knolle was always known locally as "The Cassel".) "It would give you the chance to get a bit of sleep."

"Oh, no, I couldn't do that!" said Rudolph hastily. "Perhaps I could park down in the waiting-room or something. In any case, I'll take a bit of a stroll round now and come back later. I feel like a stretch and it's a lovely night."

It was just a series of unfortunate coincidences, so that when Clara wrote at white-heat and explained what had transpired, Rudolph went hot all over. He was in a jam. A really nasty jam. It would take a lot to convince even his aunt that he hadn't been near Old Knolle that night. If Mr. Richardson put the matter into the hands of the police, they would probably make inquiries at the station. The station master had recognized him. So all was for the worst in this most damnable of worlds! He wrote evasively to his Aunt Clara and claimed to have stayed in his rooms, writing. On receiving his letter, a horrible suspicion shot through Clara's mind that Deirdre after all might have been telling the truth. But she did her best with Sam by adopting a semi-jovial sort of what-did-I-tell-you approach, which left Sam satisfied.

And then, to fill Rudolph's cup of misery, he received a polite note from Angela announcing that she had just become engaged to Basil Barnes. She pleaded with him to cease all correspondence forthwith.

On the day following Deirdre's visit to Fallow Cottage, Inspector Harting came up to Old Knolle and had a long interview with Sam. Sam told him everything, including Deirdre's belief that she had recognized the figure at the desk.

"But I'm in the happy position now, Inspector," said Sam, "of being able to prove that the young lady was mistaken. Mr. Millar was in London that night. He wasn't even in the vicinity of Lambdon."

"I take it you've been able to check up on this?"

"Well, no—not exactly. I prefer to take people at their word. If he *said* he was in Town, that's good enough for me, Inspector."

"Well, it's not good enough for me, Mr. Richardson. You see that? My job is to take statements and then check up on them. As a simple matter of routine, I shall have to ask you for a full description of the young man."

Sam sighed. The police, though excellent fellows in themselves, always seemed to take this sordid view of human nature. Guilty unless proved innocent. They had no living faith.

"All right," he said. "I'll give you the details."

Then there was the question of fingerprints, explained the Inspector; but Mrs. Dreed was called in and cut short that line of inquiry with a tart, "My staff here, Mr. Inspector, are properly trained. We never neglect to dust and polish our furniture *every* day, as Mr. Richardson well knows!"

Four hours later, the Inspector was back in Sam's study. His investigations had led him, naturally, to the railway station.

"I'm sorry, Mr. Richardson, but I have to inform you that your Mr. Millar *was* in the vicinity of Old Knolle that Friday night. He got off the 10.45 from Victoria at Lambdon Halt. He returned to Town in the small hours. In the meantime he'd been walking around the neighbourhood. In my opinion it looks fishy. Very fishy. Very fishy, indeed!"

"I'm more upset than I can say," said Sam. "And I still uphold he didn't take the money."

"I shall have to cross-examine him. I can't do less. Have you got his London address?"

"No, but I can get it from his aunt. She's staying here. She'll take this sadly, I'm afraid. She thinks the world of the boy."

Somehow, as such things do, the story leaked out that young Millar had been prowling about "The Cassel" on the night of the theft. The story probably originated with the station master, whose sister-in-law had an uncle whose nephew was second gardener at Old Knolle and a great friend of the between-maid, who told Mrs. Dreed, who simply could not contain herself. Nobody was more surprised by the news than Deirdre. She was fascinated by the manner in which Fate was weaving this shoddy pattern. Elated by the success of her tremendous lie, she hurried off and dropped a few more poisonous words into Angela's shell-like ear. The combination of facts was too much for her. She was horrified and relieved. Horrified by Rudolph's unexpected moral rottenness. Relieved to think that she had not followed up her wrong judgment of his character by further intimacies. But for the grace of God, she might have made a luncheon date with a common thief! The thought shocked her to the core.

Clara was stunned. Sam was closer to cynicism than at any other period in his life. Willy was dumbfounded by his own good fortune. Basil was smugly virtuous about the matter. He took the line that appearances were deceptive and that Angela must be careful in the future to rely on *his* judgment and profound knowledge of human nature.

The Russian gloom deepened. Basil had now bought a samovar. The cast of *The Red Ant* sat around it and wallowed in lukewarm tea and primitive emotion. In a few days the whole company was to return to Town for the more advanced rehearsals.

CHAPTER IX

Return to Town

I

ABOUT THE SECOND WEEK IN AUGUST THE WHOLE COMPANY migrated to Town. Silence descended on Old Knolle and Mrs. Dreed was once more empress of all she surveyed. Basil returned to Byron Crescent, Kensington; Deirdre to her studio-flat in St. John's wood; Angela to her private hotel off Westbourne Grove; and Clara Maddison to her sister's house in Hampstead. Willy was a member of a small exclusive bachelors' club in Chelsea, which, at a price, pandered (as no woman could ever have done) to the prejudices and comforts of its professional clientele. Sam always booked a suite of rooms at the Regency Buck Hotel, the sedate and hooded windows of which looked out on to the Green Park and a distant view of Buckingham Palace. It was as if a time-bomb had exploded and scattered the house-party over half London.

Yet, as component parts of a delicate machine, five mornings a week they were collected and reassembled at the Beaumont. Punctually at ten-thirty, coagulating by means of tube and bus and taxi, they met again on the empty stage. Gone was the sketchy, rather amateurish atmosphere of the first rehearsals. Under the naked bulb of the pilot-light, with the composite odour of dust and glue and distemper in their nostrils, they metaphorically stripped themselves to the buff and made ready for some serious sparring. The common denominator of the two atmospheres was, of course, the Russian gloom. But here, at the Beaumont, it was even more apparent. A theatre during rehearsals is full of shadows. There is the yawning black pit of the auditorium with the ghostly mist of dust-sheets protecting the higher-priced stalls. There are ubiquitous black cats like small animated pieces of darkness broken off the general gloom. There was the shuffle-shuffle, slip-slop of Madame Rameau's carpet slippers as she moved about her job as wardrobe mistress. There were steps which led nowhere; pillars that supported nothing; doors that opened on to space, and windows on to blank walls. Above all, there was the vast tenebrous tower of the flies, with its latticed grid, its festoons of rope, its backcloths, borders and running battens. In such a setting Toulippski's masterpiece was fated to gain in power and effectiveness.

As rehearsals progressed the strain on the cast increased. Once in the theatre, Basil grew more autocratic. For some reason Toulippski's simple and often repetitive dialogue proved formidable stuff to memorize. When the time came for the cast to "drop their books", they fumbled and staggered through their parts like a collection of mental cripples. Willy, with other things to think about, was a particularly bad offender. Basil, who had now reached that stage in his production where he desired to etch in a little light and shade, was tried beyond the limits of his patience. He stormed. He raved. He pleaded. He threatened. From the obscurity of the stalls he was to the actors a disembodied curse.

"In heaven's name, Willy, what the deuce has come over you? I asked you to be word perfect in the first act by this morning. Just the first act. And you've had six 'dries' on the first page. It's damned disgraceful. All right. All right. I know Clara's been no help to you. Really, my dear Olga Dennikin, we might just as well cut you out of the plot and bury you in the first act instead of the third, for all the use you are to the plot! You've given Willy the wrong cue at least half a dozen times. Oh, I agree, he's just as bad! Now we'll go back to, 'Look here, Fyodor Petrovka, have the goodness to stick to the point. The pig is sick of swine fever, and that's all there is to it.' Have you got the place? Right! Off you go, Clara, and remember you're aggressive here. You're verbally thumping Petrovka over the ears. You talk as if he were to blame for the pig being sick. Got it? Off you go, then."

And the harried, exhausted couple pulled themselves together for the umpteenth time and plunged with despair into another morass of paraphrase and faulty cues. Then from the stalls the crack of a hand and an infuriated:

"No! Stop! Stop! It's hopeless! Hopeless! How many times have I told you, Petrovka, to move up right centre on 'God forbid, my dears, that I should waste the day in listening to your cackle'? And have you moved up? You know damn well you haven't. You're masking Olga completely if you insist on staying down by the table. And your exit line is, 'I'm not a grand talker but I speak to the point.' God knows, Willy, I only wish you *did* speak to the point. And remember—you go off in a petty huff, not like an insulted emperor. You're stepping slap out of your part at the moment. And Clara, my angel, if you could handle that stewpot more like a Russian peasant and less like the vicar's lady at a charity tea, I should be profoundly grateful. All right! All right! We'll go back once more. Top of page two. 'Look here, Fyodor Petrovka, have the goodness to stick to the point.' Got it? All right, then—off we go!"

Away in a remote corner of the pit, quiet as a mouse, Angela waited her entry cue. Her heart bled for Basil as he poured out his energy in what seemed a hopeless cause. The night before, like a good little girl, she had sat up until the small hours conning her part. She, at any rate, would help Basil all she could by being word perfect. She did not feel smug when later he praised her and held her up as an example, but warmed by the glow of duty done. Behind her back, some of the lesser lights began to speak of her as "the Producer's Pet". In her innocence, Angela never suspected that she was giving any cause for unpopularity.

She, too, was not without her background of trouble. No sooner had she arrived back at her ladies' hostel off Westbourne Grove, than Rudolph rang her up. After perfunctory congratulations on her engagement, he begged her to fix a luncheon date. He wanted to talk to her.

"I'm sorry," said Angela, "but I just can't make it. We're being rushed off our feet at rehearsals."

"Is that just an excuse?"

"Don't be unkind."

"I've a feeling that you don't want to meet me."

"Don't be stupid."

"I suppose," went on Rudolph with some bitterness, "that you've heard these foul rumours that have been going round about me?"

Angela hedged. "I don't quite know what—"

"Of course you do! You can't kid me. That Lehaye woman couldn't hold her tongue, even if she wanted to. You know jolly well that I've been accused of stealing money from Mr. Richardson's study."

"Well, I—"

"I don't care a hoot what anybody thinks except you!" broke in Rudolph vigorously. "As long as you believe it's a rotten lie, I don't care. Honestly, Angela, you don't think I took the money, do you?"

"No, of course not!"

"I've had a police inspector here asking questions."

"Oh, how beastly for you!"

"Yes, and I told him the truth. He wanted to know if I was anywhere near Old Knolle on that particular Friday night, and I told him I was. I *was*, you know. I felt so mad keen to see you that I took a train down to Lambdon, and when I got there—well, my courage failed me. I just walked the lanes and took the milk train back to Town."

"Oh, Rudolph, you shouldn't have been so reckless. I suppose it's all my fault that you've been landed into this mess."

"I can't tell them that I came to see you. It looks so fearfully stupid, Angela, particularly now you're engaged to Basil. But I could see at once that the inspector fellow just didn't swallow my story that I'd gone down there for a country walk. It does sound a bit thin, doesn't it?"

"Oh, I *am* sorry, Rudolph!" Angela was quite genuine. "What can you do about it?"

"That's why I want to meet you—to discuss things. *Can't* you lunch to-morrow?"

"No—really I can't."

"You're afraid of what Basil might think?"

Angela flared up. "I'm not. He's got complete faith in me, as I have in him. He'd let me lunch with any man I wanted to."

"I'm sorry. I'm fearfully sorry," apologized Rudolph, ashamed of himself. "This nasty business has put me on edge. It's all that Lehaye woman's fault. She started the whole story. I'd—I'd like to strangle her! I know Aunt Clara had a few words with her and nearly pushed her into the lake. She told me. She says they got quite heated." There was a brief pause, then Rudolph made a final appeal. "If you can't lunch, may I meet you near the Beaumont after rehearsal and take you out to tea somewhere?"

"No, Rudolph, I'm sorry—I can't, really."

"Could we meet in the evening?"

"No, really, I can't."

"I see. So we can't meet at all?"

"No, not really."

"I see. So that's that. Good-bye."

"Good-bye."

But the moment after she had hung up, Angela had a fierce fit of remorse. All her natural sympathy went out to Rudolph in his obvious misery. After all, he *had* taken that train down to Lambdon in order to see her, and if he hadn't taken that train he would have had his— now, what was the word?—yes, alibi. Instead, it really did look terribly suspicious. *She* knew he couldn't possible have taken that money, but other people...

Yes, Angela was not without her private tribulations even though she was still in the first flush of her engagement. She wondered if she ought to tell Sam Richardson about Rudolph's chance visit to her bedroom, and how it seemed to have fostered a false air of intimacy and driven Rudolph to catch that fateful train. It was the decent thing to do, and it came naturally to Angela to do the decent thing.

2

Rudolph could no longer work. Concentration was impossible. The more meagre his chances of seeing Angela, the more he longed to see her. The greater his effort of will to dispel the cloud which was hanging over him, the more it distracted him. The inspector had not been officious, merely business-like. He had asked a lot of questions and taken a lot of notes, thanked Rudolph for his co-operation, and gone back to Lambdon. Since his departure there had been no further developments; but Rudolph knew well enough that until the genuine criminal were found he would have to shoulder the burden of another man's guilt. He found out from his aunt where Sam was staying and tried to get an interview. On two occasions Sam was ostensibly out, but on the third he was able to waylay him in the hotel lounge. Sam was patient, polite, apologetic; but, of course, the moment arrived when he asked with excusable curiosity: "But why did you take a train down to Lambdon at that time of the night, Mr. Millar? That's what I can't understand." And the country-walk explanation sounded thinner and more futile than ever. Rudolph left the Regency Buck with the feeling that Mr. Richardson would have given away half his fortune to believe him innocent and the other half to convince himself that he wasn't guilty.

He descended on his Aunt Clara at Hampstead one evening shortly after his telephone talk with Angela.

"But see here, Auntie, *this* is the point. We happen to know that I wasn't in the study. That Lehaye wretch swears she saw me there. Why? That's what I can't fathom."

"Oh, can't you? Well, I've already told Sam—she put this story around to cover her own tracks. *She* took the money—the horrid creature!"

Rudolph shook his head. "I don't want to be uppish, but I can't agree. I mean, if she took the money in the dead of night and nobody *knew* she took it, why worry to cover up anything? It would have been far better to have said absolutely nothing."

His aunt looked at him, first with doubt and surprise, then with admiration.

"Do you know, Rudie darling, you've been rather clever. It *is* curious. If the odious creature didn't take the money, then who did? That's what I'd like to know."

"You're not the only one!" said Rudolph warmly. "Until we can find who did swipe that two hundred quid, I'm liable to be cut by my nearest and dearest. This sort of libel gets round quicker than you can imagine. Angela suspects. I know she does. She's fearfully nice about it, but she refuses to touch pitch lest she herself, dear soul, be defiled. Oh, you can't blame her!" Rudie took a cigarette from his aunt's proffered case with an absent-minded nod. "Look here, Auntie, I'm going to hold a sort of post-mortem on Mr. Richardson's house-party. Was there anybody staying at Old Knolle who *needed* the money?"

"It may have been one of the servants or a proper burglar," pointed out Clara.

"Yes, but apart from that, if the Lehaye woman did catch somebody red-handed, then she wouldn't try to switch the blame on to me just to cover one of the domestics. She's obviously trying to shield somebody."

"Well, darling, I'm always in need of money. Although I've separated from your Uncle Peter, I just can't let the poor dear go bankrupt. He does so love his little shop, but, in spite of the financial strain, I haven't the heart to cut him off with a shilling."

"Don't be funny. You didn't take the cash."

"Then there's Basil." Clara shook her head. "No, he's feathered his nest very nicely. All his vices are of the inexpensive kind. And, of course, there's Angela."

"Don't be ridiculous!" said Rudolph hotly.

"I'm sorry, Rudie dear. Caesar's wife, of course. How naughty of me. Well, that leaves Willy Farnham." She added on a louder, more excited note, "Willy! Yes! I wonder if Willy took that money? He's always running into gambling debts and snooping round for the loan of a fiver. A perfect dear, but not in the least practical. Yes, Rudie, the more I think of it, the more convinced I am that Willy *might* have taken that money. I don't say he did, but it's on the cards."

"But would the Lehaye woman have any interest in wanting to shield him?"

"None, unless she's his illegitimate daughter. In crime fiction her kind usually are. Now I come to think of it, Rudie darling, she *looks* illegitimate. But this much I do know—she wouldn't raise a finger to help anybody unless it benefited her. You might take that as a basis to work on."

"Couldn't *you* tackle Mr. Farnham on the subject? Tactfully, I mean. You always could get anybody to confide in you, Auntie, if you wanted them to."

"Don't flatter! I may be your business agent, but I'm not a private detective. I won't promise."

"It's fearfully sporting of you."

"Now don't get excited."

"I'd give anything," declared Rudolph emphatically, "to clear myself of this foul business. It's hateful when marvellous people like Angela look on one as a kind of social leper. She *is* marvellous, isn't she? Absolutely marvellous."

"She's also engaged," concluded his aunt sharply. "And by that token, my dear, an untouchable. Kindly remember that. You've made a big enough fool of yourself over her already."

3

Angela, true to her instincts, rang the Regency Buck the evening after her 'phone talk with Rudolph and asked to be put through to Mr. Richardson. Sam himself answered the call, and on learning that she urgently desired to have a private talk with him, told her to "make herself prettier than ever" and come along to dinner. Sam liked to do things in a spacious manner and Angela had always been his favourite.

He had dinner served in his suite. Trails of some rare clematis wriggled between the cutlery and the salt-cellars. Gauging the tastes of his young guest to perfection, he ordered a bottle of sparkling Moselle. Angela drank very sparingly, but she had the social sense to acclaim Sam's choice. It was not until a waiter had left them with their Turkish coffee that Sam allowed Angela to come to the point of the meeting.

"Serious conversation during meals," he explained, "has a very bad effect on the digestion. It's as much to be deplored, young lady, as smoking between courses. Now what exactly do you want to talk to me about?"

"Rudolph Millar."

"Ah!"

"I want to explain, Mr. Richardson, just why he caught the train down to Lambdon that night."

"He told me it was to indulge in a country walk."

"But that's not strictly true. He came down with the intention of seeing me."

"You?" Sam was startled. "But in the middle of the night like that— surely not?" Was he due for another disillusionment?

"Oh, we didn't actually, meet, Mr. Richardson. When he arrived at the station he just hadn't the courage to approach Old Knolle. I felt I had to tell you this. You see, Mr. Millar, I—that is, we—no, actually, it was he—" Angela sipped her coffee and gazed at Sam with a stricken look. It is not easy to tell anybody, without appearing boastful, that a man has fallen in love with you more or less at first sight. Sam, with his unfailing generosity, helped her out.

"You mean that before the young man returned to Town he was violently in love with you?"

Angela nodded shyly.

Sam went on, "Well, he can't be blamed for that. I can only admire his sound judgment, young lady. And I understand his judgment is only to be equalled by his enterprise?"

"I don't quite follow."

"Well, a little bird whispered that he had the audacity to walk into your bedroom."

"By accident?" put in Angela swiftly. "And nothing—really happened."

"By accident and nothing really happened," repeated Sam. "After that, of course—" He smiled and chuckled and wriggled in his chair.

"Oh, you *are* a dear, Mr. Richardson! I knew you'd understand. You're quite right—after that he seemed to lose his head over me. It was awfully sweet of him, but awfully awkward because of Basil. I didn't want to hurt Mr. Millar's feelings."

"I'm sure of that!" put in Sam warmly.

"He wrote me every day from London. Really he didn't make any bones about it. I mean, he kept on telling me how much he was in love with me and trying to fix luncheon dates and all that. You *do* see what I'm getting at, Mr. Richardson?"

Sam nodded and, leaning forward, patted Angela on her silk-clad knee.

"Perfectly. You've pocketed your pride, my dear, to come here and convince me that young Millar had a very definite reason for going down to Lambdon that night. And thank heaven you *have* convinced me. I didn't like the idea of suspecting the boy from the start. I told Inspector Harting so, but when I learned about his visit that night, it was very difficult to sustain my faith in his innocence. Now I can quite see how it all came about. I was young myself once, and that's just the headstrong, foolish way in which I would have behaved. Well, you can leave here in good heart, young lady, because I'm going to ring that lad up and tell him that, as far as I'm concerned, he's entirely cleared of suspicion. What's more, I'll see that the rest of the company come into line."

"That's really nice of you."

"Oh, and there's one other thing."

"Yes?"

"I owe Mr. Millar an apology, and, I'm sure you'll agree, the best form of apology I can make is to produce his play."

"Oh! Mr. Richardson!" Angela clapped her hands like a child. Her blue eyes shone with delight.

"I know Basil's a splendid critic, but I *liked* that play. For once I'll have the courage to back my own Philistine opinion. Provided the rest of the company rally round."

"Oh, we will! We will! We all liked it except Basil."

"Then that's as good as settled, isn't it?"

"There's just one thing, Mr. Richardson."

"Um?"

"Who told you about Rudie coming into my bedroom?"

"A little bird with a very long beak. Shall we leave it at that?"

"All right," smiled Angela. "And thank you."

4

Whilst the Beaumont company wrestled on the stage with Toulippski's masterpiece, Deirdre was at work with ruler and compass in the catacombs below. For the moment her work insulated her from the cast, but to certain of the members this was a loss they were more than willing to sustain. In a bedaubed and bedraggled overall Deirdre now spent most of her time in the paint and carpenter shops, making sure that Teddy and Alf and Syd Scorfe translated her visions into reality with a forthright eye for colour and proportion. But even these troglodytes had their time off in the evenings, and, somewhere about six o'clock, Deirdre would emerge from her catacombs and step back, as spruce and sophisticated as ever, into her private life. There she was ready to complicate the web which she had started to spin at Old Knolle. Intrigue was as meat and wine to her. Much as one woman was dedicated to bridge and another to squash or the singing of madrigals, intrigue was her hobby.

Her "business arrangement" with Willy was now functioning perfectly. With the regularity of night and day his weekly five one-pound notes came to her through the post. It was all clear profit with no clogging overhead and she spent it with a light heart. But Deirdre, now well up the ladder of her ambition, no longer took a provincial view of life. Hers was the metropolitan outlook. She had now developed the habit of thinking in a Big Way. Willy was only a start.

Coincident with Angela's visit to the Regency Buck, Deirdre, leaving the Beaumont that evening, made her way down the crumbling glory of Ladbroke Grove to a small, little-known street called Dickers Place. It was an unsavoury backwater, fringed by dingy houses of impeccable similarity. Most of them, judging from their little tiers of brass bell-knobs and dog's-eared visiting cards, had been converted into flats. Arriving at Number 12, she rang a bell marked Barron—this time in indelible pencil on a snippet from a plain postcard. Since this Mrs. Barron lived in the cheapest flat up under the slate roof, Deirdre was not in the least surprised when an upper window was flung open and an unmusical voice demanded:

"Yes, who is it?"

"It's me, Miss Lehaye."

"Oh, Miss Lehaye, is it? All right, you can come up. The door's off the latch. You know your way, don't you?" Miss Lehaye did. It was up a carpetless stairway beyond a narrow hall, redolent of the odour of cooked greens and musty potted plants. It was past a gently hissing water-closet and glimpses of unmade beds through half-open doors; past an enormous framed reproduction of Reynold's "Age of Innocence"; past a cylindrical umbrella-stand full of empty stout bottles; up a narrower stretch of staircase as steep as a ship's companion-way to the threshold of Evandine Barron's undesirable flat.

She was there to greet her visitor—a tarnished blonde with a pale face and blue smudges under her eyes. She was thirty-five, but looked ten years older; in part due to the fact that she dressed with the seedy jauntiness of a down-at-heel actress and liberally smothered herself with cheap jewellery. Once she had been pretty, very pretty. Now she looked faded and anæmic. Her voice was the most strident factor in her personality.

An eight-year-old boy with a humbug bulging his cheek hovered round his mother's skirts. Deirdre flashed him an artificial smile. Very slowly and deliberately the pasty-faced child put out its tongue.

"Won't you come in?" said Mrs. Barron.

"Thanks."

The room smelt of stale talcum powder and coal gas. In the centre of the room was a large mahogany table littered with the remains of a meal, an untidy pile of school-books, a work-basket, several overloaded ash-trays and a pair of pink corsets. Deirdre dropped into a wicker-chair by the unlit grate and offered her cigarette-case. Mrs. Barron accepted a cigarette with orange-stained fingers and a nod of her rusty blonde head.

"And how is Horace to-day?" asked Deirdre with the stiff joviality of a duchess out slumming.

"He's been bilious," said Evandine. "He's gotta weak stomach that comes back on him if he doesn't watch himself."

"Then surely he shouldn't be sucking sweets?"

"Well, *you* try and stop him."

"I'd as soon snatch a lump of meat from a ravening lion. By the way, Mrs. Barron, you know why I've come round this evening?"

"I can well guess." She looked across at the unprepossessing child. "Horry—you nip down and amuse yourself for a time in the Place. This lady and me want to have a private talk. And no swinging on lamp-posts, else it'll be the worse for you. Remember!"

"Yah!"

Horry snapped up a bag of sweets and a grubby school cap from a chair and bolted without another word down the stairs. A few seconds later they heard him shouting a popular ditty in the street. He had definitely inherited his mother's unmusical voice.

"Well, Mrs. Barron, we won't be so foolish as to waste each other's time. On my last visit I laid a certain proposition before you. This time I've come for your answer."

5

Over the week-ends Angela and Basil slipped down to Fallow Cottage and had, so to speak, a preview of married bliss. She insisted, of course, on sleeping over at Old Knolle; not, as she hastened to explain, that she didn't trust Basil, but it was sensible to consider the uneducated minds of Other People. She cooked his meals and was sweetly managing in a way that Basil found totally irresistible.

But on the week-end following Angela's *tête-à-tête* with Sam at the Regency Buck, Basil went down alone to the cottage. Angela, who was an orphan, had promised to spend a day or two with her guardian at Maidenhead—doubtless to discuss the details of her impending marriage. Hearing about this, Sam decided to go down to Old Knolle so that he could break the news of his decision about *Pigs in Porcelain* to Basil, away from other members of the company. He anticipated a scene, and he wanted Basil to get over his ill-humour before he returned to Town.

On Sunday morning, therefore, a dismal weeping September day, he marched off under an umbrella across the fields to the cottage. To his surprise, he found Basil in gumboots and decrepit mackintosh digging a trench under the kitchen window. He looked hot and exasperated.

"Hullo?" said Sam. "And what may you be up to?"

"Drains," said Basil tersely.

"Drains?"

"Yes, I told you so," snapped Basil. "These Tudor gems are all very fascinating, but their sanitary arrangements are damned discouraging. There's a stoppage somewhere."

Sam peered into the muddy trench with the judicial air of a plumber about to deliver himself of a verdict. A certain amount of water had already collected in the bottom of the trench.

"Looks more like a water-main than a drain-pipe," he said. "You're excavating in the wrong place."

"Well, old Bill Ewing told me the land-drains run under this window and empty themselves into that ditch. His great-great-grandfather or somebody was present when the confounded things were put in."

"Let's forget drains," suggested Sam jovially, "and join each other in a tot of your excellent whisky, old chap. It's a wretched morning. There's something important I want to see you about."

"Oh, all right."

Basil drove his spade into the slush-heap beside the trench, threw aside his damp cigarette which had frizzled out in the rain, and followed Sam into the cottage. A cheerful log fire was burning in the inglenook and a considerable amount of smoke was belching into the room. Sam sniffed the pungent air.

"Homely," he observed. "Nice to see a fire, even in September, when it's wet. A pity more of the smoke doesn't go up the chimney."

Basil poured the drinks in grim silence. Sam had the impression that he wasn't a particularly welcome visitor.

"What d'you want to see me about, Sam?"

Sam looked apprehensive. He disliked any form of scene and arguments always disturbed his digestion. However, out of fairness to young Millar, he must go through with it.

"It's a matter of that play—er—*Pigs in Porcelain*."

Basil glanced up wearily, almost disinterested. "Well, what about it?"

"I'm going to rescind my decision. I want to do it this season." Sam went on hastily before Basil could marshal any arguments: "It may not be up your street, Basil, but it's very much up mine. Oh, I know I only represent the average theatre-goer—I'm not educated up to Toulippski and Strindberg and all the other intellectual giants. But we do get a number of quite ordinary theatre-goers visiting the Beaumont. And their money being as good as the other man's, I really don't—no, I really *don't* see why we shouldn't pander to them on this occasion. Just for once, my dear chap. Let's step aside from our fixed policy for just this one show. After all, there's enough cleverness in Millar's dialogue to titillate the brains of the intellectuals. They won't stay away. They'll come, even if it's only out of curiosity, to assess the value of an entirely new playwright. You follow? As for the average playgoer, he'll get a proper Grand Guignol shiver up the spine and rush to tell his very average friends about it. It means putting the Beaumont on the map for thousands of new patrons. It means a display of enterprise. It means avoiding a policy that's too cut and dried. Oh, I quite realize, old chap, that this sort of psychological thriller isn't really worthy of your talents—but to please me. Just this once. Let me have my own pig-headed, unimaginative, rather commercial way. Well, Basil, well, what do you say?"

At the conclusion of this long and breathless speech, Sam braced himself for the inevitable onslaught. He was prepared to see his powers of persuasion hacked to shreds. He was prepared for a biting criticism of his artistic sense. He was prepared to be called a Philistine, an amateur, a "box-office" manager, even a biscuit millionaire. He was prepared for anything, save the casual answer which he actually received.

"All right," said Basil. "When do you intend to produce the show?"

"When do I intend? Then you agree—my dear Basil, you *agree* to its inclusion in our season's programme?"

Sam was positively beaming with delight. No row, no argument, no recriminations, no criticism. Yes, he was delighted, delighted.

"Why not? The rest of the company seemed to think it a winner."

"But I thought—?" gasped Sam.

"Forget it!" snapped Basil. "We all make mistakes, Sam. I was probably wrong about it. And now, if you don't mind, I want to get back to those drains."

"Of course you do," said Sam obligingly. "Most important. We'll have another talk later on about young Millar's contract and the proposed date of production."

"All right," said Basil, without enthusiasm.

"Well, good-bye, old chap. This smoke's a trifle hard on the throat, isn't it? You ought to have that chimney seen to. It's quite made my eyes sting. But nice to see a fire, even in September. Very nice. Good-bye."

Like a good-humoured spaniel that has anticipated a whipping and got away with a lump of sugar, Sam trotted off down the flagstone path and went bobbing off happily over the sodden fields under his umbrella.

Now, what on earth, he thought, had come over the fellow? Was his indifference due to his engagement and approaching marriage? After all, many things which previously appear to be of great importance pale before the enormous adventure of matrimony. Or was it that, aware of Millar's devotion to Angela, Basil was now in a magnanimous mood and ready to give his defeated rival a leg up the ladder of his career?

CHAPTER X

Phone Calls and a Phantom

I

WHATEVER CLARA MADDISON'S ABILITIES WERE AS A BUSINESS agent, as a private detective she was rotten. She hadn't the necessary guile. But Rudie's plight had roused all her maternal instincts, and she was determined to do her utmost for him. She began by adopting a solicitous attitude towards Willy's health, following him around and getting him to talk on every possible occasion. She thought he looked paler and thinner than usual. Was he getting enough sleep and feeding himself properly? Perhaps he was smoking and drinking more than was compatible with his increasing years? He looked worried. Was he worried? If so, what was he worried about? Perhaps, if he cared to confide in her, she could help him with her advice and understanding.

At first Willy thought this increased interest in his wellbeing was due to the simple fact that they were playing opposite each other in *The Red Ant*. He could quite see that if, due to sudden ill-health, he had to drop out of the part, Clara's own rôle would suffer an incurable relapse. They were, in fact, just beginning to squeeze the juice out of Toulippski's characters and their particular scenes were growing in strength and realism every day.

Then Willy began to wonder, and a new worry was added to his already overstocked storehouse of trouble. Was the impetus of Clara's interest amorous? It did happen, he knew, that late in life, actresses were inclined to become over-emotionalized. A constant strumming on emotional strings loosened up their sense of morality and left them the sad prey of their impulses. Clara was an old and long-admired professional friend, but that was no reason why she should not suffer a change of heart. After all, she was separated from her husband and, apart from her life in the theatre, was probably a lonely and dissatisfied old woman. He began to appraise her with an apprehensive eye; the kind of glance that measures the distance to the nearest exit. He claimed that, like Cassius, she had, if not a lean, at least a hungry look about her.

Then, one day, sitting side by side on a rostrum in a dark corner up-stage during rehearsal, she asked him if he were suffering from "a secret trouble"? This was too much for Willy. He made some feeble excuse about a 'phone call and bolted to his dressing-room. Thereafter he devoted his waning energies to side-stepping his old friend whenever she buttonholed him for a *tête-à-tête*.

For the first time, Clara's suspicions were definitely aroused. Willy was acting strangely. He seemed uneasy in her presence, watchful, impatient, and now he was doing all he could to avoid her. She felt pretty sure at the end of a few days that Willy had filched Sam's petty cash.

Into this unpleasant interlude crashed an hilarious, almost inarticulate 'phone call from Rudolph. Sam Richardson had just informed him that he intended to put on *Pigs in Porcelain*. Could he come over to Hampstead without delay and talk over the superb news with his aunt? Of course, said Clara, and wasn't it all too, too thrilling?

In this manner, with Sam's subsequent invitation to Rudie and his aunt to visit him at Old Knolle the next week-end, events moved a step nearer to their fateful conclusion. Life was evolving a far more subtle and harrowing drama than any conceived by the fertile brain of Igor Toulippski, although the actors in the two dramas were destined to be more or less the same.

2

Other apparently irrelevant incidents cropped up like poison weeds. Basil, under pressure of work connected with the new production, was forced to spend the Saturday of that same week-end in the theatre. It was a matter of technical conferences with the stage staff. He apologized to Angela and suggested that if she were at a loose end she should trespass on Sam's kindness and go down to Old Knolle. Deirdre, also under pressure of work, had asked earlier in the week if Basil would lend her Fallow Cottage for a few days; so in any case, explained Basil, they couldn't have had their customary time together at the week-end. Basil promised, however, to join the Old Knolle house-party at Sunday lunch. Much to Angela's surprise, he concluded:

"But you won't be bored, my darling. I understand Sam has asked young Millar down there to talk over the contract. But mind you behave yourself."

"Oh, Basil!" Her mock-anger was charming. She went on enthusiasti-cally: "I was thrilled when Sam told me he was going to do *Pigs in Porcelain*. I knew you'd relent and agree with the rest of us, you darling man."

"Huh!" grunted Basil.

"And of course I'll behave, you jealous stupid."

As they happened at the time to be in the producer's private office, her arms at this juncture enlaced themselves round Basil's neck and her lips brushed his with the promise of a kiss. He lifted her off her feet, kissed her in a manner that was much more than a promise and, giving her a little pat on the posterior, shooed her paternally from his office.

So, on the night of Friday, September 11th, Clara, Angela and Rudolph, after dining with Sam at the Regency Buck, piled into his luxurious Forty Daimler and sped away in the direction of Sussex. Basil, who had also been present at the dinner, heaved a sigh of-ever-increasing depression, watched the tail-light of the Daimler slide away in the stream of traffic, and ambled off along Piccadilly in the direction of the Circus.

The stage staff hadn't been too pleased about having to show up at the Beaumont on Saturday; particularly in the afternoon, which they usually spent losing hard-earned money on temperamental greyhounds. Nor was Willy exactly enthusiastic when, later that Friday evening, Basil rang up his club and suggested they should put in an hour on the stage the next morning, polishing up Petrovka's soliloquy in the third act.

"I know it's a damned bore, old fellow," he said. "I'm no keener on week-end work than you are—but it's a chance for us to get together on the Q.T. without the rest of the company milling around. What do you say?"

"Oh, all right! All right!" piped Willy. "I'm of an opinion that my present rendering of the speech can't be improved upon, but after forty years on the stage I'm quite ready to learn."

"That's my co-operative Willy!" cried Basil heartily. "Shall we say ten-thirty?"

"Ten-thirty? Damme! we will *not* say ten-thirty. I refuse to tread the boards before noon on a Saturday morning. Expect me at twelve o'clock. Good night."

3

Saturday, September 12th, dawned mistily, but the sun still had strength behind the mist, and by the time breakfast at Old Knolle was finished, the day was clear and sparkling beyond the terrace windows. Clara, Rudolph and Sam closeted themselves in the study to talk business. Angela, after mooning about the garden for a time, feeding the pigeons and peacocks, decided to slip over and see how Deirdre was coping with life at Fallow Cottage. She missed Basil enormously, but it was pleasant to sniff the clean country air again and to hear the lawn-mower whirring over the ancient sward of "The Cassel". Her heart ached for Basil, shut away from this jewel of a morning in the dark and dusty emptiness of the Beaumont.

An hour or so later she left Fallow Cottage in a furious temper. Deirdre's cynicism and mockery could always be relied upon to upset her, but that particular morning her remarks had carried unusually toxic stings in their tails: It was all innuendo and mostly directed at Basil, but the implication was as clear as the September morning. Angela, according to Deirdre, was about to commit the craziest blunder in her life. She was about to marry a man whose past reputation was something to shudder at, whose future behaviour was something to be dreaded. If, explained Deirdre sweetly, she hadn't been so fond of Angela, she wouldn't have bothered to warn her, but even now it wasn't too late to withdraw. The result was, of course, that Angela felt murderous and left Fallow Cottage more in love with Basil than ever. She thought Deirdre quite the nastiest and meanest creature she had ever met.

Unfortunately, Sam, unaware of all this undercurrent of bad feeling, had asked Deirdre over to lunch. Clara and Rudolph, leaving Sam's study with an encouraging contract well on the way, had a sudden cold douche emptied over their elation when they came face to face with Deirdre in the hall. They exchanged a few frozen nods. Sam was polite with the sherry. Angela brightly talkative. Deirdre maliciously amused. She turned to Sam.

"By the way, Mr. Richardson, I forgot to ask—have you found out anything more about that loathsome burglary?"

Clara and Rudolph stiffened. Deirdre's ice-green eyes rested for an instant on the young man's disconcerted countenance, then stared impudently at Clara.

"No! No! Nothing further," put in Sam hastily. "It's a complete mystery."

"Yes, isn't it?" said Deirdre. "I wonder if it will ever be cleared up?"

"Oh, I'm sure it will!" cried Angela, who knew just how Rudolph must be feeling. "And then—then—" She stammered to a full-stop and looked helpless. "And then we—"

"And then," added Deirdre, "we shall *all* be cleared of suspicion, shan't we, Mr. Richardson? At the moment I feel you can't really be sure of *any* of us, can you? It's frightfully disagreeable for you, I'm sure."

"My dear young lady, of course it isn't! It was an outside job. There's no doubt about it. Now let's drop the miserable subject. It's too nice a day to spoil." He turned to Rudolph and Angela, who found themselves almost rubbing shoulders by the fire-place. "And what are you young people going to do this afternoon? Tennis? Boating? Eh?"

"Tennis would be fun if you're game, Mr. Millar," said Angela.

"Well, I haven't brought my things, but—"

"Oh, I can manage that!" cut in Sam cheerily. "I've a complete sports department always at the disposal of my guests. No country house is complete without it." Adding, as the gong throbbed in a crescendo down the corridor: "Ah, lunch! Well, I don't know about you, Miss Maddison, but business discussions always leave me peckish. Shall we go in?"

4

If it hadn't been for Deirdre's presence in a hammock-chair, Rudolph would have been in heaven that afternoon. What more could he ask of life? His play to be produced; Angela, a cool vision in white on the far side of the net; his back-hand working with a dreamlike efficiency; the sun overhead; the garden a blaze of autumn flowers—everything conspired to pander to his happiness. Everything save the watchful soignée creature in the hammock-chair. There was so much he wanted to say to Angela; but how could he be natural with those mocking eyes following his every movement and those pendant-embroidered ears harvesting his every word?

When he realized that Angela was to be at Old Knolle that week-end, he knew his luck had changed. When Deirdre turned up with her foul insinuations before lunch, he was not so sure. Her very presence made him awkward and boorish. He felt he wanted to take her by the scruff of the neck and run her out of the garden.

Angela was no less disconcerted when Deirdre had tailed them down to the tennis court. Her hints about Basil's unreliability still rankled. She knew Deirdre was making Rudolph uncomfortable, and was furious with her because, in the first place, she had been responsible for spreading the beastly rumour that Rudolph had been in Sam's study on the night of the theft.

It was with a general feeling of relief that, after a strained and unusually silent tea on the terrace, Deirdre betook herself back to Fallow Cottage. Sam then buttonholed Rudolph for further talks about the production of his play, so that he was still unable to see Angela alone. Angela and Clara walked down to the village and back to fill in the time until dinner. After dinner they sat about in the music-room talking shop, which foiled Rudolph yet again of the chance he was seeking. Once more Deirdre had succeeded in dealing him a pretty shabby hand!

It was about five minutes to ten that evening when Mrs. Dreed came in to tell Mr. Richardson that he was wanted on the telephone.

"I'll take it in the study," said Sam.

It was Deirdre ringing from Fallow Cottage. "Hullo, young lady, is there anything wrong?"

"Not exactly, but Basil's just rung through from Town to know if Willy has come down to the cottage or Old Knolle. I told him he hadn't been here."

"No, and he's not here either."

"I see, only Basil appears to be rather anxious about him."

"Anxious?"

"Yes. They met at the Beaumont this morning for an extra rehearsal, and Basil says poor Willy seemed rather queer. I don't mean ill, but acting rather strangely. Basil says he seemed terribly keyed-up and unnatural."

"I suppose," suggested Sam diffidently, "that he hadn't been—er—imbibing? I'm afraid it's one of poor Willy's little weaknesses."

"I asked Basil the same question. He says definitely *not*! It's been worrying Basil all day. And this evening, when he rang Willy's club in Chelsea, the manager told him he'd left the place shortly after six and hadn't returned since. The manager said he'd also noticed that Willy wasn't normal. It's frightfully worrying, Mr. Richardson."

"It is," agreed Sam. "I'm only sorry he *hasn't* turned up here."

"It's curious, because Basil went round at once to Victoria and both the booking-clerk and the man at the barrier swear that somebody answering to Willy's description caught the seven-forty-three to Lambdon. I'll ring back to Basil at once and tell him that he hasn't shown up. He may like to put the matter in the hands of the police in Town."

When Sam conveyed the news post-haste to the music-room, it caused honest consternation. Willy was popular with everybody at the Beaumont. He had his faults, but he was a lovable character and, in the right part, a brilliant actor. Now it looked as if trouble were in ambush for him.

Clara and Rudolph exchanged a meaning glance. Had they been right in their supposition about the theft of that money? Had this lapse overwhelmed poor Willy with remorse and driven him half out of his mind? They had all noticed his fumbling for words and false moves at rehearsal; his air of preoccupation; his nervous, bird-like glances; his appearance of inner tension.

"My dears," said Clara forlornly. "I don't want to be melodramatic, but if Willy *has* got something preying on his mind he's quite capable of suicide."

"Oh, no!" cried Angela with a shiver.

Rudolph, who was sitting beside her on the settee, dared everything and placed a comforting hand on her bare arm. She turned and flashed him a little smile.

"It's highly disturbing," observed Sam. "I feel I ought to do something about it."

"Well, Basil will do all he can at his end," pointed out Clara, who having started a hare now seemed anxious to draw attention away from it. "If he's any common sense, which I doubt, he'll inform the police. If he *does* learn anything to-night, he's sure to ring through to Deirdre or direct to us here. He'll realize how anxious we all are. Oh, dear, it *is* distressing! But we can't really *do* anything. I'm all for an early night."

This seemed to be the general feeling, and, after a further brief but lively discussion, the party broke up and made their way to their rooms. All save Sam, who, observing that the news would prevent him from sleeping, went through to his study and a biography of Napoleon, which he felt would take his mind off poor Willy. The time then was exactly twenty-five minutes past ten.

6

About an hour later the telephone rang in Sam's study, where the extension lead was still plugged in after the Fallow Cottage call. As luck would have it, he had become so absorbed in his biography that he still hadn't made his way to bed. He seized the instrument with alacrity.

"Hullo? Yes?"

"Is that you, Sam? It's Basil here. I say, I'm coming down to Old Knolle, and I'm coming pronto."

"You've heard something about Willy?"

"No, that's just it. He was certainly seen catching the seven-forty-three down to Lambdon, and when Deirdre rang me up about an hour ago to say he hadn't turned up at Old Knolle or the Cottage, I was more worried than ever, Sam. I felt sure he'd be at Fallow Cottage."

"But, my dear chap, why should he want to go there? To see Deirdre?"

"Exactly."

"But why should he want to see her at this time of night?"

"I can't tell you over the 'phone, Sam. But about ten minutes ago I rang Deirdre again and couldn't get any reply. That's why I'm driving down without delay. But I'm anxious, damned anxious. We may already be too late. Look here, Sam, is it too much to ask you to nip over to the cottage and see if everything's all right?"

"But you don't suspect that poor Willy—"

"In his present queer state of mind I'm inclined to suspect anything—even the worst! He's got something against Deirdre. I guessed that from something he said after our rehearsal this morning. The whole thing looks pretty serious and urgent. And *urgent*, Sam. You follow?"

"All right. I'll go over at once. I'll get young Millar to come along, too."

"Good! I should be at Old Knolle about one o'clock if I drive flat out. Till we meet, then, Sam. *Au revoir.*"

Sam turned from the telephone puzzled and shaken. That something ominous had taken or was about to take place seemed certain. Basil thought it might already be too late. Willy had evidently got a set against Deirdre, and—Sam shivered. No—that sort of thing just didn't happen within the circle of one's own friends.

However, spurred on by the genuine anxiety in Basil's voice, he loped off along the corridor, ascended the main staircase and knocked on the door of Rudolph's bedroom. There was no reply. He knocked louder. Still no reply. Without further ceremony he opened the door and switched on the light. The room was empty. The bed-clothes were turned down and young Millar's threadbare pyjamas set out, rather pathetically, on the expensive eiderdown—but there was no sign of the man who should have been inside them.

For a moment Sam was at a loss, then, before his fine faith in human nature could assert itself, a nasty suspicion wriggled into his mind. Once before when Mr. Millar had slept under his roof his nocturnal peregrinations had not been all they should have been! He recalled Mrs. Dreed's story about a somewhat impulsive visit to Angela's bedroom. Angela had assured him that young Millar's intrusion had been purely accidental. And yet—

Without more ado, now frankly perturbed, Sam moved off down the lighted corridor until he came to Angela's room. Again he knocked; gently at first, then louder. The profound stillness was like a blow in the face. Surely he was not to suffer a disillusionment over Angela? His charming little Angela? The child he always looked upon as his adopted niece? For the second time he pushed open a door and switched on a light. Angela's room, like Rudolph's, was empty!

The bedclothes had been turned down and a totally inadequate slip of a nightdress was set out on the eiderdown, but there was no sign of the girl who should have been filling this pretty garment with the shapely curves and limbs of her innocent young person.

For some reason, best known to themselves, neither Angela nor Rudolph had gone to bed. Sam's heart sank. Surely they had not sneaked out of the house together? Angela was engaged to Basil. Young Millar was a guest under his roof!

Then, recalling Willy, Sam whipped himself into more violent action and pounded down the stairs on his way to Fallow Cottage.

7

The moon was rising as Sam started on his jog-trot along the bridle-path which led to Fallow Cottage. A faint wash of light, gradually growing stronger, was laving the landscape. A sedentary career and a tricky diges-tion had left him with the conviction that it was possible to get through life quite comfortably at a walking pace. If he wanted to go quicker there was always the car, a taxi, a bus or a train. So this sudden demand on his physical energies found him abominably and abdominally out of trim. He arrived at the cottage, breathless, giddy, hotter than a griddle-cake.

To his intense relief, a light was burning behind the drawn curtains of the sitting-room window and the front door was wide open. After a casual ring, he called out in a merry voice, "Miss Lehaye there? Ahoy! Can I come in? It's Sam Richardson! Miss Lehaye!"

For the third time that night, however, Sam passed through a door into silence and mystery. There was no doubt that the cottage was deserted, for Sam's voice had good penetrative powers and the place itself was compact. He went first into the sitting-room. Nothing appeared to be out of order; a scattered pile of charcoal sketches on the centre table; Deirdre's overall flung carelessly over a chair; a little heap of gold-tipped

Turkish cigarette stubs in an ashtray—all factors indicating that Deirdre had recently been working in the room. The tiny dining-room was unlit and the curtains had not even been closed, suggesting that the place had not been used since dark. In the kitchen a slow fire glowed in the domestic heater and a few unwashed crocks had been left on the draining-board. Upstairs Sam found nothing untoward, save the fact that Deirdre's bed was unrumpled and that she, herself, appeared to have vanished from the cottage like a puff of smoke down the wind.

"Strange," thought Sam. "Her exit must have been somewhat pre-cipitate since the young lady left the lounge light burning and the door wide open. Careless. Doubt if Basil would like it. Anybody could walk into the place, eh? I don't really like this. After Basil's recent warning one could put a pretty uncomfortable interpretation on all this. Puzzling and unnatural. No—I really don't like it."

As he was about to turn out the light in the sitting-room, he noticed a handkerchief that had been dropped near the doorway. In the ordinary course of events Sam was the sort of fellow to let sleeping handkerchiefs lie, but this was a man's handkerchief. He picked it up. Yes, an outsize silk handkerchief with the single letter F embroidered in black in one corner. Without further thought he stuffed the thing into his pocket and, having turned out the light and closed the front door, he hurried back across the fields.

Scarcely had he entered the boundaries of his extensive gardens when he stopped dead and held his breath. Floating like a ghost between him and the yew hedges of the Dutch garden was the unmistakable figure of a woman. Her progress in the filmy moonlight was eerie to a degree, for she seemed to move over the ground swiftly and silently without moving her legs. But Sam had not made a cool million by believing in psychic phenomena. If his eyes saw something, then his brain was always ready with a perfectly normal exposition of what his eyes had seen. In this case he had no doubts at all. His relief was intense.

"Hi! Miss Lehaye!" he boomed. "Miss Lehaye! It's me—Sam Richardson. Is there anything the matter?"

For a split second the figure seemed to hover in mid-flight and then, without sign or answer, whisked itself away into the deep shadows. By the time he reached the head of the yew-lined walk which led through the centre of the Dutch garden to the east door of the house, the figure was no longer to be seen.

"Well, I'll be—!" said Sam petulantly under his breath. "What in the name of—?"

All his thoughts seemed to be tailing off into space like this without reaching any logical end. He was beginning to feel the slightest bit moonstruck and stupefied by this pressure of odd events. Old Knolle had lost for the moment its reassuring stolidity. Its crazy little turrets and bonneted roofs might well have been those of some ogre's castle. The moon glimmered coldly on its numberless windows. An owl hooted in the walnut tree.

In Sam's estimation the person, whoever it was, must have gone direct into the house, but a quick search of all the likely rooms on the lower floor was without result. The bedrooms he felt, were outside his domain; and, in any case, it *was* possible that the uncatalogued phantom (whom he believed to be Deirdre) had skirted the house and was still somewhere on the estate. He returned, now somewhat exhausted, to the warm familiarity of his study.

What now? he wondered. Presumably he'd have to wait up until Basil arrived. He'd probably have some masterly scheme up his sleeve for coping with this present situation. Deirdre, of course, may have just been out for a breath of air after a long spell of work, and his sudden shouts had probably frightened her. It had been inconsiderate of him and very ill-mannered. Even the most worldly of young women does not expect to be accosted by an unseen Boanerges in the calm of a moonlit garden!

Then Sam came bolt upright in his chair. Half a minute—perhaps it had *not* been Deirdre Lehaye! It might well have been Angela. Poor child! What an unforgivable shock he must have given her. He ought to apologize—yes, really—there and then. It would only be fair to the girl's peace of mind to let her know that his was the rude voice which had shattered the stillness of the night. Without more ado, like all men of action, Sam strode to her bedroom and knocked on the door. This time he was answered.

"Yes, who is it?" came the drowsy inquiry.

"It's me, Sam Richardson."

This seemed to be his tag-line for the night.

"Oh, come in, please, and turn on the light."

Sam did so, modestly lowering his glance before the feminine vision which appraised him anxiously from a nest of snowy bedclothes. Angela's round blue eyes were filled with innocent amazement.

"Please, tell me quickly, it isn't bad news about Willy?"

"No, I've heard nothing further. You must excuse me breaking in on you like this, my dear young lady, but I felt I must apologize for shouting at you so unexpectedly in the garden just now."

The round, blue eyes grew rounder and bluer. "In the garden? Just now? Oh, you made a mistake. Just now I was in bed and nearly asleep."

"Yes, quite, I see that now." Sam was nonplussed. "In fact, I—er—realized my error the moment I switched on the light and saw you in bed. It must have been somebody else. I'm—I'm sorry, my dear. I'm afraid I've ruined your beauty sleep. Most stupid of me."

"Oh, that's all right," said Angela handsomely. "I—we—we all make silly mistakes sometimes, don't we? Good night, Mr. Richardson."

"Good night, my dear."

Sam turned out the light and softly closed the door. The dream-like quality of the night was growing stronger. He couldn't grasp the implications of all these queer happenings. People who ought to be in bed were abroad in the moonlight. People whom he imagined to be abroad in the moonlight were snug and sleepy in bed! Was it possible that Angela had merely been in the bathroom when he had paid his first visit to her bedroom? He ought to have thought of that. In which case the figure in white was almost certainly Deirdre. But did the girl ever wear white? Sam, although the type of man who never noticed if a girl were in slacks or a shimmy, had a feeling that Deirdre favoured rather colourful creations. At some time or another he had evolved the private phrase "a bird of paradise". He had not meant it unkindly, of course, but that was the effect Deirdre's attire must have produced on him. Angela was muted strings. Deirdre was *fortissimo* brass. He thought that rather neat.

But the rush of curious events was not yet over. Before Sam regained his study, a panting, agitated figure with wild hair and wilder eyes came dashing down the east wing into the dimly lit hall.

"Good God!" cried Sam, now thoroughly exasperated. "Who the devil's that?"

He jammed on more lights.

"It's me, sir."

"Millar! And what's the matter with you?"

"Nothing—really. I just felt I couldn't sleep, so I took a stroll round the lake. Then, as I felt a bit chilly, I put in a sprint to warm me up. I'm sorry if I gave you a turn, crashing in on you like that, sir."

"Oh, I'm getting used to this sort of thing," said Sam, out of temper for the first time that evening. "And now, I take it, you intend to go to bed?" Rudolph nodded. "Well, I'll wish you a very good night, young fellow. A *very* good night."

"Good night, sir."

In his study, Sam indulged in a very large whisky with very little soda.

8

It was a few minutes after one when Sam detected the approaching drone of Basil's M.G. He went through into the entrance hall and switched on the porch light. With a skidding of tyres on the loose gravel Basil braked up and vaulted from the car.

"Deirdre?" he snapped, recognizing Sam. "She's all right? She's at the cottage?"

"No, she isn't!" In a few terse phrases Sam described his visit to Fallow Cottage. "But about twenty minutes or more ago," concluded Sam, "I saw a figure in white running towards the house near the Dutch garden."

"Then she's here!" cried Basil, with obvious relief as they crossed into the main hall. "Thank God for that!"

"That's just where you're wrong. She certainly hasn't taken refuge anywhere in the lower part of the house. At least not in the rooms you'd naturally expect to find her. In any case, does Deirdre wear white?"

"For heaven's sake, give me a drink, Sam, and I'll think this out. White? No, she never wears white. Never! Too virginal. It *couldn't* have been her." They passed into the study. "But wait a minute, Sam."

"Whisky?"

"Yes, by heaven, and have the decency to make it a large one. Wait a minute, Sam!"

"Well?"

"I suppose she couldn't have been in her pyjamas?"

"I was too far off. I couldn't really say. But does she wear pyjamas?"

"It's quite possible."

"White pyjamas?"

"Why not?"

Basil seized on the proffered tumbler and took a long gulp with his eyes closed. "Sam, we've got no time to waste. Willy's down here—I'm sure of it—and if he's got to the cottage before us—"

"But what would Willy be up to chasing the girl in her pyjamas all over the garden?"

"Ask me another. But I don't like it, Sam. I don't like it at all. I'm going to be honest with you, and you'd better prepare yourself for a very nasty jar. Willy Farnham took that money from your desk. He confessed to me this morning at the Beaumont. The old chap simply broke down and blubbered like a kid. Deirdre, the hell-cat, caught him red-handed at this desk. Result—blackmail! Her silence was costing poor Willy five pounds a week. To cap it all he had no sense of security. You see that, Sam? He knew at any moment the damn girl might change her mind and blab. It was driving him crazy. I hate having to tell you this. It's rotten news, isn't it?"

"Shocking," murmured Sam. "Absolutely shocking. That people can *do* such vile things!" His sigh was full of pity for the inherent frailty of the human race. His faith in the fundamental decency of his fellow-men was moribund. "You think Willy has come down here with the intention of doing bodily harm to the girl?"

"What else can I think? He hinted at the idea this morning. 'Of putting an end to the intolerable suspense'—those were his words, Sam. Come on, we mustn't hang around! We must rouse the whole crowd and search the house and grounds. Young Millar had better dash over to Fallow Cottage and make sure Deirdre hasn't turned up there in the interim. Come on!"

Within five minutes Old Knolle was seething with activity. All over "The Cassel" lights were springing on in windows, and guests and servants alike scrambling into the oddest collection of garments. Sam had faltered about bringing in the domestic staff; but, as Basil explained, they were bound to realize that something unusual was afoot and, in such circumstances, truth was far better than conjecture. In fact, it was Basil who promoted Mrs. Dreed—gaunt and unappetizing, with a black-belted mackintosh over a voluminous quilted dressing-gown—to the rank of officer commanding the indoor search-party. He himself led the guests into the moon-laved garden. He paused for an instant to comfort Angela, who was shivering with cold and apprehension. She looked like a wistful schoolgirl, with her tumbled hair and sleep-laden eyes, her piquant little face emerging from the collar of Sam's fur-lined motor-coat. Basil gave her a quick hug.

"Oh, Basil, I know something beastly has happened!"

"Keep smiling. Don't let's cross our bridges till we come to them, my dear. It may all turn out to be a storm in a teacup."

But in this Basil proved to be drastically wrong. By the time young Millar had returned from Fallow Cottage with the news that it was still deserted, the rest of the party had searched the terrace and passed on to the lake. Sam was the first to notice the luminous patch against the dark waters. It was like some giant-petalled water-lily, suspended and gently swaying on the slow ripples. At his curt summons the others came hurrying up and, peering forward, they knew their search was at an end. As their eyes gained strength over the shifting interplay of light and shade which fretted the moonlit water, they could discern the blurred outlines of a human form. It was floating, face down, not four feet from the bank— one cold white arm flung out like a tendril, moving eerily on the heave and fall of the surface, lending the spectral shape a sickening animation.

In silence Basil fetched the boat-hook from the nearby punt and cautiously edged the half-submerged figure to the bank. The water was shallow there and the bank shelving, so that he and Sam and Millar were soon able to get their hands under the body and lift it clear of the lake.

In silence they stared down on the pearly outlines of what had once been the soignée and disturbing entity known as Deirdre Lehaye. Even in death she was relaxed in an elegant and disdainful posture. Her white satin pyjamas moulded her figure with a bold indifference to the accepted canons of modesty. A single red sandal encased her left foot, suggesting that the other had come loose and sunk to the bed of the lake. Her wet bare arms glistened in the moonlight. Only her eyes and mouth were unnatural. For her eyes were staring and horrible and totally without expression; and the malicious smile, so often the perfect materialization of her inmost thoughts, was erased for ever from the crimson gash of her mouth!

CHAPTER XI

A Case of Brandy

I

A S A STRUGGLING PHYSICIAN IN A NOTORIOUSLY HEALTHY PARISH, Doctor Bredhurst, despite the lateness of the hour, was delighted to be summoned to Old Knolle. He had been up to "The Cassel" once or twice to deal with the minor ailments and injuries of the domestic staff, but he never made the acquaintance of Sam Richardson. Apart from his digestion, which was in the care of a Wimpole Street dietitian, Sam was fairly tough. One does not amass a million out of biscuits without a strong constitution. Doctor Bredhurst was one of those incurable romanticists who look upon millionaires as supermen, as beings but once removed from archangels. This urgent 'phone call, therefore, found him on his toes, dressed to the last button, black bag in hand, before one could have said Jack Robinson.

Sam was waiting for him, teetering with impatience on the impressive front steps. The body had been laid out on a mattress in the conservatory; and it was there, amid the humid perfumes and lush tropicality of Sam's hothouse plants, that Doctor Bredhurst made his examination. Only the men of the party were present. The women were huddled over an electric fire in the music-room, sipping strong tea.

"Ah, excellent! I see you're trying the effects of artificial respiration as I suggested over the telephone, Mr. Richardson," said Bredhurst, in the cultured tones he employed when addressing the wealthier members of his clientele.

Basil was, in fact, doing his utmost according to the instructions young Millar had read out to him from the *Encyclopædia Britannica*. Nobody at Old Knolle had any first-hand knowledge of the process, but even an amateurish attempt was better, they felt, than complete inactivity.

"Are there any signs of returning respiration?" added the doctor.

Basil, breathless from his efforts, shook his head. "I've an idea that life was extinct before we lifted her from the water. Take a look at that."

He pointed to the top of Deirdre's sleekly raven head. A big contusion was visible under the hair, which was itself matted with a considerable patch of coagulated blood which even the water hadn't washed away. Doctor Bredhurst examined the wound in silence, then asked sagaciously:

"Was the body found in deep water?"

"Far from it," said Sam. "In quite shallow water, only a few feet from the bank."

"Are there any large stones in the bottom of the lake, Mr. Richardson?"

"None. It was recently dredged and restocked with trout."

"I see." Bredhurst passed his hand with an habitual gesture round his chin and realized, to his dismay, that he badly needed a shave. "I only ask," he went on, turning his face slightly away from the direct rays of the light, "because of this blow on the head. If I were asked to reconstruct the probable sequence of events, without having visited the locale of the accident, I should say that the unfortunate young woman was walking along the bank, slipped, hit her head against some hard object, and rolled into the lake. Being unconscious, she was powerless to save herself from drowning, even in shallow water. You see my point, Mr. Richardson?"

"I think it shows considerable perspicacity and common sense, doctor."

Bredhurst flushed with pleasure. He quite forgot the dark stubble ringing his jowl. He looked as if he could have crawled into Sam's pocket and wagged his tail. To be complimented by a man who owned a million! He completed his careful examination, and announced in a suitably hushed voice:

"I'm afraid there's no hope—no hope at all. But I intend to continue with the artificial respiration for a little longer." He took off his coat, rolled up his sleeves and knelt down, straddling the girl, "I take it you've rung up the police, Mr. Richardson?"

Sam nodded. "Inspector Harting is coming over from Millward Heath at once." At this stage of the proceedings Sam was not prepared to inform the doctor that they suspected foul play. He glanced up at Basil and added meaningly, "Perhaps it would be as well, old chap, if you and Millar took a more comprehensive look round the grounds. You follow, eh?"

"Perfectly," said Basil. "Come on, Millar. Let's get cracking."

As they went out into the corridor, they heard the sycophant voice of Doctor Bredhurst saying, "You grasp the arms thus, Mr. Richardson—just below the elbows—and actuate them in an arc to a point above the head about fourteen times a minute—if you follow me?"

Once clear of the house, Basil turned to Rudolph, "Look here, young fellow, you probably don't know what all this is about. We suspect that Willy came down here to-night half out of his mind, in order to do Miss Lehaye some sort of bodily harm. Events rather suggest that he succeeded. Get me?"

"You mean—?" gasped Rudolph.

"Yes—murder. No good going all sissy. If ever there was a case of murder 'most foul, strange and unnatural', this is it!"

"But why?" Rudolph looked strained and shaken.

"Oh, well," said Basil lightly, "as you're really an interested party, I may as well let you in on it. Willy pinched that cash and Deirdre *knew* he pinched it. She was blackmailing the old boy."

"Good God!" Rudolph was staggered. "So *that* was it! I guessed it might have been Farnham. I say—this is pretty frightful, isn't it?"

"And now," cut in Basil incisively, "we've got to find the poor devil. It's my opinion that if he lost his head and did commit murder, he'd try to follow it up with suicide. Probably on the spot. Now, you take that side of the garden and I'll take this. Work your way gradually down to the lake through the shrubberies. Look in every possible hiding-place."

They parted company and began to pad like a couple of bloodhounds this way and that over the sloping lawns. Much of the ground had been covered in their search for Deirdre, but they were taking no chances. Just as they started on the job, they saw the headlights of a car swing through the drive-gates and swiftly approach "The Cassel". Inspector Harting, ignoring all speed limits, had done the journey from Millward Heath in record time. But this, he realized, was big-time stuff. "Lovely Lady Loses

Life in Lonely Lake." "Mystery of Millionaire's Mansion!" It was due for a splash in the big dailies; and, as such, was a case worth handling.

                                2

Doctor Bredhurst was lying back on a couch, recuperating from his barren attempts at artificial respiration, when Mrs. Dreed showed Inspector Harting into the conservatory. The Inspector knew Bredhurst well, as they had often met in their professional capacities in court and elsewhere. They got together at once over the case.

"And the cause of death, doctor?"

"I'm inclined to think asphyxiation due to drowning—that is the primary cause. There was absolutely no sign of heat in the body, which suggests it had been in the water for some time. A secondary cause may well have been a severe blow on the vault of the head."

Harting turned to Sam. "Can you let me have full details of the discovery of the body and so on, sir?"

"I suggest we go through to my study," said Sam. "Doctor, you'll join us in a tot before you return home?"

"Ah, thank you! Thank you!" Bredhurst only just stopped himself from washing his hands in invisible soap and water. It was a habit he found most distasteful in other people.

Over their drinks, Sam gave Harting a general picture of events; but it was not until Bredhurst had withdrawn that he could speak really frankly to the Inspector.

"You imagine the poor girl lost her life through an accident, eh, Harting?"

"Yes—either that or suicide. You agree?"

"I wish I could," said Sam, "but there may be more to this tragedy than appears on the surface. There's just a chance, a fair chance, Harting, that there's been foul play."

"What makes you think that?"

Sam outlined briefly the astonishing information that Basil had so recently handed out—about Willy and the money; about Deirdre's untimely appearance on the scene of the theft; about her subsequent blackmail, and Willy's tempestuous threat to "put an end to the intoler-able suspense".

"And what's more," concluded Sam, "we're pretty sure that Farnham actually caught a train down to Lambdon to-night."

Harting whistled. This unexpected pattern of events was intriguing. There was a possibility, a distinct possibility, that he would be called upon to exercise his not undeveloped powers of deduction.

"So there's just a chance that it's neither accident nor suicide, Mr. Richardson, but— "

Harting never rid himself of the dread word, for at that moment Basil, white and anxious, rushed into the study.

"Young Millar's just found him, Sam! Semi-conscious and blind drunk in the thatched summer-house. He looks just about all in. We need a stretcher or something to bring him over."

"Inspector Harting," said Sam, "this is Mr. Barnes."

"'Evening, Mr. Barnes, I take it that this fellow you've just found is Farnham, eh? Mr. Richardson has just been telling me—"

"Yes. He caught the train down here to-night."

"Umph—let's take a look at him. Once he's recovered, he'll be ready to talk. Have you got such a thing as a stretcher, Mr. Richardson?"

"No—but there's a canvas camp bed in the hall lobby."

The little party trooped out of the east door and made their way down the lawn to the summer-house. Millar was sitting beside Willy, propping him up with the crook of his arm. The old fellow's head hung forward slackly and several dried runnels of blood streaked his neck and jowl. His breath was quick and rasping. Every now and then he muttered through closed lips. Harting bent down in an effort to catch an isolated word, but it was nightmare stuff, without rhyme and reason.

"Pity we let the doctor slip away," said Sam, as Basil and Millar lifted the inert figure on to the canvas bed. "He looks in pretty poor shape, eh, Harting?"

The Inspector smiled. "I'd not take a bet on that, sir. I noticed his clothes were fairly reeking of brandy. I think he's more fuddled than hurt. The sooner we can get him warmly wrapped up and some strong coffee inside him, the sooner we shall know how bad he is."

With Basil and Rudolph acting as stretcher-bearers, the little procession filed into the house and re-entered the study. There Willy was made comfortable on the big leather settee, with cushions under his head and blankets under his meagre shivering frame. Lifting an eyelid, Harting brought a lighted match close to the dilated pupil. There was no reaction. But after a few minutes it was obvious that Willy was coming, slowly but surely, out of his coma. His eyes began to rove questioningly over the ceiling and his left hand, true to the instinct of years, fumbled over his waistcoat, searching for his shattered monocle. Mrs. Dreed had speedily brought the hot coffee, and Harting had soon forced a little between his bloodless lips. He addressed the others, who were gazing down to record the result of the stimulant.

"And now, gentlemen, if you'd leave me alone with the patient for a few minutes—er—not you, Mr. Richardson. I think it would be as well to get Bredhurst over without delay. With any luck you'll catch him before he gets back to bed."

Basil and Rudolph retired with some reluctance, followed by a typical slice of Sam's unfailing thoughtfulness.

"Don't tell the ladies about this, Basil, old chap. They're greatly upset, as it is. They needn't even know that Willy's here until the morning."

"Don't worry, Sam. I'll do my best to shoo them off to bed. Angela looked like the ghost of a spectre, poor kid. I think we're all pretty played out. Er—Millar and I will be around if you want us, Inspector."

It was while Sam was getting through to Bredhurst, that Willy suddenly called out in a thin, unnatural treble:

"I tell you it's gone too far! Damme! you'll agree—limits even to my patience. Like a rat in a trap—round and round. But I'll break free, my dear fellah. You see! There's always that way out." Then with mournful distaste, "Oh, very bloody and violent. *Most* plebian. But needs must when the devil—oh, the she-devil, the she-devil—the *she*-devil— Who questions it? Exquisitely unpopular. Makes an *art* of unpopularity. Growing sleek on hate. Aaaak!"

"Steady there," crooned Harting. "Take another sip of this, old fellow."

Willy's myopic eyes focussed themselves on the cup and he seized it with a hand that resembled a talon. He gulped noisily. Five minutes later the nightmare reeked up from his mind and, through a darkness that was like oily smoke, he emerged once more into the normal world. His eyes, watering under the glare of the light, fastened themselves on Sam.

"Hullo, Sam."

"Hullo, Willy. Feeling better, dear chap?"

"A trifle weak and shaky. I can't quite—can't quite—"

"Don't trouble your head at the moment, sir," put in Harting. "Just take it easy. You've had a bit of a crack. Nothing serious. Must have slipped and fallen."

Willy relapsed into a luxurious and deeply appreciated silence. He wanted time; time to consider how he came to be in Sam's study at Old Knolle. They did not hurry him. Until Bredhurst had made his examination, Harting was not anxious to press forward with his interrogation.

3

Out in the corridor beyond the closed door of the study, Bredhurst shook his head.

"Frankly, Harting, I don't know what to make of it. If it's intoxication, well that's not the whole story. He's had a very nasty crack on the right occiput—a little more drastic and it might well have proved fatal. I know it's none of my business, but is there any connection between this and the other tragedy?"

Harting glanced at Sam. Sam nodded.

"We suspect that there *may* be," acknowledged the Inspector. "If so, could this be a case of attempted suicide?"

"No, I don't think so," said Bredhurst slowly. "He certainly didn't attempt to kill himself by hitting himself on the head. That's out of the question, even absurd. And I would hazard a guess that any amount of brandy wouldn't have had a fatal effect. He's too accustomed to it. But he's certainly been drinking heavily this evening. You noticed the dilatation of the pupils yourself, Harting, and their lack of response to light. Both symptoms of an alcoholic collapse."

"And how did he incur that blow on the side of the head?" asked Sam.

"Well, there's somebody," observed Harting with a sardonic glance, "who *should* know the answers to all these questions, and that's Farnham himself. Dare say he tried to negotiate a step that wasn't there. Any objections if I put him through a very gentle dose of third degree to-night, Bredhurst?"

"Better not," said the doctor. "He's still suffering from shock. I should let him stay where he is. He's quite comfortable, and he'll probably fall asleep. Perhaps you could detail somebody to sit up with him, Mr. Richardson. I'll be over first thing in the morning. Question him then, Harting, if you must, but don't harry him. He's a frail-looking fellow."

"I'm sure the inspector's far too tactful to do that, Doctor Bredhurst," Sam held out his hand. "Good night, and thank you for your prompt and willing services."

"You'll be issued with a subpœna for the inquest on the girl," Harting reminded him, as he took up his black bag. "But it should prove straightforward. At least, that's my opinion *now*!"

CHAPTER XII

Inspector Harting Runs
Around the Evidence

I

DESPITE THE LATENESS OF THE HOUR, SAM WAS NOT ONLY READY but eager to accompany the inspector down to the lakeside. Harting had already gathered in a fairly comprehensive catalogue of facts concerning the events which had led up to the discovery of the girl's body. He was puzzled by Sam's statement about the figure he had seen careering down the yew valley in the direction of the house. At the moment he was inclined to believe that this *was* Deirdre Lehaye. After all, when taken from the water, she had been wearing white pyjamas, and since she must have been abroad in the vicinity of Old Knolle, the supposition was perfectly logical.

As they walked down to the lake, Harting asked, "What time was it when you saw this unknown figure?"

Sam made a rapid calculation. "It must have been just after midnight."

"And you took the body from the lake?"

"About one o'clock."

"So Miss Lehaye probably fell into the lake between those times. Now let's take a look at the exact locale of the accident."

Harting noticed one important factor at once. The lake was edged with a stone wall, the cement coping of which was flush with the bank. He commented on the fact.

"After dredging we found there was a certain amount of seepage," explained Sam. "So I had the wall built to retain a proper level."

The inspector tested the depth of the water with the boat-hook. Then, flashing on his pocket-torch, he went down on his hands and knees and made a close examination of the ground. Although there had been a certain amount of rain, the close-shorn grass was far from soggy, and no clear footprints were visible. In any case, the search-party had trampled pretty freely over this stretch of the turf. There was a large wet patch where the body had lain and the cement coping had been drenched with water.

Harting rose. "Not much to be gained here, I'm afraid. That coping may explain away the contusion on the girl's head."

Sam asked anxiously, "You still think it was an accident, Harting?"

"I'm keeping an open mind," was the cautious answer. "There are a number of peculiar facts that I can't pigeonhole. For one thing, I see absolutely no reason why anybody should slip at this particular point. The grass is nearly dry and there are no obstructions over which anybody could trip. Did you notice the exact position of that contusion, Mr. Richardson?"

"Yes—on the crown of the head."

"Ah, that's just it! It *wasn't* on the crown, but on the vault of the skull! And if you trip and fall it's almost impossible to catch yourself a crack on the *vault* of your cranium—you admit that? The only way in which Miss Lehaye could have sustained such a blow is an utterly fantastic one—that she attempted to *dive* into the lake, misjudged the distance and hit her head on the coping. Again, that's improbable if you're not diving from a height."

"Then it doesn't have the appearance of an accident?" persisted Sam as they moved up towards the terrace.

"I don't know what to think yet. But I do claim, even if it's not accident, it isn't suicide. Nobody would attempt to drown themselves in about three feet of water. Oh, you *could* do it, I admit, but it would require the will-power of an Indian fakir! Even in moments of mental aberration the instinct of self-preservation is always uppermost. Then we've still got to take that bump into account. As you noticed, I had a good feel around with that boat-hook. It's all shelving mud—no stones of any sort on the bed of the lake."

They went into the hall, where Basil and Rudolph were crouched in desultory conversation over the electric fire. The womenfolk had allowed themselves to be persuaded that they could be of no further assistance and had gone meekly to their beds. All save Mrs. Dreed, who was to keep vigil in the study, for fear that Willy, now sleeping the sleep of exhaustion, should suddenly awake and need attention.

"My God, Sam!" cried Basil as the others entered, "you look ghastly. You ought to get some sleep."

"Well, you don't look too chirpy yourself, my dear chap. Nor do you, Millar. What a shocking night it's been, eh? Shocking! And somehow, you know, I don't feel that we've touched even the fringe of the truth. Now, if Inspector Harting's agreeable, I think we all ought to get some rest. Nothing more we can do to-night, is there, Harting?"

"No, sir," said the inspector. "But I'd like to have a brief word with Mr. Barnes before he retires. I'll be over early to-morrow to take further depositions. In particular, I'm anxious to get a statement from Mr. Farnham. He's the one person, I imagine, who may be able to lighten our darkness."

2

"Now, Mr. Barnes," said Harting when the others had gone out. "Suppose you tell me the full story—everything you know about Mr. Farnham's relationship with the dead girl. Mr. Richardson had the idea that the girl was blackmailing Farnham. D'you think this is true?"

"I know it is. Ask Farnham himself. He'll be only too ready to tell you."

"Unless, of course, he still wants to conceal the fact that he took the money," contested Harting. "If he hadn't wanted to conceal it the girl would have had no hold over him. Tell me—is it also true that Farnham made definite threats to get even with Miss Lehaye as recently as this morning?" Harting smiled and nodded at the clock. "Or rather yesterday morning."

"Yes, that's right."

"Suppose you tell me all you know about Farnham's movements from the time he met you at the theatre yesterday morning until you discovered him in the summer-house."

"Very well, Inspector. Only you're asking me a damn sight more than I can fairly answer. When you glibly demand his movements prior to finding him in the summer-house, well—I can't oblige. Actually I last set eyes on him when he left the theatre yesterday morning. I do know from reliable evidence that he took a ticket for Lambdon at Victoria, and was seen boarding the seven-forty-three. Since we discovered him in the locality, it's pretty safe to assume that he stepped off the seven-forty-three at Lambdon Halt. The train gets in about nine-ten. So up to that point I've been able to more or less check up on his movements. After that time—" Basil threw out his hands to suggest the vacuum in his mind. "Anything, anywhere, Inspector! A brain-storm. A drinking bout. Temporary black-out of all reason. Attempted suicide. Take your choice. God alone knows where he went and what he did—*I* don't!"

"But you heard him threaten Miss Lehaye when you met him at the Beaumont?"

"Yes. Not any specific threat. He kept referring to her as a 'malignant harpy'. Then he broke down and confessed to me about the theft of the money."

"Yes—I was called in on that case, as you know." Barnes nodded. "So that young woman deliberately put out false information in order to pluck her pigeon?"

"You've said it, Inspector!"

"Your information at Victoria was reliable?"

"I think so. Both the booking-clerk and the ticket-collector cottoned on to him at once. I made the inquiries just after his train had pulled out. Willy's got a very odd walk for a man—more a prance than a walk. Our stage hands call him 'the ballet-master'. He also wears a monocle."

"Your suggestion is that he's responsible for Miss Lehaye's death?" inquired Harting casually.

"It naturally entered my mind—but now I've had time to think about it I don't believe he could have done the job."

"Why?"

"Because Deirdre was in pyjamas."

"What the devil's that got to do with it?"

"Well, how did Willy—supposing he did visit Fallow Cottage—get her to take a walk in the grounds of Old Knolle clad only in her night attire? She was an unconventional girl, I admit, but gifted with lashings of common sense. It's a trifle late in the year for *al fresco* pyjama parties!"

"Does it occur to you that he might have attacked the girl in the cottage and then carried her unconscious body across the fields and dumped it in the lake? That head wound certainly makes this a possibility."

"But, good God, Inspector! you've seen Willy for yourself," cried Basil, almost derisively. "Now, I ask you: could a puny old chap like Willy lug a well-developed girl like Miss Lehaye across half a mile of rough country with at least three stiles to negotiate en route? You know it's damned nonsense! There's no suggestion that Willy even went near the lake."

Harting smiled. This was his opportunity for a little mild derision.

"Really? That's where *you* slip up, Mr. Barnes. I'm probably the only one that noticed it. Oh, nothing to boast about. I've been training myself for twenty years or more to observe what other people don't usually see. This particular clue stuck out a mile, but you were all naturally so worried about the old chap's condition that you never troubled to examine his shoes and trouser-legs."

"What the hell's that got to do with it?"

"Possibly quite a lot," concluded Harting, knocking out his pipe and getting lazily to his feet. "You see, they were coated with half-dried mud and sodden with water. There *may* be other places in the locality where he could have sloshed about in a duck-pond or something—but you must admit it's reasonable to suspect, Mr. Barnes, that he had been down to the lake. And not only down to it—but in it! Well, I won't keep you from your bed any longer. I shall be over after breakfast. Thanks for your statement. It's been a great help. Good night."

3

Inspector Harting drove back to Millward Heath in a reflective mood. The roads, in the small hours of the morning, were deserted and he was able to give more attention to the case than the car. Already he saw factors in it which formed the basis of a first-class mystery. Too soon to put up any well-founded deductions, but there was no harm, he felt, in letting his powers of reasoning have a run around.

First big problem: was there any connection between the girl in the lake and the old fellow in the summer-house? Answer—definitely yes. The fellow had stolen that two hundred odd pounds. The girl knew he had stolen it. Result—blackmail. Assumption—he had motive for the murder. But half a minute, *had* Lehaye been murdered? This was the second big problem. He had now heard the medical evidence and visited the spot on the lakeside where the body had been discovered. And taking into consideration all he had learnt to date, *there was every reason to believe that it was murder.*

The position of the large contusion on the girl's head and the fact that she had been found in shallow water seemed to preclude the idea of both accident and suicide. If he accepted murder, what then? Plausible reconstruction of events—Lehaye had been attacked without warning on the edge of the lake. She had been rendered unconscious by a severe blow on the head and then thrown into the water. If Farnham were responsible, the attack *must* have occurred very close to the spot where the body had been found. Reason—Farnham was an elderly, undersized man, incapable of carrying the dead weight of the unconscious woman more than a few yards. All right. After the attack Farnham loses his head, takes swig after swig of brandy to steady his nerves, crawls into the summer-house, collapses and catches himself an almighty crack on the side of the head.

Not much profit to be gained at present, thought Harting, by following up this theory. Final conclusions—Lehaye had been murdered and Farnham could well have been the murderer. Powerful evidence of the mud on his shoes and trouser-legs. He had strong motive.

Now for the side-shoots. The figure seen by Richardson moving down the yew alley towards the house just after midnight—was it Lehaye? Why not? Figure was in white. Lehaye was dressed in white satin pyjamas.

Second off-shoot—if so, what had brought the girl over to Old Knolle on a somewhat chilly night clad in her night attire? Suggests an abnormal state of mind—but so far there's been nothing to back up this assumption. According to Richardson's evidence, the girl had rung up Old Knolle shortly before ten to inquire if Farnham had shown up at the manor. Barnes had just rung her from Town to say that he was worried about the old fellow. Well, she seemed to have handled those 'phone calls with perfect common sense. Nothing abnormal there.

Had Farnham somehow managed to fix a rendezvous with her at the lakeside? When Richardson saw her was she on her way to keep the appointment? Double objection—(a) If it were a prearranged "date", surely she would have worn an overcoat over her pyjamas, even if Farnham's 'phone-message had reached her after she was in bed? (b) She was not going in the direction of the lake when seen. Conclusion— damned curious and, at the moment inexplicable.

And at this, with his customary common sense, Harting decided to forget all about the case until the following morning. His crying need now, of course, was bigger and better depositions.

CHAPTER XIII

Actions and Reactions

I

S AM RICHARDSON WAS THE INSPECTOR'S FIRST CONCERN WHEN HE arrived at Old Knolle about nine-thirty the next morning. The whole party was collected in the music-room, where the French windows had been flung open to another perfect September morning. The bells of Lambdon church came thrilling over the still air. The scent of late roses was discernible in the room. Nature was doing her utmost to counteract the doleful effects of tragedy.

"How's Farnham?" asked Harting the moment he and Sam had withdrawn to the privacy of the latter's study.

"Splendid! Splendid!" beamed Sam. "Bredhurst has just been, and we've moved the patient into a bed upstairs. Thank heaven we can place that much on the credit side, Inspector. He appears to have made a complete recovery. He had a fillet of sole boiled in milk for breakfast. Great, isn't it?"

Harting laughed. "You're a true Christian, Mr. Richardson! Here's a man who stole a couple of hundred pounds from you when staying as a guest in your house. And here are you crowing your head off because this same gentleman, after a veritable skyscraper of a tall night, manages to sit up and eat a little boiled fish, *still* an honoured guest in your house, mark you!"

"Do you know why I feel like that?" asked Sam.

"Can't say."

"Because I'm convinced there isn't an ounce of real vice in Willy Farnham. Circumstances drove him to take that money. I admit he was wrong there. He should have come to me openly and told me of his trouble. But that's beside the point. He's one of those child-like men of near genius who just can't keep their private affairs in order. Clever people make fools of them—drive them into corners. You see, Harting, Willy's an artist, not a man of the world in a world of hard-boiled men."

"If I'm right in my assumption that Miss Lehaye was murdered, you wouldn't cast Farnham for the part of First Murderer?"

"Never! Impossible! Ridiculous!"

"He had motive."

"He may not be the only one." Then anxiously, "But do you frankly think Miss Lehaye was murdered?"

"I do."

"It's a terrible thought."

"Quite, but I must deal in facts, Mr. Richardson. That means evidence. Tell me, was there any sign of a struggle having taken place over at Fallow Cottage last night?"

"No. Everything was disturbingly normal. That was what first made me uneasy."

"You noticed nothing out of the ordinary?"

"Nothing. No—wait a minute—that isn't strictly true. This!" Sam whipped out the monogrammed handkerchief and tossed it to Harting. "It was on the floor of the sitting-room."

"F!" exclaimed the Inspector after a brief examination. "F for Farnham, eh? I wonder if you're not a little prejudiced in your judgment of his character because he happens to be a good actor."

"Willy's? Good God, Harting, I never thought of that! So Willy *was* over at the cottage last night?"

"It's on the cards, isn't it? Now what about Miss Lehaye? Any relations?"

"None as far as we can make out. I rang Tom Fullaby, her agent, at his private address just before you came in. He's an old friend of mine. He says there's a friend of hers living in Bournemouth—a Miss Honisett. He's had to forward letters when she's been holidaying there. I suppose we ought to get in touch—after all, there's the question of the funeral. Oh, and the inquest, of course. I'll send a wire to Bournemouth and explain what's happened. Fullaby says Deirdre's always been a bit of a mystery to him. Seems to have no past and no ties of any sort. A queer girl, Harting. I never took a very favourable view of her, apart from her brilliance as an artist. I admit I wasn't in the least surprised when Basil told me she'd been blackmailing poor Farnham."

"The rest of your household were in bed, I take it, between the hours of, say, eleven and one?"

"Yes, of course. Er—that is, no!" stuttered Sam, with a sudden quickening of his heart. "Now I come to think of it, young Millar said he'd been out for a stroll round the lake. He rushed into the hall just as I came down the stairs. He seemed excited, I thought, and out of breath. He told me he'd got rather chilly and had run back to the house to warm himself up."

"What time was this?"

"About twenty past twelve."

"Had he any reason to dislike Miss Lehaye?"

"No, of course not. Er—that is—now I come to think of it—" Sam's blood, for all the quickening of his pulse, went cold. The Inspector's pertinent questions seemed to be outlining new and yet more foreboding possibilities. Was there anything untoward in young Millar's precipitate entry and somewhat wild-eyed appearance? He went on, "I must be quite frank with you, Harting. That's my bounden duty as a good citizen of the realm, eh? Millar *did* dislike Miss Lehaye, and you know the reason as well as I do. It was on her evidence that we suspected Millar of the theft. At the time you felt pretty sure yourself that he was guilty. Well, as he happened to be innocent, you can imagine how the girl's false accusation must have rankled."

"Naturally. Does he know yet that Farnham has confessed to the crime?"

"No. I've kept Barnes's information under the punkah. I've asked him to do the same."

"So last night Millar was still, in a sense, under a cloud? At least he *felt* he was?"

"Quite, although I'd told him most emphatically that I didn't believe Miss Lehaye's story."

"Umph. Anybody else out of bed or wandering about?" Sam had a fleeting vision of Angela's empty bed on the occasion of his first visit to her room, but this was swiftly erased by a second vision of Angela, drowsy and innocent, peering at him from the bedclothes. He held stoutly to the theory that on the first occasion she had merely been in the bathroom.

"No," he said with a sigh of relief. "As far as I know, everybody was snugly in bed, probably asleep. Except me," he added with a gentle smile.

"Where were you, Mr. Richardson?"

"Here in the study, until Barnes rang me up about eleven-thirty asking me to go over to the cottage. Then I walked across the fields, found the place empty and returned to Old Knolle."

"Meeting the figure in white on your way back?"

"Quite so."

"You say you were coming down the stairs when you met Millar rushing into the hall. Had you been to bed in the meantime?"

"Er—no," said Sam uncomfortably.

"Then where?"

"You're confoundedly persistent, Harting," said Sam with a hollow laugh. "You make me feel like a criminal myself."

"No! No!" replied the inspector with a boisterous denial. "That's not my intention at all! I must know just where everybody was during the hours the crime might have been committed. When you came into the house you apparently went upstairs—why?"

"Well, if you must know," blurted out Sam, "I went up to Miss Walsh's bedroom."

"She's the young lady with the blue eyes and fair hair?"

Sam nodded. "Angela Walsh. A charming girl and a very promising young actress. She's always been a favourite of mine."

"I take it," grinned Harting, "that you're not offering this as the reason for your visit to her bedroom."

"Don't be facetious! I went to her room to make sure that she was safely in bed."

"Had you any reason to think otherwise?"

Sam sighed. There was no getting round this gruesomely efficient fellow. He had a proper nose for smelling out the facts. He'd have to tell the truth, confound it!

"Well, frankly, I had. Earlier in the evening I'd been to her room and found she wasn't there. It didn't occur to me until later that she was probably having a bath. Then, when I saw that white figure flitting about the garden, I half thought it might be Miss Walsh, so I went direct to her bedroom to make sure."

"And you found her in bed and asleep?"

"Well, in bed and sleepy," corrected Sam.

"In her night attire?"

"Er—yes."

"What was she wearing?"

"Er—a nightdress."

"A white nightdress."

"No—a sort of orangy affair. But I didn't take specific notice. It certainly wasn't white."

"So you feel pretty sure that it wasn't Miss Walsh in the yew alley?"

"Yes."

"All right, Mr. Richardson—I'm not going to worry you any further. I'd just like to have a full list of the people sleeping in Old Knolle last night. Perhaps, when you've done that, you'd be good enough to send Millar in to me."

2

Rudolph, who had already experienced Inspector Harting's unhurried methods of interrogation, knew more or less what to expect when he entered the study—a slow, almost persuasive leading up to certain points of elucidation. He was all the more unprepared, therefore, when Harting shot out, "What made you take a walk in the grounds last night, Mr. Millar, when everybody else had gone to bed?"

"I—I—who told you about that?"

Harting smiled. "Now, Mr. Millar, I'm here to ask the questions, not answer them. The point is I *know* you were in the grounds sometime after eleven o'clock. Why?"

"Well, I've just had a fearfully good slice of luck. Mr. Richardson's going to put on my first play at the Beaumont next season. It's a tremendous break for me, as you can imagine, and naturally I'm pretty excited about it all. Mr. Richardson asked me down this week-end to discuss the contract. He's been frightfully generous, and when I got to my room last night I was so het up that I knew I wouldn't sleep, even if I went to bed. So I decided to take a turn round the lake to cool off."

"What time was it when you left the house?"

"Shortly after eleven. I can't be certain to the minute."

"Mr. Richardson met you returning from your walk about twenty past twelve?"

"I dare say that *was* about the time—yes."

"Where exactly did you go when you left the house?"

"I just took a stroll round the lake. There's a path that leads through the woods on the far side. But perhaps you know that?"

Harting rose and, crossing up to the French windows, stepped out on to the terrace.

"A minute, Mr. Millar." Puzzled, Rudolph joined the inspector. "Take a look at the view, will you? You agree that we can see the whole of the lake from here?"

"Certainly."

"Even at a most generous estimate it can't be more than half a mile in circumference, eh?"

"No, just about that."

"Then can you tell me why you took about an hour and twenty minutes to walk half a mile?"

Rudolph seemed embarrassed. An answer to this perfectly simple question seemed momentarily to elude him. Then he said with an air of (what he hoped would pass for) nonchalance, "Well, Inspector, it was more of a stroll than a walk. I just drifted along, stopping now and then to look at the moonlight on the lake. It was marvellous out there last night. Absolutely wizard. Tranquil and romantic, you know—like a Chopin prelude or a landscape by Corot."

"Quite," agreed Harting dryly. "But also, as you yourself admitted, chilly! It wasn't exactly the sort of night to hang about admiring the view. Or *was* it, Mr. Millar?"

"It's not easy to describe one's moods on these occasions," explained Rudolph. "I was carried away. Don't you ever experience a disembodied effect in the moonlight? One just doesn't notice physical discomforts until the mood passes and you… well, come to your right senses again. I just meandered round, stopping here and there to—" He broke off and added with a stare of incredulity, "I say, Inspector, it's just occurred to me—you don't imagine I had anything to do with poor Miss Lehaye's—er—accident, do you?"

As they moved back into the study, Harting chuckled.

"I ask the questions. You answer them," he reminded Rudolph. "I'm convinced Miss Lehaye—shall we say?—*fell* into the lake sometime between midnight and one o'clock. For the first twenty minutes of that period you were in the vicinity of the lake. To me that's important. If you saw or heard nothing of the accident during those twenty minutes, then I can narrow down the time of the tragedy still further. You see how we slowly but surely arrive at the facts?"

"I saw and heard absolutely nothing unusual. Nothing!"

"You're sure?"

"Quite sure, Inspector."

"All right, Mr. Millar, we'll have to leave it at that. I was hoping you'd be able to tell me something more definite. However, negative evidence is not to he despised. Now I'd like to have a word with"—Harting consulted the list which Sam had drawn up for him—"Miss Angela Walsh. Would you ask her to come along?"

3

But before Rudolph could summon Angela, before he was even clear of the study, the door was flung open and Clara Maddison entered.

"Ah, Rudie, I wondered if you were still here. I understand we're to be interviewed one at a time. That's right, isn't it, Inspector Harting?"

"Quite right, madam. And in due course—"

"My name's Clara Maddison. You've probably never heard of me, but I'm a member of the Beaumont Company. I'm also this young man's aunt. All right, Rudie darling, there's no need to stay on. I want to see the inspector alone. Trot along, there's a good boy." With a brief nod to

Harting, Rudolph dutifully trotted. Clara faced the inspector. "My dear
man, I just couldn't wait my turn to be called into the witness-box. I
simply had to come at once. There's no need to tell me—I know I ought
to have spoken up about this last night, but I've only just realized its full
significance. Can I talk?"

"Nothing could suit me better," smiled Harting, indicating one of
the big leather arm-chairs. Clara sank into it with a sigh of thankfulness.
She was one of those comfortable people who find an almost sensuous
pleasure in removing the weight from their feet. "Now, Miss Maddison?"

"Really, it's very, very horrible having to sit here and talk with you in
this icy official manner. I'm no fool, Inspector. You suspect Deirdre was
murdered—you can't deny that. Sam thinks so, too. But we mustn't lose
our heads, however gruesome, must we? We *must* be logical. If Deirdre
were murdered somebody must have murdered her."

"That's the kind of assumption I'm always ready to condone,"
Harting's blue-grey eyes twinkled.

"Now don't mock me! I've had to exert considerable will-power to
drag myself here and talk like this. I'd be far, more comfortable, my dear
Inspector, having hysterics in my bedroom. But last night *I saw the figure
of a man prowling about the lawns quite close to the lake.*" Harting slipped the
pencil from his notebook and looked inquiring. Clara went on, "It was
when I returned to my bedroom after my tub. I wasted a certain amount
of time—no, no, I'm ready to confess it!—at my mirror. Then I switched
out the light and drew back the curtains. The garden and lake looked so
breathlessly beautiful that I stayed there a minute quite spellbound. It
was then I noticed this prowling figure."

"And the time would be?"

"About a quarter-past eleven—perhaps a little later."

Harting rose and moved up again to the French windows. "Perhaps
you'd be good enough, Miss Maddison, to point out to me just *where* you
saw this figure. By the way, you're quite sure it was a man?"

"That was my immediate impression. I admit it could have been
a woman in slacks, but I thought at the time it was a man." Clara had
now joined the inspector on the terrace. She pointed down at the lake.
"You know where we discovered poor Miss Lehaye? Well, that was the

spot where I first noticed the figure. You can see now why I thought this information might be significant? The figure was kneeling close to the edge of the lake and seemed, for some unearthly reason, to be peering into the water. It then got up and moved away at a fairly rapid pace across the garden towards the paddock over there."

"Let me see," reflected Harting, "that's in the opposite direction to Fallow Cottage and the village of Lambdon?"

"Yes. If you cross the paddock you come out on to the main road, not far from Lambdon Halt. Like so many of these quaint country stations, it's nearly a mile from the actual village."

"Now, don't get me wrong about this, Miss Maddison, but was there anything about the shape or walk of that figure which suggested it might have been your nephew?"

"Rudie? How could it have been? Rudie was in bed."

"No, you're wrong there. He was taking a stroll round the lake."

"Good gracious, I knew nothing about that! What a stupid thing to do—I mean, it was a chilly night for stargazing, wasn't it? But darling Rudie's so impulsive. Of course it *might* have been my nephew; on the other hand, it was probably not. I'd like very much to say with absolute conviction that it *wasn't* Rudie, but prevarication's not going to help you, is it? You want the truth, the whole truth and—" Clara broke off and added after a pause, "I wonder if we shall ever get at the whole truth? Tragedies of this kind so often remain unsolved. I admit things look very black against dear Willy Farnham, but I refuse to believe that he pushed that unfortunate creature into the lake. If he had nothing to do with it, I ask you, my dear man, why was he down here in Sam's summer-house sleeping off a drunken orgy?"

"Exactly. And here's another poser, Miss Maddison—if the figure you saw wasn't your nephew, how was it Mr. Millar didn't notice this other person when he set out on his walk? He says he left the house shortly after eleven. You saw this unknown prowler about ten minutes later. It's puzzling."

"You're not suggesting that my nephew dumped that unhappy wretch in the water?"

"I'm not suggesting anybody did," smiled Harting. "For the very simple reason that to have dumped Miss Lehaye into the water wouldn't have been enough. At that point the water's barely three feet deep. If

anybody had pushed her in, she could have walked out again. I'm absolutely convinced that she was rendered unconscious by a blow on the
head *before* her body was placed in the lake. I'll be frank, Miss Maddison,
this isn't any casual, hot-tempered affair. It was something brought to
a climax after long and careful deliberation. Unfortunately, that young
woman appears to have collected enemies with as much energy as less
perverted people collect postage stamps!"

4

Unemotional efficient unit of machinery that he was, even Inspector
Harting was moved by Angela's obvious timidity as she entered the study.
She looked tired and frail and defenceless, with heavy shadows under her
wide blue eyes, and her lips struggling to form a courageous, if quivering,
smile. In cross-questioning her he felt rather like a man who bludgeons a
butterfly with a coal-hammer. Her *naïveté* was disarming. At the end of
five minutes he was feeling quite as uncomfortable as his witness.

But the interview was, luckily, short. Angela's evidence had the charm
of utter simplicity. She had gone up to bed about ten-thirty, read through
her part in *The Red Ant* once or twice to keep her memory green, taken
a leisured bath and gone to bed. But the news about Willy had so worried her that she found it impossible to sleep. At length, just as she was
slipping off, Mr. Richardson had looked in to apologize for something he
hadn't done; and after that she had drowsed until the whole household
was awakened to go in search of Deirdre. She was awfully sorry she
couldn't tell the inspector more. She was afraid her little thimbleful of
information hadn't been very helpful.

"One point, Miss Walsh. What time was it when you visited the
bathroom?"

"The bathroom? Oh, I really can't say. I'm an awful duffer about time,
and—and my watch had stopped."

"Was it after eleven o'clock?"

"I suppose it could have been. I read through my part more than once.
Yes—I think it must have been after eleven, don't you?"

"You say you didn't hurry over your bath?"

"No, I'm simply dreadful. I adore drowsing in the bath when there's unlimited hot water. It's supposed to be unhealthy, but I think that's nonsense. It's so marvellously relaxing."

"Shall we say half an hour in the bathroom?"

"That's probably a very fair estimate. But don't write it all down and use it against me, please! I know the Law does something like that with evidence. But I really am so terribly vague about time, and—and my watch *had* stopped and"—Angela appeared to be on the brink of tears—"and really—that's all I can tell you, Inspector."

"All right, Miss Walsh, thank you. I needn't worry you further. You've been very frank with me."

And yet it was curious that, the moment Angela's swimming blue eyes were no longer gazing into his, Harting felt convinced that the girl hadn't been telling the truth. At least, not the whole truth. There was a peculiar negative quality about her evidence which seemed unnatural. For all her innocent expression, her melting helplessness, hadn't there been a clever, cautious little piece of mechanism at work behind her sculptured brow? These *ingénue* little wenches were the very devil, thought Harting. They could twist your heart-strings and tweak your nose at one and the same time. They wanted more watching than a cartload of monkeys!

5

For his final interview that morning, as the mountain couldn't come to Mahomet, Mahomet went to the mountain; though, as Harting slipped into the bedside chair which Mrs. Dreed had set ready for him, he thought Willy Farnham looked more like a molehill than a mountain. The ravages of his overnight tipple had left him a generous legacy. Wrinkled pouches sagged under his eyes, his cheeks were sunken and his lips bloodless. It seemed that a puff of wind would blow him from the bed. Yet mentally he was as sprightly as ever and he greeted the inspector, if not with gusto, at least with some show of interest. Sam had already been up and warned him to make ready for this official visit. So far nobody had spoken to him of the death of Deirdre Lehaye.

"Well, sir," said Harting cheerily. "You look a trifle more perky than you did last night."

"Yes, I am! I am! Though, to tell you the truth, I still can't grasp what it's all about. It's all featherweight stuff—flies away—pouff! They tell me I was lying unconscious in the summer-house last night. Why? How did I get there? Damme! can *you* tell me, because I don't know. It's all drifting smoke."

"Suppose you tell me what you *do* remember, Mr. Farnham? Take your time. Perhaps I can fill in the blanks afterwards."

"I'll do my best. Can't say more, my dear fellah. It all started with a telegram."

"Eh?"

"I say, it all started with a telegram—delivered to me at my club about five o'clock yesterday afternoon. It was from a young woman called Deirdre Lehaye—you may have heard of her—asking me to catch the seven-forty-three down to Lambdon Halt and to meet her without delay at Fallow Cottage. She's staying there for a few days. The telegram said it was urgent. Mark that! *Urgent*. Damme! Inspector, if you'd received a telegram like that what would you have done?"

"Caught the seven-forty-three out of sheer damned curiosity."

"Which is precisely what I did. You can't blame me. I had specific reasons for wanting to see that young woman alone. Perhaps Sam Richardson—?"

"Yes, he's told me all I need to know. Blackmail, wasn't it?"

"Ah, blackmail! Slow poison—that's what it really is, Inspector. God knows what induced me to take that money. I was in a cramped corner. Debts, y'know—gambling debts. No—I'm not playing for sympathy. The whole cataclysmic affair was my own stupid fault. I ought to have kept my nerve and made a clean breast of my difficulties to Sam. He'd have put me on my feet again. But in moments of extreme mental tension our morality seems to suffer from a blind spot, doesn't it? I didn't stop to think—that's about it. Impetuous, a bit frightened, a sense of frustration, and there y'are!—a criminal before you can shake any common sense into yourself. I created the idea that it was just a loan, and, in the long run, I'd pay the money back. I'm a past-master at self-delusion, y'know. I can always find a noble excuse for doing an ignoble thing. And then that malignant harpy came on the scene and it didn't take her two seconds to cut the ground from under my feet. I was faultlessly cornered, and that cold-eyed creature knew it! She knew that it was the finish of my career if I didn't dance to her tune.

"An artist of my calibre can be involved in certain types of scandal and gain a modicum of useful notoriety. But common or garden theft is the kind of lapse the public refuse to condone—even in an artist. Too sordid. Too unimaginative. Too inartistic. So there I was, my dear fellah, faced with a lifelong obligation to a young woman I detested with every fibre of my being. Damme! I still detest her! But when I received that telegram I entertained a hope—doubtless a very foolish hope—that a trickle of the milk of human kindness had somehow got into her veins. I thought perhaps she was ready to relent. So I hurried off to Fallow Cottage before that female viper could change her mind."

At the conclusion of this long recital Willy lay back on his pillows breathing heavily. His emotions seemed to have been too much for his frail frame and left him exhausted to a point where he could barely continue. Harting did not hurry him. He was slowly but surely absorbing the personality of his witness; formulating his own judgment of Farnham's complex character; weighing up his evidence.

After a lengthy silence the inspector said quietly, "You don't happen to have that telegram at hand, do you?"

"Yes. Yes. Of course. It's in the breast-pocket of my coat hanging over that chair. Take a look at it if it interests you."

But although Harting went meticulously through every pocket in Willy's bedraggled suit, there was no sign of the telegram.

"Damme! that's funny!" exclaimed Willy. "I *know* I slipped it into my pocket after I'd read it."

"Where was it handed in?"

"I didn't notice. I'm not observant over that kind of thing. Presumably Lambdon, eh? That's the nearest post office to Fallow Cottage."

Harting nodded. For the first time a suspicion shot through his mind that Farnham's story might not be true. Perhaps true in its main outline, but embellished with a number of carefully considered strokes of the imagination with the intention of concealing his actual movements. This telegram may never have been dispatched. But if Farnham could persuade him, the inspector, that Lehaye had really sent for him, it would provide a natural excuse for his precipitate descent on Lambdon. In confessing to the theft of the money, he might have entertained the supposition that to confess to the minor crime would clear him of all suspicion concerning the major one. It was an old and well-tried trick.

"You arrived at Lambdon Halt, I take it?"

"Yes, at nine-ten."

"And then what?"

Willy made a rounded gesture suggestive of complete bewilderment. Even at this moment the technique of his profession never deserted him.

"Vacuum! A rushing darkness! A horrible negation!"

"I don't follow."

"Just this, I had only walked a little way down the lane from the station, when my head seemed to split open and everything went black."

"You mean you received an actual blow on the head?"

"Yes, I think so," said Willy reflectively. "I can't be positive, of course. But you'll notice, my dear fellah, that I've a very nasty contusion behind my right ear. And, damme! unless somebody hit me on the head, how did it get there? Lumps like that don't sprout on the human form like gooseberries on a gooseberry bush. But *who* assaulted me, and *why* I was assaulted I can't say. It was brutal and sudden. Most inconsiderate."

"After this presumed blow you don't remember anything until you recovered your senses in Mr. Richardson's study?"

"That's perfectly correct."

Harting paused and then cleared his throat. "Now look here, sir, don't take offence, but I want to get this point quite clear. When you arrived at Lambdon Halt, had you, perhaps, been drinking a little more than was good for you?"

Willy, haggard and shattered as he was and half shrouded in the bedclothes, succeeded in drawing himself up with tremendous dignity.

"Drinking? Me, my dear fellah? My—dear—fellah!"

"Just a nip or two of brandy, perhaps?" insisted Harting. "A little nip or two in the train, eh?"

"Brandy!" cried Willy, with a sudden flare-up of excitement. "That's it! That's the operative word. That's the key to one of the locked doors. Brandy! Let me reflect for a moment. Things are becoming clearer—yes—but still fogged over by a strange lack of sequence. There *was* brandy in the nightmare—I'm sure of that—but I can't say where. Ah, yes, yes! The vague outline of a shape against the sky and the clink of glass against my teeth—the unmistakable *smell* of brandy. But where and when—don't ask me! I believe I swallowed brandy, but how much and under what conditions—" Willy stopped short and lay back once more, damp and filleted, against the pillows. "I'm sorry, my dear fellah, the effort is too much. The facts elude me. I can't clarify something which, in its essence, is no more than a miasma. No man can ring a clear note on a cracked bell."

"And what," thought Harting as he rose to ease his crossed legs, "am I to make of this? Is it a clever and calculating phantasmagoria put up to hide his real actions? Or is it the result of an alcoholic nightmare?"

Looking down, he suddenly realized that the contents of Farnham's pockets were still in a heap on the bedside table. With a quick movement he stretched out his hand.

"This is yours, Mr. Farnham?"

"Of course. Of course. The single black initial is a little foible of mine. They're rather elegant, I think. There's a charming sempstress in the King's Road who stitches them specially for me. But what the deuce—?"

"You're not in the habit," cut in Harting, "of lending out such expensive handkerchiefs, eh?"

"I am not."

"Not even to Miss Lehaye?"

"She would be the last person—"

"Then why was *this*," Harting drew out the replica which he was carrying in his wallet, carefully wrapped in tissue, "found on the floor of the sitting-room over at Fallow Cottage last night? Did you visit the cottage last night?"

Willy began to work his feet under the bedclothes. A storm of petty anger was threatening. To question his word had always been to prick his honour in a most insulting place.

"I've already told you," he piped, "that after leaving the station I remember nothing until I found myself in Sam's study. Now please don't bother me any more. I'm not myself. I'm far from well. Doctor Bredhurst will be most annoyed if he hears you've been badgering me. I'm bewildered as it is. Dizzy, damme! with all these senseless questions. I can't see the point of half of them. I suppose you think I'm the victim of assault and battery? That *is* the official term, I believe? But what handkerchiefs have to do with it…"

"I'm afraid there's more to it than that," said Harting, in that solemn voice which is the normal prelude to bad news. "Miss Lehaye was found dead in the lake last night. There is every indication that she was—murdered."

The inspector's eyes never left Willy's face during this revelation, but with an old actor it was impossible to tell if the facial reflection of any particular emotion was genuine or not. Was it in this case? Was the horrified surprise real or simulated?

"Deirdre? Murdered?" Then with a swift and totally unexpected change of mood, "Ah, thank God! No, no, no! You needn't stare at me like that. I'm not out of my mind. I say it again. I thank God for it. You think it callous of me to accept this news with such egotistical relief, eh?"

"I can well understand."

"That's just it—you can't begin to understand. Murder is abhorrent to me. It is brutal, unæsthetic. That Deirdre should have been murdered horrifies me. That she is dead and can no longer scheme to upset other people's lives—to that I say thank God! Of one thing I'm convinced, Inspector."

"And that?"

"She brought this sudden eclipse on herself. She had a preposterous flair for making the mildest of us hate her. She enjoyed being hated. For that young woman, just round the corner, there was always trouble in ambush. I believe she found a strange and overpowering excitement in the thought of danger ahead." Then with a queer, weary little smile Willy concluded, "But if, as this cross-examination suggests, you think I had anything to do with her premature end—well, damme! go on thinking it. It won't get you an inch along the road to promotion."

"You claim you didn't go near the lake last night?"

"I claim nothing of the kind. What happened to me after darkness descended on Station Lane, and before I was discovered in the summer-house—who can tell? I can't. If I went near the lake, then I have no knowledge of it."

"I only ask because your shoes and trouser-legs are caked with mud, and with a type of mud that is only found in the bed of ponds. Such mud has a peculiar and characteristic odour." Harting thrust a hand under the bedside chair and held up one of Willy's elegant pointed shoes. "Perhaps you hadn't noticed this?"

Willy shook his head, more weary and defeated than ever. "I've already told you, my dear fellah, that I can't explain what to me is still inexplicable."

"There's just one thing more. Can you describe the exact spot in Station Lane where you collapsed?"

"Yes, quite clearly. That much I can recall. It was a few yards short of a milestone on the same side of the road as the wood. It was the last thing I remember seeing—the white-painted milestone glimmering in the half darkness."

CHAPTER XIV

The Stone Pavilions

I

WITH HIS CROSS-EXAMINATION OF WILLY FARNHAM THE INSPEC-
tor had done with his immediate depositions. The domestic staff,
including Mrs. Dreed, had all been in bed and had heard and seen nothing
unusual. They had had no inkling of the tragedy until Mr. Richardson
had summoned them to join in the search for the missing girl. But before
leaving the house Harting took fingerprints of every soul under Sam's
hospitable roof.

His next concern was to make a sketch of the Old Knolle estate.*
In particular he wanted to make sure just how it was situated in regard
to Lambdon Halt and Fallow Cottage, which he now looked upon as
two vital points in the topographical aspects of the crime. After a walk
across the fields he came to the cottage. The front door, which Sam had
slammed behind him the previous night, was locked, since it was fitted
with a Yale; but Harting had sensibly obtained a key from Basil before
setting out. Everything was as Sam had found it—uninterestingly in
order. Deirdre's clothes were laid carelessly over a bedside chair, but the
bed itself was undisturbed. It meant, therefore, that Lehaye had left the
cottage *after* she had got into her night attire and slipped on her sandals,
but *before* she had got into bed. It suggested that the reason which had
sent her scuttling across to Old Knolle must have been an urgent and
unexpected one. The fact that she hadn't stayed to slip a warm coat over
her pyjamas strengthened this suggestion. Her departure must have been
half-sister to a panic!

* See beginning of this book, facing first page.

But *what* had drawn her from the cottage? A 'phone call? An actual visitor? A call from the garden?

According to Richardson, when Barnes had rung Fallow Cottage for the second time, shortly before eleven-thirty, he had received no reply. This meant that the girl had already left the cottage. But Richardson had not seen her in the yew-alley until after midnight, at least forty minutes later. Where had she been in the meantime? To walk directly across the fields to Old Knolle could not have taken her more than twenty minutes at the utmost, and further, if she *had* taken the bridle-path about that time Richardson would have encountered her on his way *out* to Fallow Cottage. The most plausible theory was that the girl had left the cottage some time earlier and had reached the gardens well before Richardson had taken the path across the fields. Perhaps, when later he had seen her, she had been making for the manor, and his shouts had upset her plans. Why hadn't she answered his call? For two simple reasons: (*a*) she wanted to conceal her identity; (*b*) she was out and about for some nefarious or, at least, private purpose.

"So much for Lehaye," thought Harting as he completed his survey of the cottage and set off once more across the meadows. (He had carefully locked all the doors again, intending to return that afternoon for a more detailed investigation.) "Now what about this Farnham chap? A queer, unbalanced devil! Not exactly shifty, I admit, but elusive. Difficult to make head or tail of his information. At a guess I should say it's a subtle blend of truth and fiction. If he *is* the murderer—and, damn it! he had motive—that mental black-out is very, very opportune. It saves him from having to account for his movements, say, between nine-twenty, just after he'd left the train, and about four hours later when he was discovered in the summer-house. Assuming he did the job, what are his possible movements?"

Perched on one of the stiles, the inspector slowly filled his pipe. The case was complex and bristling with novelty. He'd have to enlist the aid of his customary official shadow, Sergeant Dane, as he had done in all his major cases. He'd have to get the Chief Constable to give him *carte blanche* to investigate, without the threat of imminent interference from the Yard. Luckily Major Frost had a fine faith in the abilities of his county C.I.D., and preferred to give them a fair run for their money before appealing for outside help. But Dane must be sent for without delay to cope with some of the routine work which Harting now saw confronting him. As for the inquest, it was essential—failing a murder verdict—to obtain a postponement. Time would be needed to get to the bottom of this double mystery.

And once more his mind swung back to Farnham.

Was this a reasonable reconstruction of the crime? From the moment he had decided to murder the girl, Farnham had started to bolster up his courage with brandy. He arrives at Lambdon and, after frequent refreshment on the way from a brandy flask, he reaches Fallow Cottage—say about ten o'clock. He finds the door open and goes in. The girl's clothes are beside the bed, but the girl herself is no longer there. (No—wait a minute—what time had Lehaye rung Richardson? He consulted his notebook. No, that was all right. The call had gone through before ten o'clock, so it was still a possible theory.) While in the cottage, Farnham inadvertently drops his handkerchief. So much for that!

Now what? He goes off in search of the girl, no doubt wondering (as Harting wondered) what had taken her abroad into the night clad only in her pyjamas. Though, of course, he wasn't to know, admitted the inspector, that the girl hadn't changed out of one set of clothes into another. Her most likely destination would be Old Knolle. So to Old Knolle he goes and starts to prowl around, searching for his victim. Doubtless he imagined that she was in the house itself, and determined to lie in wait for her until she should return to the cottage.

In this manner he must have hung about, still drinking heavily, until well after midnight. At length he sees the girl in her white pyjamas wandering along the edge of the lake. He realizes his opportunity has come and, arming himself with some form of club, creeps up behind her, his footsteps deadened by the turf. A violent blow on the head and the girl collapses. Half fuddled with drink, Farnham rolls her body into the lake and, in doing so, slips and steps into the shallow water himself. Then, hardly aware of what he is doing, he moves away from the scene of the crime, reaches the summer-house and falls to the floor in a drunken stupor, hitting the side of his head. And there he remains unconscious until discovered.

Well, it was all fine and dandy as far as it went, but did it go far enough?

By far the most inexplicable factor in the case was not the possible *modus operandi* of the murder but the reason for the girl's presence by the lake at a late hour on a chilly September night, clad only in a pair of white satin pyjamas. Find out what had lured her from the cottage and the mystery would be half solved. That was Harting's opinion.

He decided, before ringing up Sergeant Dane, to take another look at the summer-house. Lighting his pipe, which had gone out twice during his reflections, he slipped from the stile and continued on his way.

Suddenly he snapped his fingers. Hold on a minute! Rudolph Millar! Hadn't he got something there? Was it possible that it was Millar who had fixed the rendezvous with the girl, and not Farnham? Millar had seen Lehaye earlier in the day and may have arranged the meeting with her then—a secret meeting; a meeting in which he determined to have it out with her about the false news she had spread about the theft; a meeting to demand an apology or a signed statement to say that she had deliberately lied; a meeting, even, to extract money from the girl by way of recompense for her false evidence. He may have obtained some hold over her himself—a lever which he was using to force her to keep this appointment.

Well and good. Millar left the house at eleven o'clock. And yes, by heaven! when Barnes rang up the cottage some time after eleven he got no reply! It was fitting in very prettily, eh? At, say, eleven-twenty Millar and the girl met somewhere near the lake, perhaps in one of the two little stone pavilions which he, Harting, had marked on his sketch-map. If this were the case, then there was no doubt that the male figure Miss Maddison had seen on the lakeside at eleven-fifteen *was* her nephew. Why he was kneeling on the bank and peering into the water the Lord alone knew! Perhaps in his disembodied mood he was sounding a visual variation on his moon-across-the-water theme. On leaving the bank, according to his aunt, he had gone in the direction of the paddock and, *ipso facto*, the east pavilion. Yes, it was dovetailing quite snugly. The fact that Miss Maddison had not mentioned the girl suggested that Lehaye was already waiting for Millar at the rendezvous; that she was waiting there *before* eleven-fifteen.

Now what? Lehaye and Millar stay arguing in the pavilion until about midnight, when the girl sets off again for the cottage. But a little short of the Dutch garden she sees Richardson climbing over the stile on the very track she wishes to take. She moves, therefore, up the side of the Dutch garden and, when hailed by Richardson, runs through the yew alley towards Old Knolle and away from the cottage. Her intention was doubtless to make a détour and return to the stile when Richardson had gone indoors. Her détour brings her back close to the bank of the lake, which gives the concealed Farnham the opportunity he seeks. Lehaye is murdered. In the meantime Millar, after lingering for a time, returns to the house and arrives in the hall just as Richardson comes down the stairs.

Why did Millar appear breathless and distraught? Was it because, on his way across the garden, he had seen Farnham's attack on the girl? Was it fear and horror which had sent him running like a madman back into the house? Why hadn't he come forward with this vital evidence when cross-examined that morning? Well, there was a feasible explanation. When a man arranges a secret rendezvous with a woman on the edge of a lake, and when, some little time later, that woman's dead body is lifted from the lake, a certain amount of justifiable suspicion is bound to fall on the man who fixed the rendezvous. Better to say nothing about it. Nothing about the secret meeting. Nothing about the witnessed assault. Just profess complete ignorance and say one went for a stroll round the lake because one couldn't sleep.

In the light of this new theory there was just one correction to be made with regard to Farnham's possible movements. He couldn't have reached the cottage by ten o'clock if the rendezvous with Millar had been fixed for, say, eleven-twenty. Otherwise he would have seen the girl. But the dropped handkerchief definitely indicated that he *had* visited the cottage—presumably some time after eleven-twenty and before eleven forty-five, which was about the time Sam Richardson must have entered to search the place.

As Harting approached the summer-house he felt quite pleased with himself. A certain amount of order was being fashioned out of chaos. He was getting somewhere. Pieces of the puzzle were fitting in.

But the tremendous, irritating, insistent query still remained. *Why was the girl in white satin pyjamas?*

2

Harting had decided at once against the acceptance of Sam's invitation to lunch at Old Knolle. In the opening stages of a case he liked to have spacious fields of silence and solitude over which his mind could wander undisturbed. The Railway Hotel would serve his purpose *and* his lunch. In the meantime he was cleaning up on his investigations en route, first by another look at the thatched summer-house, then at the two stone pavilions which he had noticed facing the lake on the east and south sides.

One thing had struck him when the excitable old actor had concluded his evidence. Somewhere in his story there was unquestionably brandy. When discovered, his breath and clothes reeked of it. He himself was convinced that after his "black-out" he had smelt, if not tasted, brandy. Brandy was apparently his favourite tipple. And brandy had to come out of a flask or bottle, if it were to be taken in any quantity. But there had been no flask tucked away in the pockets of his suit and, a few seconds later, Harting found that there was no sign of flask or bottle in the summer-house. Further, there was no sign of blood on the wooden floor or walls from the gash on his right occiput. Negative evidence, but significant. It meant that he had suffered that wound and taken his last nip of brandy *before* collapsing in the summer-house—in all probability before the murder itself.

From the summer-house Harting proceeded to the east pavilion—a squat, pillared place of rag-stone and Cornish slate. Inside was a massive stone bench, a heavy teak table and a vague smell of damp and lichens. But this time his careful search did not go unrewarded. On the stone flags he discovered two long cigarette stubs faintly rimed with lipstick and, what his wife always referred to as a "kurby-grip", and he, a hairpin. The butts had not been there long enough to absorb the sweat from the stone and the kurby-grip was untarnished. In fact, Harting was prepared to take his oath that *this* had been the prearranged rendezvous between Millar and the dead girl. And what place more suitable? It was both accessible and isolated. He felt even more pleased with himself.

The south pavilion stood on a little promontory on the wooded side of the lake, opposite the lawns which sloped down from the terrace. It was in a commanding position, and gave a comprehensive view of the lake and the well-wooded island in the middle of it. The lakeside path ran just behind the pavilion as it wandered through the trees and under-growth of the copse. The pavilion itself was furnished with an identical bench and table; and it was here that Harting found further and, in this case, puzzling evidence. Admitted there were no kurby-grips, but from the stone floor he collected no less than ten cigarette-butts of a brand known as Churchman Number 1—a cigarette which is slightly larger than the average. The butts were smoked far shorter and there was no hint of lipstick. In brief, the smoker in this case had not been of the female sex.

But what the deuce did it mean? Once again it was obvious that the butts had only recently been thrown on to the damp floor. Had they any connection with the movements of any of the various people who seemed to have been prowling the grounds the night before? Or had the smoker occupied the place earlier in the day? His wait must have been prolonged, for it takes a considerable time to smoke ten outsize cigarettes, even if one is lit from the stub of the other. That man had been chain-smoking, Harting deduced at once, for among the ten butts was one solitary spent match. It suggested nervousness or boredom or impatience on the part of the smoker.

Retracing his steps along the south side of the lake, Harting climbed the iron-railed fence into the paddock—a seven-acre field dotted with huge oaks and grazed by a herd of pedigree Jersey cows. This, he found, was a short cut to the main road and, *ipso facto*, the railway station. Doubtless, Farnham, anxious to avoid Old Knolle, had gained the lake across the paddock.

For the last few hundred yards the road rose steeply to the station itself; on one side bordered by a high bank, on the other by a tangled, derelict and fenceless wood. Halfway up this hill, on the same side as the wood, was Farnham's "white-painted milestone". It was here that the old fellow claimed to have been attacked, or at least overcome by unconsciousness.

But was there any truth in this claim? Wasn't it more likely that it was on this deserted stretch of road that he had squatted down and started his really serious drinking?

A cursory examination of the road verge brought to light one undeniable fact. Somebody had been lying recently in the tangled undergrowth on the edge of the wood, only a few yards from the milestone. The imprint of a human form was clearly discernible. The odour of crushed garlic and nettles was still pungent. Whipping out his flexible steel rule, Harting measured up the imprint. Roughly—five foot three.

"And, by heaven!" thought the inspector, "five foot three is just about Farnham's measure, eh? The devil take the old chap, but is his story true? Was he attacked at this spot and knocked unconscious? Did he then partly come to and wander off in a dazed condition to commit the crime and end up in the summer-house? Umph! I doubt it. These wanderings would have to include a visit to Fallow Cottage. And to get across country, even on a moonlit night, requires a pretty clear brain. Still, somebody's dossed down here quite recently, and there's every reason to believe that it *was* Farnham. If he were attacked—who attacked him?"

3

After ringing up Sergeant Dane from the public call-box outside the Railway Hotel, Harting went into the inn and ordered his lunch. While waiting for it to be served he drifted into the saloon bar for a light ale and a discreet chat with the landlord. He was anxious to find out if Willy Farnham had picked up any fuel for his culminative binge at the Railway Hotel. But Bert Twining was emphatic.

"Brandies, Inspector? Naow! Oi don't reckon to sell moren'a couple o' tots o' brandy over this bar in a week. We're what you might call an agricolltour house. For all that we're nigh the station, there's not many 'oo drop in off the trains and have one in here. Locals—that's our trade. Farm hands from round about 'oo come in for their pint o' mild and such. So when I *do* sell a brandy—it's an event. Oi'd remember it even from a week since. So when Oi tell 'ee that no chap come in here for a brandy last night, you can take it as a fac'!"

Harting did. It was no more than he had anticipated. A veteran, and probably fastidious, brandy-drinker like the old actor would carry his source of supply about with him. There was the question of his favourite brand and the limitations imposed by the licensing hours if he relied on local amenities. Then where, in heaven's name, was the flask or bottle responsible for last night's little orgy? Had Farnham, with a buccaneering gesture, taken a final swig, chucked the empty bottle into the lake and staggered forward to commit the murder?

Harting gave the matter up and devoted the next three-quarters of an hour to an unexpectedly excellent lunch. He roofed his meal with a slice of crusty new bread, farm butter and a wedge of tasty cheddar; then he went through into the dingy, deserted lounge, ordered his coffee and waited for the sergeant.

A few minutes later a high-powered motor-cycle roared up to the hotel entrance, emitted a single deafening backfire, coughed twice and went silent. Sergeant Dane entered the lounge.

The sergeant never walked anywhere. He waddled. He was the Falstaffian type of Englishman, popular to a degree, who wheezes and chuckles and roars his way through life, as amiable and deceptive as a hippo. Tiny twinkling eyes in a pudding-bag face; a rosebud mouth above a massive tier of chins; hands like hams; and a high, whistling voice which emerged from his enormous person with as much incongruity as a pea might emerge from the mouth of a cannon. Yet encased in that shaking good-natured mass of flesh was a brain as quick and shrewd as any at County H.Q. Harting valued him as he valued no other subordinate, for, on top of these other qualities, Sergeant Dane, like the bulldog he was, never let go of a problem once he'd got his teeth into it.

"Well, Sergeant?"

"Mine's a pint, thank you, sir. Dry work on that bone-shaker."

Harting laughed. "True to form, eh? Old and bold, isn't it?"

Dane nodded and the hovering landlord took the order. Five minutes later in the deserted lounge Harting swiftly and succinctly laid all the relevant facts of the double case before the sergeant. When he came to a stop, Dane ran a hand round the third chin from the bottom of his massive jowl.

"Like a bit of knitting the cat's been at, sir. All taggly ends. We're going to have a stiff pull up the grade before we get anywhere."

"Well, there are three immediate jobs I want you to do. Question the stationmaster and make sure that Farnham stepped off the nine-ten. Find out if Lehaye sent a telegram to Chelsea from Lambdon post office. Then comb about round that milestone and see if you can find the bottle which produced Farnham's outsize hangover. I'm sure there's a bottle somewhere in the set-up."

"O.K., sir." He drained the last of his pint and smacked his lips. "Has it struck you in the case of them two stone pavilions you were talking of, that Millar may have been waiting in one and Lehaye in the other? According to the evidence we've got here"—he thumped his open note-book with a pudgy hand—"in one pavilion there was a hair-slide and some red-tipped cigarette butts, suggesting the female of the species. In the other about a dozen supersized butts without trimmings, suggesting the male of the species. Now, to my daft way of looking at things, if Lehaye and Millar had met, we'd get the leavings of a male-female combination—butts with and without lipstick. Common sense, eh?"

"But you're assuming," argued Harting, "that I imagined it was Millar in the south pavilion. But I didn't and I don't. If Farnham's black-out story is all hookum, then I think *he* was the man who stood in the pavilion and smoked ten Churchmans in a line. In the meantime, Millar and the girl met in the east pavilion. She smoked. He didn't. And that's all there is to it."

"You think the old boy knew they were going to meet there?"

"I can't say. It seems that he must have done. Otherwise why did he wait for her near the lake instead of tackling her in the cottage which is far more isolated? No. My idea is that he knew where and when Millar and the girl were meeting, stood waiting in the south pavilion until the meeting broke up, followed the girl and—"

"But half a mo', sir—where's Millar in the meantime?"

"He's run ahead into the house."

"But look ye here, sir, look ye here! Let's get this straight." Dane consulted his notebook with a sort of coy sidelong glance which he always adopted when reading, holding the book not directly in front of him, but somewhere out beyond his left ear. "Millar was seen by Richardson in the hall twenty minutes after midnight—and twenty minutes earlier Richardson saw the girl flittering about in the garden. She wasn't being followed by Farnham *then*. Leastways not according to the evidence. What's more, it proves that Millar didn't kiss the girl good night and rush smack into the house. He hung around the lake."

Harting admitted, "You're right there. I slipped up. Any better ideas yourself?"

Dane puffed out his cheeks, pursed his lips and allowed his repressed breath to escape through the minute aperture of his mouth. He never thought without, as the inspector told him, "pulling his face about". The mobility of his vast countenance was alarming.

"Roundabouts!" he announced. "More or less. This way, sir. The girl leaves the east pavilion and makes for the track across the fields to the cottage, meets Richardson, scuttles back towards the house, makes a big détour and comes down towards the lake again. In the meantime, Millar, after hanging on for a few minutes in the pavilion, moves off along the lake and thus up the lawns to the house. The two not meeting, as you see. As for the old boy in the south pavilion, he starts off and comes in behind the girl, as it were, just as she makes her second attempt to get back to the cottage. Farnham overtakes her half-way along the bank, however, dots her a fourpenny one and dumps her in the water. Three of 'em all on the move, sir, and none of 'em meeting." Dane pushed out his legs and undid the top button of his trousers. "I reckon we're getting places, sir."

"Well and good, Sergeant, provided we're getting to the *right* places. Has it occurred to you that the figure in white might not have been Lehaye?"

"But, heavens above, sir, we can't possibly postulate two young women prancing round the estate in their pi-jams! That one of 'em should be doing it is puzzling enough. Now don't let's make things more difficult!"

Harting argued, "But the point is, Richardson was too far off to say whether the girl *was* in her night attire. Dressed in white—that's all he'll swear to. I still think it might have been—"

Dane pushed his notebook out beyond his left ear. "Miss Angela Walsh, eh? You think she's been telling you fairy tales?"

"I do. A lovely piece of blue-eyed innocence, Dane, but intelligent. I believe she was out and about last night, possibly when Richardson first called into her bedroom at half-past eleven. The chances are that half an hour later Richardson saw her returning to her bedroom."

"But he followed her up and took a dekko at her room, didn't he? And found her safe and snug and sleepy."

"Fake!" exclaimed Harting. "Richardson says she was wearing an orange-coloured nightdress. But that means damn all! She might have left the house in a white coat or wrap. Knowing Richardson, he wouldn't spot the difference between an evening frock and a nightie. I'm going over to Old Knolle this afternoon to carry out two specific jobs. I'm going to, poke my nose into Miss Angela Walsh's wardrobe. I'm also going to cadge a cigarette of Millar and, if necessary, Farnham. They can't both smoke Churchman Number One."

"Smart enough," nodded Dane. "If Miss Walsh was a-roaming round—how come, sir?"

"For some reason she's anxious to conceal. Very anxious. She's not the sort to tell a lie unless it's absolutely necessary. Maybe there's something between her and young Millar. She's engaged to Barnes, but that doesn't preclude the possibility."

"Quite, sir. My old woman married me when she was in love with another chap. So she *said*! Took her five years to get over it. God! fairly held him up as an example, she did. Always 'Cecil did this' and 'Cecil did that'. Damn silly name, anyway!"

Harting ignored this sidelight on Dane's domestic career. "Well, I can deal with all these matters without delay." He got to his feet. "I'll show you just where that milestone is on my way over to the manor. I have to go that way."

"Righto, sir. I'll leave the bone-shaker to cool off in the yard here. A bit of foot-slogging's good for my waistline."

As they stepped out into the burning sunlight, Harting said with enthusiasm, "I think we've made progress already. You're a grand whetstone for my wits, Dane. Always were, y'know. The facts are beginning to line up and take their dressing from the right."

Dane emitted one of his wheezy deep-throated chuckles. "We always were a couple of optimists at the start of a case. Remember the Lankstone Park mystery—them Vemeers and Van Whatsisnames, sir? Remember the case of 'Nosey' Babbington and the Groaning Bridge? Remember—but, lordy lordy! I could go on indefinite. Quick off the mark in every investigation we were, and then, dammit! if we didn't run slap into one bloomin' big snag. And in this particular case—"

"I know! I know!" broke in Harting. "Why was the dead girl in pyjamas? I keep on coming back to it. When I die, guess I'll have 'white satin pyjamas' written across my heart. It's the most puzzling factor in the case."

CHAPTER XV

Clue at the Cottage

I

LUNCH AT OLD KNOLLE WAS FAR FROM BLITHE, BUT ALREADY THE high temperature of events was cooling. Minds were probing into the immediate future. Could Deirdre's unfinished sketches of the first productions be completed by another artist? Would Willy be fit enough to take his part on the first night of *The Red Ant*? What about the coming week's rehearsals? Sam voiced an opinion on this over the *poulet en casserolle*.

"We shall have to abandon all idea of rehearsing for the next few days. I'm sure you'll all agree. Several of us will have to appear at the inquest. We may be needed for further cross-examination. Then there's the funeral. What's your idea, Basil?"

"Agreed absolutely, Sam. We couldn't do any good work in our present frame of mind. If that inspector chap allows it, I'll move into the cottage for the rest of the week."

"Is he coming here again?" asked Millar, with a hint of anxiety in his voice.

Sam nodded. "This afternoon, I think. A sound fellow, Harting. He knows his job."

Clara said, with a meaning glance that took in the whole table, "Too well for somebody's peace of mind. If I'd anything on my conscience, I should feel decidedly nervous with Inspector Harting on my track. Quite terrifyingly thorough!"

"You're thinking of poor Willy?" asked Sam gently.

"Oh, I'm sure he had nothing to do with it!" cried Angela with an appealing glance at Basil.

"You know, Sam, I rather agree there," put in Basil. "As far as I can see, Harting's mind hasn't travelled much beyond this immediate circle. Why not? There's no reason at all why somebody quite outside the company—you see my point? He suspects all of us. Otherwise, why did he take a specimen of our fingerprints before he left this morning? The chief reason why he suspects us is simply because we happened to know Deirdre rather well, and were on the spot when she was murdered."

"By the way," said Sam, "I succeeded in getting a telephone call through to that friend of hers in Bournemouth. I'm sending a car over to meet her at Brighton. She should be here this evening."

"No relations?" asked Basil.

"According to Miss Honisett—none. A couple of cousins in South Africa. She and Miss Honisett met in Paris four years ago."

The meal progressed for a time in silence. Everybody seemed occupied with their thoughts, and, of course, the really excellent *poulet en casserolle*. Suddenly Clara looked across at her nephew.

"Rudie, darling, I don't want to seem unduly curious, but did you go down to the lake about a quarter-past eleven last night? I saw somebody kneeling on the bank and peering into the water. It was just where we found—er—Deirdre later on."

"It certainly wasn't me, then, Auntie," answered Rudolph with some spirit. "I walked round the lake as I told the inspector, but I didn't go near that particular spot. I looked at the moonlight on the water, I admit that, but I didn't go down on my knees to do it. What a damn silly idea!"

"All right. Don't get heated, darling. Now I wonder," mused Clara, "who it could have been?"

"I suppose it wasn't Willy?" asked Sam. "He must have been wandering about the garden. He was drunk enough to have done anything, however damned silly it might have seemed to a sober man. Everything, that is, save murder."

"The inspector has clear proof that Willy *did* go near the lake," broke in Basil.

"But I'm absolutely sure he had nothing to do with poor Deirdre's death," Angela reiterated. "Off-stage he's such a muddle-headed helpless sort of baby. I don't think it's fair to accuse him just because he happened to be found in the summer-house."

"Funny finding that handkerchief of his at the cottage," observed Sam.

"*Not* for Willy," replied Clara tartly.

The party again fell silent. It was all very bewildering. It was also horrible to think that somebody at the table *might* prove to be a murderer!

2

Harting was there soon after lunch. He went to work with the directness born of impatience. Five minutes after his arrival he was following Angela along the corridor to her bedroom. Once there he asked, "Tell me, young lady, when Mr. Richardson looked into your room for the second time, were you in your night attire?"

"Yes, of course. In my nightdress."

"And the colour?"

"Pale blue." She went to the bed, picked up a small Scotch terrier, ripped open its abdomen by means of a zip and shook out the garment in question. "There, Inspector."

"I see." Harting's eyes were roving round the room. "You play tennis?"

"Yes. We were playing yesterday afternoon."

"Ah, I thought so!" He pointed to a racquet leaning against a chair, over the back of which was flung a long white tennis-coat. "You ought to keep your racquet in a press, you know." His hand encountered the handle of the wardrobe. The next minute he was peering inside. "Don't misunderstand my curiosity, young lady. Just routine."

"But—but what on earth are you looking for?"

"This!" exclaimed Harting with an air of triumph as he unhooked a coat-hanger. Suspended from it was a tangerine evening frock! Little things were falling into place. He faced Angela with a stern look. "Now, young lady, I want the truth. I think I *know* the truth, but I want your confirmation. Last night you changed for dinner, eh?"

"Yes."

"Into this frock?"

After a moment's hesitation, Angela nodded. "When Mr. Richardson looked in you were *still* in this frock? You were wearing it in bed? You hadn't undressed. This is all true, isn't it?"

"Yes," admitted Angela in an almost inaudible voice, "it's quite true."

"Then why, in heaven's name, did you lie to me?"

"I—I had to. You see—I thought that if Basil—But why must I answer all these questions? I know nothing about Miss Lehaye's death. Absolutely nothing. Nor does Rudie. I swear that, Inspector. I've just been terribly foolish and awfully thoughtless. That's all."

"You were in the grounds last night?"

"Yes."

"Before you went out you put on that white tennis-coat?"

"How did you—?"

"And it was *you* Mr. Richardson saw about midnight near the Dutch garden? Why didn't you answer him when he called out?"

For a moment Angela stood there, trembling, without defence. But in the heat of the chase her melting looks cut no ice with Inspector Harting. He was getting places. The truth was burgeoning. "Well, why didn't you?" he repeated.

"Because I didn't want anybody to know that I'd been out of the house."

"But—"

"No, please—let me explain in my own way, Inspector. It's all so frightfully stupid and yet so simple. Rudie—that is Mr. Millar—wanted to see me alone. He had no chance during the day, but just as we were going up to bed he made me promise to meet him in the garden. He said it was fearfully important that he should see me, and promised not to breathe a word to Basil—that is Mr. Barnes. I've always felt sorry for Mr. Millar. He went through a wretched, wretched time when he was accused of taking that money. Somehow I just couldn't refuse him. After all, Inspector, I wasn't doing anything very terrible, was I? If Basil were not so horribly jealous, I shouldn't have thought twice about it."

"Quite. And so you went?"

"Yes. I promised to meet him in the pavilion about eleven o'clock. But his aunt was dodging about round the bathroom, and I didn't dare leave until she had gone to bed. So I actually didn't leave the house until five and twenty past. And then, when I got to the pavilion, I found Rudie wasn't there!"

"Which pavilion is this?"

"The one at the end of the lake—with the larches round it."

"You say he wasn't there?"

"No. I couldn't make out what had happened. I naturally thought he must have got tired of waiting and gone back to bed. Then, somehow, I felt that wasn't like Rudie. He's a sticker, if you know what I mean, Inspector? And he'd seemed so frightfully keen on seeing me alone. So I lit a cigarette and hung on, expecting him to turn up at any minute. Well, I actually waited there until midnight, and then I got so chilly that I couldn't stand it any longer. I ran back into the house."

"But why the détour round the Dutch garden? Why not straight up the lawn to the terrace?"

"Because as I was crossing the lawn I saw somebody getting over the stile which leads to Fallow Cottage. They were silhouetted against the moon. I thought it looked like Rudie. Then when Mr. Richardson called out I realized my mistake. And that," concluded Angela, "is just about all that really happened. I'm sorry now that I told such fibs, but I didn't want to get Mr. Millar into trouble. Basil would have half killed him if he'd found out."

"And what actually *did* happen to the young man?" asked Harting, who had already guessed the probable answer.

"Weren't we stupid? We both forgot that there were *two* pavilions. Rudie was naturally thinking of the one in the wood on the far side of the lake. He thought it would be safer. So there we were, each in our own little pavilion, both waiting for each other. Weren't we perfect idiots? Oh, I can laugh about it now, but it seemed so risky at the time. I'm afraid I'm an awful duffer at intrigue, Inspector. I've had so little experience."

She sighed. But at that moment Inspector Harting thought this lack of experience was her greatest charm. She had told him far more than he had dared to anticipate.

3

Rudolph was just as open. The moment he knew there was no longer any need to shield Angela, he told Harting the whole story. Quite simple. He had left the house about eleven o'clock and walked straight round the east end of the lake to the pavilion in the wood. There, for the best part of an hour and twenty minutes, he had waited. (As Angela had said, Rudolph was certainly a sticker!) The pavilion was damp and draughty, and the cold air from the lake rose up and hung about under the trees. When at last he was convinced that Angela had decided not to keep their tryst, he was stiff and chilled to the marrow; but a sprint back to the house had soon stimulated his circulation. By the time he met Richardson in the hall he was thoroughly warm and out of breath.

"And that, believe it or not, Inspector, is the whole story. You can't crime me for fixing a rendezvous with another fellow's girl, eh?"

Harting laughed. "No, we won't pull you in for that! Now one point, Mr. Millar. Did you notice anybody on that stretch of the bank where the body was recovered? I imagine you could see the far side of the lake fairly clearly from the pavilion."

"As it happens, I couldn't. You see, the island blots out most of the far bank. The trees on the island are pretty dense."

"Well, thanks a lot, young fellow." Harting patted his pockets and then looked annoyed. "Damn!"

"What's the trouble, Inspector?"

"Left my cigarette-case in the car."

"Here, have one of mine."

"Thanks."

Rudolph held a match. A surreptitious glance and Harting had found out all he needed to know. The cigarette was a Churchman Number 1. In brief, Angela and Rudolph, unless his reading of the facts was myopic, had been telling the truth.

4

The inspector had interviewed Rudolph in the study and no sooner had the latter withdrawn than Basil came in.

"Look here, Inspector; I wonder if you'd give me permission to go over to the cottage? Rehearsals are a washout for at least a week. I'd like to stay there in the meantime. Any objections?"

Harting considered the point. "I'm afraid I can't give you permission yet. I'd fixed to meet my sergeant there at three o'clock. I want to make a more detailed examination of Miss Lehaye's effects. So if you want to collect a few clothes and so forth, you'd better come along with me."

"Thanks." Basil glanced at the clock. "If you fixed that meeting for three, isn't it time you got cracking?"

"Good heavens! No idea it was so late."

Harting moved up briskly to the French windows on to the terrace. He exuded energy and self-satisfaction. As they strode off together across the gardens towards the stile, Basil observed, "You seem pretty tickled up, Inspector. Things going well?"

"Ah, so-so! So-so!"

"The official mute, eh?"

"That's our fixed policy, Mr. Barnes."

Presently they arrived at the cottage to find that Sergeant Dane had not yet shown up. Harting took out his borrowed key and unlocked the door.

"Mind your head!" warned Basil automatically.

They went in. Basil offered Harting a drink. He refused. "Kind of you, but time's evidence on this job. I want to go through the pockets of the young woman's clothes, also her hand-bag."

All was just as it had been left after Deirdre's departure the previous night—bed neatly made; clothes in a pile over a chair; walking shoes side by side in front of the antique tall-boy; her hand-bag on the dressing-table. It was the latter article which first attracted Harting's attention. He picked it up.

"Women carry half their lives round in these things," he declared. "Give me the contents of a woman's hand-bag and I'll give you a pretty accurate reading of her character and status in life."

He undid the bag and emptied it on to the bed. The usual clutter dropped out—lipstick, powder compact, nail-file, rouge and so forth. Among the documentary articles were one or two letters addressed to her St. John's Wood studio. Harting fanned them out like a hand of cards. Basil glanced at them idly and then gave an almost imperceptible start.

"I say, you're not going to read them, are you? Not exactly cricket, is it? I mean to say—"

"Cricket or not, Mr. Barnes, I *am* going to read 'em. I'm not playing a parlour game. I'm investigating a murder."

"But surely—?"

Harting looked up in surprise. "None of these is in your handwriting, surely?"

"No, of course not."

"Very well."

Harting opened the first—an invitation to dinner from a St. John's Wood neighbour—quite without interest. He opened the second, the address of which had been written in indelible pencil. The handwriting was obviously uneducated. Basil's uneasiness seemed to increase. Harting was just about to smooth out the folded sheet enclosed in the envelope, when the cottage was shaken by an almighty thud.

"Good God! what's that?"

From the hall below came the full, fine fury of a man versed in the gentle art of swearing. From this bloodthirsty welter of words Harting gathered that the door-lintel was not all it should have been. It was something different. Quite different. It was a——!

"That you, Dane?" The sergeant grunted and attempted to mount the stairs. "All right. I'll come down."

"You'd better, sir, because I very much doubt if I can come up!" He hadn't noticed Barnes, who was still lingering by the bedroom door. "Well, sir, I've struck oil from the start. A fair gusher! Not two yards from that damned milestone—"

"Sssh!" cautioned Harting, jerking his thumb upwards.

"Sorry, sir. I didn't know you had company."

Basil came down, smiling like a cat that has swallowed the canary. Harting noticed it at once and felt a sudden leap of excitement and exhilaration.

"Look here, Inspector, if I'm in the way, I'll take a hammock chair under the mulberry tree. You'll find it easier without me cluttering up the place."

"All right. Thanks."

No sooner had Basil lounged into the garden than Harting took the stairs two at a time. It was just as he had anticipated. Of the three letters he had so carelessly thrown aside on the bed, one was missing. The one addressed in indelible pencil! He chuckled to himself and pulled out the folded note, which he had pretended to replace in the envelope.

Dane, who had come up the stairs sideways, holding his breath, joined him in the bedroom.

"Coo! what a joint, sir. Can't understand chaps paying out good money for such relics. Make a nice tea-shoppe, eh?"

"Shut up and listen to this!" Harting had now unfolded the note.

Dear Miss Lehaye,

You asked me to write and let you know if everything was working out according to plan. Well, it is, and well we can do with it. Jim's taken it all right without any questions the same as you guessed he would. We teamed up in a good act that night, didn't we? When I think of what it means to us I can never thank you enough.

Respectfully yours,
Evandine Barron.

"Now what the hell?" breathed Dane. "What's it all about, sir?"

"Can't say yet. But this much I *do* know. It has some bearing on Mr. Basil Barnes. That's the gentleman you met downstairs. He saw his chance, just as I meant him to, and stuffed the envelope in his pocket thinking he'd got the note." With a couple of swift strides, Harting was at the window. "Ah-ha! just as I thought. Look at that, Sergeant!"

Having set up his hammock-chair, Barnes was standing under the mulberry tree casually lighting his pipe. But not with a match. He had made a spill from a folded envelope, and he took care to hold it until it all but burnt his fingers.

"And the funny thing is," chuckled Dane, "he thinks he's burnt the evidence."

"Quite. If I said the letter was missing, he'd claim it must have been mislaid and offer to help me look for it. A cool card, Dane. He wants watching."

"And that note, sir?"

"I can't say. I should judge from that phrase 'and well we can do with it' that it's in some way connected with money. Somehow Lehaye has been instrumental in doing this Evandine Barron a good turn. Luckily she's scrawled her address across the top. Twelve, Dickers Place, Ladbroke Grove. It's worth following up, in my opinion. Now let's take a look at the girl's effects, then I'll listen to your tale of triumph."

But there was nothing more of interest, save one rather curious point. With his customary thoroughness Harting turned down the bedclothes to make quite sure that the bed had not been slept in and then casually covered with the counterpane. And there, just under the turn-down of the blankets, was *a pair of white satin pyjamas*! They were identical with the pair found on the dead girl!

5

Sergeant Dane had waddled round the parish of Lambdon to good effect. Within fifteen minutes of Harting's departure he had learnt from the station-master that Farnham *had* stepped off the nine-ten. Within half an hour he had gingerly collected a square-necked brandy bottle from a bed of nettles. It lay not five yards from the spot where the inspector had first noticed the imprint of a human form. The bottle had obviously been flung aside. Although the screw-top was missing, a few dregs of the spirit still remained at the bottom of the bottle. He had wrapped this exhibit in a big square of silk, and making sure that Basil was now comfortably seated, he proudly displayed it to the inspector.

"Notice the brand, sir? The old boy has good taste. You'll want to run over it for fingerprints, eh?"

"Yes, I took specimens at Old Knolle this morning. And the telegram?"

"Post office was shut, of course, being a Sunday—but I soon cottoned on to the postmistress's private address. Smart old biddy. Truly rural, but intelligent. Says she knew Miss Lehaye by sight, and what she'd seen she didn't like. But that's on the side. This is what counts. No telegram was dispatched by Miss Lehaye on Saturday and no telegram went through Lambdon post office addressed to Farnham in Chelsea. The nearest telegraph office, apart from Lambdon, is five miles away at a place called Dewbourne. So that, sir, is *that*!"

CHAPTER XVI

The Pyjama Puzzle

I

THE INQUEST HAD BEEN FIXED FOR TUESDAY MORNING AT OLD Knolle, and the funeral was to take place that same afternoon. Miss Honisett had turned up from Bournemouth on Sunday evening, and Harting had questioned her before driving back to Millward Heath. He learnt little enough. Save for those cousins in South Africa, Deirdre Lehaye seemed utterly unattached. According to Miss Honisett, she was "difficult", reserved and cynical in her attitude to the past, and preferred not to talk about it. She had lived in South Africa until the death of her parents; at the age of seventeen she had come to England, unescorted, and had gone on the stage. She had had a hard time, said Miss Honisett, and it had made her rather bitter. Then, under de Sulemann's influence in Paris, she had gradually emerged as an artist. But, as Miss Honisett confessed, although devoted to her art, money was her god. She saw her career not in terms of artistic evolution, but as a means of making money. About her work with the Beaumont company and its members she seldom spoke. Miss Honisett admitted she had heard of Willy Farnham and Basil Barnes, but Deirdre had never appeared to set them apart from her other theatrical acquaintances.

Harting's first task on Monday morning, when he arrived at Millward Heath headquarters, was to lift the prints off the brandy bottle. Within fifteen minutes he knew he was face to face with one of those negative clues which may mean anything or nothing. There was only one set of recent prints on the bottle, and those were Willy Farnham's!

But even if Farnham's story were true, surely there was something queer about this evidence? He claimed to remember "the vague outline of a shape against the sky and the clink of glass against my teeth". In other words the brandy had been administered by a second person. Allowing for the fact that Farnham had instinctively clutched the bottle when it was applied to his lips, *why were there not other prints on the glass?*

Two reasons occurred to Harting at once. Either Farnham's story was all my eye and Betty Martin, or the person who had placed the bottle to his mouth had been wearing gloves. It was, Harting admitted, not exactly the weather for gloves, but if anybody had come to his assistance from a passing car it was a definite possibility.

But if Farnham had suffered a stroke or had been knocked down by some reckless driver, why had this good Samaritan given him the brandy and then, instead of ringing up a doctor or the police, deposited the old actor in the summer-house? No, the more Harting worried this bone, the more he was convinced that Farnham had either lied like hell or been the victim of foul play. This meant that somebody *had* attacked him in Station Lane. But who?

Harting suddenly straightened up. There *was* somebody who knew that Farnham would be stepping off the nine-ten and that was Barnes. His inquiries at Victoria would make sure of that—but steady, steady! The old boy collapsed in Station Lane at nine-twenty and at nine-twenty Barnes was in Town. He must have been, because just before ten o'clock he had put through a call from London to Lehaye at Fallow Cottage to say he was worried about Farnham. And later, at eleven-thirty, Barnes had rung Old Knolle to tell Richardson that he was more worried than ever and was driving down to Lambdon without delay. So that was that!

But damn it! thought Harting after a brief reflection, *was* it? Barnes's alibi at the moment depended on that most tenuous of factors—a telephone wire. What if *both* calls had been put through from a local kiosk? No chance then of tracing the calls, and no reason for either Lehaye or Richardson to suspect that he was *not* ringing from London. This meant that at nine-twenty Barnes could have been in Lambdon; could have been waiting for the nine-ten; could have seen Farnham collapse in Station Lane; could have brought him round with brandy. But why, why? What was the damfool idea? And surely Farnham hadn't allowed Barnes to pour brandy down his gullet to such an extent that he was rendered blind drunk? Above all, why should Barnes have been on the spot just as Farnham collapsed with a bottle of brandy in his hand? Ridiculous, eh? Something more to it than that.

Since it was easy to check up with the railway officials, those inquiries at Victoria *must* have been genuine. But even then, since the inquiries had been made just after the train's departure (Barnes's own evidence) he would have had time to drive all out in his M.G. sports and reach Lambdon Halt *before* the train.

Again, had Barnes sent that telegram purporting to come from Lehaye? Why not? Knowing his man, he took a risk on the "office of origin" and dispatched the telegram from a London post office; and he had done this because he wanted to get Farnham on to that seven-forty-three train. Why? Was it—yes, by heaven!—was it because he intended to *murder* him?

The motive for the major crime was not, of course, available, nor was the precise reason why Farnham had been left in the summer-house. But the means by which Barnes hoped to bamfoozle the law was already formulating in Harting's mind. What if the bottle had contained something other than brandy? Or, rather, something *as well as* brandy? Something in the nature of a drug or poison? Barnes's idea was simply this: When Farnham was found dead (as Barnes had actually anticipated) in the summer-house, the police would naturally think he had died of heart failure due to an excess of alcohol. That he was in fact discovered alive was just too bad for Mr. Basil Barnes!

But wait, thought Harting, there's another point to consider. Suppose Lehaye hadn't been murdered by the lake, wasn't it possible that Farnham would not have been discovered that night? What then? Exposure might well have tipped the scales and dropped him into oblivion. When Barnes had dumped the fellow there, he had not anticipated the Lehaye complication. Granted he had built up the idea that Farnham was on his way to Lambdon in order to get even with the girl, but the astounding fact that she was actually destined to be murdered that night had never occurred to him.

All very fine as far as it went, but it was a long way from going far enough! Attempted murder is one thing—successful murder another.

The big problem still confronting him was—who had murdered Lehaye?

Accept this latest theory, and Farnham was erased from the list. Angela Walsh and young Millar had apparently cleared themselves of all suspicion. There was Sam, of course. Harting only had his word for it that he had spent the time from ten-thirty to eleven-thirty reading in his study. There was the domestic staff to consider, and it was quite within the bounds of possibility that the job had been done by some-body outside the Old Knolle ménage. Finally, if he were not in London, there was Barnes.

But what motive had Barnes for killing the girl? He knew that she was alone at the cottage, and the cottage offered a far safer place in which to commit the crime than the open lawns at the manor. Even in his attempts to pin the Farnham affair on to Barnes, wasn't he going too fast? When Barnes had rung up Lehaye he had asked her to ring him back the moment she had been in touch with Richardson. If she had rung him back, then he must have called Fallow Cottage from his flat in Kensington. After all, unless Barnes had murdered the girl, he wasn't to know that she would be unavailable as a witness. No, on second thoughts it looked as if Barnes had his alibi and this hyper-subtle theory about the attempted murder of Farnham was all moonshine.

For all that, with his customary caution, the Inspector decided to have an immediate analysis made of the dregs left in the brandy bottle. If the bottle contained brandy—well and good. If it contained more than brandy—well, he'd have to start his deductions all over again!

2

An hour and a half later Dane came into Harting's office direct from the laboratory. The sergeant was beaming with delight.

"Come on, Dane, get it off your chest. I can see you're tickled to death about something."

"I am, sir."

"That analysis, eh?"

Dane nodded. "Peterson's made a grand job of it. There's no loophole for error. About seventy-five per cent. of the residue was brandy."

"And the other twenty-five?"

"Veronal!"

"Good God! So Farnham *was* drugged."

"And how, sir? But I notice you haven't cottoned on to the full beauty of the trick."

"Don't look so damned smug. Go on."

"Brandy laced with veronal. Mark that, sir. The brilliance of the scheme lies in the fact that brandy in excess has exactly the same effects as a shot of veronal. Enlarged pupils, no reaction to light, lowered temperature, feeble pulse and coma. So unless you'd been a bit suspicious about them lack of fingerprints and decided on this analysis, we should still be ready to kid ourselves that Farnham was drunk. Oh, it's smart, sir—lovely and smart. You've got to admit it."

"It's even more. It's *proof*! It's proof that Farnham's telling the truth and that somebody has been up to a lot of devilish sculduggery. So far as we can say, Barnes is the only person who knew Farnham would be stepping off the nine-ten. So let's assume for the moment that Barnes is our man."

"That contusion on the old boy's right occiput—we can explain that now."

"You mean Barnes rendered Farnham unconscious with a blow on the head?"

"Yes. He had to knock him silly first, otherwise he couldn't have got that veronal cocktail down his throat. I reckon Mr. Basil Blooming Barnes didn't have to pour a whole bottle down his gullet. The veronal was pretty concentrated. He'd have passed out like a baby after a full meal. What's more, if they hadn't found the old chap when they did, he'd have probably passed out altogether."

"Exactly. But could Barnes have done it? His alibi looks good to me. Then there's the time factor. Don't forget this: if he attacked Farnham at, say, nine-twenty, at nine-fifty or thereabouts, he was on the 'phone to Lehaye. I doubt if he'd have time to carry Farnham the half-mile or so to the summer-house and then get back to a call-box all in a matter of half an hour."

"Why not, sir? He had his car."

"Damn it! so he had. I was forgetting. So he could have placed the fellow in the car, driven to a point just beyond the Old Knolle entrance and carried him the necessary couple of hundred yards down to the summer-house. And the call-box?"

"Well, the only public call-box in the near vicinity, as far as I know, is the one outside the Railway Hotel. There's one outside the Lambdon post office, but that's nearly twice as far from Old Knolle."

"So in all probability," said Harting, "he then drove back to Station Lane and put through his call from the kiosk, making out that he was 'phoning Lehaye from London."

"Half a mo', sir. He couldn't have done that, because he definitely told Lehaye to ring him back in ten minutes."

"Hell!" breathed Harting. "I can't begin to see it all. But let's waive that point for the moment and assume that he *did* ring Lehaye from the kiosk. What then, eh, Sergeant?"

"The next thing we know about him, sir, is that he rang Richardson up at eleven-thirty. So he probably hung about up a dark lane and then returned to the same call-box."

"And finally, after hanging about for another hour and a half, he turned up at Old Knolle," concluded the Inspector, "with all the appearance of having driven direct down from London. Umph! I wonder if we've got it right?"

Harting sensibly realized that there was little more to be gained by theorizing at this stage of his investigations. His next move was to re-examine Barnes in the light of this new assumption.

But all this, of course, was getting him nowhere in the major case. The question still remained, who murdered Deirdre Lehaye? For the rest of that Monday morning he sat in his office viewing the facts from every possible angle. When he arrived home for lunch he was still in no position to point even an uncertain finger at the murderer. But a plausible reconstruction of the crime had now occurred to him, and the moment he was back at H.Q. he summoned Dane to his office.

"I've been thinking hard about the Lehaye problem, Sergeant, and I've tried to evolve a common-sense explanation for all the known facts.

With Farnham, Millar and the Walsh child now out of the running, we've got to view the problem from a totally different angle. To begin with, we mustn't ignore Miss Maddison's evidence, because I think it's really important. So far we've been inclined to ignore it because it just didn't fit in with our previous theories. You recall, Dane? Miss Maddison saw a male figure kneeling by the lake, peering into the water *at the exact spot where the body of Lehaye was recovered.* In other words, there's every reason to believe that Miss Maddison was the one witness who actually set eyes on the murderer. The time was eleven-fifteen. Hang on to that. Lehaye was alive at ten o'clock, or as near that time as dammit, because she then rang through to Old Knolle. So we can take a fairly safe bet on it that she was murdered between ten and eleven-fifteen. As to the actual events, I think the murderer must have visited the cottage and attacked her before she could defend herself. She was knocked unconscious by that blow on the head. The murderer then carried her across the fields before she regained her senses and dumped her in the water. I imagine it would take him about twenty-five minutes to get from Fallow Cottage to the lake, carrying the girl. So the actual attack on her probably occurred at ten-fifty. Agreed?"

"So far so good, sir."

"At the same time, Dane, we have some very curious points to consider. To clarify matters I've tabulated the various snags. Here you are—take a squint at that."

Dane took the paper, held it well out beyond his ear and cocked his head sideways.

Points in the Lehaye Case which need elucidation.

1. *Why did the murderer leave the light on in the cottage sitting-room and the front door wide open?*
2. *Why were there no bloodstains to be found from the head wound?*
3. *Why was Farnham's handkerchief found on the premises?*
4. *Why were the girl's clothes on the bedside chair and her pyjamas still in the bed?*
5. *Above all, why was she dressed in a second pair of white pyjamas?*

"Now I'm going to do the talking for a bit longer," said Harting as the other handed back the memo. "You butt in if you don't agree. I think we can answer that first point quite satisfactorily. The light was on and the door open because the murderer wanted to get to hell out of the cottage just as soon as he could. Natural reaction, eh? The bloodstains problem is more tricky. But it *is* possible that the murderer had something to hand in which to swathe the girl's head before she actually fell. Farnham's handkerchief is a puzzle. But it may be a mere coincidence. After all, he might have dropped one in the theatre and Lehaye picked it up meaning to return it, and then failed to do so. I doubt if we should place too much stress on the handkerchief. It's probably quite irrelevant." He paused for a moment, relit his pipe and sighed profoundly. "And now," he went on with a scowl, "we come to these confounded pyjamas. I reiterate, Dane, the most peculiar factor in the crime. If you've got an explanation, well, put it on the table."

Dane shook his head. "I'm as bamfoozled as you are, sir. I mean to say—look at the known facts. Clothes on bedside chair; bed undisturbed; pyjamas still between the sheets—fair to deduce that the girl had undressed in the bedroom and been attacked by the murderer before she had had time to get into her night clothes."

"But damn it, Dane, she *wasn't* attacked in the bedroom. At least, I don't think so. Remember, it was the sitting-room light which was left burning. No, she must have heard the murderer moving about, gone downstairs to investigate, turned on the sitting-room light and then been assaulted."

"But blimey, sir, *not* in her birthday suit?"

"No, that's just it. In pyjamas. For some inexplicable reason, instead of putting on the pair set out in the bed, she snatched up a second pair. That's about as far as we can go, Dane. And in my humble opinion it's not far enough."

The sergeant gave added weight to his look of depression by a doleful shake of his head.

"It's not, sir—not by a long chalk. Even if we *can* reconstruct the crime, we're still a helluva long way from knowing who did it." Dane meditatively scratched his array of chins. "I suppose Mr. Basil Blooming Barnes—?"

"You mean because of his fishy behaviour over that note?" cut in Harting. "Yes, I thought of that. I can't quite see how it connects him with Lehaye. He seemed on pretty good terms with the girl, as far as I can gather. Again, even if we can break his alibi and pin the Farnham affair on to him, he couldn't possibly have done both jobs in the time available. However, Dane, we'll take nothing on trust. I suggest you get a spot of tea and catch the next train up to Town. Check up on Barnes's statement about his inquiries at Victoria—then get round to Dickers Place and see what you can pick up from this Evandine Barron woman. Go easy with her. Don't twist her tail too hard or she'll shut up like a clam. If she's seen this morning's papers she'll know that Lehaye has been murdered. This may induce her to talk. Report back to me here first thing to-morrow morning before we go over for the inquest."

"O.K., sir."

"In the meantime, Dane, I'm going to drive over to Old Knolle and have another talk with Barnes. I'm going to assume that he did kill the girl and cross-question him from that angle. I'll see how he reacts."

3

After a cup of tea in his office, the Inspector drove all out for Old Knolle. Now that the case was slowly moving forward, he was racked with impatience. Evidence and yet more evidence—that's what he wanted—all the minutiæ of police investigation which, added together, makes proof.

He discovered Barnes in a hammock-chair in the Dutch garden. Coiled at his feet like an adoring spaniel was his blue-eyed fiancée eating chocolate truffles. In any other circumstances Harting would have looked upon the idyll with a favourable, even sentimental, eye; but the girl was an unexpected encumbrance.

On seeing Harting, Barnes languidly got to his feet, upsetting the box of chocolates which the girl had placed on his knee.

"Oh, hullo! Hullo! This *is* a surprise. What the deuce brings you over here, Inspector? Something cooking?" Then glancing down at his humble inamorata, he added: "Don't worry about the chocolates, my child; run and fetch the Inspector a chair from the summer-house."

Harting smiled. He liked the fellow's sublime egoism; the cool manner in which he used the girl's obvious infatuation to save his own legs.

"Thanks, Miss Walsh," he cut in quickly. "Please don't bother. As a matter of fact, I want a word with Mr. Barnes—alone."

Angela took the hint immediately. "Of course. I was just going on to make a few purchases in the village. I've been trying to persuade Mr. Barnes to come with me, but he's so frightfully slack. I'll see you later, darling."

"I'll be waiting," said Basil. The two men watched the girl cross the lawn. "Now, Inspector?"

"Well, look here, Barnes, I'm not going to beat about the bush. It's my job to check up on the statements of every witness. I've taken a deposition from you and I'm not quite satisfied with what you've told me. For example, after you'd made those inquiries about Farnham at Victoria, what did you do?"

"I went back to my flat in Kensington."

"Very worried, of course, about Farnham's curious behaviour?"

"Naturally."

"I mean, from what he'd let slip at the Beaumont on Saturday morning you were convinced he'd gone down to Lambdon to see Miss Lehaye?"

"Yes."

"Then why didn't you ring Miss Lehaye until nearly ten o'clock? That is to say, until at least two hours later."

"I didn't want to upset her unduly. She was a nervy sort of girl, you know. Besides, I wasn't sure that Willy's chatter wasn't half moonshine. He's excitable and uncontrolled—inclined to talk a lot of hot air."

"But dammit, man!" broke out Harting explosively, "two hours later you rang through *convinced* that something pretty dangerous was afoot. You had no compunction then about warning the girl. Why the sudden change of heart? Had anything occurred in the meantime?"

"Nothing. Except that I'd had time to think—and brood."

"You just sat quietly in your flat for two hours—brooding?"

"Why not?"

"Because it just doesn't make sense! But let that pass. What happened then? You rang Miss Lehaye from your flat?"

"Yes, and asked if Willy had shown up either at the cottage or Old Knolle. I told her to get through to Sam and ring me back in ten minutes."

"Which she did?"

"Naturally."

"Then what?"

"Well, when I discovered that Willy hadn't shown up in Lambdon I was more puzzled than ever. Disturbed, too. I knew the train got in at nine-ten, so he would have had plenty of time to reach either the cottage or Old Knolle. Point was—he hadn't!"

"Your next call went through to Mr. Richardson at eleven-thirty?"

"It did."

"An hour and a half later?"

"That sounds mathematically correct."

"I suppose you spent that hour and a half sitting quietly in your flat—er—*still* brooding?"

"Any objection?" Basil lit a cigarette. He smiled rather sardonically. "You know, Inspector, you hide-bound officials amuse me. You have absolutely no knowledge of ordinary everyday psychology. Because you expected me to dash about impulsively all over the countryside looking for Willy Farnham, you're highly suspicious when I tell you that I didn't. But, my dear fellow, do have a sense of proportion. I wasn't all that interested in Miss Lehaye. Oh, I admit she was very clever at her job and we really got along quite well, but she's never been my type. As for dear old Willy, he was always making a fool of himself; so when he started calling Deirdre rude names and threatening to do all manner of rough things to her—well, I just didn't take him seriously. Not at first, that is. But the more I thought about it the more I—"

"Now let's get this straight," cut in Harting. "You say you didn't take his threats seriously?"

"No—not at first."

"Then why the hell did you rush off to Victoria to see if he'd boarded that Lambdon train?"

For the first time Basil uncrossed his legs and came upright in his chair. "Why did I? Well—why not?"

"Shall I tell you what *I* think, Barnes? Shall I tell you something which you appear to have forgotten?"

"Certainly—if it amuses you."

"It does—but it won't amuse you. When you left Victoria Station you never returned to your flat! You drove straight down to Lambdon!"

"My dear chap!" Basil's eyebrows went up in an expression of! quizzical derision which Harting found infuriating.

"What proof have you that you were still in Town? Those 'phone calls mean damn all, and *you* know it!"

"Proof? Well, really I have not had time to consider the matter. One doesn't waste one's energies searching for proof of an accepted fact. It never occurred to me that anybody would ask me so many lunatic questions. But since you want proof—now let me see. Ah, yes, of course. You may recall that I asked Miss Lehaye to ring me back at my flat. She actually mentioned this to Mr. Richardson—a fact which I'm sure he'll be only too charmed to corroborate. Further, I believe you sleuths like evidence from what you call 'independent witnesses.' It's just occurred to me that I may be able to produce the very witness you want."

"Really?"

"Yes. When I drove down to Old Knolle after my 'phone talk with Sam, I had to take in petrol en route. It was late, as you know, and it so happened that I had to knock this fellow up before I could get any service. Do you know a place called Flimwell, on the main London-Hastings road?"

"Yes."

"You also realize that one turns off there for Lambdon?"

"I do."

"Well, about half a mile down the Flimwell-Hawkhurst road there's an isolated garage."

"I know it," broke in Harting. "It's called the Fillem. It's owned by a man called Ted Carstairs."

"Then you know a damn sight more about it than I do!"

For a moment, somewhat put off his stride, Harting was silent, then he said, "I'd like to clear this point up without delay. My car's outside. I suggest I drive you over to see Ted Carstairs straightaway. He can then corroborate your story and identify you at the same time."

"O.K., Inspector." The sardonic smile was even more irritating. "That suits me fine. There's nothing I appreciate more in life than to see a minor official of our national bureaucracy making a fool of himself. You know, I'm going to enjoy this!"

CHAPTER XVII

Mrs. Barron Tells a Story

I

SHORTLY AFTER NINE O'CLOCK ON TUESDAY MORNING. HARTING AND Dane met in the former's office. The inspector was in an irritable frame of mind and Dane, who knew his superior's moods like the back of his hand, went warily. He realized only too well what was the cause of the trouble—their investigations after trotting along a straight road had been brought to a snorting standstill in a *cul de sac*. Unfortunately his own news from London was none too rosy.

"Let's hear the worst, Sergeant," said Harting tersely. "Barnes was at Victoria, eh?"

"Yes, sir. Those inquiries were genuine enough. He turned up there about five minutes after the seven forty-three had left. I managed to track down both the booking clerk and the ticket collector."

"Well, it's no more than I anticipated. And Evandine Barron?"

Dane described the environment in which he had found the woman, her somewhat tawdry and slipshod appearance, her faded prettiness.

"Ex-vaudeville—that's what she is, sir. I got her story after a sticky start. Says she met Lehaye some years back when they were both struggling to make a career in the profession."

"And the note?"

"Oh she admitted that she wrote it. But I may as well tell you now, sir, there's nothing in it for us. As you guessed, she'd seen the Monday papers and knew all about Lehaye's death. No doubt that it had knocked her all cock-a-hoop. You see, sir, it's all very simple: One night when Lehaye was leaving the Beaumont they came face to face and recognized each other. It appears they hadn't met for eight years. I'll cut it short, but this is the general layout. Barron had the usual hard luck story to put over—genuine, too, I reckon. Jim Barron, her husband, out of a job for six months, kid to look after, she herself pulling no weight at the theatrical agencies. Well, Lehaye fell for it good and proper—old times' sake and all that. Offered to make the girl a weekly allowance until things should improve. But the snag, according to Barron, was her husband. Seems that he's an independent sort of chap and touchy when it comes to charity. Anyway, Lehaye told her to have it out with her hubby and let her know how things went. Hence this letter. Seems that Jim Barron swallowed his pride, eh, sir? And that's all there is to it."

Harting scowled. "Another confounded dead-end and more time wasted! Though why the devil Barnes should show any interest in the letter I can't see. You're sure Barron was telling the truth?"

"She seemed slick enough—but you can never be sure with a woman. I mean to say, we're both married men and—"

"All right. You can cut out the philosophy. The point is, Barnes doesn't seem implicated. What's more, I'm damned if I can break his alibi. I've now got absolute proof that he took in petrol at a garage on the Flimwell-Hawkhurst road at twelve twenty-five on Saturday night. We can't get round the fact that he asked Lehaye to ring him back at his flat. The girl's no longer available for cross-examination, but Richardson has no cause to lie, and he says Lehaye mentioned this fact when she rang Old Knolle. Finally, we know Barnes was at Victoria just before eight o'clock. So there you are—eight o'clock at Victoria, just before ten o'clock at his flat ringing Lehaye, just before twelve thirty taking in petrol at this garage en route from Town. Personally, Dane, I think we've been barking up the wrong tree."

"If he left London at eleven-thirty, as he said, what time *would* he have arrived at this garage?"

"More or less at the time stated. The garage is about forty-five miles out of Town. The roads would be clear and he has an M.G. Sports. No, Barnes has his alibi all right. What's more, I can't pin any motive on him for either the Farnham or Lehaye affair. The only reasons we have for suspecting him at all are (*a*) that he knew Farnham would be getting off the nine-ten, and (*b*) his curious anxiety about that note."

"So we're right back where we started, sir?"

"We are. With Farnham as our only plausible suspect. I suppose he couldn't have placed that bottle there to mislead us? I mean to lend colour to the story that he had been attacked and dumped in the summer-house. After all, he was quite ready to draw attention to the exact spot where he was supposed to have been assaulted. He knew damn well that if we started snooping round about that milestone we should soon stumble on the discarded bottle. It would also explain why his were the only finger-prints on it."

"You know," said. Dane slowly, "I believe you've got something there. The veronal was only mixed with the dregs of brandy in that bottle left near the milestone, and the brandy he swiped, sir, was the real stuff, eh? I mean after he'd chucked the girl in the lake he must have squatted down in that summer-house and drunk himself silly. Otherwise the doc wouldn't have found the usual symptoms of an alcoholic collapse, which are more or less identical with those of veronal. You know, I reckon that's smart."

Harting's depression lifted a little at the sergeant's ingenuous flattery.

"What's more, Dane, he had that little extra which the others haven't got—*motive!*"

2

They arrived just in time for the inquest, which was lucky, since Mr. Bibsee, the coroner, was a stickler for punctuality. By now, however, Harting had no doubt that a murder verdict would be brought in, and he wasn't disappointed.

As the proceedings broke up, Harting drifted over to Barnes, who had moved out on to the terrace.

"I should like you to inform us of any change of address, Mr. Barnes. We may still need your help."

"Well, if you'll let me return to the cottage I shall be there until the end of the week. After that I shall return to my flat in Byron Crescent, Kensington. For the rest of the day I shall be over here at Old Knolle, as we're all attending the funeral this afternoon. I wish you luck, Inspector."

"Thanks," said Harting.

As he and Dane took their places in the little black police car, he said, "We're going over to Fallow Cottage. The coast's all clear. I still think we've missed something of importance over there."

The two officials concerned themselves first with the sitting-room. Once there they examined every inch of the floor and upholstery for possible bloodstains, but, as before, they drew a blank. Taking an arm-chair to either side of the inglenook, they spent a solid hour analysing and re-analysing every factor in the case.

Dane started a fresh hare by asserting that the Inspector had wiped Millar off the suspect slate without going deep enough into his alibi. Dane's theory (which Harting admitted was quite a sound one) was that Millar had distinctly told Angela Walsh to meet him in the east pavilion. He himself had no intention of keeping the tryst since he had already fixed a rendezvous with Lehaye in the *south* pavilion. He waited there, chain-smoking until Lehaye turned up and, probably after a violent quarrel, knocked her unconscious. He then carried her round to the far side of the lake, placed her in the water and dashed helter-skelter into the house, where he was met by Richardson.

"You see," concluded Dane, "he used the Walsh girl as the basis of his alibi and an excuse for getting out into the grounds."

Harting objected. "But look here! What about Walsh's evidence? If he'd specifically told her the east pavilion she would have recalled the fact and told me in cross-examination. According to her, he merely said 'the pavilion,' with the result that they made a muddle of the whole thing."

"That's all very well, sir." Dane winked and chuckled. "But you know what these young wenches are when there's a lad in the case. By the time you cross-questioned her, she and young Millar could have laid their heads together. She might well have altered the facts a little, with the mistaken idea that it was her duty to shield the boy. Women are funny that way. No sense of civic obligations, but ready to perjure themselves blue in the face when somebody they're fond of gets into a jam."

"Umph, there may be something to it. Millar had motive, though not a strong one. So we've got to decide between Farnham and Millar; is that it?"

Dane nodded.

Harting went on, "What about taking a walk across the fields to the lake? We might find some clue on the way. It's a bit of routine I've neglected. We might at least discover if Lehaye was attacked here in the cottage or beside the lake itself."

"I don't like walking," grinned Dane. "But you're the boss."

It was just before they reached the second stile that Harting knew his hunch had been a sound one. The path at this point ran through some fairly extensive clumps of gorse, and the grass to the sides of the track was long and sere. It was in this straggling grass that the Inspector spotted a woman's scarlet sandal. There was no doubt about it, it paired up perfectly with the one found on the dead girl!

"So that settles that!" exclaimed the inspector with great satisfaction. "We can now safely assume that Lehaye *was* attacked in the cottage. Damn it all, Dane! I'm absolutely certain that we've missed some vital clue in the place. Let's go back and take one final look. Perseverance pays good dividends, y'know."

As they walked back over the fields Dane observed, "Well, this knocks young Millar out of it. He wouldn't have had time to smoke those ten cigarettes in the pavilion *and* nip across to the cottage to attack the girl."

"Unless the cigarette stubs were placed there as a deliberate blind." Harting lifted his shoulders and added in a surly voice, "But all this high-faluting theory makes me tired. If only we could get our hands on a couple of first-class clues. We're in the clouds. I want to bring the case down to earth—and *pronto!*"

3

But a hair-fine investigation landed no further catch. Harting and Dane dropped into the arm-chairs on either side of the inglenook, grouchy and defeated. There, for the umpteenth time, they let their minds travel over the ramifications of the case. Farnham? Millar? Richardson? Barnes? An outside job? Query after query they took up, harried and set aside. But the deeper they went into this tricky morass, the worse they got bogged. At the end of an hour they were no nearer to driving the case home to a logical conclusion.

It was then that Harting's acute powers of observation stumbled on an astounding and totally unexpected clue. At first the detail seemed so trivial and irrelevant that he did not trouble to draw attention to it. Yet his roving eye kept coming back to this curious little discrepancy. At length he could curb his curiosity no longer.

"I say, Dane, have you noticed anything peculiar about that pair of tumbler switches by the door?"

"Tumbler switches, sir? What the—?"

"Sorry, but I'm tidy-minded. Come over and I'll show you what I mean."

Fallow Cottage, like most domiciles in the remoter rural areas, drew its electricity from the grid. In the interests of expense the majority of these places had been converted from oil-lamps to electricity by the installation of what was called "outside wiring." In other words, the wires, instead of being concealed behind the plaster of the walls, were visible as narrow lead tubes leading from the mains to the switches and the switches to the lamp-holders.

The curious fact which had aroused Harting's interest was simply this: although there were two switches screwed on to the panel, only one of them was wired.

"Funny," agreed Dane. "But I don't see that it—"

He never completed the sentence, for Harting, with typical curiosity, had clicked on the unwired switch. Almost coincident with the click there was the sound of a strangely reverberant bang from a point directly behind the wall; a sound which suggested that something of considerable weight had been slammed home like a door!

"Good God, sir, what's that?" exclaimed Dane.

"The devil only knows! Come on, let's take a look. It's the kitchen through there. Something must have fallen."

4

It did not take Harting two seconds to realize what *had* fallen. At a spot on the kitchen wall, somewhat to the left of the switch-panel in the sitting-room, was a sturdy metal clasp. Directly below the clasp was an enormous oak-panelled chest. Without hesitation, Harting lifted the lid.

"Well, I'll be b... blowed, sir! It's a blooming bath! Cunning idea, eh? Lid must have been propped up and you mucking about with that switch must have set up a vibration and jerked it forward."

Harting shook his head. "Not on your life, Dane. We're on to something here. By heaven we are! Look, man, the lid clips into this spring clasp. It would have taken a devil of a shake on the wall to have loosened it. Quick! Run round and work the switch again, will you? I'll stay here and watch."

The result was just as the Inspector had anticipated. No sooner had Dane actuated the switch than the metal clasp lifted and the heavy oak lid crashed down. Harting caught it before it slammed against the tall wooden sides which boxed in the enamel bath. Its weight was surprising, and as he gently lowered it into place he noticed another peculiar detail. There was a species of spring-lock on the front of the chest which could be made to engage with the lid by the release of a small knob—rather like the little knob which frees the action of a Yale lock. The moment he had clicked over this knob he found it impossible to lift the lid.

Suddenly an amazing, a monstrous, a sickening idea came to him!

It was this. *Had Deirdre Lehaye been drowned in this infernal contraption which passed as an ordinary but somewhat outsized bath?*

The moment Dane had waddled back into the kitchen, Harting snapped out, "My God, Dane, we've found what we're looking for—a nice fat clue! I'm ready to lay a penny to the Bank of England that Lehaye was not drowned in the lake. She was drowned here in this bath! The lake was a blind. She was dumped there to draw our attention away from the cottage. Heavens above! I'm beginning to see daylight now!" The inspector's excitement was growing with every breath he drew. Dane teetered about the kitchen, sucking his teeth and "tut-tutting" with surprise and delight. "That blow on the vault of the girl's head—she was never attacked and struck with a blunt instrument as we imagined. That contusion was the result of this lid crashing on to her cranium as she sat in the bath. It probably knocked her silly. Her nose and mouth were under water, and... hey presto!... napoo! What's more, she couldn't have struggled out of the damn thing, because there's a spring lock on the chest, which had obviously been set to engage the lid as it fell. So there she was—trapped and tricked and done for!"

"Lordy-lordy," breathed Dane. "What lovely ideas some people do get, don't they, sir?"

"Some people?" inquired Harting. "This bath has been deliberately tinkered with for a specific purpose, Dane. There's only one person who could have done it, and that, without any shadow of doubt, is Barnes! Barnes was down here last night. Barnes murdered the girl. Barnes carried her across to the lake. And Barnes's alibi, m'lad, is about as rotten as a worm-eaten twig!"

"And Farnham?"

"I'll hazard a guess that Barnes was responsible for that job, too. But first things first, Sergeant. You're agreed that Lehaye *was* murdered as I suggest, eh?"

The ham-like hand caressed the manifold chins.

"Well," admitted Dane with irritating caution, "it's more than possible, sir. But there's something that still puzzles me." He jerked a stubby thumb at the boxed-in bath. "That contraption as it stands isn't fool-proof. This way—there wouldn't be more than eight to twelve inches of water in the bath, I reckon. That's about average, say. When the lid came down, it's more than likely the girl would have fallen back with her head still clear of the water. Then there's another point, sir. What if the girl had been lying right down, having a soak, so to speak?"

"I can clear up that last objection at once," said Harting. "We can take it that Barnes was in the sitting-room waiting to work that switch. The walls in these old places aren't exactly sound-proof, you know. He'd hear the girl turn off the water and get into the bath. That would, more or less, be his signal. You see, Dane, nine hundred and ninety-nine people out of a thousand sit upright when they first get into a hot bath. The splash and soak ritual comes later. The other point is more tricky, and at the moment I can't see how it was overcome. Quite frankly, I refuse to bother my head with it. We've more important things to do. First and foremost, we've got to break Barnes's alibi. Now that we really suspect the fellow, there's one way we can do it without wasting time. We must find out from the respective telephone exchanges if those three calls were put through—the two that Barnes claimed to have made from Kensington to Lehaye and Richardson, and the call Lehaye was supposed to have put through to his flat. The latter can be traced here at the Lambdon exchange, the others through Kensington. My suggestion is this. You walk down to the village and deal with the Lambdon call; I'll drive direct to Town and deal with the others."

"Wouldn't it save time to ring up and make the London inquiries, sir?"

"It would, Dane; but I also intend to look in on Mrs. Evandine Barron and see if I can't make her come a bit cleaner than she did with you. I'm convinced now that her note to Lehaye is connected with Barnes. If I can find out *just* how it's connected, we'll probably get his motive for the murder."

"And after I've been to the exchange, sir?"

"Get up to Old Knolle and tell Barnes—er—with the Chief Constable's compliments, that we should deem it a favour if he'd keep clear of Fallow Cottage for another twenty four hours. Say no more than that—understand? We'll get together again at H.Q. this evening—say eight o'clock."

5

"Strange," thought Harting when, about a couple of hours later, he left the Kensington exchange for Dickers Place, "how things begin to happen thick and fast the moment one's rounded a sticky corner. After the inquest to-day Barnes was a doubtful starter in the Hangman's Stakes, and now, damn it, he's a hot favourite. So those calls were *not* put through to Lambdon from his flat in Byron Crescent, eh? Admit that doesn't preclude the possibility that he rang up from a London call-box. But Barnes swore they were put through from his flat, which is good enough for me. If he troubled to lie, then he lied because he wanted to conceal something of importance from the police. In other words, his actual whereabouts between the hours of nine-ten and one a.m. last Saturday. Now for Mrs. Evandine Barron!"

As luck would have it, the Inspector found Mrs. Barron free of her horrific incubus which so far had not returned from school. Visualizing the elegant and self-possessed Mr. Barnes, Harting could forge no link between him and this faded creature with the dyed hair and strident voice. That she was uneasy in his presence he sensed at once, and he decided to take advantage of this perturbation before it wore thin.

"See here, Mrs. Barron, you've read all about Miss Lehaye in the papers, so I'm not going to bother you with details. I've come, more or less, direct from the inquest, and in case you haven't seen the stop-press of the midday editions, the coroner brought in a verdict of murder. I'll say no more than that. I'm investigating the case. I want information, and I've an idea that you can supply it."

"But really I hardly knew Miss Lehaye. Not since she's come up in the world. But of course, in the old days, when we were on the boards—"

"Yes, you've explained all that to Sergeant Dane. I'm not here to question you about your relationship with Miss Lehaye. I want to know just how Mr. Barnes fits into the picture."

"Barnes? Mr. Barnes? But I don't—"

"There's no need to tell me you don't know," cut in Harting, bluffing for all he was worth. "We've found out that you do. If you care to deny it, so much the worse for you. I needn't stress the fact, I take it, that I'm investigating a murder case, Mrs. Barron? I repeat—how does Mr. Barnes enter into the picture?"

"But really—I don' see what you're driving at."

"Just this. Barnes had got something against Miss Lehaye, hadn't he? He detested her. And you know what that 'something' is."

"Even if I do—" began Mrs. Barron, with a certain desperate perkiness. "I don't see that it's up to me—"

"You realize that it's a crime to withhold information from the police?"

"Maybe. But Miss Lehaye has been pretty fair to me and Jim. I owe her a lot, and the best way I can repay her now, I guess, is to keep my mouth shut about her affairs."

"That's just about the worst way, Mrs. Barron. If you want to see justice done in this case, you've got to talk and talk now!"

For a moment Mrs. Barron hesitated, aware with acute discomfort that Harting's blue-grey eyes were fixed unwaveringly on hers. Her glance fell. She jerked out her cigarette and crossed to the window. All her movements were tense. The inspector waited with baited breath. Was his bluff going to draw a dividend or not?

Then suddenly, to his great relief, he heard Mrs. Barron say, "It's a long story, you know, and I'd have given a lot to have kept quiet about all this. But they say the truth *will* out, don't they? So better now than in the police court, I suppose."

"I've plenty of time," said Harting, drawing out his notebook and settling himself more comfortably in his chair. "Well, Mrs. Barron?"

"Well, it all began about eight years ago in Manchester, when I was teamed up with old Sammy West in a conjuring act. We were booked in for a season at the Palladion, where Ike Finnestein was running one of his hack revues. *Music and Magic*, it was called, and it was just about the lousiest show ever seen on the road. And that's saying plenty! Well, I got pally with a girl in the second row of the beauty chorus, who was digging in the same joint. We were both trying to make out, and I guess that drew us together a lot. She called herself Deirdre Deane then, which was no more her real name than Deirdre Lehaye is now. But that's off the point. There was a chap in Ike's revue doing monologues—a dude number—who fell for me good and hard. I was fool enough to swallow his blarney, and before I could straighten out the kinks in my heart I was married." Mrs. Barron paused, stuck a cigarette jauntily in her mouth and struck a vesta on the sole of her shoe. "I told you it was a long story, Inspector, but you asked for it."

"Go on, Mrs. Barron, please. I'm interested—very!"

"Well, this is where I show myself up as a prize sucker, and don't think I'm kidding. I ought to have guessed that the fellow wasn't a sticker, and when he knew there was a kid on the way he just walked out on me. So there I was, stranded in Manchester, with a baby in the making and the usual reputation that sticks to a girl when she looks as unmarried as I did then! My double act with old Sammy West went by the boards when I was nearing my time. I hadn't got the right outline for a conjuror's stooge. Oh, Sammy was fair enough, but he had to think of the act. When I dropped out he teamed up with a bad 'un and his act went to blazes."

"And then Jim Barron came along?" Harting had heard this kind of yarn before.

Mrs. Barron nodded. "He was living in the same lodgings as me at the time. A decent chap in a steady job—he's a bricklayer—and he fell hard for me and did the one thing I was dreading."

"You mean he asked you to marry him to legitimize the child that was on the way?"

"That's about it." Mrs. Barron's eyes glistened with a sudden flood of tears. "Somehow, like the fool I was, I hadn't the heart to tell him the truth. I made up some cock-and-bull story about not being the marrying sort and tried to edge him off. But there was no stopping Jimmy—bless him! 'All right,' he says, 'if there's to be no blooming wedding bells and orange blossom, we'll run in double harness *without* a wedding. There's the nipper to think of,' he says. We've had eight years of it now, Inspector, and never once has he mentioned the idea of us getting properly married. I've got his name and so has Horry. He seems to think that's all that matters. Oh, he's been a real good sort, has Jimmy!" Mrs. Barron dabbed her eyes with a dainty, yet none too clean, handkerchief and took a quick puff at her cigarette. "And—well, that's about all there is to it, I guess."

"But what the devil has all this got to do with Barnes?" shot out Harting, annoyed by this anti-climax.

"Oh, didn't I make it clear? *He was the dirty twister that married me and walked out before the kid was born!* He was the dude with the fancy suiting and toothbrush moustache. And God help me, according to the Law I'm still Mrs. Basil Barnes—that's all."

Inspector Harting emitted a whistle of perfect comprehension. So that was it? Why the devil hadn't it occurred to him before? The whole meaning of the note to Lehaye was now as transparent as glass.

He said briskly, "And just lately you chanced to meet Miss Lehaye again?"

Mrs. Barron smiled. "It was no chance. She went round the agencies, found out my address and looked me up. Need I tell you the rest of the story, Inspector?"

"I think I can guess it." He had Willy Farnham in mind. "Blackmail, wasn't it? With a rake-off for you?"

"Increased maintenance more like!" said Mrs. Barron tartly. "You can't pin anything on to me. I didn't like the idea, and that's straight. But

Miss Lehaye knew how to get round me. Seems that Basil had just got himself engaged to a pretty little bit in the legitimate. Crazy about her, so Miss Lehaye said. So we just teamed up on our last double act and called round at his flat one night. After that he came quietly, Inspector. Signed on the dotted line, as it were, and paid up like a lamb."

"How much?"

"Fifteen quid a week. Ten for Miss Lehaye. A fiver for me."

"Good God!"

"Well, do you blame me?" flared up Mrs. Basil Barnes. "Jim and me have had a hard time. The poor lad's been stood off for months on end. When Miss Lehaye came along with her proposition it didn't take me long to see that she was first cousin to an angel."

"Barnes realized he'd met Miss Lehaye before?" asked Harting.

"No. That's the funny thing. He had a feeling that her face was familiar, but he couldn't place her. But she re-membered *him* all right, even though he was minus his ducky little moustache and ebony cane. My God! his was a bad act, too—real right-down lousy!"

Harting rose and held out his hand. "Well, Mrs. Barnes, you've been very sensible and most helpful. A pity you weren't so frank with the sergeant. It would have saved me a lot of time."

"Don't mention it. But kindly lay off the 'Mrs. Barnes' slant. I've spent eight years trying to live it down and the sound of that name still turns my stomach over. Mind the stair-rail. It's rickety like the rest of this damned joint. S'long, Inspector."

CHAPTER XVIII

Inspector Harting Tells Another

I

WHEN HARTING ARRIVED BACK AT MILLWARD HEATH HE DID FULL justice to the meal which his wife had waiting for him, and drove round at once to headquarters. Dane was already in the office.

"Lordy-lordy, sir! you look as pleased as a kitten with two tails."

Harting dug his subordinate playfully in the ribs, proof that he was in an abnormal state of jubilation.

"I am, Dane, I am! I've succeeded in doing something that you failed to do."

"What's that?"

"Getting a woman to tell the truth."

"Mrs. Evandine Barron, eh, sir?"

"Mrs. Basil Barnes."

"Phew!"

"Very apt, Dane. It *is* 'phew'! There's no need to tell me how you got on at the Lambdon exchange. I know the answer already. Lehaye never put through that call to Town."

"Right first time, sir. Oh, and I explained to Mr. Basil Blooming Barnes about Fallow Cottage. He seemed a bit annoyed about it, so I took the precaution of posting a local constable in the place."

"You're improving. One day you'll make quite a good policeman."

Dane chuckled his way into an arm-chair and then suddenly grew serious. "So Barnes *did* murder Lehaye, eh, sir? I mean there's no getting away from the fact now, is there?"

"There isn't. What's more, I'm convinced that he attacked and doped Farnham in Station Lane."

"For what reason, sir?"

"Well, I've been puzzling about this facet of the case all the way down from London. Suddenly I saw the whole thing as clear as crystal. I'll tell you just what occurred to me. To begin with, I reckon Barnes knew that Lehaye was blackmailing Farnham. He knew Farnham had stolen that money. Well and good, there was the old boy's motive for wanting to murder the girl. So with devilish ingenuity Barnes worked out what he considered a foolproof alibi. Firstly, he was out to build up the illusion that he didn't leave Kensington until eleven-thirty on Saturday night. Secondly, Farnham was to be planted in an incriminating spot close to the lake, where he intended to dump the body. In order to do this he had to get Farnham down to Lambdon, so he sent that telegram purporting to come from Lehaye. He knew only too well that the absent-minded old fellow wouldn't trouble to glance at the office of origin. What's more, he knew Farnham wouldn't be able to resist the invitation, I will say, Dane, his psychology is quite brilliant throughout. At the same time he wanted to let everybody at Old Knolle realize that Farnham was on his way to get even with the girl. He spoke of the old chap's outburst against Lehaye and subsequent confession to the theft, which had taken place that morning at the Beaumont."

"Surely that was a bit of luck, sir? I mean that Farnham happened to threaten the girl on the morning of the murder."

Harting smiled. "Not a bit of it. Barnes obviously led the old boy on. He's a simple sort of chap, and if he thought Barnes were in sympathy he'd open up without a thought. But this was the point. Barnes knew he had taken the money. The others didn't. So he had to let them know, otherwise Farnham's motive for wanting to kill the girl wouldn't be obvious. Get that?"

"Lovely, sir."

"Right!" Harting seemed to gather energy and enthusiasm as his reconstruction proceeded. "Now this is how I see it. Barnes went to Victoria to make sure that Farnham had reacted to his bogus telegram and had boarded the seven forty-three. Barnes then drove all out for Lambdon and arrived there before the train. He parked his car well out of sight and waited in the shadow of the trees unti Farnham came down Station Lane.

Then he caught the old boy a crack on the head from behind, probably with a rubber truncheon or something similar. Farnham went down for the count. But the moment he came round, Barnes was ready with the brandy-cum-veronal mixture and the old fellow swallowed it like a lamb before he was fully conscious. In brief, he never recognized Barnes. The crack on the head was essential, of course, otherwise he couldn't have got the veronal into Farnham's system. Neat, eh, Dane?"

"It's like a ruddy fairy tale, sir—but for Gawd's sake go on."

"Now this," said Harting, "is where I think I've been really smart. Not boasting, mark you—it's just due to the proper application of common sense. Note the time factor, Dane. It must have been about nine-thirty when Farnham passed out for the second time under the influence of the narcotic. We know Lehaye rang Old Knolle at nine forty-five. So, in my opinion, Barnes simply left Farnham lying in the nettles and long grass in the shadow of the trees and drove straight to Fallow Cottage."

Dane looked quizzical. "But what the devil—?"

"Listen, you blockhead! When Lehaye rang up Old Knolle, *Barnes was already at the cottage standing at the girl's elbow.*"

"What?"

"I'm sure of it. It's the only way we can explain Lehaye's remark about Barnes having asked her to ring back to his flat."

"But even then—"

"This way, Dane. Barnes simply burst in on Lehaye and told her that Farnham was out for her blood. Said he'd made sure that the old fellow had boarded the seven forty-three, so suggested that she should ring Old Knolle to make sure he hadn't shown up there."

"But what excuse did he make for not putting through the call himself?" objected Dane.

"Engaged to Angela Walsh, isn't he?" rapped out Harting. "Well, there's his excuse. He obviously made out that his fiancée would be in a pet if she learnt that he was alone with Lehaye in the cottage. Probably quite true, in its way. You know how jealous a young girl can be when she's gone down for the count. To make things even more plausible, he got Lehaye to slip in that remark about ringing back to his flat in Town. You like it?"

"It's the goods, sir," wheezed Dane with genuine admiration. "No doubt about it."

"Right! Now what happens? Barnes says something to this effect: 'Look here, it's not safe for you to sleep here alone to-night in case Farnham turns up, so I'll do the decent thing and keep you company.' He then suggests she might as well have her bath and get to bed."

"But could he be sure of that bath, sir?"

"He probably knew this nightly bath was a fetish with the girl. It *is* with some people. They fondly imagine that if they don't soak themselves half silly in boiling water every night they won't get a wink of sleep. It's nothing to do with cleanliness. I understand Lehaye suffered from insomnia. So there you are."

"O.K. I'll accept the bath, sir."

"That's handsome of you. Thanks. Can I proceed? Very well. Lehaye undresses and gets into the bath. Barnes presses that infernal switch and down comes the lid. In a very short time the girl is dead—asphyxiation due to drowning. The time now is probably about ten-fifteen or ten-twenty. Barnes then lets the water out of the bath and adorns the girl's nakedness with those confounded white satin pyjamas arid a pair of heelless slippers, taking care to leave no wet patches on the floor."

"But half a mo', sir," broke in the sergeant, perplexed. "Them pyjamas was still in her bed."

"Quite. But why shouldn't a second pair be airing in the kitchen? There was a domestic heater in the room. What more natural? They're close at hand, so Barnes obviously makes use of them. Her frock and underwear he gathers up and places on the chair beside her bed. Everything, you see, to draw our attention away from the kitchen. Then, before carrying the dead girl across the fields to the lake, he makes sure that the sitting-room light is left on, the front door wide open, and the handkerchief he has lifted from Farnham dropped in a conspicuous place."

"Then he ups with the corpse," went on Dane with ever-increasing enthusiasm, "and offs with it over the fields, not noticing that one of them sandals had come adrift."

"Correct, Dane. And at eleven-fifteen he dumps the body in the lake."

"You seem pretty sure of the time, sir."

"I am, Dane. You see, that was the time Miss Maddison looked out of her window and saw the figure kneeling by the lake and looking into the water. This done, Barnes returns to the cottage to collect his car."

"But didn't that Maddison woman say he moved off towards the paddock?"

"Yes. He probably made a deliberate détour, just in case he'd been seen. Now follow what happens. We'll assume he's at the wheel of his car again by eleven twenty-five. At eleven-thirty he's in the telephone kiosk outside the Railway Hotel at Lambdon Halt ringing up Richardson at Old Knolle. He speaks of getting down to Lambdon at one o'clock. All clear?"

"Perfectly, sir."

"Right! It's now eleven-forty or thereabouts, and our next check-up on Barnes is when he called at Ted Carstairs's garage at twelve twenty-five, to take in petrol. Well, that's simple enough. All he had to do was to drive to a point beyond the garage, turn and approach the garage from the London direction. The Hawkhurst-Lambdon road, as you know, passes Lambdon Halt, and in Station Lane Barnes stops the car and takes Farnham on board. The old boy, of course, is still under the influence of the drug. Just short of the drive gates he stops the car, carries the old boy down to the lake and shoves his legs into the shallow water, coating his shoes and trouser legs with mud. He then dumps him in the summer-house, returns to the car, and drives up to the manor almost on the dot of one. To clarify the time factor I jotted down these notes over supper. Take a look at them."

BARNES'S MOVEMENTS	ESTIMATED TIME	
Enquires Victoria	7.50	p.m.
Arrives Lambdon Halt (in car)	9.10	"
Attacks Farnham in Station Lane	9.25	"
Arrives Fallow Cottage (in car)	9.40	"
Gets Lehaye to ring Old Knolle	9.55	"
Murders her in cottage	10.0	"
Places body in lake	11.15	"
Rings Old Knolle from call-box (Railway Hotel)	11.30	"
Takes in petrol on Flimwell-Hawkhurst road	12.25	a.m
Gets Farnham into summer-house	12.55	"
Arrives Old Knolle	1.0	"

"The rest was as easy as kiss your hand. The whole household roused to search for the girl, Barnes having sworn that he'd put a phone-call through to her about eleven-fifteen and got no reply. You sense the atmosphere he'd created, Dane? Naturally he more or less took command of the outdoor search-party, with the result that it wasn't many minutes before the body of Lehaye was discovered. Later, when he and young Millar went to look for Farnham, it wasn't chance that took them to the summer-house. And that, unless I'm sadly mistaken, is how the whole thing was worked."

Sergeant Dane was just one big, beaming acolyte at the feet of his very superior officer.

"Where do we go from here, sir?"

Harting glanced at the wall clock. "Nine forty-five, eh? I think we'll pick up Richardson at Old Knolle and give him some inkling of what we suspect. We'll also get Sanders, the borough engineer, to come along with us and take another look at that infernal bath."

2

By clever manipulation Sergeant Dane succeeded in withdrawing Sam Richardson from Old Knolle without the rest of the house-party knowing anything about it. Sanders had willingly offered his expert services and the four of them drove over at once to Fallow Cottage. The constable who had been left in charge opened up to them; and while Dane and the borough engineer examined the switch apparatus, Harting drew Sam aside into the little dining-room.

A few general hints were enough to let Sam see which way the wind was blowing. His astonishment was intense; his regret profound. But in the light of all that had taken place and the calculating manner in which the crime had been conceived and executed, even *his* warm sympathies were chilled to the marrow. If he did not see Barnes as an inhuman monster, he could only view him as a man destitute of all pity and decency. Granted that Deirdre's behaviour had roused Barnes to a state of acute desperation, but the revenge he had taken on the girl was out of all proportion to the mental suffering she had inflicted on him. Above all,

Sam's thoughts hovered around Angela, who was destined, poor child, to walk through the shadows before coming once more into the sunlight. The shock to her would be sharp, but not, he prayed, ineradicable. He sighed. How frail and merciless and stupid was human nature; how vastly difficult to keep faith in and idealize!

"You will make the arrest to-night?"

Harting nodded. "I'm afraid so, Mr. Richardson. I obtained the warrant before I left Millward Heath. Once I have the expert advice of Sanders, I think we can claim to have driven the case to its absolute conclusion."

They moved back into the sitting-room, where Sanders had unscrewed the switch and carefully opened up a section of the plaster wall.

"Quite elementary," he said. "The switch merely actuated a wire which runs through this metal tube let into the wall. See for yourself, Inspector. The wire was hooked to the back of the spring clasp which held the lid in position when it was raised. A small tug on the wire, the clasp lifted and the lid crashed down. There's also a second hook inside the tumbler which enabled him to disengage the apparatus in case anybody clicked over the bogus switch by accident. I repeat, it's all very simple, but it's foolproof!"

"I still come back to my point, gentlemen," said Dane stoutly. "If the girl just fell back after the blow on the head, it's more than possible her nose and mouth would be above water. In my opinion, Barnes isn't the sort of chap to overlook such a point."

"You're suggesting that he got over this dangerous possibility in some ingenious way, is that it, Sergeant?" asked Sanders.

"I do, sir."

"You mean he might have dashed in, lifted the lid and turned on the tap until the bath was full, and then closed the lid again?"

Dane shook his head. "Too risky, sir. He couldn't be sure that the fall of the lid would knock the girl unconscious, could he? Suppose she recognized him? Suppose she managed to struggle out of the bath? What then? She might not suspect attempted murder, but Barnes might well have missed his opportunity to work out his devil-spawned scheme." He turned to Harting. "After all, sir, there's the Farnham angle of the case to take into account."

"Quite," agreed the Inspector. "So what? Could Barnes have tampered with the water-mains in any way and—?"

Suddenly Sam broke into the conversation. His excitement was undisguised.

"Half a minute, Harting! I believe I can help you over this. Yes, yes, the more I think about it, the more odd it seems. Some little time ago I walked over from Old Knolle to see Barnes, who was week-ending down here on his own. When I arrived I found him digging a trench under the kitchen window."

"A trench?" exclaimed the Inspector.

"Yes; he claimed that the drains were stopped. But I can't help feeling that it was odd, as I said before. Barnes is not the type of fellow to take any pride in being a handyman about his own house. He'd call in an expert. Moreover, it was a very wet morning and he looked soaked to the skin."

The hunt was on again.

In a little under half an hour Harting realized that the last piece of the puzzle had clicked into place. Sanders knew just what to look for and he found it! Under the gravel of the garden path was a clumsily contrived manhole. Barnes's plumbing was crude but effective. The water-main had been tapped at this point and the flow of water controlled by means of a stopcock sunk inside the manhole. From there the pipe had been directed through the kitchen wall, under the floorboards and thus up inside the enormous box-bath. The jet was so arranged that the water spurted into the bath through the grilled waste-hole just below the actual taps.

"Ingenuity and foresight could go no further!" thought Harting, amazed at the fellow's diabolical cunning.

There was no doubt that he had learnt through practice just how long to keep the stopcock open in order to raise the water level to the appropriate height. Imprisoned there under the locked and heavy lid, even if she were still conscious, what hope had the girl of freeing herself from this gruesome trap? A brief and frantic struggle, perhaps, and then—silence.

When Inspector Harting looked back on this case he always marvelled; for his reconstruction of the crime, set out in his office to Sergeant Dane that Tuesday night, was subsequently proved up to the hilt. He had, in his extremely comprehensive theory, been a hundred per cent. correct!

CHAPTER XIX

Logical Conclusions

I

DURING THE COURSE OF THE FOLLOWING YEAR THESE NOTICES appeared respectively in the *Notting Hill Journal* and the *London Evening Tidings*.

The first was set up under the bald column-heading which newspapers reserve for the reporting of man's three greatest adventures in life—*Births, Marriages, Deaths*. It read:

BARRON—BARNES—*At St. Mary's Church, Notting Hill, on May 16th, by the Rev. Peter Franks—Evandine Amelia, only daughter of the late Mr. and Mrs. J. Preece of Redhill, Surrey, to James William, second son of Mr. and Mrs. T. Barron, of Beckenham, Kent.*

The second read:

The marriage took place to-day at St. George's, Hanover Square, of Mr. Rudolph Millar, the playwright, and Miss Angela Walsh, the well-known young actress now appearing in Mr. Millar's play "Pigs in Porcelain" at the New Theatre. "Pigs in Porcelain" was an instantaneous success when it was first produced at the Beaumont Theatre some months ago. It was hailed by the critics as heralding the arrival of yet another brilliant young dramatist. Miss Walsh's performance in the play has been described as "one of the most tender and sympathetic interpretations seen in years". Among those present at to-day's ceremony were Mr. Sam Richardson, the millionaire philanthropist, Miss Clara Maddison, Mr. Willy Farnham...

DEATH KNOWS
NO CALENDAR

CHAPTER I

The Littel Bottel

I

Mr. and Mrs. John Arundel
request the pleasure
of
your company
at
the formal opening of their recently completed licensed premises
known as
The Littel Bottel
Opening Time—6 p.m. Tuesday, June 7th.

R.S.V.P. The Oasts, Beckwood.

THE REV. PETER SWALE-REID GLANCED AT THE EXPENSIVE INVITA-
tion card with an expression of disgust. He was seated at his desk
in the study of Beckwood Rectory, jotting down notes for his sermon. A
sheet of noble thoughts, in fact, was still clutched in his left hand as if to
balance up the darker implications of the Arundels' invitation. The word-
ing at first puzzled him, until he recalled a rumour which had reached him
via Lady Dingle concerning the Arundels' latest and most vulgar excess.

"My dear man," said Lady Dingle. "It's really very amusing and
most original. But then you'll admit, Lydia and John are *always* original.
We've come to expect it and take it too much for granted. But they do *so*
much to brighten our little lives in Beckwood. I hear—of course it may
be no more than parochial gossip—but I hear they've fitted up John's
old workroom as a bar. A perfect replica, my dear man—including the

beer-engines. I *do* think it's enterprising of them, don't you? They're sure to invite you to the formal opening because you've always been such a close friend of Lydia's, haven't you? I'm sure she admires the wonderful way in which you can cast aside your cloth and enter into the worldly fun of us ordinary mortals."

Swale-Reid had left Beckwood Court in a tortured frame of mind. He wondered if Lady Dingle had been hinting at anything unseemly in her reference to his friendship with Lydia. For five years he had been on the alert for such innuendo, hypersensitive to criticism, swift to believe that the parish slighted him behind his back, suspecting some personal sneer whenever two heads were laid together. For five years the ceaseless battle had been waged—his faith set in the scales against the dead weight of his evil-doing. But the vision persisted none the less—the vision of Lydia Arundel, flamboyant, dynamic, dark-haired, armoured with her light and mocking laugh against any sense of morality. Even now the memory of that ghastly night, five years ago, filled him with the wildest remorse. Slowly he tore the invitation card into small pieces and dropped them into the waste-paper basket. Then, shuddering as if with cold, he buried his face in his hands.

His one horror had been that his parishioners suspected; that for all this time they had looked upon him as a hypocrite, a whited sepulchre, a man unworthy to be their spiritual guide. But how should they know? For all her twisted values Lydia was not one, praise the Lord! to put her private life on show. Sometimes (it even happened in church!) she caught his eye with a long teasing look of complicity which sent the blood rushing to his face. The brazen Jezebel! But she was clever enough to conceal this secret glance from other people. To her that dreadful night had been an amusing and unexpected incident. She could not see that it had cut his life in two. Time and again, aware of his sinfulness, he had taken the revolver from his drawer and walked in the Rectory fields on the verge of suicide. But he believed that one could not sidestep God's judgment. He had, in a dark moment, fallen from grace, and from that moment he must dedicate himself with redoubled vigour to the furtherance of God's word in his parish of Lower Beckwood. Lydia Arundel was his evil star, but he believed that, at last, his prayers had been answered. The spell of her worldly lures was waning. The star was in the descendant.

He would *not* attend the opening of The Littel Bottel, however original and amusing it might seem to Lady Dingle.

2

The invitation that morning had cropped up at many a Beckwood break-fast-table. Major Boddy, slowly savouring his kedgeree, had chuckled thickly at the little joke and wondered if John would have stocked his private bar with Irish whisky. He'd accept, of course. He had never taken kindly to social engagements, tea-parties in particular, but the Arundels' functions always went with a swing. Free-and-easy affairs, eh? Bohemian! That word wasn't much used nowadays, but it fitted Lydia like a glove. Fine figure of a woman, an accomplished artist, outspoken, witty, generous to a degree. After Sarah Dingle, his oldest and best friend in Beckwood.

Once, some seven years ago, before John Arundel had appeared on the scene— Major Boddy grunted and shook his head. Better forget it. Never had a sporting chance. He'd been in the Army then, seeing her only on leave. No money and no life to offer to a woman of Lydia's tastes and temperament. Well, he hadn't made an ass of himself, thank God! When the time came for him to retire he found Lydia waiting for him as a friend. And in the meantime she'd married John Arundel and moved into The Oasts, with her reputation as a painter already assured.

The Major's expression hardened and, taking a piece of toast, he snapped it with a certain satisfaction. Damned curious chap, John Arundel. Difficult to place. Difficult to assess. Women found him charming and unusual, but in his presence Boddy always felt on edge. Outwardly they were good friends, but behind this friendly façade the Major was uneasy and Arundel watchful. Boddy was only too ready to admit that their ways of life had been poles apart—he following a traditional, hide-bound career in the Army and Arundel the slip-shod, emotional vagaries of the stage. He'd never made a name for himself and he'd certainly made no money. His marriage with Lydia had hauled him at a single pull out of obscurity and poverty and set him up in Beckwood as a person of some consequence. Not that Arundel was a bad mixer or in any way a snob. On the contrary, he went out of his way to be pleasant to everybody in the parish. But that was just the point—this affability was not natural, it was assumed, cultivated, a part of the actor's stock-in-trade. And to Major Boddy, with his direct, unimaginative mind, John's charm and polish was anathema. It was only for Lydia's sake that he had the fellow round to bridge or gave him a round of golf. On the other hand, he was ready to admit that John Arundel was just the type for Lydia to have married. They had much in common—an easy morality, quick wits, imagination and if Lydia was content to feather their mutual nest with a not inconsiderable fortune, that was *her* pidgin. Her husband was a wonderful host. He spent her money with an air, dispersing it in the grand manner as if the cornucopia was inexhaustible. He was reputed to be working on a novel, but nobody had ever been privileged to see the manuscript.

3

This same invitation card was propped up against the scarred and dented pewter coffee-pot at Claydown Farm. With its gilt edges and richly embossed printing it looked out of place beside the homely appointments of Hawkinge's breakfast-table. From the chipped egg-cup to the thick willow-pattern cup and white-metal spoon everything breathed of utility. No sense of the æsthetic had ever penetrated the earth-bound skull of Stanley Hawkinge. He walked as if two enormous clods of clay were permanently stuck to his boots. His thoughts were as slow as his speech and, like a heaven-born writer, he never used two words where one was enough. He lived in an atmosphere of dour bachelordom in the big rambling farmhouse, tended by an ancient housekeeper who had once changed his nappies and sluiced him in a hip-bath. He still used the hip-bath, but now he sluiced himself and did not take kindly to Mrs. Pelt's reminiscences of the nursery.

Beckwood liked Hawkinge because he was a good farmer, a hard worker, a fearless rider to hounds and the finest shot in the district. The womenfolk put their heads together in sympathy and wondered why he had never married. Mothers with eligible daughters dangled them like gay trout-flies before his brooding eye, but for some reason he never rose to the bait. Only two people in Beckwood knew of the calamity which had overtaken him—one of these was his greatest confidant, Major Tom Boddy; the other was the cause of the calamity, Lydia Arundel. For Stanley Hawkinge, slow to kindle, had burst into a great erotic conflagration at the age of twenty-eight and for ten years Lydia had been the only woman in his life. His devotion was pathetic, dog-like and, in some ways, danger-ous. The very fact that he, the simplest of men, had been able to conceal it, showed that it was no ordinary passion. It had survived Lydia's own peculiar brand of mockery, her lack of amorous response, her subsequent marriage. It had even survived the hard-headed advice of Major Boddy.

In the dingy rooms of Claydown Farm, Hawkinge brooded over this one-sided affair, but always with a ray of hope sliding through the gloom. One day his slow devotion would be recognized and, in a blaze of passion, a veritable fire-ball of love, he would come into his own.

Wasn't this invitation a hint? She had not forgotten him in his lonely existence down in the valley. In the midst of her butterfly pleasures, these ridiculous poodle-faking parties, she needed him—the shady oak, the bastion of rock, the honest tankard amid the cocktail glasses.

4

That same morning Tite and Merry's grocery-van was drawn up on the side-drive of The Oasts. Jed Willis, the house-boy, aged sixty and a bit, was unloading it with the help of the van-driver. John Arundel, in a light twill suit and white-and-tan shoes, was supervising the work. He was doing it with the fussy importance of a supercargo directing the discharge of high explosives.

"No! No! Steady there, Willis. Make sure you've got the crate the right way up. Let me see now." He stuck a monocle into his left eye and appraised the label. "By heaven, yes! Careful with that one, Willis. Best

Irish blended. The Major would never forgive me if— No! No! Get sideways to it through the door. Mind the mat! You too, driver. Now get your
left hands *under* the crate and—oh, *do* take care, Willis!"

"Oi nearly 'ad un over that time, sir," observed Willis jovially. "It's
these 'ere boots. They're too big."

"You should buy boots that fit, my dear fellow."

"Oi didn't buy un. Oi 'ad un given to me."

"Really?"

"Aye—you gave un to me. They're too big."

"Well, we can't worry about that now. I'll see to it, Willis, at the proper
time. Now ease the crate on to the floor here, will you? Gently! Gently!
Now let me see, driver, how much more is there to come?"

The driver consulted a list. "One doz: Cinzano. One doz: Orange
bitters. One doz: Martell's gin. One doz: lime-juice—"

"Lime-juice? You're sure about that? It doesn't sound right to me,
y'know."

"Well, it's down on my list, sir. Together with twelve doz: pints light
ale. Six doz: pints milk stout—"

"All right! All right! We'll check up later. Come on now. Back to the
van. Back to the van, Willis."

"About them boots, sir."

"Some other time, Willis, *if* you please!"

"There's them ole brown shootin'-boots…"

"Possibly, possibly."

"Oh, and fifteen botts: maraschino cherries, sir."

"Botts?"

"Trade abbreviation for bottles, sir. Oh, and one half-doz: boxes fancy
cocktail-sticks."

"Oi like the look o' them boots, sir."

"So do I, Willis."

"That'll be the lot, sir."

"Good."

"Not fit for 'e to be seen about in, Oi reckon. Cracked uppers."

"Some other time, Willis."

"If you'll kindly sign here, sir. Receipt of delivery—see?"

5

For the remainder of the morning John worked like a beaver, splitting open crates, scattering straw, ranging the bottles along the glass-backed shelves. At eleven o'clock the publican from The Seven Bells came up and showed him how to charge and work the beer-engines. From twelve onwards John was busy tacking up notices and advertisements. Then he fixed the dartboard, tried out a lone "hand" on his own account, mixed himself a whisky-and-soda behind the bar-counter, and silently drank to the fortunes of The Littel Bottel. This done he crossed to the double-doors and flung them wide open to the murmurous beauty of the June morning. Stepping out on to the terrace, he mounted his monocle, turned and viewed this new offspring of his fertile but totally useless brain.

It was, he admitted, an extremely clever imitation of a small old-fashioned saloon-bar. From the gasolier to the red-rep curtains and brass foot-rail the illusion was perfect. Here, in his own house, he had created a corner that brought back to him with astonishing clarity his early days upon the boards. Days when he had drifted round the agents, hands in pockets because he had no gloves, coat-collar up to conceal a frayed under-collar. Raw and foggy mornings in the Charing Cross Road when he had sidled into the pungent warmth of many a saloon-bar for a "quick one" with the "boys". Dead, dispiriting days of seedy jauntiness, grand bluff and empty stomach. Days when he had learnt to listen and absorb the genteel accents of his betters, mastered those small, careless *nuances* of dress which marked down the gentleman. Palmy, spacious days which in retrospect distilled a gentle, glamorous sentimentality.

And now, viewing his latest masterpiece, John Arundel could well afford a smirk of satisfaction. He had travelled far since then. His eye took in appreciatively the warm brick façade of the house, the twin turrets of the converted oasts, the great clusters of climbing roses, a glimpse of Janet, the parlourmaid, setting the luncheon-table in the Georgian dining-room. Ease, wealth, an assured position in the community, a well-stocked wardrobe, unlimited alcohol, a spacious and artistic setting in which to play this greatest of all rôles—the country gentleman. He lit a cigarette and swung round to gaze over the garden. A lovely expanse of turf dipped to a little belt of conifers, above which rose the roof of Lydia's studio. A blue cedar cast its shade over flowering borders and rose-beds, beyond which, the perfect background, reared a high wall of mellow brick embroidered with espaliered pears and peaches.

Arundel sighed. It was a ripe idea, this little Edwardian bar. It was a reminder of his progress, a homely monument to his charm and cunning. He was about to turn back into the house when there was a flash of scarlet amid the conifers and a rich contralto voice calling him from the far end of the lawn. Like an old actor bracing himself for an entry, he altered his stance, fixed a welcoming smile upon his bland features and waved an elegant hand. Then in a voice vibrant with pleasure, he called back: "Welcome to The Littel Bottel! Welcome to The Littel Bottel, my angel!"

6

Lydia Arundel advanced down the lawn like a galleon in full sail. Over her scarlet frock she wore an unbuttoned overall smeared with the multi-coloured stains of brushes. Her blue-black hair, faultlessly coiffured, had about it, however, an air of carelessness. Her make-up, too, though beautifully contrived, suggested that Lydia was not over-anxious about her personal appearance. It was all fake, of course. This was studied untidiness brought to a fine art, for Lydia knew only too well just what the world demanded of her. First she had to be the woman, groomed and gowned for effect—then the painter, a little wild and "different", with a hint of the flamboyant, a veiled immorality. She gained her effect effortlessly, aided by a magnificent figure, a rich, rather husky voice and eyes which smouldered with an inner fire. Her self-assurance was immense. She moved through the world perfectly aware of the spells she cast over others less gifted.

Her husband seemed to shrink a little at her approach. He became less than life size. It was a feeling that he resented. She dominated him and pricked his *amour-propre* at every turn. But try as he would he could do nothing about it and because of this, deep, deep down, John hated his wife with a cold and calculated hatred. Sometimes he had great difficulty in hiding the fact.

"But how life-like! How perfect! How *fin de siècle!*" cried Lydia. "How cleverly you've managed to convey the atmosphere, my darling. You could only have achieved such a delicious result from first-hand observation."

"Are you suggesting—?" began John, at once on the defensive.

"I'm *never* suggestive," corrected Lydia. "What fun it will all be! I hope we have kind weather. 'The Littel Bottel'," she read from the Neon lights over the entrance. "It sounds so cosy and intimate. You didn't forget to send a card to the Rectory, my darling?"

"No, no, my angel. But I can't see Swale-Reid being interested in this sort of thing. A bit off his beat, eh?"

"Still I think he will come," said Lydia with a faint smile. "He's so devoted to me, you know. I've an idea that his Reverence is just the teeny-weeniest scrap in love with me, John darling."

"Fantastic!"

"Yes, isn't it? Oh, and John, I know it's most unladylike, but do you think you could draw me a nice glass of beer with one of those quaint-handled things? I've had a gruelling, despairing morning."

"The Dingle portrait?" inquired John as he strolled into The Littel Bottel and took up his post behind the bar.

Lydia nodded. "The trouble is that the dear woman has a face like a horse, so *intensely* like, my darling, that it's impossible to disguise the fact." She dropped on to a high stool before the bar. "Oh, isn't this fun!" John, catching her mood, whipped a handkerchief from his breast pocket and laid it over his arm. "A mild and bitter, John."

"A mild and bitter it shall be, my angel."

He worked the handle in a series of brief jerks as Parkinson had shown him that morning. He obtained a fine "head", pushed the glass across the counter and mixed himself another whisky-and-soda.

"To us!" he said heartily.

"To the future of our little enterprise," said Lydia, adding after an appreciative sip: "The Dingle has promised to bring her niece to the opening ceremony. Have you seen her, my darling? She's devastatingly pretty. We think of parading her before poor Stanley. Such big blue eyes! Such innocence! Really, darling, she makes me feel like a raddled old harridan."

"Tut, tut!" said John with tactful disapproval. "What's her name?"

"Honororia."

"Good God! I can't see that dumb fish Hawkinge falling for a wench with a name like that."

"Oh, it's a *sweet* name," protested Lydia. "Poor Stanley, he looks so stricken, doesn't he?"

"Secret sorrow, my angel." John laughed gaily. "Like the rest of this unenterprising parish, he's probably in love with you. The Beckwood males have no originality."

Lydia bridled with becoming girlishness. "How silly you are, John. So jealous, my darling. I won't have you thinking such things. It's not very nice for *me*, is it?"

"Sorry, my angel." He leant in confidential manner across the bar and declaimed in a thick voice redolent of whisky:

> *"Beauty itself doth of itself persuade*
> *The eyes of men without an orator."*

"How neat! How nice of you, darling. Shakespeare, of course. A mental hangover from your barn-storming days—it *must* be. What a pity your talents as an actor were never really appreciated by the best people."

John scowled. These were the kind of pin-pricks he had to suffer. Little poisonous darts aimed unerringly into the very heart of his vanity. God knew, he *earned* his living as Lydia Arundel's husband. Life at The Oasts was not all cakes and ale!

CHAPTER II

Party at The Oasts

I

I T SEEMED THAT LYDIA WAS NOT ONLY *persona grata* WITH GOOD-fortune but with the weather gods, for the following Tuesday dawned bright and beautiful. As the hours advanced there descended on Beckwood, like an inverted shining cup, one of those peerless June days that transform the face of rural England into an earthly paradise. The scent of the Étoile d'Hollande was heavy on the still air and the bees were working in the clover fields. The red tiles of The Oasts threw off an aura of shimmering heat. A few birds piped languidly in the feathery branches of the conifers and peace, clear and perfect, seemed to have settled over the village.

But in the heart of one man all was darkness and confusion. For the Rev. Peter Swale-Reid, meeting Lydia the day before at a garden-fête, had capitulated—weakly, completely and, what was so shameful, almost willingly. He had accepted her invitation to be present at the inauguration of The Littel Bottel. No matter that he advanced all manner of excuses, she took them lightly, mockingly and tossed them aside. He was left in her presence without defences; just a frail adolescent Adam confronted by a mature and sophisticated Eve. Why wouldn't she acknowledge the tortures inflicted upon him by that terrible memory? Why didn't she realize that his dreams were haunted by sinful visions and his waking hours hounded by the sound of her voice, the rich langour of her laughter? It was wrong, wrong! Armoured in his faith he should have turned a deaf ear to her persuasions, closed his eyes to that Gioconda smile and walked steadfastly along the paths of righteousness. Now he was committed to attend her vulgar party. He'd probably drink far more sherry than was good for him and wake up with a liver. His sermon would suffer. So would his temper. And once again he would fail in his duties as shepherd to his small but wayward flock.

"But Peter darling," she had said in a tearful voice. "It wouldn't *be* a party without you. You simply must come, if only to lend tone to the event. I'm so terrified that John will grow rowdy. You know how he does when he gets overexcited and you're the only one who can manage him in his cups." Then in a small voice: "And I've planned a special surprise for you. *So* original. We've bought a monk's costume from Clarkson's, and Willis is to go round with a collection-box for the Church Restoration Fund. And without you, Peter darling, it would be a dreadful flop. *Nobody* would give! But if you stand beside Willis and just glare, nobody will dare withhold. I thought it was such a lovely idea and now—now—"

The thought of Lydia in tears on *his* account had terrified Swale-Reid. It was at this point that he had capitulated.

2

By six-thirty that evening the party was in full swing. Major Boddy had made an inarticulate speech on the terrace. Lady Dingle had advanced with an enormous gilt key, unlocked the swing-doors and with a coy giggle declared The Littel Bottel to be open. The crowd had surged in. Thereafter conversation was brighter, wittier and far far louder. Soon the lawn and terrace were dotted with colourful groups like clusters of flowers, among which Lydia passed, a gaudy butterfly, to sip the honey of gossip and blind with the glory of her presence.

At seven o'clock Stanley Hawkinge appeared in a tight tweed suit and starched collar. He looked and was damned uncomfortable. Lydia saw him at once and descended with a blare of *bonhomie* that startled the pigeons off the roof. Hawkinge gripped her hand, stared dumbly into her eyes and stumbled off to where John, in a white jacket, was wise-cracking behind the bar. Later, fortified by two pint tankards, Stanley swayed forth to inspect "the menagerie", as he called it. And in this manner, fearlessly stalked by Lady Dingle, he came face to face with Honororia Preece. With greater alacrity than tact Lady Dingle rushed off and left them stranded.

For a moment, like two dumb beasts, they eyed each other. She, shy and anxious; he, awkward and sullen.

"Stupid stunt, this," he said at length.

She agreed.

"Waste of good money," he added.

She agreed again. His interest awakened, he looked at her with a less bovine eye.

"Simple things—that's what I like."

"Tho do I," lisped Honororia. "The thimple life. Thith thort of thing ith all tho thilly."

They decided to slip out through the wicket-gate beyond the studio and walk over the fields to Claydown Farm. He wanted to show her the horses and cows and pigs. She trotted along behind him like a meek and dutiful spaniel at the heel of its master, agreeing with everything he said. It was a new experience for Hawkinge to feel this domination over a woman, and he was enjoying it. Before they had visited the second cow-byre he had kissed her, with such force that she had no breath with which to make a formal protest. On their way back across the meadows, as the dusk was falling, Hawkinge clamped his arm round her waist and kept it there. She nestled up against his rough tweeds and closed her eyes. If this were her Auntie Dingle's choice, she was well content.

It was John who saw them approaching and reported the good news to Duenna Dingle. He had climbed one of the conifers for a bet, with a glass of water in one hand and a piece of anchovy-toast in the other.

"'Gone already! Inch-thick, knee-deep, o'er head and ears, a forked one,'" he declaimed. "It's worked, my dear lady! It's worked!"

They carried the grand tidings to Lydia, who was seated in quiet conversation with Major Boddy. She seemed to accept the news somewhat flatly, perhaps at heart a little piqued by Honororia's amazingly swift capture. Stanley had been a nuisance, but a pleasant, passive nuisance. His dumb admiration had become a habit and Lydia was not prepared to see him change his habits without first consulting her!

"Well, well," observed Tom Boddy. "It's a good thing if it comes off. Sound chap, Hawkinge. Cracking good shot! Wants a woman in his house. You agree, eh, Lydia?"

"Yes, I think so," said Lydia slowly. "But it's a trifle unexpected. The thought of Stanley in love is like a contradiction in terms. I've had no time to get used to it."

"Sssh! Look out!" hissed Lady Dingle. "Here they come."

Although no longer entwined, the couple advanced with a certain sheepishness. Hawkinge deliberately avoided Lydia's eye.

"Stanley darling, where *have* you been?" she asked. "The party's half over. We've already sent Willis to switch on the fairy-lights."

"Mithter Hawkinge hath been thowing me all hith lovely, lovely animalth," explained Honororia. "I know it wath dreadfully rude, Mitheth Arundel, but we thlipped away."

"No manners!" barked Lady Dingle with a broad wink at John and the Major. Then with a sigh: "But there's no gainsaying a really masterful man, is there, Mr. Hawkinge?"

"Pigs," explained Stanley. "Cows."

"Quite," said Lydia.

She accepted the Major's hand and rose imperiously from the garden-seat, as the fairy-lights suddenly came on and drew a round of applause from the guests.

"You'll excuse me," she added, with a pointed look at Hawkinge. "There are still so *many* people I haven't met."

"Umph!" thought the Major as he watched her departure. "Bit huffy, eh? Wonder why. Queer!"

He didn't realize that a woman nearing her forties is reluctant to sever any thread that links her with the past. Hawkinge, after all, was just one more spoon (honest pewter though it were) feeding her insatiable vanity. She had thought Stanley proof against any other woman's attractions. Otherwise she would never have conspired with Lady Dingle to parade that simpering schoolgirl before him!

3

Behind a clump of rhododendrons John and Willis were in heated argument.

"Come on, my dear fellow, don't be obstinate. It's all quite simple. You've only got to tie this girdle round your middle and pull the cowl over your head."

"Oi doan't like it," said Willis stubbornly. "It's blaspheemy in my 'umble opinion. Parson woan't like it neither. 'Tain't proper."

"Mr. Swale-Reid has given his full approval, Willis. Damn it, you'll be collecting for the church."

"Maybe. It's this 'ere dressin' up Oi doan't 'old with. Mockin' the cloth, this is."

"Oh, for heaven's sake—hurry! We don't want half the donors to sober up before you get round with the box. You want to strike the iron while it's hot on these occasions."

"Then there's another thing," argued Willis. "'Tain't Anglican."

"What the devil do you mean?"

"Monks," explained Willis. "'Tain't Church o' England."

Being uncertain about this delicate ethical point, John sidestepped the issue and led into another suit.

"It's worth ten bob to you, isn't it, Willis?"

"Oi never 'eld with monks. Oi've 'eard tales about they," insisted Willis.

"Fifteen bob then."

"Oi'd be deserting my faith to put on this 'ere garb, sir."

"Damn it all, man, I'll make it a quid!"

Willis considered the offer with a ferrety look, then slowly shook his head. "Tell 'e what Oi might do, sir. There's them pair o' ole shootin'-boots what ain't fit for a—"

"They're yours!" cried John promptly.

Willis nodded his satisfaction. "'And Oi that cloak then. Oi'll chance it."

4

On leaving Hawkinge and Honororia, Lydia had exercised a little fascination on some of the less exalted guests and then, somewhat exhausted, she had taken the flagged path through the conifers to the studio. The door was unlocked and the place in darkness and Lydia, knowing every inch of this territory, entered soundlessly. But once inside she was arrested by a conviction that somebody was already in the room. She froze into immobility and listened with all her senses at full stretch. She was not wrong in her judgment. Somebody was breathing gustily in the stillness, breathing that was now and then interrupted by a curious choking sob. Then suddenly a voice whispered into the darkness—an intense, shaken, sibilant voice that cut through her good-humour like a knife.

"Give me strength, O Lord, to withstand the lures of that painted Jezebel, that wanton daughter of joy who—"

At this uncomplimentary and highly personal remark, Lydia coughed and, with brutal unconcern, switched on the light. Mr. Swale-Reid, kneeling in the very centre of the studio, sprang up with an inarticulate cry and stood glaring at the scarlet woman smiling at him from the doorway.

"You!"

"This is all highly dramatic, Peter darling, and totally unnecessary. Particularly in my studio. Why can't you be reasonable? Come along now—don't you remember your Khayyám? 'The moving finger writes and having writ moves on.'"

"Pagan!" hissed Swale-Reid, gathering up his black felt hat from the model's throne. "Go away! Go away!"

"I *won't* go away!" said Lydia with emphasis. "You're acting like a spoilt child. I can't tolerate the manner, Peter darling, in which you revel so in your remorse. Good gracious! you're no more to blame than many another man in similar circumstances."

"Why did I come here to-night?" he wailed in anguish. "I was weak—weak!"

"Nothing of the sort! You came because I asked you to as a special favour, and being a gentleman you naturally accepted. As for these unhealthy histrionics—" Lydia placed a gentle hand on his sleeve. "Don't torture yourself, my dear man. I feel sure the parish would appreciate you far more if they knew."

"Don't touch me!"

"How very rude you are this evening. And don't look like that, Peter darling. You remind me of Savonarola, Cæsar Borgia and Torquemada all rolled into one. Quite murderous! It terrifies me. You wouldn't really like to put weed-killer in my breakfast porridge, would you, darling?"

"Yes," said Swale-Reid flatly. "I would." He added as postscript: "If I thought it would expiate my sin in the eyes of God."

"How delicious you are. So quaint." Then hastily: "Quick! Quick! Dust your knees and straighten your bib. You look like the Other Man in a French farce, my darling. I can hear footsteps."

The footsteps ended in the appearance of John Arundel and a hooded figure smoking a pipe.

"Ah, there you are, Swale-Reid! Having a little *tête-à-tête* with my wife, eh? Can't blame you, old man. She looks ravishing to-night, doesn't she? You do really, my angel. Well, here's Willis all togged up and ready to make his entry. Got the cigar-box, Willis? We'll drop in a bob's worth of coppers for a start so that it'll rattle properly. Then if you're ready, Swale-Reid, we'll start to pluck our pigeons, eh? Coming, my angel?"

"Later, John."

"What about you, Padre?"

Swale-Reid gulped and loosened his professional collar.

"For the sake of the Fund!" he said.

"'Lead on, Macduff!' cried John heartily, clapping Willis on the back. Then in horror: "Good God! Willis, you can't smoke that pipe. Out of character, my dear fellow. An anachronism. Pipes hadn't been invented, y'know, in the days of the Cistercians."

"Oi doan't 'old with monks," said Willis stoutly, reverting to his *leitmotiv.*

"That's got nothing to do with it!"

"Oi doan't like it," concluded Willis. "Pipe or no pipe, Oi doan't!"

The little *cortège* set off.

5

While Willis and the Rector were making their round, Major Boddy cornered John in the thatched summer-house. He had half-promised Lydia to keep an eye on her husband after the tree-climbing incident. But the

tussle with Willis behind the rhododendrons had done much to sober
John up. He had now passed into a maudlin phase in which everything
was tinged with a delicious sadness and everybody was his friend.

"Going with a swing, eh?" said Boddy. "Damned smart idea, that pub.
How's the book going?"

"Book?"

"The novel?"

"Oh, that." Then earnestly: "It's like giving birth to a child. Frankly,
old man, I sometimes wonder if the strain is worth while. After all, what
is a book? What *is* it, my dear fellow? One's soul, like a slice of indigestible ham, sandwiched between two cardboard covers. There, one says,
is all that I am and strive to be—on exhibition!" He shuddered. "Yes, I
sometimes wonder if I shall go on with it."

"It's a big work?" inquired Boddy.

"Colossal!"

"Ah!" breathed Boddy.

"Historical, of course," went on John. "It means continual research.
In fact I'm off again next month, old man. London—the British Museum.
Then on to Cambridge—the Bodleian, of course. Always chasing, chasing
after the Irrefutable Fact. Exhausting!"

"Quite."

"And furthermore," continued John in a thin voice. "This desire to
create comes between me and my marital happiness. Half the time I am
separated from Lydia. The last time I was away three months, old man—a
recluse, an anchorite, chained to the chariot of the Irrefutable Fact and all
this"—he waved a hand over the garden and the fairy-lights—"forsaken.
You ask me why I tolerate the pain of these separations?"

"I do," said Major Boddy obligingly.

"Because deep down I feel that one day I shall be appreciated. I shall
have made something worth-while. After all, old man, would you have
me live here in luxury and idleness at Lydia's expense? Evil tongues have
already wagged."

"Does Lydia approve?"

"She, too, is an artist," said John expansively.

"Has she seen the manuscript?"

"Never!" cried John. "It is an unfinished portrait. I'm never allowed to see a single canvas of Lydia's until it's finished. It's reciprocity, old man. She's so sensitive about her painting that she always locks the studio door when she's at work."

"Y'know, Arundel, I've never been able to make out why you don't return to the stage."

"The boards?" John raised a shocked hand and swept two or three cocktail glasses off the summer-house table. "My talents were never appreciated in the profession. Too subtle. Too delicate. Thistledown stuff, old man. Authorship is my *métier*. 'Whate'er my fate is, 'tis my fate to write.' Know it?"

"I think not," said Boddy after due reflection.

6

John had barely left the summer-house en route for the bar, when a massive figure loomed up in the entrance and, without a word, lowered itself into the chair facing Major Boddy. For a moment there was silence. Then, knowing his man, Boddy started the ball rolling.

"Enjoying yourself, Hawkinge?" A grunt from the semi-darkness. The Major went on: "Knowing how you feel about our hostess—surprised you showed up. Strategic error, m'boy. Only make you damned miserable."

A longer, even more profound silence descended, broken only by the distant raucous laughter of the best people enjoying themselves. The Major coughed. Hawkinge cleared his throat. An owl hooted. (Or was it Lady Dingle calling to her niece?) The Major lit his pipe. Hawkinge blew his nose.

"That niece of Lady Dingle's—a personable wench, eh, Hawkinge? Needs protecting. Unassuming little thing. Fluffy."

Another grunt and an even longer silence. Damn it all, would the fellah never speak? And then, suddenly, he did. "I'm in love with her," said Stanley hoarsely.

"By gad, that's quick work! You only met the girl to-night. Besides—er—what about Lydia? I always thought—"

"Mutton," asserted Stanley, "dressed as lamb."

The Major whistled softly. "I say! that sounds damned funny from you. Don't forget, m'boy, you've confided in me. I know pretty much what you've been through. Once went through the same sort of thing myself. Didn't last, thank God! But you've had ten years of it. Ten years of silent devotion, eh? Good show, that. You've been a sticker, Hawkinge."

"I wrote," growled Stanley fiercely, "letters. She never answered 'em."

"Tut-tut. Bad policy. Showed you were over keen."

"But she kept 'em," argued Stanley assertively. "She told me."

"I think she cared for you a little. Still does."

Stanley thumped the table with his ham-like fist. "I don't give a damn now! I'm free of her. Free! Think of it, Boddy, after ten rotten, awful years. And I've Honororia to thank for it." He paused and added in a husky bass: "Honororia Preece. Isn't it a grand name, Boddy?"

It was the longest speech he had ever made in the Major's hearing. The effort had apparently exhausted him for he threw himself back in his chair, breathing hard.

"You'll marry her, Hawkinge?"

"If she'll have me."

"Good. You need a woman, m'boy. Brood too much. Bad for your spleen. Makes you melancholic. Feel on top of the world to-night, eh? Push a bus over, what?"

A gay and blithesome grunt from the ponderous mass sprawled in the chair seemed to confirm Major Boddy's suspicions. Stanley was in heaven.

7

In twos and threes the guests were melting away. On the far side of the house cars were started up and driven with caution, with *extreme* caution, out on to the road. Farewell shrieks echoed under the stars. Soon the lawn was deserted and one by one the strings of fairy-lamps went out until only the Neon sign over the doorway of The Littel Bottel remained alight. Mr. Swale-Reid had long since departed with the cigar-box under his arm. Willis had slunk round to the kitchen to join his wife in a bottle or so of light ale which he had managed to secrete under his Cistercian cassock. Lydia, John and Tom Boddy were seated alone in the bar, where the latter was having his customary "one for the road". John was now in a beatific mood, full of self-approval.

"Well! Well! Well! What a success. Exceeded even *my* expectations. You're satisfied with the organization, my angel?"

"Perfectly," said Lydia without enthusiasm.

The Major cocked an eyebrow. "An eventful evening, eh, Lydia? Poor Hawkinge, taken a proper tumble this time. Mark my words, he'll marry that girl. Obstinate fellow when he gets his hackles up."

"Don't be vulgar, Tom," said Lydia crossly. "She hasn't accepted him yet. Such a simple little thing. Did you ever *see* such a frock?"

"Umph!" The Major was non-committal. "Surprised to see the Padre on parade," he went on.

"Looked very seedy, if you ask me," put in John. "A proper ghoul at the feast. Still, the old boy got a handsome collection. Mind you, I don't trust Willis. I think he appropriated some of the donations when they were in the shadows. A mercenary fellow. Too open to bribery and corruption. No loyalties."

Lydia rose and stifled a polite yawn. "Well, Tom darling, if you'll forgive me I'm going to bed. Beckwood *en masse* is a little overwhelming. Sweet of you to come."

She extended her hand. With a gallant gesture Boddy seized it and raised it to his lips. "For you, dear lady—anything."

With a little nod to her husband, she swept out of the bar, leaving a faint distillation of Coty's L'Aiment suspended on the alcoholic air. The Major looked after her with a nostalgic expression.

"A grand woman!" he sighed. "A thoroughbred!"

"'A child of our grandmother Eve, a female,'" declaimed John, striking an appropriate posture. "'Or, for thy more sweet understanding, a woman!'"

CHAPTER III

Odd Behaviour

I

MAJOR BODDY LIVED IN A SMALL HEAVILY BEAMED TUDOR COTTAGE on the main village street. Behind a neatly clipped quickset hedge he had a well-trained garden, interlaced with brick paths. Two small cannon, picked up cheap at some Army Ordnance Store, flanked the front door, with a pyramid of cannon-balls beneath them. Unfortunately they were of an entirely different calibre from that of the cannon. Apart from this oddity, everything about the place was on parade. Boddy's existence was orderly. His well-being was in the hands of a small bird-like man with ginger hair who had once been his batman. His name was Syd Gammon, who, quite apart from his exceptional curries and chop-sueys, had an astonishingly light hand with pastry. Many a Beckwood housewife, up against some little culinary problem, had slipped in through the back door of Ladysmith to consult Syd.

Boddy lived a simple life and his hobbies were a perfect reflection of his type—golf, shooting, fishing, bridge, crossword puzzles and detective fiction. The latter recreation was a passion with Boddy. He had saturated himself in this bastard form of literature and probably retained in his head more ingenious murder methods than any living man. He had a vast knowledge of time-factors, alibis, motives, ballistics, moulage, photo-micography and police procedure. As Syd had once expressed it to Jed Willis: "If the ole man wanted to do a chap in, 'e'd do him in so ruddy well that nobody would never know 'oo 'e was done in by!"

In keeping with this, it was natural that Tom Boddy, meeting the Chief Constable of the County Police at a neighbouring shoot, had struck up a lasting friendship. The Major was never absent from the public gallery at the Quarter Sessions and once, a high-spot in his retirement, he had shaken hands with a murderer. For two years he had been a Justice of the Peace. There were few detective writers in the country who had not, at one time or another, received a letter from Major Boddy beginning:

> *Dear Sir,*
> *Much as I appreciated your really capable novel, Title So-and-so, I should like to point out that on Page So-and-so you have made a regrettable slip which you might care to correct in any later editions, etc.*

2

The fire-ball which had been set in motion at the Arundels' party had, in a week, gathered momentum. Stanley Hawkinge dropped in to dinner at Beckwood Court with such tactless regularity that Lady Dingle felt he was already one of the family. He spoke little. He simply masticated with bored jaws and gazed dumbly at his Honororia. Within ten days their engagement was announced, a fact triumphantly conveyed by Lady Dingle to Lydia over the telephone.

"How nice, how very nice," said Lydia. "I trust Honororia is not rheumatic. Claydown is so *very* damp and I hear the drains are not all they should be, darling."

But Honororia—the simple little soul!—was far too enthralled to notice the mildew or the medieval plumbing. One Sunday, shortly after their engagement, she took tea with Stanley, under the acid eye of Mrs. Pelt, and lisped happily of the future.

"It theemth impothible that we thall really run thith great big plathe together—jutht you and I, Thtanley dear—alone! You're thure you thtill want to marry me?"

Stanley made a forcible and affirmative noise in his throat and re-declared his passion.

"I only athk becauthe I notithed you looking in thuch a *peculiar* way at Mitheth Arundel in church thith morning. I know you've alwayth been friendth with her, Thtanley dear, but it would break my heart if I thought it had been anything more than a thimple friendthip."

"Damn it all, Honororia!" protested Stanley uneasily.

But at once she had been contrite and gay as a kitten as she presided over the tea-pot. It was, she explained, only because she adored him so much that she felt these little twinges of jealousy. She didn't want to share her happiness with any woman, not even with the shadow of his past conquests. Although flattered by this suggestion, Stanley took up the cudgels in his own defence and like a fool declared that she was the first and only woman in his life. Reassured, Honororia let the delicate matter drop and began to discuss the new curtains and chair-covers for the sitting-room. Later they went out, hand in hand, to feed the pigs and inspect the new disk-harrow, an extravagance that Stanley had allowed himself in the first flush of his delight. But behind his outward enthusiasm, he seemed preoccupied. There was a worried expression on his rugged features as he drove her back to Beckwood Court and, for the first time since the party, he refused Lady Dingle's invitation to stay to dinner.

3

It was the following Tuesday that Major Boddy blundered into the beginnings of a mystery. It had come about quite naturally. His recreations were divided into two sections—physical, such as deep-digging, lawn-mowing, bicycling, dumbbell exercises and so forth; mental, such as bridge, letters to *The Times*, detective fiction and so forth. But at one period in the day these two forms of recreation joined hands and took an outing together. It was the Major's habit after dinner during the summer months to take a leisured walk through the woods and fields with his nose buried in his latest crime book. Once or twice he had come rather nasty croppers over mole-hills, but on the whole it was the most enjoyable hour of his day. He liked to feel that he was cheating Time by indulging in two forms of exercise at once. Nearly all his greatest triumphs as an amateur sleuth had been won during these perambulations.

On that particular Tuesday he had set off by the forge, crossed the stile into Beddow's Bottom, walked along the bank of Braddock's stream, turned off at Wilkinson's Spinney and entered the gloomy, sprawling expanse of Parker's Wood. The moss-covered paths deadened his footsteps and, dusk already falling, he advanced with the uncanny precision of a ghost. It was in this manner, coming to a small clearing in the very heart of the wood, that he saw two figures in deep and earnest conversation. With the instinct of an old soldier, Boddy took cover behind an oak-tree. There was something conspiratorial in the men's attitude, but who they were and what they were talking about he was unable to say. For some ten minutes he stood there listening to the low murmur of their voices, and then, stiffening with embarrassment, he realized that one of the men was coming in his direction. By careful timing he succeeded in edging round the tree so that it was always between him and the approaching figure. But for all that, before the man padded away into the gloom, he did not fail to record his identity.

There was no mistake about it, it was Jed Willis, the house-boy up at The Oasts.

4

After that, a whole series of strange events began to stalk in the parish. To Boddy, at the time, none of them seemed to be related; they were no more than isolated oddities of behaviour which did not reveal their full significance until many weeks later.

The first of these events was brought to the Major's notice by Miss Finnigan, of the Beckwood Post Office. She was a thin, dough-faced spinster with a huge coil of black hair piled on top of her head like a pudding and retained in position by an elaborate Spanish comb. She was the nerve-centre of village gossip and the post office itself a veritable clearing-house of scandal. Miss Finnigan also sold sweets, cigarettes, tobacco and walking-sticks and, on the principle that it is always good to stimulate local trade, Boddy bought his special Navy Cut at her counter. On this particular morning it was obvious that

Miss Finnigan was suffering from repressed emotional strain. Her hands shook as she tied up the Major's little parcel and handed him his change.

"Something wrong?" asked Boddy. "Don't look yourself, Miss Finnigan. Worried, eh?"

"Oh, dear me, Major Boddy, I hardly know what I'm up to this morning. All at sixes and sevens, I am. I'm surprised you haven't *heard*, Major Boddy. It's all over Beckwood already. Terrible! I can't tell you how upset I am. It's all to do with the poor Rector, Major Boddy!"

"The Padre, eh?"

"Last night it was, Major Boddy, as I was coming home from the Institute jam-making class. As you well know, the lane passes right under the Rectory wall. Really and truly, Major Boddy, I couldn't help overhearing. It wasn't that I wished to pry into matters which didn't concern me. I just couldn't *help* it!"

"Could have blocked your ears," said Boddy jovially. "Never thought of it, eh, Miss Finnigan?" Then roguishly: "You women. Ha!"

"Well, really, Major Boddy—"

"No! No! Pulling your leg, Miss Finnigan. Mustn't take me seriously. Point is, what did y'hear?"

"I heard," said Miss Finnigan with round eyes, "the Rector praying in his garden."

"Well! Well!" The Major cleared his throat in discomfort. "Nothing funny about that, surely? Got to pray somewhere, eh? Warm night. Why not in the garden?"

"It was his *words*, Major Boddy; that's what so took me aback. It wasn't proper praying to my way of thinking. His voice was all shaky and horrible, and the things he said, Major Boddy! It made me blush to hear him. It wasn't *like* the Rector."

"How d'you mean?" The Major coughed and fixed his eye on an advertisement for toilet soap. "No need to beat about the bush with me, Miss Finnigan. I've knocked about, y'know. Nothing—er—improper, eh?"

"No, Major Boddy, not improper but, in my opinion, unnatural in a clergyman. All about being in the toils of sin and following the lures of the flesh." Miss Finnigan glanced out into the sunlit village street through the sweet bottles and, leaning over the counter, lowered her voice. "And he kept talking about a woman, Major Boddy—a *scarlet* woman!"

"Umph—that's queer."

"It upset me, Major Boddy. Dear me, it did! It was like madness to hear him going on and on in that horrible voice. It made me fear for his reason, Major Boddy, it did really! 'The devil's in me,' he said over and over again. 'I have fallen from grace,' he said. Just like that, Major Boddy. I thought perhaps you could slip into the Rectory and have a talk with him. It might turn to something dangerous. I had a brother-in-law, Major Boddy, who was taken that way. Knelt down in the middle of the street and confessed his sins at the top of his voice to a crowd in a charabanc. Awful, it was, Major Boddy. And that night he went for my sister with a bread-knife."

"Guess she was taken by surprise, eh? Awkward." The Major stooped and put on his trouser-clips. "Well, Miss Finnigan, I'll do what I can. I'll cycle up to the Rectory. Shouldn't like anything awkward to happen here, y'know. Perhaps the poor fellah's ill. Been overworking."

But on rounding the Portuguese laurels into the Rectory drive, Boddy was somewhat reassured. Swale-Reid, hatless, in a green-baize apron, was kneeling on a little rubber mat, weeding his rock garden. On seeing Boddy he raised his trowel in salutation and scrambled to his feet. The Major dismounted with athletic vigour, propped his bicycle against the house and marched across the lawn.

"Ha! Padre, hard at it? Confounded hot work, eh?"

"It is—rather sultry," said Swale-Reid in a tired voice. "You wished to see me?"

"Ah, yes. That is—I thought I'd just look in."

"A spiritual matter?" Swale-Reid glanced at him suspiciously.

"No! No! I wanted to see if you—confound it all, Swale-Reid, what *did* I want to see you about?"

"Really, Boddy." The Rector flapped his arms like a tired penguin. "I'm not a mind-reader."

"No, thank God!" Then hastily: "That is—how *are* you, Padre? Keeping on your toes? Fit, eh?"

"You're very solicitous concerning my health," said Swale-Reid, now definitely uneasy and on guard.

"Been a bit worried, y'know. Looked a bit pale about the gills, I thought, last Sunday. Not overworking? Not burning the candle at both ends, eh?"

"And what," demanded Swale-Reid stiffly, "do you mean by that, precisely?"

"Oh, nothing! Nothing! Wondered if you needed a little holiday, that's all. As a member of the Church Council—see how I mean, Padre?"

"You're dissatisfied with my work in the parish?" flashed Swale-Reid. "Er—as a body?"

"Balderdash! Wrong end of the stick, my dear fellah. Personal visit, this." The Major removed his trouser-clips and twiddled them on a finger. There was a long uncomfortable silence. Then: "Just wanted to make sure," he said. "Looked seedy. Er—worried about your health—that's all."

"Quite," said Swale-Reid.

"Well—er—" The Major remounted his trouser-clips. "Good-bye, my dear fellah. Glad you're fit."

"Thank you."

"Come round for a hand of bridge soon, eh?"

"Thank you."

"Good! Good! Pleased to find you well, Padre. Yes. Really. Er—good-bye. Good-bye."

The Major walked back across the lawn as if wading through the depths of a slimy pool. He mounted his bicycle with great pomp and, in his anxiety not to look self-conscious, missed the pedal and jarred himself unpleasantly. Then bolt upright, and very stately, he careered down the drive, rang his bell with undue caution at the gate and vanished into the lane.

"Damn it!" he thought with acute astonishment. "I made a bloody fool of myself!"

5

It was that same evening, when returning a gardening book to The Oasts, that John drew him aside and said darkly: "I've had rather a worrying time, old man, since I saw you last. Things have been happening here that need explanation. 'Things',," added John, savouring his quotation like a connoisseur of verbal gems, "'that do almost mock the grasp of thought.'"

"Ha! Really?"

"It's upset Lydia, too, because it was she who really came in contact with events. In an inspirational mood last night, old man, and she didn't come over to the house from the studio until well past midnight. The Dingle portrait, you know. Well, the poor angel was just going upstairs to her bed when she thought she heard noises in the sitting-room. Of course, Boddy, she *should* have called for me, but you *know* Lydia. Independent. Brimful of feminine curiosity, so the dear woman just had to find out things for herself. So she creeps along the hall, pushes open the door and looks in."

John paused, smiled to himself and placed the tips of his fingers fastidiously together. Boddy looked at him with irritation. "Well, damn it all, Arundel—don't leave me in suspense!"

"Nothing," breathed John. "Nothing, old man. An empty room with a shadow slipping through the open French windows. No more than that. My bureau, mark you, open and papers in confusion. No further sign of the intruder."

"You searched the grounds?"

"Naturally," protested John. "As you know, Willis and the cook—that's his wife—sleep in the east wing, and the moment Lydia roused me I routed out Willis and we quartered every inch of the garden. Again—nothing. Disturbing, old man."

"Anything missing from your desk?"

"No. No. Just a damned muddle—that's all."

"Ha! Keep anything of value there? Money? Jewellery? So forth?"

Major Boddy had slipped into the skin of his part. He was now Detective-Inspector Boddy of the C.I.D.

"Far from it, old man. Accounts, receipts, gardening-notes—the usual conglomeration of personal oddments. Hadn't even troubled to abscond with my automatic, which was in one of the pigeon-holes—a Colt .45 which I was left with after the last war. The whole business is extremely ominous, eh?"

"What did Lydia make of the figure?"

"Damn it all, old man, just a featureless silhouette. She didn't have time to switch on the light. Tall, she believed, thin, in black clothing, wearing a queer-shaped hat. The dear lady seems convinced that it was a woman. What's your theory, Boddy?"

"Umph. Tricky business. No circumstantial evidence worth a row of beans. Any ideas yourself?"

"None."

"Queer, eh?"

"Very."

6

And then it was Jed Willis's turn to add a link to this crooked chain of events. Boddy found him the following afternoon sitting in the potting-shed at Ladysmith, chatting with Syd Gammon. On seeing the Major, the latter sprang to attention and said in a toneless voice: "Beg to report, sir, Private Willis has just returned that Dutch hoe we lent him. Return three months overdue, sir."

"All right, Gammon. Dismiss!" Syd clicked his heels and marched off up the garden with a tell-tale trail of cigarette smoke oozing from his clenched hand. Boddy smiled. "Passing the time of day, eh, Willis? Wasting your employer's time, what?"

"Oi was," said Willis with a certain truculence. "But Oi 'ad good reasons for so to do, sir. There's been some queer going-ons up to The Oasts as Oi was just a-tellin' Syd. First there was that figger the missus come on—"

"Yes! Yes! I've heard all about that. Nothing more happened since, surely?"

"That's just where you be all wrong, sir. There's a 'ell of a lot 'appened since, as Oi was just a-tellin' Syd. Last night—or more proper like, the early hours o' this morning—Oi was took up with a touch of indy-gestion, see? Fetched me out o' bed, it did, an' when Oi chanced to look out o' the windy, jigger me if Oi don't see a bit of a light a-bobbin' in the garridge. No more than through a chink o' the door, sir, but enough to set me a-thinkin'. So Oi pulls on my boots an' 'ops out quick through the back door. But darn me, when Oi gets to the garridge there ain't no sign o' nobody nor nothin'. Just a queer smell like, same as if a chap 'ad just done a bit o' soldering at the garridge-bench. As Oi was a-tellin' Syd, sir, the soldering-iron was still 'ot. No mistake. Oi doan't like it. It doan't fit in with what's proper, do it?"

"You told Mr. Arundel?"

"There an' then, sir. Flummoxed 'e was, same as me. There's folk around this 'ere parish as is up to no good, in my 'umble opinion. Oi tell 'e, sir, Oi doan't like it!"

"Neither do I, Willis."

"Things," concluded Willis, "is 'appening."

"'Things'," said the Major with a superior smirk, "'that do almost mock the grasp of thought.' That's a quotation, Willis. You wouldn't know it. But apt—damned apt! We must keep on our toes, what?"

CHAPTER IV

Romance off the Rails

I

ABOUT ONCE EVERY FORTNIGHT TOM BODDY HAD DINNER WITH Lady Dingle at Beckwood Court. It was a long-standing arrangement. After dinner they always retired to a corner of the vast stone hall and played cribbage behind a screen—as Lady Dingle waggishly put it, "So that the servants can't see how much you drink, Tom dear." On this occasion, however, she had warned him, over the telephone, "We shall have to forego our little *tête-à-tête*. You see it's really to be Honororia's party. Just the happy couple and you and I. I thought possibly that Lexicon might meet the case. Stanley can't spell for little apples, naturally; but perhaps we could arrange a handicap."

There was no need. When Boddy arrived at the Court all was chaos and confusion. Honororia, half-extended over a sofa in the chilly lounge, was having hysterics, not half-heartedly but with the full fine fury of an operatic star crossed in love or cheated of a contract. Lady Dingle was rushing round with a bunch of lighted feathers in her hand and, in her agitation, was absent-minded enough to thrust them under Honororia's nose before blowing out the flames. The result was not gratifying. The poor girl, already fully extended, found herself unable to cap her previous performance and promptly fainted. The parlourmaid and chambermaid, who had been grappling with her contortions, now found themselves without a job, until Lady Dingle sent one to 'phone the doctor and the other for her smelling-salts. It was at this comparatively idle moment, during a hiatus in the pressure of events, that Major Boddy arrived.

"Oh, Tom dear! thank God! A man! So essential on these occasions. So solid and calming."

"What the devil's the matter?"

"It's Stanley."

"He's knocked her out, eh?"

"Don't be ridiculous, Tom. He's not here. Honororia's just had hysterics and now she's fainted. Oh, can't you, can't you help to bring her round? She looks so very ashen. I'm sure she's dead."

"Balderdash! Got any brandy?"

"Brandy! Brandy!" Lady Dingle spun like a teetotum and shot off across the room. "Why didn't I think of it? Oh, what a comfort you are, Tom. Yes! Yes! Here's a full decanter *and* a glass. How opportune."

"Here, I'll have it!" said Boddy anxiously. "You'll spill the damned stuff, Sarah. Your hand's trembling like an aspen leaf. Raise her a bit. Can't administer in that position."

Between them they forced the inanimate girl to accept their administrations. Suddenly she made a wry face, shuddered and opened her eyes.

"Where am I?" she fluttered. "Whath happened?"

"Fainted," explained Boddy. "All right now. Nothing to worry about."

Taking advantage of Lady Dingle's concern over the patient, he swallowed down the brandy left in the glass and hastily refilled it. The parlourmaid returned with the news that the doctor was on the way.

"Cancel the call," said Boddy firmly. "*I've* got this in hand. Unnecessary to take up his time."

The girl departed as the second maid entered with the smelling-salts.

"Don't need 'em," said Boddy. "Waste of time. Brandy. Understand?" The chambermaid also departed. "Now," added Boddy, feeling like a General in the heat of a great campaign, "let's get to the root of this trouble, young woman. Possible I can help. Used to tight corners. Can confide in me, y'know."

2

The tearful facts of the matter emerged haltingly from the depths of Honororia's misery. With a girlish delight in springing surprises, she had set off for Claydown Farm earlier that evening, intending to accompany

Stanley back to Beckwood Court for the dinner-party. She had taken intense pains over her appearance, daring an old-fashioned poke-bonnet and full flounced skirt only once removed from a crinoline. She had pictured the scene. Stanley, breeched and booted, still invested in the honest effluvia of the farmyard, sluicing his sunburned arms over the wash-basin—a dark, enigmatic male in the true D. H. Lawrence tradition. Then herself entering, fresh, shining, innocent as a daisy, a piece of thistledown blown across his brooding vision. His strangled grunt of desire and his soap-flecked arms, regardless of her flimsies, closing about her like a steel trap—*that* was her vision!

The reality, alas, had been very different—disastrously different, as Boddy was swift to appreciate. Honororia's path across the fields led along the border of the Arundels' garden and passed Lydia's studio only a few yards away. It was the same path, in fact, that she and Stanley had taken on the night of the party when they had slipped through the wicket-gate. It was seldom used and Lydia had not worried about her privacy, and, in any case, needing the light, she had been unable to plant a screen between the studio and this ancient right-of-way. In consequence the big east window made a perfect frame for Honororia's disillusionment. Within it Lydia had painted one of her finest and most characteristic pictures, not with brush and oils, but with flesh and blood, with the arresting colours of her own personality. For there she stood, flaunting the ripe curves of her maturity not eighteen inches from Stanley Hawkinge and every instant closing the fateful gap between them. Stanley was staring at her with the glassy expression of a rabbit hypnotized by a basilisk and, even as Honororia took in the grouping, the gap closed and Lydia, with a laugh of triumph, coiled her arms round his neck and kissed him on the brow. Granted, Stanley seemed to reel back from the assault; granted, his expression was one of horrified disgust; nonetheless, the general lay-out of the drama was enough even for the innocent Honororia. Gathering up the hem of her crinoline, choking back her sobs, she fled back across the meadows to Beckwood Court.

There, in its essence, was the tragedy.

"And now, Tom," said Lady Dingle briskly, when the last lisping echo of Honororia's lament had died away; "what are we going to do? Of course the moment poor Honororia returned, I rang Claydown and left a message to say that the dinner-party was cancelled. I couldn't, you'll admit, do less."

"Not tactful," declared Boddy after due consideration. "Accepts the worst without giving the best a chance. Put his hackles up, if he realizes."

"There *is* no best," cried Lady Dingle with vehemence. "He, engaged to poor Honororia, was making love to another woman, a married woman."

"Stand fast! Stand fast, Sarah! Confound it all, that don't conform with the facts. *Her* arms went round *his* neck—admit that? Then, damn it, *she* was making love to *him*, eh?"

"Oh, yeth! Yeth!" said Honororia plaintively. "There ith that way of looking at it, Auntie Tharah."

"You don't want to lose the fellah, eh, young woman? Don't want to give him his *congé*?"

"No. No. Of courthe not, Major. It wath jutht what I thaw—"

"Precisely—through the window. Well, I say, have the fellah up. Give him a chance to explain. Put him in the witness-box. After all, Sarah, you *know* Lydia. Damn fine woman but—er—unrestrained. No sense of sexual *meum* and *tuum*. Crude way of putting it but you know what I mean."

"Very well, Tom, if *you* say so, I'll ring Claydown and tell Stanley that the dinner's *on* again. He'll think we're mad, of course, but we mustn't let any personal scruples stand in the way of this poor child's happiness."

"You're prepared to see him, young woman?"

"Oh yeth, yeth," breathed Honororia. "Dethpite everything I thtill believe in dear Thtanley's innothenthe."

"You shall be closeted alone," announced Lady Dingle darkly, as she swept towards the telephone. "And if you're satisfied with his explanation, he may stop to dinner."

3

What transpired behind the closed doors of the study Lady Dingle and Major Boddy were never to know in detail. At the end of some twenty minutes, Honororia tottered out into the hall, white and sobbing, with a small wet handkerchief held to her large wet eyes.

"It'th all over! I can't underthtand him! Oh pleathe, pleathe, Major Boddy, thee if you can make thenthe of what he thayth."

"Very well." The Major rose, straightened his tie, squared his shoulders and marched into the study.

He found Stanley's massive bulk blocking the light of a window. His back was to the room and he appeared to be breathing heavily. On hearing the click of the door, he swung round and said in a dull voice: "Oh, it's you."

"Yes," said Boddy sternly. "It's me, Hawkinge. Now, tell me—what the devil have you been up to? Fine mess you've made of things. Can't have any hocus-pocus with other women when you're engaged, y'know. Bad policy. Bad form. Confound it all, Hawkinge, why did you go to Lydia's studio at all? Dangerous places—studios. General public look upon 'em as cesspits of iniquity. Strong way of putting it, I admit, but you've got to see things from the girl's point of view."

"Had to meet the woman," growled Stanley, with an evasive eye.

"Why?" barked Boddy.

"Reasons," said Stanley. "Private reasons."

"But damn it all, Hawkinge, that's bad. That's very bad. Suspicious. Can't you do better than that? Tell me; did you make love to her?"

"Good God, no!"

"Do you still care for her?"

"Good God, no!"

"Then why did you go?"

"I wanted something from her."

"You mean—?" began the Major in a shocked voice.

"No. No. Not that!" protested Stanley. "But I swear, if Honororia insists, I'll never see Lydia Arundel again, Boddy. Not if it will make things right. Tell her that, for heaven's sake! I can't bear to see her cry."

"Umph. I'll do my best. But I can't promise a favourable result. That young lady's pretty cut-up. Shouldn't try to see her again to-night. Slip out through those French windows. I'll let you know over the 'phone how I get on."

About an hour later Boddy was on to Claydown Farm from Ladysmith. He had swallowed a hasty, uncomfortable dinner at Beckwood Court and bolted from the place as soon as politeness allowed. Lady Dingle was in no mood for cribbage. He, himself, felt, as he expressed it, all "cock-a-hoopla!"

"That you, Hawkinge?" A queer farmyard noise winged back in answer. "Well, I've had no luck. She won't see you."

"Hell!" said Stanley softly; then in a crescendo of despair, "Hell! Hell! HELL!"

"Your own fault," pointed out Boddy brutally. "You should have left Lydia strictly alone. Damn it, you know what she is."

"I do," said Hawkinge succinctly. "She's a—" He uttered a low word and finished in a frenzy of wrath. "I'd like to strangle that woman, Boddy, with my own two hands I'd like to strangle her!"

"Well don't," advised Boddy. "Murder wouldn't get you anywhere—at least, not with Honororia. You've got to keep a stiff upper lip and stick it out. No, damn it, I don't mean your lip. Patience, see? I'll work on the girl. Get through her defences. There's still a chance she'll relent."

4

It was, therefore, in a strained and foreboding atmosphere that the last days of June came to the little parish of Lower Beckwood. As if to lend colour to this mood, the weather, hitherto unbelievably fine and settled, suddenly broke up and darkened. A wind rose and great black clouds scudded across the sky, later to split apart and drench the countryside with rain. And once the rain had started it went on, relentless, chilling, depressing. The fields grew sodden, the trees dripped, the summer flowers lay battered and flattened along the borders. The small birds humped their backs and looked upon the world with tiny, miserable eyes.

Misery, too, was rife among the human element of the village. Down at Claydown, Stanley sprawled over his solitary meals or plodded cheerlessly over his muddy acres with two female faces for ever glowering at him. At the Rectory, a similar drama was slowly working itself out, except that on Swale-Reid's mental horizon there glowered only one female face—a vivid, gargantuan enlargement like an advertisement for bath-salts. Boxed in his dingy study he struggled with his sermons, knowing that all he wrote was tainted by his preoccupation with this fateful woman.

At The Oasts things were little better. Lydia, wrestling with the Dingle portrait, was in a highly irritable and explosive frame of mind and, as usual, John was her whipping-post. Her sarcasms grew more bitter, her innuendos more biting, her mockery more acid, until John felt cheap and withered and desperate. He was buoyed up by his secret thoughts, by the knowledge that he would not have to endure the rôle of second fiddle much longer. The time was drawing near for him to break into action. His ideas were ripe for execution. In spite of everything he felt keyed up, like an old actor who has been cast in the part of a lifetime and waits in the wings for the curtain-rise. Let her taunt him! Let her rail and sneer and mock! For the time being he would lift his shoulders, throw out his hands and with this Gallic gesture dismiss her ill-humour as of no importance.

Willis, too, was in a bad temper, for Lydia, having found him in John's shooting-boots, was furious. First with John, then with Willis himself. She lectured John on the false generosity of giving away something which had been paid for by somebody else. (A particularly nasty pill, this!) She accused Willis of cadging, and touched lightly on the strange disappearance of a cigarette-casket, a bottle of sherry, two baskets of peaches and the *Illustrated London News*. Willis, naturally, took umbrage and with truly rural independence threatened to throw up his job and take his wife with him. Lydia was hounded into an apology, though this retreat was not due to the possible loss of her house-boy, but of that pearl without price, her cook. For all that, she forced Willis to surrender the boots—"Just," as he complained, "when the darned things 'ad worn nice and comfortable to my corns."

And last but not least, caged like a princess in the west tower of Beckwood Court, there was Honororia. The skies wept with no more abandon than did she. Nature's horizons were no blacker than hers. She was of a piece with the stormy landscape, the lowering clouds, the desolate, sodden earth. She toyed with the meals that Lady Dingle so thoughtfully sent up on trays, and developed a passion for playing *Finlandia* over and over again on the gramophone. Faces loomed in her mind, too—Stanley's and Lydia's—sensual features, heavy with passion, faces which every now and then came together in a prolonged and devilish kiss! No matter that Stanley rang up every day, she refused to speak to him. His daily letters remained unanswered. Even Major Boddy, now acting as liaison officer between the two camps, was unable to break through her defences. She wept and grew thin, but she would not give in.

It seemed that the atmosphere of Beckwood parish was charged with electricity. The local soothsayer prophesied the end of the world. A fireball passed over the church. A puppy with two heads was delivered in the house of the District Nurse. Old Mrs. Faddian slipped on a wet brick path and broke her wrist. A hooded figure was seen near Beddow's Bottom.

Tragedy, swore Beckwood, was in the air!

CHAPTER V

The Sealed Box

I

MAJOR BODDY HAD JUST ALLOWED *The Times* TO SLIP FROM HIS hand, preparatory to a little pre-bedtime doze, when the door was flung violently open and Syd Gammon entered. With a species of muscular quiver he sprang to attention and announced in a barrack-square voice: "Beg to report, sir, urgent call from Mr. Arundel. Would you go up at once. Something's 'appened."

"Eh? Eh? What's this? What the deuce d'you mean, Gammon, *happened?*"

"According to information received, it's Mrs. Arundel, sir."

"Well? Well?"

"Beg to report, sir—she's dead."

"Dead!"

"Discovered 17.45 hours, sir, in her stoodio. Revolver by her side. Suspected suicide."

"*Suicide!* Good God, Gammon, get my hat and start up the car." Gammon quivered again and made for the door. "Wait! Did Mr. Arundel tell you all this over the 'phone?"

"No, sir. The information was received from Private Willis, acting on behalf of his C.O., sir."

"Right. Dismiss!"

"Very good, sir."

2

Lydia dead! That dynamic, restless, flamboyant personality emptied of life and by her own hand! Incredible! Boddy's hand shook as he steered his neat little saloon through the lamplit slithers of rain. This abrupt and unexpected news seemed, in a moment, to underpin his security. He had been comfortable in his stout stone tower of a pensioned retirement, and now a *saboteur* had packed its foundations with fulminate of mercury and touched off the detonator. "In the midst of life we are in death." He suddenly felt old and worried and full of foreboding.

He swung the car recklessly between the brick pillars of the drive-entrance and skidded to a stop at the portico of The Oasts. The door was open and a flood of light streamed into the rain. The silhouetted figure was obviously awaiting his arrival. It lumbered forward and clumsily wrenched open the door of the driving-seat.

"Major Boddy, sir? 'Tis Willis. Oi've 'ad instructions to take 'e down to the stoodio at once. The police 'as just arrived."

"Police!" The thought of Constable Belling coldly taking notes over the inert figure of poor Lydia shocked the Major acutely. This was a sordid aspect of the tragedy which had not previously occurred to him. He recovered himself. "Of course! Of course! Very necessary. A dreadful business, Willis. Dreadful!"

The house-boy flicked on an electric torch and, his boots scrunching on the wet gravel, guided the Major between the blanched and battered flower borders. The studio, behind its circle of conifers, was a blaze of light, and as Boddy drew near he heard the murmur of voices. With unusual politeness Willis stood aside and allowed him to pass first into the room.

This was the final picture conjured out of space by that enigmatic, contradictory creature Lydia Arundel. It was a piece of unrelieved realism in harsh colours, its subject-matter stark, its grouping dramatic. In the centre foreground of this self-portrait lay the artist herself, one hand outstretched above her raven head, the other folded away beneath her hip. A gleam of emerald silk showed below the hem of her drab overall. She stretched in silence, one ear to the floor, as if listening. A few feet away from that out-thrust arm was a small metal object upon which the whole conception pivoted—a Colt .45. Three minor figures were spaced with an unconscious sense of balance in the near background. On a small Récamier couch near the slow-combustion stove which heated the studio in winter sat Mrs. Willis, softly and interminably sobbing. Standing directly beneath one of the unshaded electric bulbs, suspended from the transomes of the skylight, was Constable Belling—a solid block of Prussian blue picked out in silver—with a notebook in his podgy hand and a red rim across his brow from which, in deference, he had removed his helmet. And finally, brilliantly and tragically posed against the wine-coloured velvet window-curtains, stood John Arundel in pyjamas and brocaded dressing-gown. His bland face was pale, and in its grief, franked with the stamp of nobility. But even in that moment of hushed dismay, within that chill circle of death, Boddy was caught up with the thought that John's attitude was not genuine. He was, as ever, acting a part and, stimulated by the sublimity of his rôle, acting it well.

On seeing Boddy he slowly shook his head, and crossing to Mrs. Willis laid a comforting hand upon her shoulder. Belling gave a perfunctory salute and said in a reverential voice: "A terrible affair this, Major. Unexpected like. Shot herself through the side of the head. The automatic's where we found it. Nothing's been touched. The Inspector's on his way from Cobbleden."

"Who found the—er—?"

The constable nodded towards Arundel who, noticing the gesture, came over and took Boddy by the arm. "Glad to have you here, old friend. I felt I must send for you. At the moment, you understand, it's all beyond my comprehension. Ghastly!"

"How did it—?" began the Major with a tentative air.

"Mrs. Willis heard the shot and rushed up to tell me. I was, unfortunately, in the bath at the time. Willis was out and didn't show up until after we'd broken in here."

"Broken in, eh?"

"Yes, old man. The door was locked on the inside. Poor Lydia always locked herself in when she was working. She was terribly, terribly sensitive to interruption, you know."

"And you found—?"

"Poor Lydia"—John waved an indicatory hand—"like that. She was already dead. A frightful wound, old man, to the right base of the occiput. She must have taken my Colt from the desk." Then with a burst of bitterness: "God in Heaven, Boddy, why didn't I lock the damned thing away? If I had, this—this might never have happened!"

"But why? Why did she?"

John shook his head, then with a spectral gleam of his old jauntiness, he said in a hollow voice: "'Who is't can read a woman?'—eh, old man? There was one side of her life she always kept hidden from me. That, perhaps, was her mistake and her tragedy."

3

Inspector North, from the headquarters of the County Police at Cobbleden, cut through the emotional atmosphere of the little group like a knife. He brought balance, reason and hard fact into the highly charged air of the studio. Constable Belling had already sent Mrs. Willis over to the house and dismissed Jed Willis, who had been hovering outside the door like a watch-dog. Only Arundel and the Major remained to confront officialdom.

"Major Boddy, a close friend of mine and—er—my wife's," explained John to Inspector North. "I should like him to be present while you gather in your data. I trust you have no objections?"

"None at all, sir. He may be able to help us." North knelt by the strangely impersonal shape and examined it critically. "The body has not been moved?"

"No," said John in a strangled voice. "No, Inspector. I could see that life was—er—extinct without that necessity."

"And the automatic?"

"It has not been touched," asserted John. "Mrs. Willis will be able to tell us the same thing."

North drew out his notebook and, after the others had seated themselves, took down a full statement from John Arundel. The facts, as Boddy afterwards clearly remembered them, were these:

Mrs. Willis, fastening the French windows on the south side of the house about a quarter to ten, had heard a single shot fired from the direction of the studio. The report in the stillness had startled her considerably and she had rushed through to the kitchen-quarters to tell her husband of the incident. Then, realizing that Willis had gone up to The Green Dragon about half an hour before, she ran from the kitchen and mounted the stairs to the bathroom. Banging on the door, she told her master of the shot.

"At that precise moment," went on John, "I happened to be in the bath, but the woman's voice sounded so urgent that I got out in great haste, roughly dried myself and got into pyjamas and dressing-gown. Mrs. Willis and I then ran through the rain to the studio and tried to open the door. It was locked. We called out, but got no answer. As you can well imagine, Inspector, by that time I was in a state of great uneasiness. I tried to break in the door with my shoulder, but without success. I then fetched an axe from the wood-lodge, splintered open the panel near the lock, as you can see, Inspector, and managed to push my hand through the gap. My wife was lying just as you see her. The moment I had made sure that there was no hope, I left Mrs. Willis, who had more or less collapsed, and 'phoned the constable from the house. Belling said he'd 'phone the doctor. Willis had come back in the meantime and I told him what had happened. I then suggested that he should get on to Major Boddy and ask him to come up without delay. After that I stayed in here until Constable Belling arrived."

North turned to the constable. "Mr. Arundel's statement fits in with the facts noted in here when you first turned up?"

"Yes, sir. And pending your arrival I thought it best to leave everything just as I found it."

"Sensible. Well, Constable, you'd better go over to the house and take a statement from Mrs. Willis. I shall want a signed deposition. As for you, Mr. Arundel, I don't think we need keep you hanging about here any longer. There seem to be no complications in the case. An unpleasant shock for you, sir, I admit, but from our point of view it should all be plain-sailing. There will have to be an inquest, of course, but we'll talk about that later."

"Thank you, Inspector," said John, with forlorn dignity, rising and wrapping his dressing-gown with a toga-like gesture about his plump person. "I feel, as you can well appreciate, at the end of my tether. A great ordeal. A fateful, shocking affair, Inspector." He shivered. "Yes! Yes! And I'm soaked to the skin. I really hadn't noticed—these thin pyjamas. Coming, Boddy?"

"A minute, Mr. Arundel," broke in North. "I'd rather like the Major to stay over and give me a hand with—er—you see my point?"

"Oh, quite, quite!" John gulped audibly. "I'm sorry about this, Boddy. Much appreciate your help and sympathy." He held out a shaking hand. "Thanks, old man. Have a peg before you leave. You too, Inspector. I'll be over in the bar. Good night."

Followed by the constable, the bowed and solemn figure in its flapping dressing-gown squelched away into the drizzle and darkness. The others watched his departure in silence. Then closing the shattered door, North turned to the Major.

"A pretty grim evening for Mr. Arundel, sir. Devoted to his wife, eh?"

"An idyll," declared Boddy, blowing his nose with trumpetlike ferocity to conceal his emotion. "Poor devil! It hasn't all come home to him yet. Never does at once. Numbed! Like frost-bite. Hurts like hell when the thaw sets in!"

"Why on earth did she do it?" asked North. "That's what puzzles me. They were rolling in money, weren't they?"

"*She* was," corrected Boddy. "Can't understand it. Perfect health. Perfectly happy. At the height of her powers as an artist."

North jerked a thumb at the unfinished portrait set up on the easel. "Any idea who that is, sir? Not exactly the toast of the ball, eh?"

"That," said Boddy with some dignity, "is a very old friend of mine— Lady Sarah Dingle."

"I'm—I'm sorry, sir."

"No need to be, my dear fellah. Has many excellent virtues. But no looks. No looks at all. A horse face. I admit it, Inspector. A very dear friend, but I've no illusions about her face. A homely woman."

4

With professional thoroughness North made a general examination of the studio. He had, with unexpected thought for the Major's feelings, already covered the body with the velvet pall from the model's throne. As he worked, as if to clarify his findings, he gave a running commentary of the facts.

"You'll notice, sir, that skylight overhead. It doesn't open. It's fixed with a roller-blind but there are no hinges or fastenings of any sort. The window here was closed and locked and the curtains drawn. The door, as we already know, was locked on the inside. The automatic was a few feet away from her outstretched hand. Only one shot was fired, or at any rate, *heard*. There can be absolutely no doubt about the verdict. Now, let's take a look at the Colt."

Drawing on a pair of rubber gloves, the Inspector made a chalk mark on the floor to fix the position of the gun, picked it up and examined the magazine. A single exploded case had been ejected on to the floor near the body. The other chambers were full. He exchanged a meaning nod with the Major and, wrapping the Colt in a handkerchief, slipped it into his pocket.

"I wonder where she got the gun?" he said musingly. "And the ammunition?"

"Can tell you that," said Boddy. "It belonged to her husband. Kept it in an unlocked bureau in the sitting-room. Damned careless in my opinion. Criminal!"

"Umph." North knelt again to the indeterminate shape beneath the pall of blue velvet. Gently he bared the side of Lydia's face and again examined the wound. "Curious," he muttered. "Does the position of the wound suggest anything to you, sir?"

"Yes," said Boddy, with a sudden queasy feeling in the pit of his stomach. "Not natural. That's my opinion. Confound it all, why hold the pistol so far behind the ear, eh? Obvious place is the right temple, if one's right-handed. Admit the shot has penetrated the right side of the head; but why so far back?"

"On the other hand," amended North with official caution; "it *is* possible."

"Oh, yes, it's quite *possible*," agreed Boddy. "Once saw a coolie— damn it, right under my nose it was, Inspector!—blow out his brains with the pistol held, fair and square, mark you, against the very back

of his cranium. Nothing extraordinary in this, I suppose. Just unexpected, eh?"

"Exactly, sir. If we're going out of our way to search for odd facts, I
should suggest the Colt was lying farther away from the body than we
might expect to find it. On the other hand, apart from these two small
mats, the floor is of polished parquet and if a heavy object falls on to a
polished surface, more often than not it skids."

"You realize," broke in Boddy, after a moment's reflection, "that she
was working on this portrait to-night? The left eyebrow—it's still wet.
Notice it? What's more, Inspector, this brush—" He stooped and picked
up a long-handled brush which had fallen at the foot of the easel—
"Wet paint still on the bristles, eh? What an unpredictable woman! Mrs.
Arundel, I mean. To the last minute absorbed in her work. Knew the
portrait would remain unfinished, but continues to touch up that left
eyebrow until it's time to lay down her brush and take up the gun. By
gad! Inspector, there's something sublime in women! We couldn't do that.
We'd dither and brood, write a note to the Coroner, dope ourselves with
alcohol, then shoot ourselves quickly before we lost courage, eh? Can't
see myself acting as she did. Pruning roses, eh? Put down my sécateurs,
pick up a gun and blow myself to eternity."

The Inspector nodded. He was not particularly interested in these
psychological niceties. He'd seen too many suicides. His mental palate,
so to speak, had become dulled by a "surfeit of lampreys". He was no
longer interested in the *modus operandi* of suicide. He was grateful,
therefore, for Constable Belling's timely reappearance, which cut short
the Major's dissertation.

"I've got that deposition, sir. The old girl was not easy. Difficult to
pin her down to the facts in her present state of mind. But her evidence
falls nicely into line with Mr. Arundel's. No doubt about the verdict, is
there, sir?"

"I don't imagine so, Belling. But until Dr. McBane arrives, I'm reserv-
ing my judgment. I wonder where the devil he's got to? You rang him
from the station before you came up here, didn't you?"

"Yes, sir." Belling thrust his head outside the door and listened. "This
sounds like him now, sir."

Belling was right. Sponsored by the house-boy, McBane suddenly shot in through the doorway as if propelled from a catapult. With a brusque nod to the Inspector and the Major, he crossed at once and knelt beside the body. Uttering little pig-like snorts, he made his examination. Suddenly he looked up at North and snapped: "She went oot like a knife! The bullet's lodged in the skull, you'll note. It went in but it hasna come oot again, Inspector."

"Quite so, sir."

"But she didna hold the peestol reet against her heid."

"You're sure, sir?"

"Deid sairtain, Inspector. The hair is noo singed at a'. There's leetle pooder-blackening aroond the wound. Tak' a peek for yoursel', mon."

"You're right, sir!" exclaimed North in surprise.

McBane straightened up and tugged viciously at his drooping sandy moustache. "I'm always reet, Inspector."

"Then how far do you—?"

"A foot. Maybe more."

"But considering the position of the wound, do you think that's feasible?"

"I don't doot wi' a wumman anything's posseeble. Does the rest o' your evidence suggest suicide? Verra weel, then—that's how she deed it, mon. No doot aboot it."

"There is some powder-blackening, eh?" demanded Boddy. "Important, *that*, McBane."

"You canna deny it, Major. Look for yoursel'."

The Major did. He faced the others with a solemn expression. "There seems no doubt, eh? It *is* suicide—what?"

"You'd be a fool to go lookin' for any other explanation," said McBane witheringly. "But I wonder why she deed it?"

North shook his head. "We've no line on the motive so far, sir."

"Damn all," added Boddy. "Damn all, McBane."

"Wi' a wumman," said McBane philosophically, "whatever she does 'tis a waste o' guid time to look for a motive. A wumman's motiveless, wi'oot direction—a boot wi'oot a rudder."

"Boot?" asked the Major with a puzzled look.

"Aye—a sheep, mon, a sheep wi'oot a body at the helm."

"A sheep?" inquired the Major. "Confound it all, McBane, why a sheep?"

McBane eyed him with a baleful glint. "I'm theenking your stupeed-ity is too profound to be genuine. Wull you quit your havering, mon?"

5

The Edwardian gasolier cast a greenish light over the garish appointments of The Littel Bottel. John, Boddy and the Inspector were perched like three overgrown children on the bar-stools, nibbling crisps. Three glasses stood at their elbows, freshly charged. They were talking in hushed voices of the tragedy.

"The queer, incomprehensible, cryptic thing," John was saying in lush emotional tones, "is why my poor wife committed this dreadful act? Why? Why? Why? Out of a normal happy moment springs this black beast of melancholia. Or do you think"—he swivelled his slightly bulbous eyes on the Inspector—"that it was all premeditated?"

"I'm bound to, sir. The Colt wasn't kept in the studio, was it? Mrs. Arundel must have taken it from your desk for precisely this one purpose."

"But why? What was 'the cankerous worm i' the bud' of my poor wife's mind? What Stygian sorrow was eating it away? The Dingle portrait? Artistic depression? Despair at her inability to realize some impossible ideal, to scale the Olympian heights of perfection? Do you think we've something here, Boddy old man? Or am I being too fanciful?"

"Can't say. Can't say. I tell you, John, this has knocked me for a six. She left the house in a normal frame of mind, eh?"

"Well—yes and no. Shall we say normal for her? You take the signifi-cance of the point, old man? Lydia, in my opinion, was never in a normal state of mind. Like most gifted creators in the world of art, she was balanced on the rim of a precipice. She was fretful, restless, dissatisfied and, I must be frank, old man, often unreasonable. Of late, particularly so." John lowered his voice and added dramatically: "Boddy! I've an idea it was that woman's face!"

"What face?"

"Sarah Dingle's, old man. It worried, I might even say, haunted her. It wouldn't come right. Only yesterday she said to me, 'It's driving me mad, John darling. I look away from the canvas to pick up a tube of paint. I look back again and there it is, staring at me—a horse in a bonnet with a rope of pearls round its neck!' You'll understand, of course, that a great deal of what poor Lydia claimed to experience was merely the outward projection of an inward vision. She didn't mean she had really painted a horse. It was the astral manifestation of a horse getting between her and the subject-matter. But this did worry her a lot, old man. Far more than we could realize, perhaps. She felt—ah! well I know the torture of it!—creatively thwarted! She was temporarily denied a full expression of her ego. Yes! Yes!" concluded John with a slow shake of his head; "I really do believe we have something here. Some explanation of the tragedy."

"What about money matters?" asked North, coming down with a hard practical hand on Arundel's verbal balloon. "No worries, sir?"

"Far from it, Inspector."

"And your own relations were—?"

"I have no relations," said John stiffly. "Not living, thank God!"

"I meant, your relations with your wife were—"

"Conspicuously harmonious, Inspector. You'll bear me out there, Boddy?"

"An idyll," reiterated the Major.

"And as far as you know, she had no other worries?"

"No," said John. "Apart from the racking uncertainties of her genius she was a singularly contented woman, Inspector. Er—have another drink?"

The Inspector raised a hand and glanced at the clock.

"Thank you, sir, but I must be off. I must get in touch with the Chief Constable early to-morrow and arrange for the inquest. But you'll have nothing to worry about. It should all be perfectly straightforward. I grant you, the motive is not exactly clear, but if, as you say, Mrs. Arundel was of a highly strung and imaginative temperament, I think we can take it that she suffered a kind of mental black-out." He added cheerfully, "It often happens that way, sir. I've had to deal with dozens of similar cases and we always get a 'Suicide whilst of Unsound Mind' verdict. Rest assured, sir, we'll tidy it all up very nicely for you."

"Er—thank you. Thank you," muttered John, uncertain how to accept this generous attempt to lighten his misery. "Er—*thank* you, Inspector!"

CHAPTER VI

The Rector Vanishes

I

BY THE NEXT MORNING, THE RAIN HAD CEASED, THE CLOUDS HAD thinned away and the sun was hot behind the haze. A miasmic humidity lent to the parish of Lower Beckwood an almost jungle-esque air, through which loomed the heavy foliage of elms and chestnuts and the outlines of strange beasts. Sounds came but faintly through the mist and the commonplace parishioners moved through the web of their activities like figures in a dream. It was the perfect morning for the reception of tragic news. The storm had passed and now came the still and unreal aftermath, a stock-taking of Fate's latest and grimmest prank. That Lydia Arundel had gone from their midst, swiftly, dramatically, during the night was a fact that was borne but slowly into those bucolic minds. She had been part of the village pattern, a vivid thread drawn through the drab warp of their lives. Her extinction was resented.

Barely had they recovered from this prime shock, when fresh news drifted through the mists and added to the unreality of that morning. *The Rector had vanished!* Mrs. Prescott's Milly had gone in as usual at eight o'clock with his early cup of tea, drawn aside the curtains, and turned to an empty bed. She had experienced a peculiar dread on seeing that narrow spartan bed in all its pristine freshness, undisturbed, with her master's pyjamas still neatly folded on the eiderdown. On the dressing-table, propped against his collar-box, was a note addressed to Major Boddy. Five minutes later Fred, the boot-boy, was speeding on his bicycle to Ladysmith.

The Major was in his cold tub when Syd Gammon, standing to attention on the bath-mat, delivered the note. And it was in that chill, goose-fleshed atmosphere that, to use a Fleet Street phrase, this latest story "broke". Boddy was shocked. A flash of terrible suspicion exploded across the terminals of his brain and, dismissing his batman, he hustled into his tweeds and came down to breakfast. There in a more comfortable state of mind and body he re-read the letter.

> *Dear Friend,*
>
> *The finger of God has pointed and I know now whither I must go in search of that peace which was denied me here among those that looked to me for guidance. I have sinned against the trust that was placed in me. I am no longer worthy to guide. The shame and horror of my wickedness has overwhelmed me. I echo, dear friend, the moving words of St. Luke—I go to "bring forth, therefore, fruits worthy of repentance".*

2

And so through the steaming emanations which rose from field and copse there winged the predatory bird of speculation. Down at the post office Miss Finnigan held constant court. Her story of the Rector grew and blossomed with ornament until this last strange act of his seemed nothing more than the culmination of his madness. But what in the first place had unhinged his mind? The ashes of memory were stirred with the stick of curiosity, and little sparks of suspicion floated in the air. A look here, a gesture there, a word let fall and, in remembering, Beckwood's suspicions deepened to a certainty. This woman, this scarlet woman reviled in his *alfresco* prayer? This preoccupation of the Rector's with the sins of the flesh... hadn't he always been uneasy in her presence? Hadn't there been a peculiar way in which she looked at him, an amused and challenging look? Now the veil was lifted and the stark outlines of the truth emerged from the mists. Lydia Arundel and their well-respected Rector? Impossible! And yet?

"Oh, dearie me, I just can't believe it," wailed Miss Finnigan beneath the quivering intensity of her coiffure. "Mrs. Arundel dead and the Rector stolen from our midst like a thief in the night." Then with large, incredulous eyes: "You don't think—you *don't* think that before he went—? I mean it *was* suicide? They're quite certain it's suicide, aren't they? Only if the poor Rector was out of his mind—I mean it's dreadful even to think of it, but—"

By noon these malicious whispers were hissing like arrows through the haze, criss-crossing the warm-tiled roofs, slithering this way and that, rising and falling in swift parabolas, but always in the end to find their mark. The Rector, in a fit of revengeful passion, had shot the woman who had ruined his life and brought disgrace upon his calling. His body had been found in the river with a sack of stones girdled about his waist. His body had been cut down from an oak-tree in Parker's Wood. His body, riddled with buckshot, had been dragged from the rushes in Beddow's Bottom. His body—but why continue? His body was ubiquitous, lowering out of the pearly air in a dozen horrid shapes and postures.

And then, abruptly, Hawkinge came into the picture. At nine-thirty the previous night Phœbe Dell, in the profound mystery of her swain's embrace, had drifted in from the wastes of Nirvana to see Stanley Hawkinge crossing the wide field which adjoined the studio. She had shrunk from the vision, hiding her pretty face on her lover's shoulder, for at that moment Hawkinge seemed huge and diabolical. He was striding blindly into the night, hatless, his coat-tails flapping, his hands clenched by his side, anguish instinct in very line of his body. According to Phœbe Dell, he had passed quite close to the hawthorn hedge beneath which she and her lover were sheltering from the rain, and quite clearly they had heard him muttering: "To free myself of the past—by God! I must, I must, I *must*! Otherwise—hopeless, hopeless. Oh, hell, hell, *hell*! Why haven't I the courage? Why don't I *act*!"

His agony seemed to swell out of the darkness and fade like a falling rocket in the distance. It had been no more than a curve of sound etched against the silence, but now his ravings were heavy with significance and his actions deeply suspect. And again the arrows of speculation hissed through the haze until the whole village went mad in an orgy of gossip. No matter that Willis, pregnant with inside information, insisted that "the missus done 'erself in off 'er own bat"; by then the whole drama had got out of hand. Like some distorted colossus it straddled the parish and cast its bloated shadow on the mist. There was only one wind strong enough to dispel this opacity of rumour and doubt, the chill wind of officialdom.

With bated breath Beckwood waited for the inquest. For truth—yes truth, like murder—would always, in the long run, out!

3

"The sleep that no pain shall wake", as John euphemistically dubbed it, had overtaken Lydia Arundel on the night of Wednesday, July 6th. The inquest had been arranged for Friday, the 8th, at eleven o'clock, in the long sitting-room of The Oasts. So there was a dead patch in the flowering riot of events and Beckwood was forced to turn over the old-minted coin of gossip until fresh currency should be issued at the inquest. Yet behind this temporary façade of calm, small events were taking place, little psychological shufflings that were to bear strange fruits in the not-too-distant future.

For one thing, there was the peculiar *volte-face* in Honororia's attitude to Stanley Hawkinge. High in her tower, isolated from the sordid crisis that had ended Lydia's existence, she was, however, by no means insulated from the high-voltage wires of gossip. Lady Dingle took care of that. With the calculating eye of a practised match-maker she saw her chance and grasped it with alacrity. Honororia's woodpile, as she grossly expressed it, was no longer occupied. The cause of the rupture had been removed by Fate for ever, and whatever there was or had been between Stanley and poor Lydia was now no more.

"You *must* see this point, my darling," she said to Honororia. "You really mustn't cut off that charming nose of yours to spite your own face. Stanley may have been tactless, foolish even, but there is no *status quo* in the affairs of a man's heart. Really, darling, you mustn't let self-pity blind you to the healing power of common sense. That would be quite, quite infantile."

Honororia flushed prettily but, for the time being, remained obdurate.

"When Thtanley hath proved to me that he can be loyal to hith promitheth I may reconthider hith thuit," she said. "The next advantheth mutht come from him, Auntie Tharah. He mutht pay the full prithe for hith thilly behaviour."

Then Winnie, the chambermaid, sought an interview with Lady Dingle, and the shadow that had fallen over the village crept over the towers and crenellations of Beckwood Court. The story Winnie had to tell was a simple one. The previous evening, Wednesday, she had gone up about nine-thirty to Miss Honororia's bedroom in the tower with her customary night-cap of hot milk. Miss Honororia was not there, but later, about a quarter past ten, Cook had almost collided with a figure creeping into the hall down one of the back corridors. It had, as Winnie explained, "so knocked her aback that she couldn't get her breath quick enough to call out and ask who it was". But Winnie, who was Constable Belling's eldest daughter, was not content to leave the mystery suspended in mid-air. Reheating the milk, she again went up to the tower bedroom. The evidence was unmistakable. Miss Honororia's raincoat was dark with rain, her brogues thick with clay, and a set of muddy footprints wandered up the spiral staircase.

"In the circumstances, ma'am," concluded Winnie virtuously, "I thought I should come to you."

"But why?" demanded Lady Dingle, perplexed. "Miss Honororia is free to come and go as she pleases. I'm only thankful that she *has* had some fresh air at last. It has doubtless done her a world of good. Though I *am* surprised she didn't tell me, Winnie, about this little escapade."

"You see, ma'am," explained Winnie, "if the news gets about the village, I'm afraid people will talk. There's a lot of silly talk going round already. They're saying Mrs. Arundel was murdered, ma'am."

"Murdered! Good gracious me!"

"And Miss Honororia was away from the Court, ma'am, at the very time that Mrs. Arundel—"

Lady Dingle, like a mare shying away from something unpleasant, displayed the whites of her eyes in the wildest astonishment.

"Winnie!" she neighed.

"I'm sorry, ma'am. I only want to protect Miss Honororia from any stupid gossip. Of course, if she can explain exactly where she went, ma'am—well, nobody will dare say anything more, will they?"

"I will see Miss Honororia," said Lady Dingle imperiously. "At once!"

She found her niece, languidly extended along the window-seat, perusing *The Idylls of the King* with a glass of lime-juice at her side. Lady Dingle plunged without delay.

"Honororia," she said sternly. "Where did you go last night?"

"Latht night, Auntie Tharah?"

"Yes, last night between nine-thirty and ten-fifteen? Where did you go when you left the Court? Why did you go?"

"But, Auntie Tharah—" Her round and innocent eyes gazed back in mild protest. She smiled sweetly, a small, wan, puzzled smile which infuriated her aunt.

"No nonsense, Honororia!" snapped Lady Dingle in true Wicked-Godmother style. "I *know* you left the Tower. Why?"

"Yeth, I confeth it, Auntie Tharah—I went for a walk."

"Where?"

"Jutht round the laneth."

"You kept to the roads all the time?"

"Yeth, Auntie, of courthe."

"Then why," demanded Lady Dingle with a triumphant whinny, "were your shoes thick with mud? You mustn't tell me fibs, darling, really you mustn't. I'm not used to it since your dear uncle passed over." There was a long uneasy pause. Lady Dingle waited, but if Honororia *had* an explanation, a single glance at her pursed lip and unwavering eye suggested that she was not going to give it. "Come! Come! Honororia, surely you can give me *some* account of your actions?"

Honororia shook her head. "It'th impothible."

"You mean you *won't* tell me what you were doing?" said Lady Dingle, astonished. "You won't *tell* me?"

"No, Auntie Tharah," replied Honororia with a stubborn look. "I won't!"

"Do you mean that you won't or you can't—which?"

"Both," concluded Honororia.

4

At the same time that Winnie Belling was putting a pretty crooked spoke into Honororia's wheel, her father was doing much the same thing for

Jed Willis. The constable, bloated that Thursday morning with a lusty importance, had plodded up through the mist on his customary beat. He had been gratified by the constant waylayings, the pertinent questions, the atmosphere of notoriety that dogged his passage up Main Street. But with an expression comparable to that of a Chancellor of the Exchequer on Budget Day, he said little and revealed less. The bigger the mystery, the greater his brief blaze of glory. On the threshold of The Green Dragon, which by a strange coincidence he reached just on opening time, there occurred one of those inward struggles from which, according to the poets, flowers strength of character. It was a simple matter of Duty versus Thirst. And Belling being a realist allowed Thirst to romp home with Duty lying a very poor second. After all, the suicide of a woman of such social high-standing as Mrs. Arundel called, with all due respects to her memory, for a celebration.

Constable Belling did not, of course, enter the bar. He went what was mysteriously known as "round the back". There, with a fine sense of the *sub rosa*, he was served by Mr. Tyman, the proprietor. As was natural, closeted with Belling in a little rustic arbour, Mr. Tyman began to lead up to the tragedy. Belling was discreet. He allowed Mr. Tyman to do the talking.

"Yes—'ear all the noos, I do, across one or the other of the bars. Funny thing, Constable, but you know as well as I do that once a chap gets inside a bar 'e loses all sense of 'is reserve. Family matters, business troubles, ambitions, 'opes, ideas—they all come trottin' over the bar-top. Made me a bit of a philosopher in my time. Given me a bird's-eye view, as you might say, of 'umanity as a 'ole. An' the conclusion I've reached is this—that 'arf of us is not so black as we're painted and the other 'arf is a darn sight blacker. Little chips o' chaps, with what you might call moral strength, as 'ud put some of us to shame. Bible-punchin' 'ipocrites 'oo'd do down their blind grandmothers when it come to a business deal. It's the unexpected what crops up in a chap what makes 'im interesting. Same with wimmin. Take this 'ere case of suicide. You'd 'ave said to yourself that Mrs. Arundel was the last woman in the parish to do 'erself in, wouldn't you? No nonsense! You *would*! As I was saying to Jed Willis this morning, 'If *you* was took by surprise, then what about us? You knew 'er ins-an'-outs as we never could.' Right about that, wasn't I? Well, Jed says 'e was knocked flat when 'e got in last night an' eard what 'ad 'appened. Eh, Constable? Same again? O' course.

Let's see—old-an'-mild, isn't it? Ha! as if *I* shouldn't know. Yes, shook old Jed up a lot, it 'as. What? Up 'ere? When? Last night? No—Jed wasn't up 'ere last night. Never come near the Dragon as far as I know. 'Oo told you 'e was up 'ere, then? 'E did isself, did 'e? Well, that's funny. Sort of fishy to my mind. Just goes to illerstrate what I was saying, doesn't it? There's always something under and dodging about beneath a chap's skin. People are always *up* to something which they want to 'ide from other people. What? Your old-an'-mild? Sorry, Constable. Of course I will, an' slippy too!"

Two minutes later Mr. Tyman returned to say that "speakin' of angels"—Jed Willis had just come into the public bar. Belling received the information with a cod-like expression, but the moment Mr. Tyman had retired, he gulped down his beer and went out through the tea-garden on to the misty highway. There, in a useful recess in the hedge, he waited, not impatiently, but with the uncomplaining fatalism of his species *in toto*. Long ago Belling, in common with Einstein, had posed the hypothesis that Time was a matter of Relativity. It was, paradoxically, everything and nothing. The alpha and omega of every event and yet, in itself, without end and without beginning. One simply planted one's boots staunchly on the spinning earth and surrendered one's soul to Time.

On this occasion he had barely drifted into a state of mental non-being when Jed Willis walked slap out of The Green Dragon and asked him for a light. The constable, as he set a match to the whiskery end of a self-made cigarette, was obviously taken aback.

"Oi saw 'e through the window," explained Willis. "Oi guessed 'e was waiting for me. What's the trouble, then?"

"You're the trouble, Jed," said Belling, with a dangerous grin. "You've been telling lies an', as you know, we don't like lies down at the station."

"How come, then?"

"Why did you say you was in the Dragon last night when you wasn't, Jed? Acting stupid, that was!"

Willis looked up defiantly, an argument hot on his lips, but the sight of Belling's unwavering gaze killed his protest stone-dead. He muttered something in a surly voice, pulled on his cigarette and spat into the hedge to cover his embarrassment.

"What are you trying to conceal from us, Jed Willis?"

"Oi b'ain't tryin' to—"

"Then where the devil did you go when you left The Oasts last night?"

"That be my business."

"You're sure of that, Jed? You don't think it's the business of the police to find out where you went?"

Willis considered the point, turning it over fastidiously in his mind; then he said with conviction, "No—Oi doan't!"

"So we can think what we like, eh, Jed?"

"If 'e can think at all," replied Willis provokingly. "Anybody 'ud think the missus was murdered, by the way 'e go pokin' an' pryin' about in matters which doan't concern 'e. But Oi *knows* the Law, Oi do! An' Oi knows that when 'tis a case o' suicide—"

"And who told you 'twas suicide, Jed?"

"Oi—Oi—why, dang it all, you wouldn't 'ave me believe 'twere anything else, would 'e?" Then in sudden amazement: "Jigger me, Oi believe 'e would!" He whistled softly through a gap in his front teeth, his cigarette dangling wetly from his lower lip. "So 'e thinks 'tis murder, eh? Well, if 'e wants evidence Oi'll tell 'e something. Shortly afore my missus 'eard the shot at a quarter to ten Oi see a figger come through a 'ole in the 'edge from they stoodio meadows. In Platt's Lane, Oi was."

"Platt's Lane? What where you doing in Platt's Lane, Jed?"

Willis dismissed this irrelevant question with impatience. "An' 'oo do 'e think Oi saw come through that 'ole in the 'edge?"

"No idea, Jed."

"That young niece o' Lady Dingle's, then! Fair flitterin' she were, an' breathin' more gusty than a mare with the staggers."

"But what were *you* doing in Platt's Lane, Jed?"

"Walkin' out with my gurl," said Jed with heavy sarcasm.

5

The evening after the tragedy would remain with Boddy indelibly etched on his memory until the end of his days. At seven o'clock a wild crimson sun broke through the mist and flamed in the burnished windows of

Ladysmith. High above the thinning haze of an arc of cirrous cloud threw back the lurid glow of the sunset. The lawns and trees were tinged with purple, and the scarlet ramblers, dyed double deep, were vivid against the cottage walls. For one brief spell the village was drenched in oriental colours, a fitting climax to that day of steaming heat and tropical inertia, then the dusk closed down. The cold blue of night crept into leaf and blade and petal. Major Boddy ceased his even pacing of the lawn, turned to his companion and observed in sentimental tones:

"Beautiful, what? Reminds me of Kenya. '09, I think it was. Used to sit out on the D.C.'s *stoep* with our sundowners and watch this sort of thing every damned night. After a month, confound it, we'd long for a decent English sunset. Like strong drink, Tubby, you can have too much of exuberant Mother Nature, what?"

"Oh, agreed, agreed," said Chief Constable Wilmott. "Like somebody with too overpowering a personality."

"Ha! you're meaning poor Lydia Arundel, eh?"

"If the cap fits!" Wilmott laughed huskily as they strolled into the house and entered the oak-beamed sitting-room. Then, as he lowered his sixteen stone into a massive armchair, he added more seriously, "Y'know, Boddy, I'm not at all *sure* about this case. As you know, North and I were up at The Oasts this afternoon. There are some peculiarly disturbing facts surrounding this woman's death. I know you well enough to take you into my confidence, don't I?"

The Major snorted. "My dear fellah!"

It was as if Wilmott had dared to ask if he were a British-born subject.

"All right. For heaven's sake, don't get huffy. Here's a problem to be getting on with. That automatic did *not* carry the dead woman's fingerprints."

"What?" exploded the Major.

"I thought the circumstances of her death unusual enough to warrant this elementary test. We've found one set of recent prints on the gun. But they're *not* Mrs. Arundel's."

The Major's leathery face creased in a smirk of satisfaction.

"Observation's my strong point! North should have noticed it, Tubby. *I* did, at once. Lydia was wearing gloves. Cotton gloves. To keep the paint off her hands, presumably. There's your answer."

Tubby Wilmott chuckled fatly and ran a hand round a few of his chins.

"So the amateur is one up on us bone-headed professionals, eh, Boddy? I wish the devil you'd keep your nose out of detective fiction for a time and get a better sense of proportion. North noticed those gloves. We've already taken those gloves into account, but the problem still remains, why did Mrs. Arundel leave no fingerprints on the gun?"

"Eh? Eh?"

"My dear chap, is this where *we* get the laugh? We puny, benighted, turnip-headed experts in the unsalutary game of crime. You don't know the answer to that one, do you? But that crass idiot, North, spotted the fallacy at once. From the depths of his stupidity he argued thus: If Mrs. Arundel committed suicide then it is safe to assume that *she* loaded the Colt. But could she load the Colt wearing a pair of paint-stiffened gloves? And North, with his hide-bound powers of reasoning, decided, No, she couldn't." Wilmott grinned expansively. "And I, with my second-rate and slightly shop-soiled mental equipment, was idiot enough to agree with him."

"Umph, you tested your theory?"

"This afternoon. I don't say we found it impossible, but damned difficult, Boddy. And *we're* used to handling guns. Moreover, we left paint marks on the gun-metal."

"And you're sure the Colt wasn't already loaded? Confound it, John's just the sort of blithering ass to leave it primed in his desk. Perhaps those recent fingerprints were his."

"By bringing into play our typical unimaginative police routine we questioned Arundel. He was dead certain that the Colt had been put away without a single round in the magazine. He admitted there was an unsealed box of .45 ammunition also in the desk, but we knew that already. He was kind enough to ask us into that crazy little bar of his and offer us a drink. I hope he doesn't discover that one of his cut-glass whisky-tumblers is missing." Wilmott winked broadly. "Now don't ask me why it's missing, my dear chap."

"Thundering humorous, eh? Fingerprint tests, of course. Well?"

Tubby turned down two enormous thumbs. "They were *not* his prints on the gun."

"Then whose?"

"Ask me another."

Boddy suddenly jerked himself upright and clicked his fingers. "By gad! Tubby, stand by a minute! Stand by, my dear fellah! I've got an idea. One night last week Lydia Arundel surprised somebody rifling that damned desk. Couldn't see much in the dark. Thought it was a woman. Not sure. But this is the point. Did that unknown person leave her—or his—fingerprints on the Colt?"

"But why?" drawled Wilmott.

"By mistake."

"Then how was the gun loaded?"

"Confound it! *They* loaded it. The intruder—whoever it was."

"For what reason?" drawled Wilmott.

"Well, well, with the idea of murdering poor Lydia."

"But the gun was left in the desk."

"Hell! So it was. *Cul-de-sac*, eh?"

"Looks like it. And then there's another point; that paint-brush which you picked up under the easel. It was your idea that it had fallen there, wasn't it?"

"Ha!"

"It didn't occur to you that it might have fallen from her hand when she was shot? In other words, that Mrs. Arundel was still working on that portrait when the bullet entered her brain."

"But, good God, Tubby, that postulates murder. Can't think it's murder, can you? I mean—pretty unsporting to shoot a woman like that. In any case, my dear fellah, how? How? Door was locked on the inside. Admit that? Window and skylight both shut. Curtains drawn. Even you can't crack a nut like that, eh?"

For the second time Wilmott chuckled, the soft, shivery chuckle of a really fat man. "That's a point up to you, Boddy, old man. Nobody could crack it except one of your fictional super-sleuths who work in a positive aura of inspiration. It's what they call a 'sealed-box' murder, isn't it?"

"Then you've got to accept suicide, Tubby. You've got to!"

"But, my dear chap, I can't *accept* anything. The police don't accept things, except donations to their sports clubs and an occasional 'quick one' at the back door. Our job is really very simple. We collect facts. We collate facts. We reason on facts. We pass judgment on facts. And if we haven't got enough hard facts in our bag we just don't pass judgment. And the Coroner rows in the same boat. We put up so many facts to suggest it's suicide. We put up so many facts to suggest it's murder. If the two pans of the scale just about balance, the Coroner merely suspends judgment and brings in an Open Verdict."

"And then?"

"Oh, well, after the inquest the fun begins—for us. We start intensive investigations and if that doesn't get us anywhere we call in the Yard. And if they don't get anywhere the press get snotty and the ratepayers want to know why so many millions are put aside per annum for the maintenance of a police force whose energy is devoted mainly to the prosecution of minor motoring offences. I tell you, Boddy, there are two things in England which never swerve off the norm—police procedure and public opinion. And they're both equally antiquated and equally good."

6

Just before Wilmott climbed into his car to return to Cobbleden, he asked in his fluting tenor: "By the way, is there any truth in the rumour that's going round about your local Padre? I hear he's 'moonlighted' from the Rectory."

"Quite true, my dear fellah; he has."

"Any idea why?"

Boddy hesitated a moment and then said stoutly, "No, not a notion—er—yet. Overwork, perhaps. Chap's not been normal. Probably gone home to his mater or something. Bound to turn up again."

"He'd better," said Tubby Wilmott. "Otherwise he'll be listed as missing and *we* shall be called in!"

CHAPTER VII

Major Boddy Plans a Campaign

I

THE INQUEST WAS, IF ONE CAN ADOPT SUCH AN EXPRESSION FOR so ghoulish a gathering, exclusive. Apart from the locally recruited jury and the police officials, only a few witnesses had been summoned and they, for the most part, had been intimately connected with the deceased. Lady Dingle had 'phoned John offering her services as a witness in case Lydia's personal traits should come up for discussion, but John had scotched the idea in haste. After all, it would be damned embarrassing if he had to enlarge on that ill-starred portrait, with the sitter in the room. Even in these democratic days it demands great courage to tell a titled woman that she has a face like a horse.

The proceedings opened quietly, with Mr. Titterton, the Coroner, presiding at the head of the long refectory table. John gave formal identification of the remains. McBane brought forward the cause of death and described with great accuracy the position of the wound. Belling rambled on in a stolid sing-song, recreating the picture which had met his eyes on arrival at the studio. In brief, the inquest rolled along on well-oiled wheels ably propelled by that master driver, Mr. Titterton. It was not until Inspector North took his stand that the first cold breath of the unusual passed over the assembly. He brought out with masterly effect the main points of his theory that Mrs. Arundel might not have committed suicide. (*a*) Her fingerprints were not found on the Colt. (*b*) The Colt was lying some distance away from the body. (*c*) The wet paint-brush appeared to have *fallen* from her hand. (*d*) The wound was more to the back of the head than might have been expected. (*e*) The powder-blackening was not very marked.

With dry precision Mr. Titterton took these small pieces of evidence between fastidious fingers, held them up to the light of his legal mind and analysed them. Did the Inspector think that the Colt might have skidded across the polished floor as it dropped from the hand of the deceased? Yes. Might the paint-brush have fallen from her hand *before* she picked up the automatic? Yes. Was the wound so far to the rear of the head as to preclude the possibility of suicide? No. As there was *some* powder-blackening didn't it suggest that the revolver had been fired in fairly close proximity to the head? Yes. Mr. Titterton's shrivelled face cracked into a small smirk of self-congratulation and he turned to the jury.

"You see, gentlemen, how meticulous we have to be in dealing with all circumstantial evidence? Inspector North might be attempting to suggest to us that the deceased did *not* take her own life. I do not say that it *is* so, only that his evidence on its *prima facie* value might prejudice us to believe it to be so. Ahem! But, gentlemen, in my opinion the police evidence has so far done little to convince us that this theory as to the cause of death is—ahem!—tenable. I ask you to consider the very clear and concise evidence already put forward by Mr. Arundel and Mrs. Willis. They both claim that the door was locked on the inside. The one big window in the studio was also closed and locked on the inside. The skylight, as Constable Belling explained to us, does not open. I ask you, gentlemen, in these circumstances how can we suppose that the deceased was shot by other than her own hand? Or had this imaginary criminal some—ahem!—magical power which enabled him to disintegrate and re-materialize *outside* the studio? (Subdued laughter.) On the other hand"—Mr. Titterton's gem-hard voice grew harsher—"we must not lightly dismiss the Inspector's evidence. There are, gentlemen, I admit, certain peculiar facts surrounding this case which adjure us to consider our verdict most carefully and most earnestly. I should like to bring to your notice the strange lack of motive, *if* we postulate suicide, for Mrs. Arundel's fateful act. Mr. Arundel has put before us the theory that her mind might be temporarily unhinged by—ahem!—a feeling of creative frustration. On the other hand, there seems to have been little previous manifestation of this trait in Mrs. Arundel's character. She was, if we are to believe the evidence of those witnesses who knew her intimately—and

I see no reason why—ahem!—we shouldn't—a particularly sanguine, healthy, energetic and likeable personality. So there again, gentlemen, we have a *pro* balancing a *con*. And further—"

Wilmott leaned over and touched North lightly on the shoulder. "The old boy's right, y'know. Our evidence looks pretty thin when it's laid out on the dissecting bench. It's a suicide verdict, Inspector, no doubt about it!"

"Accident? Suicide? Murder? Which?" went on the tiny rasping voice of Mr. Titterton. "I think we can rule out the idea, gentlemen, of accident. The revolver was kept in a bureau in the house, unloaded. I can see no conceivable reason why the deceased should have loaded it and taken it to the studio under the influence of an idle whim. Even less do I believe that she would then hold the revolver in such a way that its accidental discharge should prove fatal. We are left, therefore, with the other alternatives—suicide or murder. Although I admit the police have brought in *some* evidence which might confuse us in our final judgment, in my opinion this evidence bears little weight. If we seek a motive for suicide, the motive, however fanciful it may appear to us Philistines, is certainly plausible. An artist, though capable of attaining moments of the highest exultation, is also prey to moments of the profoundest depression. And furthermore, if we consider murder we must consider also the motive for murder. Has there been one single scrap of evidence, gentlemen, to suggest that any such motive exists? The deceased, on the contrary, was a highly popular, well-respected and deeply loved member of the community. I therefore charge you, gentlemen, to examine all the evidence without prejudice and propound your findings in the case. You may, if you desire, retire to consider your verdict."

The jury, suddenly smitten with acute self-consciousness, held a frantic whispered consultation. Tom Barcombe, the blacksmith, probably voiced the general opinion in his raucous remark to the Foreman: "Oi tell 'e, Bill, Oi bain't understood no more than one word in twenty o' what the chap's been a-talkin' of, but if 'e seems to think 'tis suicide, then that be good enough for Oi!"

The jury did not elect to retire.

"Have you agreed on your findings?" asked Mr. Titterton, wearily gathering together the tattered robe of his dignity.

"We 'ave, sir," said the Foreman with a defiant look. "We think as Mrs. Arundel took 'er own life whilst in a state o' unsound mind. An' we wish to extend our 'eartfelt condolences to Mr. Arundel in 'is un'appy bereavement."

2

To Beckwood the result of the inquest came as a distinct anti-climax. To those who had disseminated the theory that Mrs. Arundel had been shot by a second person, the verdict was embarrassing. There was only one line of argument left to them, however weak and unconvincing—the Coroner hadn't been apprised of all the facts. Some people were bold enough to suggest that the police had deliberately withheld evidence to save themselves the trouble of a murder investigation. A glimpse of Chief Constable Wilmott's sour expression after the inquest would have disillusioned these cynics.

"I can't help feeling, North, that Titterton was a trifle perfunctory in dealing with our evidence. During my talk with him before the inquest, he led me to believe that an open verdict was possible." He shrugged his massive shoulders. "We didn't display our particular line of goods to the best advantage. Bad showmanship, North. We failed to impress the jury. Candidly, now; do *you* honestly think that woman shot herself?"

The Inspector reflected for a moment and then said slowly: "Well, sir, taking it all in all, there is more reason to believe the Coroner's verdict was a right one than a wrong one. The weakness of a murder theory is that we know of nobody who wanted to put the woman out of the way. Granted we hadn't got that far in our investigations, but if I know anything about village life if anybody *had* got a set against Mrs. Arundel we should have heard about it."

But in this supposition the Inspector erred. He failed to realize the strictly parochial attitude of the Beckwood newsmongers. Rumour, like the postman, might make a door-to-door delivery, but it was a secret, inter-Beckwood service which was put into operation.

If there was one person who believed implicitly in Mr. Titterton's findings it was John Arundel. Alone with Major Boddy in the study after the inquest, he sighed gustily and threw wide his arms in a gesture of finality.

"And so, old man, the curtain comes down on the penultimate act of the drama. There only remains the interment this afternoon, only that, and then we must surrender our sorrow to the ministrations of 'that grand old healer, Time'. Life is a great river, it sweeps on and carries us forward into new phases whether we will it or no. A profoundly unnecessary tragedy, old man, but irrevocable."

"And you?" asked Boddy. "What are your future plans?"

"I? Oh, I shall strive to find oblivion in my creative work. It's the only sane way, old man. There are certain legal matters to clear up, papers to sign and so forth, and then I shall set out to complete my historical researches. Do you blame me? Am I too callous in my attitude?"

"When do you leave?" said Boddy bluntly, ignoring this florid display of self-pity.

"Some time next week, I trust. It depends, old man, on Burman, my solicitor. You know, of course, that I've inherited this property and that my poor dear wife has left everything unconditionally to me?"

"Quite so," said Boddy gruffly. "As I anticipated. Where are you going?"

"The Metropolis, old man. 'To merry London, my most kindly nurse, that to me gave this life's first native source.'"

"Umph. Must keep in touch. You'll give me your address, eh? Keep you posted with local news."

John said with a sidelong glance and a certain uneasiness, "As a matter of fact, old man, I'd rather draw a veil between me and Beckwood when I've departed. No offence, of course. But with the delicate mental equilibrium demanded by my work a chance word, a sudden vision, a nostalgic memory could so easily wreck my peace of mind. Perhaps, not being an artist, you consider me hypersensitive, too highly strung, too much the victim of my moods. But wasn't it Milton, old man, who said: 'Long is the way and hard, that out of hell leads up to light'?"

"Yes," said Boddy after due consideration, "I think it was."

3

That evening, after dinner, the Major sat alone in the low-ceilinged lounge of Ladysmith and allowed his thoughts to drift lazily over all that had happened so recently in the parish. He smoked in a mood of gentle melancholia, a little leggy after the funeral, at which he had been one of the bearers. It was all so depressing and yet, in some way, so far removed from reality. Even the Burial Service, which by now should have taken on a certain familiarity, had, apart from its solemn beauty, seemed strange and significant. For it was an alien Vicar standing at the graveside, borrowed from an adjoining parish, a palpable reminder that one mystery at least had not yet been cleared up in Lower Beckwood.

And now, with the shaded lamps veneering the patina of old wood with a lustrous gold, and the scent of stocks winging with the moths in through the open casements, Boddy began to think of Swale-Reid. He, above all others, *knew* now why the Rector had fled the parish. Long, long ago he had suspected that some link, forged of base metal, united those two opposites, and knowing Lydia, her charm, her casual sense of morality, he guessed just what kind of link it was. And confronted by this sinister combination, he felt convinced that the gossip flying round the village might well hold more than a grain of truth. Swale-Reid was a queer fellow, a fanatic, and in the chaos of acute remorse he might well have murdered poor Lydia.

Drawing fiercely on his pipe, he thought: "Murder, eh? Damned ugly word. But somehow I'm not convinced that Titterton brought in the right verdict. Don't know why. Intuition, eh? Backed up by an intimate knowledge of Lydia's character. Then again, the evidence. Every fact noted, capable of two interpretations. I believe Tubby felt the same thing. So did North. And daring to assume murder then, confound it all, Swale-Reid had motive. Wonder where the devil he was that night? Ought to find out. Those uncatalogued prints on the gun. Might be his. He'd know his way about The Oasts. Might well have noticed the Colt in the bureau on a previous visit. Dashed if I can see how he locked that door behind him on the *inside*! Can it be done? Doubt it. Never came across the trick in a crime yarn. Might have shot poor Lydia *through* the

wall—only weather-board and three-ply—but didn't notice the torn sliver
it would leave on the inside. And then again, why pick *only* on Swale-
Reid? What about that dunderhead, Hawkinge? Full-blooded fellah. Not
overmuch grey matter, eh? Ha! Those damned foolish letters he wrote to
Lydia. Suppose she were jealous of his sudden engagement to the Preece
wench? Suppose Lydia threatened to show those letters to the girl? Out of
feminine pique, perhaps. Pretty kettle of fish, what? The Preece wench is
the sort to raise hell over a matter of that sort. Even that idiot Hawkinge
may have tumbled to the danger. Good Gad! yes. Miss Finnigan was rattling off some yarn about Phœbe Dell. Saw the fellah, didn't she, in the
studio meadows just before the shot was fired? Agitated state. Talking to
himself. Gad! but it's fitting in as neatly as a bullet up the breech. Swale-
Reid? Hawkinge? Both had motive!"

Then, canting over in his chair, he took up a bridge-pad and pencil
and began to jot down those little oddities of behaviour which had been
brought to his notice before that fateful Wednesday night.

1. *That business I witnessed in Parker's Wood. Jed Willis. Who the
   devil was he talking to?*
2. *Finnigan's story of Swale-Reid praying aloud in his garden. Scarlet
   woman. Obvious reference to Lydia?*
3. *Who did Lydia disturb in the sitting-room of The Oasts? Desk rifled.
   Nothing gone. Why? Judging by quick glimpse of attire she thought
   it was a woman. Tall. Thin. Queer-shaped hat. But damned if I
   know who it could have been!*
4. *Later that same night Jed Willis saw light in Oasts' garage.
   Investigates. Smell of soldering on the air. Soldering-iron still hot.
   Who the devil was that?*

And how could these seemingly unrelated facts be made to fit either of his
suspects? Had Jed Willis been talking to either Hawkinge or Swale-Reid?
That, like the riddle of the Sphinx, was unanswerable—at the moment. On
the other hand it drew a third person into the net of suspicion: Jed Willis.
(Keep this in mind.) The second point was an accusing finger levelled
straight at the Rector. His frantic invocations suggested a very definite

motive. But this shadowy intruder in the Arundels' sitting-room? Swale-Reid was not tall. Hawkinge was not thin. And surely it was a psychological certainty that neither of them would have masqueraded as a woman. The thought of the Rector in— Good Gad! no! Ridiculous! Hawkinge even more so. Like a bull in a bonnet, eh? And finally that soldering escapade in the garage. *Who* was making *what*? If Swale-Reid or Hawkinge, why select the Arundels' garage for their essay in metal-work? Had it anything to do with the Colt? With the bullet itself? Had the gun been fired by means of some diabolical contraption from a point *outside* the studio?

"Confound it!" thought Boddy. "I'm getting imaginative. Won't do! Stick to facts, eh?"

Well, here was a good stout fact to be going on with: The garage was probably locked at night and only Willis and the Arundels would hold the keys. (Or at least know where they were kept.) Willis was out of the running—he reported the incident. Lydia, then? Balderdash! Damned clever woman, but soldering would scarcely be one of her accomplishments. Curling-tongs, perhaps, but *not* a soldering-iron. In any case, was she fashioning an infernal machine to use against herself? A self-anarchist? Piffle! This left John. And at once all the Major's unreasonable prejudice against the man crystallized into the conviction that Arundel was fashioned of bastard clay. He was a *poseur*, without ballast, to be trusted no further than he could be kicked. Of course, since poor Lydia's death he'd had to do the decent thing and soft-pedal this prejudice. He'd had to extend some show of sympathy. For all that, John's melodramatic grief had rung in his ears like a cracked bell. His antipathy had been fed by the fellah's self-pity. Good Gad! was this the answer? Was this sawdust *sahib* the murderer? Had *he* met Willis in Parker's Wood? Had *he*, for some abstruse reason, rifled his own desk? Had *he* been tinkering in the garage that night? Of course, Willis had gone straight up to his employer's bedroom after he had visited the garage and found Arundel asleep in bed. But confound it! that meant nothing. Arundel would have had ample time when he saw Willis's light go on to scuttle round to the other side of the house and reach his bedroom *via* the front-stairs.

Boddy sighed. By Jove! it was fascinating, fascinating, this intricate game of criminal detection. It was ripe with endless permutations and combinations, it posed a hundred problems, a *multum in parvo* puzzle—murder!

And then with a heavy heart the fire went out of that Martian eye, the stiffened sinews relaxed and Boddy slumped back unhappily in his chair. A game, eh? With that magnificent creature, the source of his fondest memories, still and cramped and walled away from him for ever. Then it was a ghoulish, perverted, unforgivable game! If indeed he were right in his suspicions, he could not stalk this problem with the insouciance of a sportsman with a shot-gun, but with the ruthless efficiency of a soldier on active service. It was not a game but a duty. Suddenly a wave of choler swept through his sluggish veins at the thought of that great-hearted, stimulating, decorative woman slain by a vile and cunning rat. It was as if a gangling pigmy had shot a lioness.

"Gad!" he thought, "if I *am* right, I won't rest until I find out who did it. Dedicate myself to the job, eh? Give up everything for it!"

He fell into another long reverie, watching his pipe-smoke rise and fan out against the low ceiling. Again and again the same picture, formed, broke and re-formed, until he had every object placed accurately before his mind's-eye—the body, there, the revolver there, the paint-brush under the easel, the painted eyes of Sarah Dingle staring down, unmoved, upon the scene. He recalled another scene, a cosier picture, a little conversation group—Lydia standing before her easel, painting; Sarah, grim and determined, posed on the model throne; he, himself, rolling his ash-stick between his palms, seated on the little couch. There were tea-cups scattered around and the scent of Turkish tobacco on the air. While she painted Lydia talked—wittily, provokingly, profoundly. He saw the long brush gripped in those sensitive, gloved fingers, the delicate play of the wrist, the unhesitating strokes of the wet bristles and the almost frightening likeness of the woman sitting so primly on the throne. And from this bright vignette, swelling and approaching his inward eye, emerged the single factor of Lydia's hand closed about the brush. For a moment he was unconvinced. His memory was at fault. But the next instant he knew he was right and a dozen more illustrations came crowding into his brain to *prove* he was right.

Lydia, that afternoon, had been painting with her left hand! She always painted with her left hand. She was, he realized it now, incurably left-handed!

Perhaps it was this realization that finally urged Major Boddy to give up his easy routine and plunge into the spacious adventure which was to follow. It might be said that Lydia's hand, like Macbeth's dagger, pointed him the way he was to go. He had no doubt that the little signs, but half interpreted by Tubby Wilmott, would now fit, if properly juggled, into a murder pattern. There was much to do. Numberless points to check. A hundred questions to ask. But somehow he looked upon this as a crusade, a crusade against cunning and blind brutality, and he was determined not to ride back into his Castle of Serenity until the campaign was over and this vile unknown Saracen laid by the heels!

Yawning with sleepiness, he again took up the bridge-pad and began to plan the opening skirmishes of the battle.

CHAPTER VIII

Lisping Evidence

I

THE MORNING AFTER THE INQUEST MAJOR BODDY CAME TO A DECI-sion. Breakfast over, he crossed into the lounge and rang for Syd Gammon.

"Look here, Gammon," he said abruptly. "Going to take you into my confidence. Need your help."

"Very good, sir."

"What was your opinion of the Coroner's verdict, eh? Don't be tactful. I want the truth. Understand?"

"Yes, sir. Quite, sir. Well, sir, it's my fixed opinion that Mrs. Arundel was done in by a second party."

"Ha! Exactly, Gammon! Now the question is, will you fall into line with me in an attempt to expose this second party, eh? Investigate on the Q.T., what? Keep our suspicions under our hat."

"Very good, sir."

"You approve of the idea, Gammon?"

"Yessir."

"Very well, Gammon. Now listen. I want you to go up to the Rectory and collect that Union Jack I lent the Rector for Empire Day. That's your *excuse* for this sortie, you follow? Want you to question that maid of his—er—Milly. Don't force the pace. Make it natural. Find out if the Rector was in the house at 21.45 hours on Wednesday. If he wasn't, well, see if the girl knows *where* he was. You understand, Gammon?"

Syd quivered with repressed intelligence, his thumbs impeccably in line with the seams of his trousers.

"Yessir. Shall I repeat orders, sir?"

"Not necessary, Gammon."

"Very good, sir."

"Right! Dismiss!"

2

The Major himself went direct to that vibrating nerve-centre of gossip, the post office. It was a perfect day. The last vestiges of the mist had been swept from the valley and the sun shone, clear and benign, upon the rain-fresh countryside. There was a sparkle in the air, a spring-like invigoration which set the pace of the Major's martial stride and took the edge off his overnight depression. For the first five minutes, with excellent strategy, he made no mention of the tragedy, at the end of which time Miss Finnigan, obviously bursting with impatience, took the lead into her own hands and romped ahead in grand style.

"I hear *you* were at the inquest, Major Boddy," she fluttered, investing her statement with a kind of hushed respect as if he had been invited to dine with Royalty. "Well, I don't know what *you* think, Major Boddy, but I *do* know what Beckwood thinks." Her Spanish comb began to quiver. She had the appearance of a bedraggled cock about to crow. "Oh, dearie me! the things I hear! The things I've heard!" Then lowering her voice: "You know, of course, that Jed Willis has been telling lies to the police, Major Boddy. He *wasn't* in The Green Dragon when Mrs. Arundel, poor soul, was shot. Oh, dear no! But it seems he won't say *where* he was. Queer, isn't it, Major Boddy? And they *say* Miss Preece slipped out of the Court on Wednesday night on the sly, just about the same time. And *she* won't say where *she* went to! There's things been going on here," added Miss Finnigan with relish, "that need looking into. I did hear, Major Boddy—mark you, I may be wrong—but I *did* hear that two figures were seen in Platt's Lane just before that gun went off. Talking in low voices, Major Boddy, with their heads together. Oh, dearie me!"

"Umph! Really. Who told you that, Miss Finnigan?"

"Well, I don't mind telling *you*, Major Boddy." Miss Finnigan seemed to shoot out invisible tentacles and draw the Major into a closer intimacy. "It was young Herbert Bull who lives down to Rosemary Cottage with his Aunt Mary. Oh, dearie me, but a fair trial he is, Major Boddy. Always slipping out of the house and up to no good. I always say that—"

"Ha! Quite! Now let me see, Miss Finnigan, did I pay you for my tobacco? I did, eh? Good. Yes. Yes. All very odd, no doubt. Shouldn't think too much about it. Probably all coincidence. After all, the police know what they're about, don't they? Mustn't make mysteries where they don't exist. Good day, Miss Finnigan. Good day to you!"

Outside the post office he glanced at his watch. If he walked quickly he should reach the school buildings at "break" time, when it might be possible to draw Master Bull aside and get him to enlarge on his evidence. After that he'd drop in at Beckwood Court—damn it!—and see what Sarah had to say about Honororia.

A screaming *mêlée* of exuberant youth streamed out of the village school as Boddy drew level, a kaleidoscope of waving arms and legs, of fluttering pigtails and leaping bodies. In the midst of this milling mass of minors Boddy had no difficulty in recognizing the stocky, pugnacious outlines of Master Bull.

"Ha! Bull! Bull there!" he thundered in his finest parade voice. "Want to see you! Come here, young fellah! Ha! Bull!"

An embarrassed hush fell over the assembly, broken only by a few nervous feminine titters, as Bull, red in the face, stumbled towards the fence over which the Major was leaning. Long ago the junior element in the parish had learnt that the Major was not an institution to be trifled with. He was discipline incarnate, vociferous, on legs, and yet somehow he held a firm place in the hearts of young Beckwood. From behind that terrifying barrage of bluster, pennies often dropped into their hot and grubby little hands, small sticky bags of sweets or juicy apples.

Master Bull, reared in the feudal tradition, touched his forelock.

"Ha! just want to have a word with you, m'boy." Then to the gaping circle beyond: "All right! Dismiss! Dismiss! Scream! Shriek! Enjoy yourselves!" The shrill cacophony broke out anew as he went on in lower tones: "I want to ask you a few questions about those two people you saw in Platt's Lane last Wednesday night, Bull."

"Aye, sir."

"Won't ask why you were there, eh? Saw them talking together in undertones, didn't you? Could you hear what they said?"

"No, sir."

"Where were you?"

"Ahind the hedge, sir."

"D'you know who these people were, Bull?"

"Aye, sir. I reckernized one of 'em. 'Twas ole Jed."

"Jed Willis, eh? And the other, m'boy?"

Bull shook his head. "Couldn't say, sir. Big chap, I reckon. No hat."

Then, "Good God!" exclaimed Boddy. "It wasn't Mr. Hawkinge, was it? Mr. Hawkinge of Claydown Farm? Think carefully, Bull."

"Come to think of it, sir, 'twas like him. Gurt big chap. No hat."

"Said that before, but let it pass, young fellah. Tell me, is that all you noticed?"

"No, sir. Just afore Jed left he seemed to hand over a little packet to t'other chap."

"Could you see what was in it?"

"No, sir; 'twas wrapped up, I reckon."

"While you were behind that hedge, did you hear the sound of a shot?"

"Aye, sir—from the direction o' The Oasts, I did. 'Course I didn't know then that—"

"All right! That's all I wanted, Bull!"

Boddy pushed a hand into his trouser's pocket and pulled out half a crown. Master Bull made great show of not having noticed the action.

"Know why I'm giving you this, young fellah?"

Bull grinned expansively, displaying a gap in his front teeth which had resulted from a slight difference of opinion with Ernie Wright concerning the ownership of a penknife.

"Yes, sir. To keep my hopper closed."

"Your hopper, eh?" Bull jerked a stubby finger into his mouth. "Ha, that's it! Silence, Bull, understand? All right, that's all. Dismiss!"

3

Hugging the purple shade of the elms and chestnuts which lined Main Street, for the heat was rising, Major Boddy walked in a reflective mood to Beckwood Court. Master Bull's evidence had proved to be more than interesting. Two pieces of the puzzle had already clicked satisfyingly into place. Phœbe Dell had seen Stanley Hawkinge crossing the Studio Meadows, hatless and agitated. Master Bull, somewhere about the same time, had seen a hatless figure talking to Jed Willis in Platt's Lane, and Platt's Lane bordered the meadows. And if Hawkinge had been talking to Jed *then*, wasn't it probable that they had also met in Parker's Wood? The reason for these clandestine pow-wows? Boddy screwed up his eyes under their bushy brows and looked out upon the blazing sunlight as if to find there an answer to this query. And strangely enough, the answer *was* there—a dazzling miniature reproduction, *a visionary bundle of letters neatly wrapped and tied!* The letters which Hawkinge, on the rack of his dumb passion, had so stupidly written to his one-time inamorata. Gad! it was all springing to attention now! Hawkinge had bribed Jed to steal those letters. Jed was the unknown intruder rifling that bureau. The letters obviously hadn't been in the desk, but later Jed must have succeeded in unearthing them, for on Wednesday night in Platt's Lane he had handed them over.

"But stand easy! Stand easy!" thought Boddy. "Lydia claimed it was a woman in that room. Tall, thin, wearing an odd-shaped hat. Confound it! Willis *is* tall and thin, but God knows he doesn't look like a woman. Surely he wouldn't have disguised himself in his wife's clothes?"

But already light was streaming through the dun-coloured fog of his first impressions. Already it seemed that Hawkinge had been near the studio for no other reason than to meet Willis and collect those awkward *billets-doux*. And Willis had not been up to The Green Dragon because he was meeting Hawkinge. Naturally he had been forced to lie to Mrs. Willis and the police. His conspiracy with Hawkinge to steal those letters was not the sort of thing he'd care to talk about. He would not only be paid for the theft of the letters but also to hold his tongue about the agreement. And if Hawkinge and Willis were off the menu of suspects, Swale-Reid was now the main dish, with John as a somewhat unsavoury savoury!

Turning in between the crested pillars of the drive-gate, Boddy walked with a more sprightly step up the long avenue of sycamores, at the end of which, impressive and ornate, reared the towers and battlements of Beckwood Court. Drawn through his melancholic thoughts of Lydia's death was a little thread of elation. He, the amateur in criminal investigation, had already made headway. For once the rococo outlines of the Court failed to outrage his sense of balance and simplicity. For once he did not shake a mental fist at those Victorian vandals who had demolished the original Tudor manor-house and erected this vulgar monstrosity in its place. He was thinking of Miss Finnigan's vicious innuendoes and wondering what part, if any, the simpering Honororia had played in this grim fantasy.

Lady Dingle herself came towards him across the lawns, two gloved hands outstretched in an all-embracing welcome. Her high whinny echoed thinly under the cedars, albeit the unself-conscious whinny of a thoroughbred. "My dear man, you don't mean to tell me you *walked*? Where's your bicycle? I thought that was your favourite form of exercise these days, Tom. How's the liver?"

"Liver? Ha! Forgotten all about it! Other things to consider."

"I know, Tom, and you have my deepest sympathy. Lydia always held rather a special place in that expansive heart of yours. Come over to the summer-house and have a gin-sling."

"Well, well, won't say no, Sarah. As a matter of fact I wanted to see you. Important."

"Now don't be impressive, Tom; it's too hot."

Linking her arm through his, she led him possessively to the reed-thatched summer-house and forced him into a wicker-chair. He accepted her solicitations thankfully and was aware, not for the first time, that beneath her equine exterior beat a heart of gold. She was a managing, noisy woman, bless her, but brimful of understanding. Poor old Horace had exercised a lot of perspicacity in marrying her. On the surface she did not seem to be the marrying sort. There was something forbidding about her face and figure which— But, damn it, she knew how to mix a gin-sling. Fifteen years in Cawnpore had left her a widow but enriched by this unique accomplishment.

"To her memory," said Boddy, solemnly raising his glass.

"A great artist," added Lady Dingle, thinking of that unfinished portrait. "And now, Tom, what is it?"

"Honororia."

"Well?"

"You know she left the Court on the night of Lydia's death? Er—at the time of Lydia's death?"

"Precisely, Tom."

"There's nasty gossip in the village, Sarah."

"There always is, Tom. But I can't help the stupid child, because she flatly refuses to help herself. Don't ask me where she went. Or why she went. The little nincompoop won't tell me. I *do* know she didn't leave the Court just to get a little fresh air, Tom."

"Awkward, eh? Throws her actions open to misinterpretation. D'you think she went to The Oasts that night? To ask Lydia, perhaps, to keep her distance with Hawkinge, eh? Heart-to-heart talk. Clear the air. *That* sort of thing."

Lady Dingle, with perfect justification, looked wise. "No, Tom, I don't. You display a singular ignorance of feminine psychology. Honororia is a great silly, but she's got her fair share of pride. I'm quite sure that Lydia was the last person of whom she would have asked a favour. Not Lydia, Tom. I think, for all her innocence, she realized that poor dear Lydia was a *femme fatale*, a creature born to pass through this world and leave nothing but trouble behind her. Er—trouble, Tom, and the fruits of her genius."

"Then, confound it, Sarah, where *did* she go?"

"Why not ask her?" Lady Dingle picked up the telephone-extension from a glass-topped table and turned a little handle. "Is that you, Winnie? Tell Miss Honororia that I'd like to speak with her in the summer-house immediately." A bell tinkled as she hung up and turned on Boddy. "I think it would be best, Tom, if you dealt with her *alone, in camera.*"

The Major sprang up in alarm. "Good God, Sarah," he stammered dumbfounded. "You can't do that! Mustn't leave me alone with the wench. Tongue-tied. Wouldn't know what to say!"

"Nonsense. I've never known you at a loss in any emergency, Tom. That's one of your greatest virtues—always *so* reliable." Lady Dingle tossed off her gin-sling with a piratical air and with the warning, "At any rate here she comes!" stumped off in the direction of the potting-shed.

With the emotions of a mariner abandoned on a scuttled ship, Major Boddy awaited the arrival of the flower-like figure drifting across the lawn. The sweet simplicity of her full-skirted white frock and wide-brimmed sun-hat transported the Major back through the years to his young Edwardian manhood. Then, it was just such charming creatures as these, fragrant and delicious, who had plucked at men's heart-strings and lured them on to all kinds of foolishness. Shy and innocent beauties, concealing beneath their foaming bodices and picture-hats adamantine hearts and calculating minds. He was not to be fooled, therefore, by the *fin de siècle* flavour of Honororia's get-up. It was deliberate camouflage, a studied sweetness with which to confuse and enfeeble the dominant male and tip him prettily from his pedestal. As she made a simpering acknowledgement of his presence, he automatically put himself on guard.

"But whereth Aunt Tharah?" asked Honororia, as she alighted petal-wise in one of the wicker-chairs. "Thee thent for me."

"Yes. Yes. Quite. On my behalf. Matter of fact, I want to have a talk with you, young lady."

"With me? Oh, pleathe *not* about Thtanley. Pleathe, Major Boddy."

The melting helplessness of her voice and posture was disarming and at once Boddy felt himself weakening. How was it possible to connect this transparent child with the sordid happenings of Wednesday night? He had never seen anybody look less like a murderer than this defenceless little butterfly. It was ridiculous to cross-question her, waste of time! He should have closed his ears to Miss Finnigan's malicious gossip. Nevertheless, once mounted, he had to ride the race. He went on in magisterial tones: "No! No! This has nothing to do with Stanley. It's about that little sally of yours on Wednesday night. You left the Court, eh? Didn't tell your aunt, eh? Tried to keep it quiet, eh? *Why*, young woman?"

"Becauthe I'm old enough to be rethponthible for my own actionth," said Honororia with unexpected tartness.

"Umph!" Major Boddy was nonplussed.

"And I know all about the horrid gothip which ith going round the village about poor little me, Major Boddy. I thuppoth you think I had thomething to do with Mitheth Arundel'th death jutht becauthe I happened to be near her thudio at the time?"

"Ha! So you acknowledge that, eh?"

"It would be thilly of me to deny it, Major Boddy. I wath theen getting through the hedge into Platt'th Lane by that dreadful old man who workth for the Arundelth."

"Willis? So Willis saw you, did he? Then why not be honest, young lady? Tell me where you'd been. Far the best policy. Confound it, I'm no tittle-tattle! Safe with me, y'know. Is there something about all this you're ashamed of—what?"

Honororia lowered her delicate blue eyelids and examined the tips of her dainty shoes. It seemed that a breath of wind would waft her from the summer-house. The Major waited. The silence became uncomfortable. Suddenly, roused by her passivity from his essential kindliness, he burst out: "Damn it all! If you won't tell, you won't! But it makes things look pretty black, y'know. Thundering black. You were on the spot when that shot was fired, young lady. Can't blame me if Beckwood turns nasty. Tell the truth and we can cram the lie down their own gizzards, eh? You see that? Common-sense thing to do. Good God! What will Hawkinge think if he gets to hear? Poisonous tongues in the parish. *Might* poison his thoughts about *you*—what?"

"Thtanley!" It was an almost inaudible whimper, forlorn, pathetic, and, at this totally unexpected manifestation of frailty, Boddy was covered with shame. Damn it! he was no better than an overgrown bully! No right to hammer at the poor little thing like this. Forgetting his manners. With an avuncular gesture he took one of her limp hands in his and went on in contrite tones: "Gad! Honororia, must apologize. Temper ran away with me. But see here, m'dear, you can confide in me. If you're in a tight corner, well, well—don't be frightened. I'd do anything to help you out of it. Your aunt's a very old friend of mine. Very old. There, there—damn it! don't cry. Can't bear to see a woman in tears. Now, what is it, m'dear?"

"Oh, it'th all tho humiliating," sobbed Honororia. "I've been tho weak. It'th Thtanley!"

"You mean?"

"I jutht couldn't go on without him. I tried to be thtrong and then
thuddenly I gave way to my feelingth. I jutht—jutht felt I *had* to thee him
that night and tell him how thilly I'd been. Oh, I wath thtupid! Thtupid!"

"So you crept out and went down to Claydown? Is that it?" Honororia
nodded dumbly and shook like a cluster of white blossom beneath a fresh
storm of weeping. He smiled down at her with fond understanding. These
foolish young people! "But, confound it, young lady, you've nothing to be
ashamed of. Sensible thing to do. Somebody's got to patch up a quarrel,
eh? And Stanley's too much of a bonehead to take the initiative."

"He'th not!" cried Honororia tempestuously, snatching away her hand.

"No! No! Of course he isn't!" said Boddy hastily. "Damn stout fellah.
Worth a dozen ordinary chaps. Admit it. Admit it." Then with relief: "So
that's where you'd been, eh? And when you reached the farmhouse you
found him out?"

"Yeth."

"As I anticipated," said Boddy gleefully, aware how tightly it was all
dovetailing together. "But tell me this, did you hear that shot fired?"

"Yeth," said Honororia dully.

"Where were you then?"

"Going down through the copthe below the thudio meadowth."

"And you noticed nothing unusual when you passed near the studio
on your return journey?"

"Why do you athk?"

"Ha! you *did* see something," exclaimed Boddy with unusual perspicacity. "Didn't you, m'dear?"

"Yeth," acknowledged Honororia in a small voice. "I did, but at the
time I didn't think much about it. There wath thomebody in the field
clothe to the thudio digging a hole." Adding after an upward glance,
"With a thpade."

"A spade? Good gad! did you notice who it was?"

Honororia shook her head and, without warning, dissolved again
into tears.

"Did they see you?"

She shook her head again, this time furiously. Boddy eyed her blankly,
as a Hottentot might have appraised a geometric rider. Why the devil

did women weep with such irritating facility? Put a fellah off his stroke. How was he to bring this interview to a close without enlisting the help of Sarah Dingle?

He made another dive at Honororia's hand and clung to it as a drowning man to a life-belt. "Now look here, young woman; no need to boo-hoo! I'll fix this up. See Stanley—understand? Knock some sense into that wooden head of— Good God! no—I don't mean that. Now, now, for heaven's sake, get control of yourself, m'dear. Won't breathe a word to him of your visit. Tell him to come up to the Court and apologize like a man. Can't have a fellah playing skittles with a woman's affection. Not cricket. It's—it's—er—skittles. Now wipe your eyes, m'dear. Chin up! Smile! Come along now!" He grinned down at her affectionately as she slowly raised two enormous tear-wet eyes and allowed a tremulous smile to flutter across her lips. "Ha! that's the way. Courage!"

Then disconcerting him utterly, Honororia flung her dimpled arms about his neck and kissed him on the brow. The next minute, a whirl of diaphanous white, she was fleeing across the lawn towards the pretentious towers and battlements of the Court. Boddy mopped his brow and with an unsteady hand mixed himself another gin-sling.

CHAPTER IX

Spadework

I

OVER A COLD LUNCH AT LADYSMITH, MAJOR BODDY REVIEWED HIS morning's work with mingled feelings. Some parts of the picture had been clarified, he felt, whilst others had grown more obscure. Hawkinge and Willis, for all their odd behaviour, now appeared on the stage as no more than the victims of coincidence. Conspiring over one matter, they had unfortunately become temporarily inculpated in another. But already Boddy felt it justifiable to cross them off his "little list". And with them, of course, went Honororia. The wind of suspicion which had blown so gustily about her snowy skirts was no more than a storm in a tea-cup. She should, upheld Boddy, never have been suspected at all. Winnie Belling and Sarah Dingle had been over-zealous in their sense of duty and done little but add complexity to an already tangled web of events. On the other hand, but for this sorry cross-questioning of Honororia he might never have learned of this man with the spade. Who? Swale-Reid? John Arundel?

Syd Gammon had brought back but little information with the Union Jack. The Rector had sat down to a solitary dinner at seven-thirty and then retired to his bedroom. The staff believed that he must have remained in his bedroom until he slipped out of the Rectory and vanished. But at what hour he had slipped away, they were unprepared to say. As Boddy saw it, Swale-Reid could well have combined the two operations in a single strategic departure from his house—murdered Lydia, as it were, *en route* to his present hide-out. He had not been cumbered with luggage, nor had he taken his car. He had probably walked across country in the dark and caught a train at some lonely, unfrequented station. But before he went, had he stayed a moment to bury some damning evidence in the studio meadow? Or had that been John Arundel?

Liberally coating his French-salad with mayonnaise, Boddy balanced the facts one against the other and suddenly he realized that John could not have been the unknown digger. Directly after the discovery in the studio, he had left Mrs. Willis and rushed into the house to 'phone the police. Surely he wouldn't have had time to slip out through the wicket-gate and dig that hole? No, as Boddy saw it, Swale-Reid was the more likely suspect, just as Swale-Reid had the stronger motive for the crime. Well, as soon as it was dark, he and Gammon would go up to the Studio Meadows and investigate that hole. It might be the premature grave of a living and very healthy clue! In the meantime—

At this point he dropped his knife and fork with a clatter and sat staring before him, working his face ferociously, eyes glinting beneath his bushy brows.

"God dammit!" he exclaimed inwardly. "I'm putting the cart before the horse! Should have realized it. Amateurish! Tubby wouldn't have been so thundering clumsy. What's the point of trailing these nebulous suspects? First problem is this—if murder, how was that confounded door locked on the inside? How was the discharged automatic planted near the body? To-night, without delay, I must get into the studio, eh? Examine every inch of the walls. Every pane of glass. Make sure poor Lydia wasn't shot from outside. If not, then how? Confound it! I'm back again where I started. Is it possible to lock a door on the inside from the outside?"

He worried this query as a terrier worries a rat. If there were some clever contrivance which enabled this to be done, then it would have to be quick and easy to operate. After all, only a very short time could have elapsed between the explosion of the shot and the arrival of John and Mrs. Willis at the studio door. And if—

For the second time Boddy dropped his knife and fork, inelegantly, on to his plate. Gad! what a numbskull! What a purblind fool! What a crass logician! How the deuce could he drag John into this? John, naked as the day, had been wallowing in a hot bath when Mrs. Willis had heard the pistol-shot. Fancy allowing this vital detail to escape his memory. That bath washed John clean of suspicion and, *ipso facto*, deepened the implication of the Rector's guilt. For a moment he felt like a marksman who, taking aim at his target with a full clip of cartridges in his magazine, finds all but one of them dud. Hawkinge, Willis, Honororia, John—all duds! Swale-Reid was the only live round left in the breech.

With this thought bedded in his brain, Boddy helped himself liberally to the summer-pudding and realized how imperative it was that this elusive Swale-Reid should be laid by the heels. In the interim he must get John away from The Oasts that evening. Willis and his wife, he felt quite confident, would respond to a little bribery and corruption. (And he a J.P.!) After lunch, therefore, he took up the 'phone and dialled Beckwood Court.

"Ha! That you, Sarah? Been thinking. Might be a neighbourly gesture to ask John up to the Court to-night. Dine him myself if I wasn't engaged. Poor devil's moping, y'know. Natural. Keep him with you as long as you can. No, dammit! I *can't* explain. Yes, play cribbage with him. Anything. What? Stanley? No, I've had no time to see him yet. But tell the little lady I always keep my promises. So she's confessed to you about that night, eh? Gad! these young idiots in love. Too damned sensitive. No! No! Not you, Sarah, bless you. Hide like a rhinoceros. Good-bye, m'dear. Can always rely on *you*, thank God. Let me know at once if John accepts, won't you?"

2

Ten minutes later Sarah Dingle 'phoned to say that John would be delighted to dine at the Court and Boddy rang off with a nod of satisfaction. Then, taking down that gloriously stained and battered relic, his shooting-hat, he crammed it on his head and whipped his ash-stick from the umbrella-stand like a sword from its sheath. For the moment he was going to forget the tragedy. He was off to see Hawkinge in an attempt to knock some sense into that great wooden head, an arbiter of sweet Honororia's future. At the same time, he admitted that this meeting would give him the opportunity to check up his theory about those letters.

He came on Stanley, a sullen, Tolstoyian hulk, planted immobile in the middle of a root crop. He appeared to be brooding.

"Ha! Hawkinge," boomed Boddy cheerily. "Watching the crops grow, eh? Thundering fine field of wurzels, what?"

"They're turnips," said Hawkinge heavily.

"So they are! Trust an old soldier not to know a wurzel from a turnip. Saw you at the funeral. Had no chance for a palaver. A shocking business, eh?"

"Huh!" grunted Stanley, non-committal.

"On the other hand," went on Boddy, "you must admit it clears the air for you. With Honororia, I mean. Can't tell you how that ridiculous tiff of yours upset me. So damned unnecessary. You shouldn't have visited Lydia in her studio. Too risky."

"Had to."

"I know! I know!" snapped Boddy. "Didn't realize *then*—do now. You went there to get back those letters, eh? Pleaded with her, and had no luck. Am I right?"

"Hell!" breathed Stanley. "So you knew?"

"I know now," corrected Boddy. "And when Lydia wouldn't hand 'em over you bribed Willis to steal the dashed things. Crude, you must admit. Not exactly cricket, but understandable."

"So Willis has been talking, eh?" said Hawkinge, pushing forward his unshaven jowl. "I'll break his bl—"

"Tut! Tut!" broke in Boddy mildly. "Got the wrong end of the stick there. He was seen handing over those letters in Platt's Lane last Wednesday night."

"So what?" demanded Stanley truculently.

"Er—nothing," said Boddy in haste, aware that Hawkinge need never know of his totally unworthy suspicions. "But this is the point, my dear fellah. That little woman—pining away. Why? Because you won't swallow your pride and apologize for that stupid *contretemps*. You weren't making the running—I'll accept that—but she thinks you were. Take my advice. *Let* her think it. Shows you're a devil with the women, eh? Pique her a lot. Put her on her toes. Exercise all her charm to keep you on the straight and narrow, what? Sound psychology, m'boy. Always want to apologize to a wench for something you haven't done. Gives 'em a chance to relent, eh? To forgive. Nothing they relish more, believe me!"

"But will she see me?" asked Stanley, kicking with manly embarrassment at a turnip-top.

"Certain of it, dear fellah."

"Does she still love me?"

"Of course."

"Eh!"

"Where are you going? Here, stand fast, my dear chap. What the devil's got into you? Hi! Hawkinge! Hawkinge! Wait a bit!"

But Boddy was alone in the field. Only a brief flash of Stanley's dorsal curve vanishing through a gap in the hedge offered proof that, a mere split second before, he had been sulking, not like Ruth "amid the alien corn", but amid the less romantic harvest of his home-grown turnips.

"Such," thought Boddy with a sentimental gleam in his eye, "is the all-transforming, omnipotent power of love. Wise men into fools, eh? And yes, by gad! fools into wise men!"

3

As dusk that same evening was dragging her sombre mantle up the valley, Boddy and Syd Gammon climbed into the car and started for The Oasts. Although Boddy, in the presence of his batman, kept a taut hold on his emotions, his nerves were surcharged with an undercurrent of excitement. It was not the tense anticipation of the hunter on *safari* but the more dubious thrill of the small boy about to rifle his neighbour's strawberry-bed. It would, thought Boddy, be damned awkward and humiliating if John caught him poking about in the studio. It might well put paid to his altruistic crusade. He was determined that the Willis pair should be nobbled "good and proper". This, as it happened, proved a simple task. Jed made no bones about the acceptance of a pound note, nor did his wife when Jed promised to split the bribe with her, fifty-fifty. In return Boddy obtained the studio key (for the door-panel had now been repaired) and a solemn promise from the Willises that they would hold their tongues about the Major's peculiar activities. It was not the only success Boddy gained from that short interview in the kitchen.

"What 'e do b'ain't nothing to do with Oi," said Jed. "Like them three 'oly monkeys, Oi doan't tell nothing, Oi doan't see nothing an' Oi doan't 'ear nothing."

"Politic," agreed Boddy. "But before you assume the rôle of a blind and deaf mute, Willis, we're going to have a little palaver. Come out on to the terrace a minute, will you?" Jed followed the Major with a certain trepidation. After all the old boy *was* a Justice of the Peace and there was the little matter of Matthew Tanner's young pheasants still... but the Major's next words reassured him. "You were in Platt's Lane on the night that Mrs. Arundel met her end, eh, Willis?"

"Oi reckon 'e knows as much as Oi do, sir."

"More, I trust, Willis. Far more. But we'll let that pass. You handed a package of letters to Mr. Hawkinge, I understand?"

Willis gaped. "How come 'e know about that then?"

"Ha! little bird, Willis—little bird. And that's not all. You were rifling Mrs. Arundel's desk that night when Mrs. Arundel surprised you in the sitting-room. Can't deny it, Willis. It *was* you, eh?"

"Oi do deny it!" contested Willis hotly. "Didn't the missus say as 'twas a woman, tall an' thin an' wearing a queer-shaped hat? That description doan't fit me, do it, sir?"

"Exactly the way I argued—*at first*. Put my thinking-cap on. Tall, thin—that fitted like a glove, but damned if I could get over that hat. Then two minutes ago, in your kitchen, had a thundering good idea. Saw something hanging on the wall. A clue, eh? Am I right, Willis?"

For a moment Jed inflated himself with righteous indignation then, suddenly, his denial passed from him in a windy sigh and he said almost jauntily: "Aye, Major, you're right. May as well be 'ung for a sheep as a lamb, Oi reckon. 'Twas smart of 'e to put two an' two together like that. But 'twas Oi in the parlour that night, 'unting for them letters Mr. 'Awkinge was so set on gettin'. Oi won't deny it. There b'ain't no use now in doing that, Major. Aye, 'twas a sudden thought o' mine to stick on that there monk's garb as a sort o' disguise. Reckon the missus see'd the 'ood against the windy an' mistook Oi for a woman. Natural, eh?"

"And the Colt? Did you handle the thing when you were searching the desk?"

"Maybe, accidental like."

"You didn't load it, Willis?"

"No, Major. Oi'll take my oath on that. 'Twasn't until the missus shot 'erself as Oi knew there was any cartridges to fit the ruddy thing."

"Those letters—Mr. Hawkinge paid you well, eh?"

"Pretty tidy, sir, pretty tidy."

"Ha! I saw you in Parker's Wood, y'know."

"Jigger me, then!"

"Small place, Beckwood, Willis."

"Might as well try to take cover on a pin'ead, Major."

"Right! That's all. And if Mr. Arundel should come back sooner than we expect, come down to the studio at the double and let me know. Tell Gammon to join me, will you?"

4

It was almost dark by the time the Major and Gammon had completed their examination of the studio walls and windows. Their search had been careful, prolonged and meticulous. It surrendered no positive clue. It merely italicized the fact that Mrs. Arundel had not been shot from outside the building. As Boddy climbed gingerly down the house steps, from which vantage-point he had been investigating the skylight, it was to find Gammon, standing forthright as a pillar-box, at the foot of them.

"Well, Gammon?"

"Beg to suggest, sir—reconnaissance complete, sir, except for one small detail overlooked."

"Overlooked, Gammon?"

"Yessir. That panel what Mr. Arundel smashed in with 'is h'axe. Been removed and a noo panel substitooted, sir. Shot might 'ave been fired through aforesaid panel, sir."

"Damned smart, Gammon. You're right. Must question Mrs. Willis about that. She saw the door before it was smashed in. Now get those steps back into the house, Gammon, pick up a spade and join me in the field."

"Very good, sir."

Syd clicked his heels, advanced on the steps, closed them and, with a very good imitation of a private sloping arms, placed them on his shoulder. Syd had this power. He could invest his slightest action with military significance. Three minutes later he marched through the wicket-gate, the steps replaced by a spade, and, halting the requisite three paces from the Major, slapped the handle of the spade with his open palm and said smartly: "Fatigue party all present and correct, sir."

"Right, Gammon. We'll find the exact spot and get to work." Boddy drew out a pocket-torch and sent its luminous circle wavering over the dew-wet grass. Syd, now carrying his spade at the trail, frisked round him like a questing terrier. For some time they quartered the ground in silence, then Boddy drew up short. "Ha! what d'you make of that, Gammon? No! No! *There*, you blithering idiot—at your feet!"

"Sod's been tampered with, sir."

"I *beg* your pardon, Gammon," said the Major in shocked surprise.

"Sorry, sir. Slipper the tongue, sir. Oblong of turf's been cut out and relaid, sir."

"Exactly, Gammon. This is the spot we wanted. Now get to work with that spade. Jump to it! But go easy, Gammon. Don't know *what's* buried—you follow?"

Cautiously Syd prised up a corner of the turf and slid the spade flatly beneath it.

"'Ope it's not a baby, sir."

"Baby, Gammon?"

"Unwanted, sir. Been done afore, sir. Quite usual."

"Don't be morbid, Gammon."

"Very good, sir."

Gingerly he rolled up the length of turf and lifted it aside to reveal a rectangle of earth some three feet long by six inches wide. Syd was just about to plunge his spade recklessly into this shallow cavity when the Major arrested him.

"Steady, there! Steady! Ground spades, Gammon! Better tackle this with our hands. Earth's—er—friable. Don't want to damage our clue, eh? Now. Now. Gently does it."

With the ritualistic concentration of two children making sand-castles, they began to scoop out the loose earth, and almost at once Syd stubbed his fingers against something hard and square.

"Beg to report, sir, digging-party encountered opposition, sir."

"Ha!"

"Feels like wood, sir."

"Wood, Gammon?"

"Yessir. Coffin, sir."

"Balderdash! Ha! I've got it now. Help me to ease it out. Extreme caution, Gammon. Important, this!"

But examining the object in the wan light of the torch, Major Boddy was not able to assess the real importance of this discovery. To begin with he had absolutely no idea of what he and Gammon had exhumed. That it was some sort of mechanical contraption was obvious, but for what reason it had been designed and to what use it could be put, he was not prepared to hazard a guess. He gazed at Gammon blankly. Syd scratched his head.

"Noo one on me, sir. Sort of h'elongated cattypault, sir."

This spontaneous description struck the Major as apt, even enlightening. Towards one end of a piece of four-by-two batten—about two foot six in length—was clamped a short section of hollow brass-tubing. This tubing had been sawn through lengthwise and the top prised open so that it formed a U-shaped groove some three inches deep. Actuating inside this metal groove was a powerful spiral spring which, as Boddy soon discovered, could be rammed back to the rear end of the groove and held in a cocked position by means of a trigger-pin. This pin could be released by tugging sharply on a length of wire ending in a loop, which ran through a screw-eye at the other end of the batten. The head of the coiled spring was capped with a small round metal disk, like the plunger on the end of a ramrod. *And this disk had been freshly soldered on to the spring!* In principle its *modus operandi* was simple. It was no more than a species of spring-gun or cross-bow. The spring was rammed back and held by the trigger-pin, the trigger was pulled by means of the wire and the spring, shooting forward up the groove, ejected any object placed against its metal head. But what kind of ammunition it was supposed to fire or for what purpose it had been designed, it was impossible to say. Syd, anxious at once to test the contraption, sought round for a medium-sized stone.

"Shall I load and fire a test round, sir?"

"Very well, Gammon, but don't point the confounded thing at me!"

"No, sir. Very good, sir."

He jammed back the spring, dropped the stone into the groove so that it was touching the metal plunger at the head of the spring and, pointing the contraption out into the field, glanced across at the Major.

"Beg to report, sir, we're loaded."

"Very well, Gammon. Fire!"

Syd jerked the wire sharply. With a faint whizz the stone winged its way into the darkness. Boddy was impressed.

"Powerful, eh, Gammon?"

"Yessir. Sort of glorified pea-shooter, sir. Same as we 'ad when we was nippers, sir."

"Er—quite, Gammon. But don't imagine it was designed to fire peas, eh? Something of a heavier calibre, what? Any ideas?"

"None, sir."

"Bit of a twister, Gammon."

"Yessir."

"Well, shove the damn thing in the back of the car. Don't want the Willises to see it. Follow me? Fill in the hole. Replace the turf. Return the spade. Then wait for me in the car, Gammon. Want to have a word with Mrs. Willis."

"Very good, sir."

"And Gammon?"

"Yessir."

"No tomfoolery with that thing."

"Me, sir? O' course not, sir. Wouldn't think o' such a thing, sir."

"Umph!"

5

"Point is this, Mrs. Willis: when you and Mr. Arundel reached the studio you found the door locked?"

"That's right, Major."

"Had you any form of light with you?"

"I had my pocket-lamp, sir."

"And when Mr. Arundel tried the door you shone the lamp on the lock, eh?" Mrs. Willis nodded. "Did you notice any hole or splinter in the panel above the lock?"

"Oh, no, Major. That door 'adn't been tampered with, I'll swear, until the master come along with 'is axe and 'acked a 'ole in it."

"After you'd broken in and discovered Mrs. Arundel—what then, Mrs. Willis?"

"Master made sure she'd passed over like, an' then said 'e'd get the police on the telephone."

"And he went straight into the house to do it?"

"I've no proper reason to think otherwise. I was that cut up and 'orrified, Major, that I didn't notice the little things. But I reckon the master must 'ave rung the police, otherwise why should that old fool Belling 'ave turned up?"

"Quite. Quite. Just an idea, Mrs. Willis. You can hold your tongue about all this."

"Of course, Major Boddy."

"One more thing. Mr. Arundel—you're certain he was in his bath when the shot was fired?"

"I'd be surprised if 'e wasn't, Major. 'E was certainly in it when I run upstairs to fetch 'im. I 'eard him fair snortin' an' wallowin'. Came out, 'e did, in 'is dressing-gown with the steam still risin' from 'im. Colour of a boiled lobster 'e was, Major. Which all goes to prove, doesn't it, that 'e *was* in 'is bath either then or a bit previous?"

Boddy was satisfied. It was no more than he had anticipated. Whoever had buried that strange contraption in the field, it couldn't have been John. There was, in fact, no single clue to connect him with Lydia's death save the somewhat nebulous one of motive. John had, by his wife's death, inherited a fortune. But that was a natural outcome of the tragedy; there was nothing unusual about a wealthy wife leaving her money to an impecunious husband. No, all the evidence seemed to point to Swale-Reid as the possible murderer. Except for one small factor: how had the Rector managed to break into the Arundels' garage and solder the head on to the spiral spring? And why the devil had he elected to do the job in the enemy's camp? He could have picked up a soldering outfit for a few shillings at any ironmongers and forged his curious weapon in the privacy of his own outhouses.

CHAPTER X

Bedside Chat

I

BACK ONCE MORE IN THE MELLOW FAMILIARITY OF HIS OWN STUDY, Boddy mixed himself a night-cap and began to assess, with a certain feeling of depression, the opening stages of his crusade. Progress, considerable progress had been made but it had been the "progress of elimination", as he liked to call it. He had taken a bunch of facts in his hand and weeded the sound from the rotten. He had proved to his own satisfaction not so much what *had* happened, but what *hadn't* happened. The results, in a way, had been encouraging; like the immortal phrase in the school report, he had "worked hard, but could do better". He had, for a start, more or less convinced himself that Swale-Reid was his pigeon, albeit a somewhat scrawny, elusive pigeon, and with this assumption went the equally strong conviction that Willis, Hawkinge, Honororia and John were armed with impregnable alibis. He drew up a brief list on his bridge-pad to show where they had been when the shot was fired.

Willis—*Platt's Lane.*

Hawkinge—*Platt's Lane.*

Honororia—*Copse below the Studio Meadows.*

John—*In the bath.*

In the cases of Willis and Hawkinge each had a couple of witnesses to corroborate his alibi. Willis had Hawkinge and Master Bull. Hawkinge had Willis and Master Bull. And even assuming such a fantastic hypothesis as a murder collaboration between Willis and Hawkinge, there was no getting round the stocky, assertive evidence of young Bull. John, too, had a witness—his cook-housekeeper. Granted Mrs. Willis had not actually *seen* him in his bath—that was expecting a little too much corroboration on the part of the housekeeper—she had heard noises distinctive of a body wallowing in water, she had noted steam rising from that body and the lobster-like colouring of those portions of that body visible to her when the bathroom door was opened. In brief, it was not pulling too long a bow to assume that her master's body *had* been in a bath when she, the bearer of evil tidings, had rapped on the door.

Honororia alone had no witness. Her evidence had to stand firm on its own shapely legs. But dammit! how could he disbelieve this innocent young puss? Much of her sweet and forlorn appearance might be no more than a lovely deceit behind which she planned, lured and trapped, with the hard-bitten cunning of a courtesan, but surely she was not a murderess? There was a vast gap between a young girl scheming and angling to hook the man she loved and the cold-blooded machinations of the criminal. Yet, with the dispassionate mind of officialdom, he could not entirely wipe Honororia off the slate. All other things being equal, she *could* have shot Lydia Arundel.

But it was exactly these "other things" that at the moment drew Boddy's brows together in perplexity. The "Who?" he felt could come later. His vital preoccupation must first be with the "How?". And the "How?", at the moment, seemed of a nature far too subtle, mechanical and diabolical to be pinned on to a mere woman! Was he justified in assuming that Gammon's "h'elongated cattypault" (now on the smoking-table at his elbow) had a definite connection with Lydia's death? If this were so, and Boddy believed it to be true, then Honororia must be credited with that clandestine soldering escapade in the Arundels' garage. Which, to borrow the Euclidean phrase, was absurd. So in full consideration of the murder method, Honororia receded farther and farther into the background. All the facts seemed to suggest that the murderer was of the male sex.

With the slow and sober movements of a man used to a leisured routine, Boddy took up the contraption and appraised it in detail. As far as he could gauge it must have served one of two purposes. (*a*) It was a lethal weapon and had actually been used in the killing. (*b*) It was an instrument designed to lock a door or window on the inside from the outside. It was here, in fact, that his main problem branched off in two laterals. Lydia had been shot either by some inexplicable means from outside the studio, and the discharged automatic, by some even more cunning jiggery-pokery, introduced into the room near the body. If this *were* the case and the murderer's idea was to suggest suicide, then it presupposed his knowledge of Lydia's eccentricity in locking the studio door when painting.

This, after all, was the star clue in a suicide theory. If the door had not been locked on the inside, then police suspicion would have been instantly aroused and a far more comprehensive investigation set afoot. If it were murder, then the murderer must have been successful in his efforts to soothe and side-track this official suspicion. Both North and Wilmott had, after a brief flare-up of doubt, been lulled into the conviction that it *was* suicide. As a footnote to this piece of reasoning, Boddy made a further mental reservation—John, Jed and Mrs. Willis would probably be the only people who knew that Lydia always locked herself in, when at work. Again, John and Jed had their proven alibis. What then of Mrs. Willis? He decided, in due course, to look closer into her *bona fides*.

Now taking the other fork, the Major constructed the second possibility. The murderer had got into the studio, shot Lydia at fairly close range, placed the Colt near the body, rushed out, and by some incomprehensible trick locked the studio door on the inside. But how? Certainly the contraption he was turning over so helplessly in his hands did not seem to be designed for turning a key in a key-hole. It was not delicate enough. Its mechanical principle was not adapted to such an operation. In a broad way, this piece of apparatus had been designed to *shoot*, to propel something through the air. But what? Surely not the bullet lodged in poor Lydia's skull?

Suddenly he straightened up and narrowed his eyes beneath their overhanging scrub of grey hairs. He was thinking back, fast and furious. The studio that Wednesday night—Belling, North, McBane, himself dithering on the edge of the official circle. McBane's pronouncement with regard to the bullet. "It went in but it hasna come oot again, Inspector!" Ha! precisely. Nobody had ever set eyes on that tiny yet shattering scrap of metal. In the circumstances the police had not thought an autopsy necessary. Was it possible that the bullet lodged in Lydia's brain was not of a .45 calibre? Had the scrap of metal been discharged from this cryptic catapult? But confound it, the shot had been heard by a number of people and an empty shell had been found near the automatic. The wound had shown some powder-blackening. So what was it after all, eh? A dead-end theory. Better back out and try another road.

But it was hopeless, discouraging! Try as he would Boddy could not find his way out of the maze. The more furiously he attempted to sever the Gordian knot of this tantalizing "How?" the more desperate and impotent he felt. He recalled with bleak nostalgia the brilliant *coups* of Poirot, Wimsey and Inspector French. Faced with just such a "sealed-box" murder they drew their inspired solutions like a conjurer out of the air—a blinding flash of intuition, a chance memory, a dazzling gem of reasoning, and there was the answer, stark and inescapable, "in the bag". With a dispirited grimace, he mixed himself a second night-cap and returned, rather shamefaced, to the secondary problem, the "Who?" angle of the case.

Mrs. Willis, eh? Well, confound it, she could have done it as well as any of his other suspects, perhaps with an even greater facility. She could have fired that shot and, having set the stage to make it look like suicide, rushed brazenly upstairs and hauled her master out of the bath. Figuratively speaking, of course. Time and again in detective novels the man or woman who dashed pell-mell into the study, office, pub or police-station, pale, agitated, horrified, turned out to be the murderer. It was one of the most conventional of alibis, this "I-discovered-the-body" sort of innocence. Just as the character with the cast-iron alibi was usually the reader's first choice as murderer. Not always, confound it! Sometimes the author did a double double-cross on the last page and left one feeling choleric and damned foolish. But, Boddy asked himself, could the ample, wheezy, good-natured Mrs. Willis really come under suspicion? There was an abyss between the assertion that she *could* have done it and that she *had* done it. There was no apparent motive. She honestly believed her husband to be in the kitchen when she stumbled through to tell him of the shot. It wasn't until she actually found the kitchen-quarters deserted that she recalled Jed had mentioned a sortie to The Green Dragon. And if she truly thought her husband was still in the house, surely she wouldn't have risked that journey to the studio and back? No, taken all round (and that was the only way Mrs. Willis *could* be taken!) the housekeeper was not even a starter in the race.

"So I'm left," thought Boddy, "with the Padre. Now what? Attempt to corner him? But how? Get Tubby on to the job? Ring him to-morrow—tell him Swale-Reid's not yet turned up. Suggest he traces his relatives—if any. Put the Rector on the Missing List. A notice in *Police Orders*, eh? But keep my detective activities under my hat. Throw myself open to leg-pulling. Friendly leg-pulling, perhaps, but not too acceptable during the delicate opening stages of my investigations. Drives it home, eh? The difference between fiction and reality. Tubby's right—must admit it! I've lost my sense of proportion by analysing too many synthetic crimes. Reprehensible!"

2

But Tubby Wilmott, the following morning, anticipated the Major's 'phone-call by half an hour. Gammon entered during the toast-and-marmalade stage of Boddy's breakfast to announce that the Chief Constable wished to speak to him on the telephone.

"Ha! 'morning, Tubby," said Boddy, with the overdone heartiness of a man with an uneasy conscience. "Promise of another hot day, eh?"

"Now look here," replied Tubby. "You know very well, my dear chap, that I haven't hauled you away from your *Times* and toast to talk about the weather. It's that Padre of yours—he's turned up. At least we think it's him."

"What! Where?"

"At the moment he's lying unconscious in the Frenshaw Cottage Hospital with superficial cuts, abrasions and slight concussion. We want you to come over at once and identify. Can do?"

"Of course, my dear fellah. But what the deuce does it mean? Attempted suicide?"

Wilmott chuckled and said with deliberate coarseness: "Suicide my—well, you know what! Have you ever heard of bathos, Boddy?"

"One of the Three Musketeers, what?"

"*Bathos*, my dear chap, not Athos; a sudden descent from the sublime to the ridiculous. Only that's what your Padre seems to have brought upon himself. He works himself up into a state of fanatical remorse, makes a high-minded flit from his plush-lined living, sets forth to rediscover his soul, and at six ack-emma this very Sunday morning he's knocked down by a bicycle on the Frenshaw-Witterton road. The perfect anti-climax! Amusing, isn't it?"

"Not for Swale-Reid," said Boddy sternly. "This is very distressing news, Tubby."

Wilmott made a handsome apology. "Sorry, Major. But after twenty years in the Force we become little more than pachydermatous louts. We're as impersonal, y'know, as the medicos. Well, can we expect you? Either come to my office here or drive over direct to Frenshaw. Suit yourself. We can meet at the hospital."

"We will! Your driving, my dear fellah, is bad for my blood-pressure."

As Boddy turned from the 'phone he was aware of Gammon quivering like a gaffed trout at the regulation three paces distance.

"Well, Gammon?"

"Shall I start up the car, sir?"

"How the devil—?" exploded Boddy, casting a penetrating glance at his batman. "Listening at doors, eh? Confounded cheek. Better fellahs than you, Gammon, have been cashiered for that sort of thing. All right. All right. Don't excuse yourself. Get my hat."

"*And* mine, sir?"

"Very well, Gammon. If you insist."

"As a matter o' that, sir, I've got a maiden h'aunt in Frenshaw what I 'aven't seen for—"

"Excuses unnecessary, Gammon. You can share the driving. Dismiss!"

"Very good, sir."

3

With Gammon at the wheel, Boddy was able to sit back and, with certain reservations, enjoy the passing panoramas of Sussex. These reservations originated in his batman's somewhat exuberant style of driving. Syd, first and foremost a yeomanry man, was not mechanical-minded. He had no "feel" for a car, no conviction, so to speak, that he and his mount were a single unit. In fact, from the moment he slipped into the driving-seat he was affected by a species of irresponsibility born of the belief that all mechanism was beneath contempt. His gear-changing (which had to be *heard* to be believed) was nonchalant; his acceleration unexpected; his steering tortuous. Only a long series of miraculous escapes from disaster had crystallized in Boddy the fatalistic attitude that Gammon "always got away with it", and this allowed him, in some measure, to relax.

He did so that lovely July morning, snatching at this interim which was slipped edgewise between his investigations. He had always favoured high-summer in England, when pink and crimson ramblers rioted in the cottage gardens and fool's-parsley foamed beneath the hedges. And Sussex was his county—with its bosky elms, its sturdy oaks, its parklands, hop-fields and hump-backed downs. It was an intimate, welcoming landscape, sunk that morning in an apathetic Sabbatical calm. The sun-shot air was rich with the sound of bells, whose sweet vibrations and lapping overtones curled and broke like invisible waves upon the senses. Here and there the white bonnets of oasts, with their wind-vanes like stiff-blown ribbons, clustered like groups of rotund gossips about a farmhouse. The road to Frenshaw dipped and rose with the elated flight of a bird, now flickering through a belt of beeches, now drawn straight and sun-swept along the crest of a ridge. And it came to Boddy, after the long tiring trek of his career, that this was a heritage he would not care to surrender lightly. For a moment, lost in this amiable appreciation, he forgot that he had dedicated himself to the solution of a puzzle that was based on brutality and violence; and then with a start he *did* remember, and the peaceful landscape only served to heighten the tragedy of poor Lydia's death. She had been an integral part of this landscape. She had loved to walk in it, to talk of it, to paint it and now—

His teeth clenched more tightly over his pipe-stem. By Jove! if he *were* right—and now he had little doubt—this malicious, cold-eyed, skulking rat of a fellah was scheduled for the long-drop! The tranquillity of this pleasant corner of England was not to be shattered with impunity!

4

He found Tubby Wilmott's sleek black car drawn up outside the Cottage Hospital. A uniformed chauffeur sat bolt upright at the wheel. Recognizing Boddy, the man saluted. "The Chief went in about twenty minutes ago, sir."

"Ha, thanks! Thanks! I'll join him."

But as he mounted the steps, Wilmott, accompanied by a short, bald man in spectacles, came through the swing-doors.

"Hullo, Major! We managed to steal a march on you, by the look of it. This is Dr. Hazlitt. We've just been in to have a look at the patient. I'm afraid he's still unconscious, but that shouldn't prevent you from setting our minds at rest about his identity. He must have cleared his pockets before he left the Manse. Nothing on his person save a couple of pound-notes and some loose change."

Piloted by Hazlitt they strolled down a spacious antiseptic corridor roofed with glass and into an even more spacious and more stringently medicated ward. Only a few of the beds were occupied and the doctor led them to a corner one at the extreme end of the ward, around which a screen had been set. Stepping aside, Hazlitt motioned the Major forward.

A single glance at the haggard, ascetic face was sufficient. Even through the disfigurements which the man's features had sustained, Boddy had no difficulty in recognizing the Rector. He turned to Wilmott and said in an undertone: "It's Swale-Reid. No doubt about it. What a damnable toss he's taken in the middle of a promising race, eh?"

Hazlitt, overhearing the remark, said blandly: "He'll be as lively as a cricket in a week or two, Major. In my opinion his trouble's more mental than physical. He has the appearance of a man who's allowed his worries to burn a big hole in his constitution. Too fine-drawn, for my liking. But plenty of rest and a well-balanced diet should soon—"

"Bring back the roses into his cheeks, eh, doctor?" broke in Wilmott facetiously. "You medicos are marvellous fellows. You've brought the job of inspiring confidence to a fine art. One honeyed word from you and you'll convince me that, for all my sixteen stone, I'm a fit man!" He chuckled thickly and turned with a wink to Boddy. "Well, Major, is the rumour correct that you're lunching me at The Black Swan? We can't drive home on the verge of starvation, you'll admit."

As they went down the ward, Boddy said uneasily: "Er—don't think I'll get back to Beckwood at once, Tubby. My man, Gammon, wants to see a maiden aunt here. And besides I—I—"

"You want a word with the Padre, eh? Quite understandable, my dear chap—and if Hazlitt agrees—"

The doctor nodded. "A brief interview may be quite possible when he comes to. I understand you're an old friend of his, Major?"

"Er, yes. I trust so. There are one or two little matters—er—*parish* matters which—"

He allowed his sentence to dissolve in silence. He was acutely anxious that Wilmott should not suspect his real reason for desiring this interview. Tubby's next words reassured him, for after they had shaken hands with Hazlitt and were walking to their cars, he said: "The Frenshaw sergeant will have to question the Padre as well, y'know. Pure routine. We want to get full details of the accident, in case there's any question of compensation. But don't let that worry you. He needn't tackle the poor devil until to-morrow."

Having told Gammon that he could drive round to see his aunt, Boddy climbed in beside Wilmott, the chauffeur sitting at the back, and they made for The Black Swan. Over lunch, a surprisingly excellent lunch for a small-town hostelry, Tubby began to hold a post-mortem on the inevitable topic.

"You know, Boddy, I've had a few nasty qualms since the inquest. I *think* Titterton directed the jury with perfect fairness in accordance with the evidence, but I'm not sure all the available evidence was laid on the table. I ought to have pressed for a postponement. It might have helped. But, of course, it's all fine and dandy to be wise after the event. One thing that worried me were those recent fingerprints on the gun. We discovered, you may remember, that they weren't Mrs. Arundel's."

"Quite so!" Boddy's innocence was enormous and convincing. His blandness was statuesque.

"So I followed the matter up—*sub rosa*, of course. I discovered whose prints they were."

"Really?" (Had he overdone his disinterest?)

"Yes, Willis's."

"Ah!"

"And you realize Willis put up an alibi that proved to be a dud. He *said* he had gone up to The Green Dragon."

"Ha! Hadn't he?"

"No, the Beckwood constable found that out. And what's more, Willis, confound him, wouldn't say *where* he was when the shot was fired."

"Suspicious, eh?"

"Damned suspicious." Tubby paused, took a long pull at his tankard of old-and-mild, then added in a flat voice, "But suspicion alone gets one nowhere. It's a car without petrol. Willis had no motive. Besides, how the devil could he have entered and left the studio when both the door and window were locked?"

"Impossible—what?"

Tubby inclined his head in sad agreement. "I only wish I could feel a hundred per cent satisfied with that verdict. The thought that Titterton may have been wrong is like an irritating speck of grit in the corner of my brain. Of course, it's probably never occurred to *you* to doubt his verdict?"

"Er—no!—no! Absurd to doubt it, eh?"

"I wonder," said Tubby musingly, running a hand round his massive chins. "I wonder. There's just a faint chance that it was *not* suicide, that we missed some vital clue in our preliminary investigations. Damn it! One minute I blow hot and the next I blow cold—don't know what to think!"

"Bad, that," observed Boddy. "Catch a mental chill, eh?" Then briskly: "Well, what about our chat? Don't want to miss the chance of a palaver with the poor old Padre. Might cheer him up. He's had a rotten deal, Tubby. Rotten!"

5

About three-thirty that afternoon Mr. Swale-Reid, pitching and tossing in a sea of darkness, glimpsed in that rushing chaos a far-away pin-point of light. It was like a promise of salvation. With all his strength and will he strove to reach out and encompass that brilliant mote within his under-standing. It was no easy task, for his thoughts were no more than splinters of imagery which floated away before he could grasp their significance. But gradually that speck of light grew and wavered outwards, the dark-ness smoking back from its luminous encroachment, until the Rector was conscious once more of his identity. A weak, uncertain smile played about his lips like the smile of a child in the sudden warmth of the sun.

Noticing that smile, Boddy leaned forward and said in a husky bass: "Feeling better, Padre? Feeling more yourself, eh?"

At the sound of his voice the Rector's face darkened and a shadow of fear and perplexity crossed his countenance. He seemed to be groping in his memory, searching for some link that would connect this voice with his past. Then, with a rush reality returned to him and the old burden of his guilt weighed implacably on his spirit. He recalled everything—his agony of indecision, his sudden flight, the long cross-country plod through hours of darkness, the daylight hours drowsing in concealment and, finally, something whizzing out of space and rushing him into oblivion. And behind these jumbled recollections loomed the fatal image of Lydia Arundel—accusing, mocking, persistent.

"Who is it?" he whispered. "I seem to know—"

"Boddy. Come to have a word with you, Padre. You've taken a bit of a toss, but you're all right now. Must just stand easy for a space."

"Yes—yes—I seem to remember—something—something ran into me."

"Ha! Shouldn't worry about that now. Just lie still. Take it calmly. Got to get fit and carry on with your job, eh? Can't do without you in Beckwood, y'know—an institution."

Swale-Reid shook his head in feeble protest. "I ran away—not worthy of their trust. I shall never go back. You—you don't understand, Boddy. Nobody has ever understood. As long as she is there I can have no rest. She has been an evil influence in my life—ever since—that night—"

"Evil influence?" Boddy made pretence to be amused. "Lydia Arundel! Nonsense, my dear fellah!"

"So you *knew*," breathed the Rector, aghast. "About Lydia? The whole parish knows! How can I ever face them again? Don't you see?"

"Listen, Padre," said Boddy, placing a friendly hand on the Rector's shoulder. "I've never known—*for certain*. Only guessed. Your parishioners haven't even done that. Can't you see, the courageous thing, the only thing is to go back and carry on. It's your duty. We're not attached to the same regiment, Padre, but dammit, we're both soldiers!"

"Apart from her—yes. I may have the strength to sustain my faith. But when we meet again—" He turned his head aside on the pillow and covered his eyes with a thin and bloodless hand. "You don't understand the frailty of the flesh, my friend. It—it—"

But Boddy was staring at him, almost blankly, in the chaos of sudden realization. He broke in gently: "But surely you knew? You've heard the sad news?"

"News?"

"About poor Lydia."

"No. I don't understand—"

"She's no longer with us, Padre. She—er—died last Wednesday."

For a moment Swale-Reid made no movement. His mind did not seem to have registered the tragic tidings. Then he uttered a curious little moan, drew the sheet up over his tired eyes and sobbed softly. Whether with pity or relief it was impossible to say. Boddy was filled with remorse. He was a clumsy fool! An oaf! The Padre was in no fit state to suffer the shock of such hard news.

With a gesture of farewell he patted the Rector's shoulder through the bedclothes and hurried off to find Hazlitt. He felt almost shamefaced as he explained to the doctor what had taken place, the more so since he could not reveal the true reason for desiring this interview. But Hazlitt was not unduly perturbed by his patient's reactions. He suggested that Boddy should visit the Rector the following afternoon and promised to 'phone if anything untoward should occur in the meantime. Then he left the Major to go through to the ward.

As Boddy emerged from the swing-doors into the blinding sunlight, he glanced at his watch. Four o'clock. He had told Gammon to meet him with the car at four, and with that virtue of military precision inherent in his nature, Gammon was standing at ease beside the little saloon. On seeing the Major, he sprang to attention and opened the car door.

"H.Q., sir?" Boddy gave a preoccupied nod. "Padre not worse, sir?"

"No, Gammon. I've an idea that when he's got over the shock he's going to be twice the man he was. Confound it all, we soldiers aren't the only ones who fight battles, y'know."

CHAPTER XI

Accommodating Address

I

THE COUNTRYSIDE WENT BY UNNOTICED ON THE HOMEWARD RUN. Boddy's thoughts were still hovering about that corner-bed behind the screen. It was not until that afternoon, perhaps, that he fully appreciated what a protracted, bitter struggle had taken place in the Rector's conscience. He had sought in the Padre's unhappy flight a motive for murder, nothing more. But now the essential kindliness of the Major's nature came uppermost and he was aware of the human element in that invisible struggle. He was tolerant enough to dismiss the Padre's lapse from grace as an incident of merely temporary importance. Granted, a Rector was expected to toe the moral line more rigorously than a member of his flock, but perversely this revealing flash of weakness seemed to make him, at least in Boddy's eyes, more of a man. After all, Swale-Reid had been horrified by this sudden surrender to temptation. He had not gloried in it. Neither was he a hypocrite. Above all, knowing something of Lydia's formidable allure, her wicked delight in charming and enslaving the male, he felt that the Rector had been not only subtly persuaded on to the slippery slope but dragged forcibly down it!

It was strange how Boddy had set out with such impersonal eagerness to test this unhappy suspect. It now seemed cruel, unthinking, that he should ever have suspected. Swale-Reid had not even realized that Lydia was dead. In that simple fact his alibi was set like a gem in a brooch. His reaction had been spontaneous. A man emerging from a coma is in no fit state to dissemble. The Rector had left Beckwood that Wednesday night without realizing that the cause of his departure was already dead. Or if not already dead, at least destined to die that very evening. This posed the only remaining doubt; had Swale-Reid left the Rectory before or after the shot was fired, and if before, was it possible he had done this dreadful thing without knowing it?

Boddy shied away from this unsavoury theory without delay. If Lydia had been murdered, then the crime had *not* been committed by a man in the throes of a brain-storm. There was too much calculation in the set-up of the murder, too many baffling points, too few clues. No, with a feeling of profound relief, he knew without question that the Padre was innocent. He had, in the past, acted foolishly, perhaps. He had suffered for this foolishness. He had thrown himself open to malicious gossip. He had temporarily lost all sense of proportion. But the Padre was no murderer.

Boddy's one thought now was to reinstate Swale-Reid in the village, to kill all gossip and free the Rector from his sense of guilt. He saw at once what line to take. The Padre, his nerves all to pieces through over-work, had wandered from the Rectory suffering from loss of memory. If he could convince Swale-Reid to put up that story, it should not be difficult to curb the tongues of his calumniators. It was strange how good seemed to blossom out of evil. Honororia and Stanley Hawkinge were now together again in perfect amity. Was it too much to hope that soon the Rector would be back not only in his familiar pulpit but in the hearts of his parishioners?

Then, this problem solved, in theory, Boddy returned abruptly to the other, even more sombre puzzle. With the Rector acquitted, who then *had* murdered Lydia Arundel? He had pulled the trigger on that final round and it, too, had proved a dud. His magazine of suspects was now emptier than Pandora's box. With a gusty sigh he realized that he would have to begin worrying the facts all over again. He was back where he had started!

2

For three days he worried at those facts—at table, half-brooding over an unopened book in the lounge, plodding down leafy lanes, or digging in his garden. The main problems of the case were never really absent from his thoughts.

"Oh, dearie me!" chattered the tireless Miss Finnigan. "I can't imagine what's come over the Major, really I can't! He's that absent-minded he only seems half there, if you follow my meaning? I've *heard*—of course I don't *know*—but I've heard he was once sweet on poor dear Mrs. Arundel, which may account for it, don't you think? Such upsets in Beckwood—I never did! I suppose you know the Rector's been found—knocked down by a bicycle near Frenshaw? Wandering with loss of memory, so the Major said, and *he* ought to know because he's visited the Rector more than once in hospital. Poor Mr. Swale-Reid. As Major Boddy said, he's been the subject of the most unpleasant tittle-tattle. 'Miss Finnigan,' the Major said to me, 'if you hear one unkind word against the Rector, kill it stone dead!' he said. 'I do believe,' he said, 'that if St. Peter walked in Beckwood, there would be *some* people, Miss Finnigan,' he said, 'who would fling mud at his saintly name!' Well, did you ever? And to think there *are* people in our very midst who delight in spreading such nasty tales. It makes one ashamed for one's very kind, it does! Mark this, if ever I *do* hear an evil word spoken against our dear Rector I'll expose them before all the parish. Believe me, I'd stand up in the House of Lords and *denounce*, them before the whole congregation. Yes! Yes! But dear Major Boddy. He seems so far away, as if half his thoughts lie, as it were, beyond the grave!"

But if the village noticed Boddy's preoccupation, they were even quicker to perceive that Lydia's death had left no real scar upon John Arundel. It might be said that his wound healed with miraculous rapidity. Within a few days his jaunty *bonhomie* had returned. On Main Street he had a quip and a ready word for everybody. Beckwood found his attitude disconcerting, for seeing him in the distance they composed their features into an expression of suitable commiseration and prepared to deliver themselves of the stock condolences. But on meeting John face to face they felt like funeral-mutes who had wandered into a cocktail-party. The village condemned John Arundel. Now that Lydia was no longer at his side, they began to look askance at his white-and-tan shoes, his suit of cream tussore and his ridiculous monocle. They didn't take kindly to the fact that he had inherited The Oasts and the whole of his wife's fortune.

But John was quite unaware of this hostility as he made ready to leave Beckwood and sink his sorrows in historical research. He hustled Burnham into clearing up the legal matters, and suggested that the Willises should shut up the house for a week and take a holiday by the sea. In less than ten days after his wife's death, John was ready to start on that long, hard way which "out of hell leads up to light".

The night before he left, more out of politeness than desire, Boddy wandered up to The Oasts to bid him farewell. As a matter of course they gyrated to The Littel Bottel.

"So you're off to-morrow early, eh?"

"The question," said John, "is purely rhetorical, old man. You know I'm off early to-morrow. Say 'When?'."

"Whoa!" cried Boddy, who had never said "When?" in his life. "In the car, eh?"

"In the car."

"To London?"

"To London," replied John, meditatively mixing himself a gin and Angostura.

"Be away long, my dear fellah?"

"It depends, old man, it depends. The life of a creative artist is not to be fettered to the hands of a clock. And now that I am alone, unencumbered by any responsibilities—" He made a circular gesture in the air expressive of his complete unattachment. "It is not the price I *would* have paid for my freedom of course, old man, but destiny has forced it upon me."

"Umph. Sorry you won't leave your address. Should keep in touch, y'know—parish matters and so forth."

"I'd rather not be bothered. But there, my dear chap, I've been into all that already. You must accept my eccentricities in good faith. We artists are of a different clay, unpracticable, difficult, elusive—and just now I—I want to forget this felicitous phase of my existence. Tragedy can embitter the sweetest of memories. I've suffered more than I dare reveal, old man, and the wound will not heal for weeks, months, perhaps—years!"

"Ha! quite." Then with a rush of frankness: "But dammit, Arundel, can't say you look off your oats. Fit as a fighting-cock. Never saw you look better!"

John eyed him with dignified astonishment. "I say, old man, you don't suggest that my dear wife's death—?"

"Oh, no! No! Good God, no!" protested Boddy, aware that this was his precise suggestion. "Mustn't take umbrage, my dear fellah. None intended."

John preened himself expansively in the warmth of the Major's apology, and for a moment they sipped their drinks in a silence broken only by the gentle hissing of the gasolier.

"I'll think of you," said Boddy at length, "boxed up in the British Museum. Miss your garden, eh? Not my pigeon, y'know, digging around in a lot of musty books."

"Ah, well," said John sententiously, "every cobbler to his last. My stage career has made me highly adaptable, old man. One day the country gentleman; the next, the academic recluse searching for that 'irrefutable fact'. There is little, I think I may safely say, to which I cannot, if necessity demands, turn my hand."

It was then that Boddy, nonplussed by his own irrelevance, heard himself saying in sarcastic tones: "Ha! quite so—soldering for example?"

"I've never had any leanings to an Army career," said John, with the suggestion that the Army had missed a great deal by his taste in jobs.

"Not soldiering—*soldering*," said Boddy with emphasis.

"Soldering?" John's face betrayed not only the veneer of surprise but the solid base of a sudden uneasiness and, in a flash, Boddy knew that his unexpected question had been inspired. "I say, Boddy old man—what the devil—?" But the laugh that followed was not a good reproduction. "Why soldering?"

"Because," lied Boddy stoutly, "I've an idea that you were the fellah in the garage that night. You recall the incident, eh? As Willis pointed out, only Mrs. Willis, Lydia and yourself had possession of the keys. Lock wasn't tampered with—admit that? It all seemed so darned mysterious—felt I had to take it up with you."

"But Willis knew I was in bed and asleep," protested John with overdone good-humour. "I really haven't the ability to be in two places at once. I'm not as adaptable as that, old man."

"Then who *was* in the garage?" John lifted his shoulders. "Confound it all, Arundel, if it *was* you, why not say so? Not criminal to tinker about in one's own garage, is it?" Then loading his voice with ominous innuendo, he added: "I'm having this out with you, my dear fellah, because I don't want to see you in an awkward corner. Point is, the police—"

John's glass clapped on to the bar-top and he stared at the Major as if to certify his sanity.

"The police? What the devil have they got to do with it? Nothing was taken from the garage, nothing was damaged, and if I'm prepared to let the matter drop, I really don't see why they should interfere. I suggest whoever rifled my desk was responsible for this other mystery."

"But damn it! I know who rifled your desk!"

"Eh?"

"Willis, my dear fellow. Hawkinge bribed him to steal some letters he'd written to Lydia. Foolish letters. Thought they'd compromise his chances with the Preece wench."

"Then I suggest it was Willis himself in the garage."

"Then why draw attention to the fact by rousing half the household in the dead of night?"

John said weakly: "Yes, old man, there is that, of course, but it's hardly necessary to pick on *me* as the answer to this mystery. I'm a little surprised by your overweening interest in these ridiculous incidents, however unusual they may be. Tell me, Boddy, is there something more behind all this than meets the eye? In my present state of nervous tension it's distracting to think that things are going on around me of which I'm being kept in ignorance."

"Then you weren't in the garage that night, my dear fellah?"

"No, old man, I was *not!*"

"Good."

But Boddy was convinced that John Arundel had been peculiarly perturbed by this unexpected cross-examination. The whole atmosphere surrounding their *tête-à-tête* had been shadowed by a certain elusiveness on the part of his host. He seemed always to be side-stepping the issues, sidling round the awkward comers of their conversation like a stage Apache slinking from the scene of his crime. Was it possible that John Arundel—?

3

Once this suspicion had been reawakened, Boddy found it difficult to maintain even the pretence of good-fellowship. He would have left The Littel Bottel there and then if John had not pressed him so urgently to remain and "have one for the road". After his little outburst of annoyance, Arundel himself had simmered down and was again the rather suave, self-satisfied host, a gentleman bar-tender. He tried, with a kind of sophisticated amusement, to pump the Major about the Hawkinge letters.

"Poor Lydia," he said with a sorrowful head-shake. "She was always being pestered by these love-lorn hangers-on. It made life very difficult for her. As for that damn rascal Willis, I've half a mind to give him his notice, old man. Not exactly in the feudal tradition to sell his allegiance to another master and act against the interest of his overlords."

"No—shouldn't do that," said Boddy hastily. "Wrong of me to have given the fellah away. After all, my dear Arundel, he's done you no harm. The whole confounded business can be well forgotten, eh? Shouldn't do anything hasty."

"You're right," said John with becoming agreement. "'Haste,' as the poet says, 'administers all things badly.' Too true. And in any case"—he made another of his broad, histrionic gestures—"to-morrow all this will be in the past, remote, another world. Willis and his incurable stupidity will be no more than a fading blurr on the photographic plate of memory." Then, liking the sound of this, he repeated it with slow and weighty emphasis, rolling each word round his tongue and nodding his appreciation like a tea-taster.

At ten-thirty Boddy made his excuses and, accompanied by John, went out to his car. As he climbed into the driving-seat he noted with satisfaction that lights were still burning in the kitchen-wing. He had an idea up his sleeve, an idea that promised to bring him profit. John's farewells were loud and effusive. He stood there slightly inebriate, plump, sleek, bland-faced, radiating hospitality. Yet his monocle seemed to gleam wickedly in the starlight, and as Boddy swung the car away round the gravel sweep, he had a feeling that this cold and glittering eye was boring into the secret places of his mind. An addle-pated *bon viveur*? An historical novelist? A Machiavellian master of crime? Which?

Some two hundred yards up the road he pulled the car into the verge, switched off his headlights, turned off his engine and padded softly back to The Oasts. A small green door let into the wall marked the tradesman's entrance, and in no time he was beyond this and making his way stealthily to the kitchen-wing. A gentle rap drew Willis, coatless and collarless, to the back door. It was obvious that he was just about to retire for the night.

"Jigger me! if 'tisn't the Major, then."

"You alone, Willis?" asked Boddy *sotto voce*.

"Aye, sir. Missus gone up some time since."

"Good. I want a word with you. Safe if I come in, eh? Don't want Mr. Arundel to know about this."

"That's all right, sir. 'E'll never come out 'ere this time o' night. Will 'e take a chair maybe?"

"Er, thank you, Willis. May think it odd, sneaking round to the back door like this—but had to see you at once. Leave on a holiday to-morrow, don't you?"

"Aye, sir. Me an' the ole woman is 'aving a week at 'Astings."

"Quite." The Major leaned forward across the kitchen-table and said urgently: "Want you to hold your tongue about all this. No questions, Willis. Things in the wind—follow?"

The house-boy nodded. During the last few weeks he had been rendered almost impervious to surprise. Events had run too fast for his bucolic mind, and now he was content to lag behind and let events go their own sweet way. He had not forgotten the pound-note the Major had handed him on a previous occasion.

"First and foremost," went on Boddy, "d'you know where Mr. Arundel is going to-morrow?"

"To Lunnon, Oi reckon. Leastways that's what 'e says."

"Precisely, Willis. But has he left you a forwarding address?" Willis's ferrety eyes darted this way and that and he shuffled his feet in embarrassment. "Ha! he has, eh? Asked you to say nothing about it? Is that it?"

"'Tisn't far short of it, Major."

"Well, I've got to have that address. Urgent reasons. Can't explain. But it will be well worth your while to let me have it. *Well* worth it."

"Oi couldn't," said Willis stoutly, eyeing the Major's hand as it delved for his wallet. "Oi made the guv'nor a proper promise, Oi did, an' 'twould be more than my job was worth to tell 'e."

"Your job's not worth a tinker's curse anyway, Willis. Mr. Arundel knows it was you who rifled his desk."

"Jigger it! 'Oo told 'e then?"

"I did, Willis. Had to. But I also persuaded Mr. Arundel not to dismiss you." Boddy drew out a pound note and fluttered it before the house-boy like an inspiring banner. "Well worth your while, eh, Willis?"

For a moment Willis hesitated, then with a stubborn expression he held up three fingers. Boddy shook his head decisively. Willis sighed. Then after further cogitation, cupidity battling with common sense, he put up two fingers and watched Boddy with morose anxiety. This time the Major nodded and thrust the two notes into the house-boy's predatory hand. Rising, Willis crossed to the big dresser and took a slip of paper from an empty tea-caddy. On it Boddy read:

c/o Mrs. Peterson,
224 Laburnum Crescent,
Ilford.

Taking out his diary, he made a rapid note of the address and returned the slip of paper to Willis.

"Tell me, Willis. Mr. Arundel often went away when Mrs. Arundel was alive, didn't he?"

"Aye, every now an' then e'd go off for as much as two or three months on end."

"What about his letters then?"

"Can't say, Major. Mrs. Arundel saw to that."

"What explanation did he give for these—er—jaunts?"

"Well, seems that 'e's writin' a book an' every now an'—"

"Ha! Ever seen any pages of this book—manuscript pages in Mr. Arundel's handwriting?"

"Can't say Oi 'ave, sir."

"Have you ever seen him at work?"

"No, sir."

"Has Mrs. Willis?"

"Never to my knowledge, Major."

"Umph—curious."

"Mind 'e, sir, the guv'nor was often locked away in 'is room upstairs, an' the missus always gave us to understand that 'e was not to be disturbed 'cause 'e was workin' on this 'ere book. So Oi reckon there's summat to it, sir."

"You think Mrs. Arundel believed in this book?"

"Aye, Major, Oi do. Otherwise, maybe she wouldn't 'ave been so ready to let the guv'nor fly off the 'ook, as it were, an' disappear for months at a time."

"Ha! Sound psychological point, Willis."

"On the other 'and, Major, 'twere no more than tit-for-tat, seeing that Mrs. Arundel always went off on 'er own account when the guv'nor was away. Painting trips, sir. We used to shut up 'ere pretty frequent in the ole days. Oi reckon it was a sort o' mootual arrangement atween the missus an' the guv'nor to 'ave a bit of a 'oliday from each other."

"So you think they needed one—what?"

"Oh, well," said Willis philosophically. "You know what 'tis with a married couple—'ammer an' anvil, Major, 'ammer an' anvil. An' Oi reckon Mr. and Mrs. A. was just about like me an' my missus. Cooin' like turtle doves one day an' touchy as 'ell the next. Okkard woman, Mrs. A. An' the guv'nor's a bit of a turkey-cock, too, in 'is own barnyard. Never come to blows, o' course, but there was 'igh words sometimes, an' a deal o' argyfying."

"Ever heard anything about Mr. Arundel's early life?"

"Comes funny like from 'e, Major. Thought 'e'd know a darn sight more'n Oi do about that."

"Very little, Willis. Very little indeed."

"Same 'ere, sir. 'E was on the stage—Oi do know that—an' Oi did 'ear that 'e met Mrs. A. at one o' them stoodio-parties in Lunnon. But if 'e's got relations livin' we've never seen 'em down these parts. Nor any of 'is ole friends. Oi tell 'e straight, Major, the guv'nor's always been a bit of a mystery chap to me an' Mrs. Willis."

Boddy glanced up at the ormolu clock, which pinged out the passing seconds with such tinny persistence on the kitchen mantelpiece, and got stiffly to his feet. It had been a long day and the thought of a hot bath was pleasant to contemplate. Willis had served him well. There was little more to be gained by prolonging the catechism. He said casually: "What time does Mr. Arundel start for London to-morrow?"

"Breakfast at eight-thirty sharp, sir; that's 'is orders. Reckon 'e'll be on the road afore nine-thirty."

"Ha! Well good night, Willis. You'll keep this under the *punkah*, eh?"

"*Punkah*, sir?"

"Under your hat."

"Aye, sir. 'Tis all very flummoxing, but Oi reckon you b'ain't so daft as 'e seems."

"Kind of you, Willis." Then as he stuck his head out of the back door: "Hullo, confound it!—raining."

He turned up the lapels of his jacket and, putting down his head like a charging bull, made a dash for the car.

4

It was not until he was seated, panting and steaming, in the driving-seat that he was aware of other occupants in the car. Two figures, closely entwined, were lolling in a back corner, the one frail, diminutive, a shimmer of white in the glow of the dash-board light; the other, dark, looming, massive.

"Good God!" cried the Major. "Who the devil? Speak up, will you?"

"Pleathe it'th uth," came the coy and piping answer. "We thaw your car and when it thtarted to rain—"

"Honororia! Hawkinge!"

"Soon will be," grunted Stanley, sunk in almost porcine ecstasy, deliberately misconstruing the Major's ejaculation. "It's on again."

"What's on, dammit?"

"The ring," boomed Stanley happily, squeezing the fragile creature at his side with such gusto that Boddy expected to hear a cracking of bones.

"Thankth to you, dear thweet Major Boddy," gasped Honororia, shivering with frightened rapture beneath these tremendous embraces. "Oh, we've been tho thupid and I don't thee how we can ever repay you."

"Balderdash, my dear young lady. Just made you both see common sense. Great virtue. National asset, eh? Well, where can I drop you? Still raining. Can't walk about in those flimsey-whimseys. Or can I persuade you both to come back and have a drink?"

"Could do with a beer," announced Stanley, with the suggestion that prolonged love-making had put an edge on his thirst.

"Splendid! When's the wedding?"

"In a fortnight'th time," lisped Honororia shyly. "And Thtanley'th in a little fix about it, aren't you, my thweet? You thee he'th got no brotherth or clothe friendth and he wondered if you'd—" Then with a small titter: "Go on, Thtanley, you athk the Major."

"Best man," growled Stanley in hoarse embarrassment. "Need a best man."

"Oh, pleathe thay yeth, Major Boddy."

"Well, dammit," said the Major gruffly, highly delighted and enormously flattered. "Not much in my line. But confound it all, I'll have a stab at it! Charmed to help. Shake the moth-balls out of my morning-suit, eh?"

"Perhapth one day," concluded Honororia pertly, "you *may* need it for an even more thpecial occathion." Adding with coy mysteriousness: "I believe I know thomebody who'th got their eye on you, Major. No! No! You muthn't try and gueth! I thall never, never give her away! But the'th a darling, a *real* darling and I know the thinkth *you're* wonderful!"

CHAPTER XII

Interviews in Ilford

I

LONG BEFORE HE DROVE THE COUPLE UP TO BECKWOOD COURT, where Stanley had left his car, Boddy had made up his mind. He had told Gammon to stay up until his return, pending important orders, and the moment he arrived back at Ladysmith, he called him into the lounge.

"Breakfast at seven sharp, Gammon."

"Very good, sir."

"We shall need the car at eight-thirty at the latest."

"Very good, sir."

"Tanks filled. Oil in the sump. Tyre pressures correct. A general overhaul, Gammon."

"Very good, sir."

"And Gammon?"

"Yessir?"

"Ever had any experience of tailing a car?"

"Well, sir, I done a bit of a sprint after a bus, sir, but it don't go much further than that!"

Boddy snorted. "We're chasing bigger game, Gammon, over longer distances."

"Good 'eavens, sir, bigger'n a bus?"

"No! No! Of course not, confound you! You know what I mean. Don't be so damned logical. We're tailing Mr. Arundel, understand? He leaves in his car to-morrow morning for London. Got to keep him under observation all the way. Can we do it, Gammon?"

"Can a duck swim, sir. Easy!"

"Good. That's all, Gammon. Dismiss!"

"Very good, sir."

2

Yes, it was all thundering fishy! This forwarding address; what the devil did it mean? Why all this secrecy? Why refuse to leave his address in a decent open manner? Queer cove, John Arundel. Bit slippery, eh? Could a fellah really believe in all this palaver about historical research? Could one even believe in this confounded novel? Not one iota of proof had been put forward to support its existence. Even Lydia had been forced to take the thing on trust. What it really came down to was this, was John Arundel fashioned of the stuff of which authors are made? Boddy doubted it. Arundel was a good mixer, a social rounder, a dilettante, but, by heaven! he was no devotee of hard work. His marriage with a wealthy woman stiffened the assumption. And Boddy, though hidebound and prejudiced by his Army tradition, was not one of those happy fools who imagined that novels wrote themselves. Even bad novels. An author, though of poor bodily fibre, needed a tough and tenacious mind. In his opinion, Arundel was devoid of this attribute. Then why this carefully prepared and sustained rôle? Was it to fool Lydia into the belief that he wasn't a drone living on her money? Or was the plot more subtle? Was it to provide an excuse for these intermittent excursions from The Oasts?

The more he pondered these questions, the more he mistrusted John's recent behaviour. Good Gad! the fellah had looked damned uneasy when he'd dragged up that garage incident. If Arundel *had* used that soldering-iron, then it was Arundel who had buried that contraption in the Studio Meadows. But hold fast! If he *had* murdered poor Lydia, what was the motive? Damned stupid to kill the goose that was still laying the golden eggs. After all, Lydia was knocking up fabulous prices for her portraits and John naturally benefited. But against this, hadn't Willis spoken of quarrels and arguments? Incompatibility, eh? A bedrock dissimilarity in their temperaments? Lydia, with far greater culture, more brains, out of the top drawer, aware of all this and slightly patronizing? Infuriate a bounder like her husband. Possibly despised him and didn't bother to hide the fact. Another damn big pin-prick to his pride. Kudos and notoriety showered upon her as a top-line artist—might make the second-rate ex-actor wriggle a bit, eh? Perhaps Arundel had anticipated which way the wind was blowing, an irretrievable row, the final split, with himself stranded high and dry once more in Poverty Street. Yet, knowing that he had not been cut out of her will, deciding to filch what golden eggs there were and be damned to those as yet unlaid. In brief, deciding to kill his golden goose. Gad, yes! there was motive enough. In Boddy's opinion, John Arundel, though unthinkable as an author, was more than conceivable as a murderer. He had the slick brains, the ready tongue, the easy charm of the heaven-born criminal. Confound it! what was the expression rife in those Yankee gangster films? A Big Shot, wasn't it?

Well, to-morrow a new phase in his investigations would open. He'd find out for certain if Arundel *was* making his headquarters at 224 Laburnum Crescent, Ilford. Or whether this, to use the police phrase, was merely an accommodation address. He had an idea that Ilford was one of those sprawling, top-heavy, amorphous boroughs of London in which people lived, not by choice, but by necessity. A dormitory for white-collared workers. Somehow the epithet didn't fit John Arundel!

3

Gammon's punctuality did not desert him the following morning, and at eight-thirty to the dot the little blue saloon edged out of Ladysmith into Main Street. Boddy had decided to take the wheel for the first stretch of the chase and he drove direct to the starting-point. It was a happy choice; a deep-sunken lane that joined the main road some two hundred yards from The Oasts driveway. Once there, he posted Gammon at the junction with orders to signal immediately Arundel left the house. Then, with his pipe drawing well, he settled himself in the driving-seat and, curbing his natural excitement, began to peruse the sober pages of his *Times*. He turned, as usual, to the latest cricket scores, that morning of vital importance as Kent and Sussex, running neck to neck for the County Championship, were hammering it out in a three-day battle at Tunbridge Wells. But somehow the little printed figures jigged before his eyes and, before he could check it, he found his mind wandering back to the case.

That catapult worried him enormously. He felt certain that it was connected with Lydia's death. He felt certain that in some oblique way it offered a solution to the "sealed-box" angle of the crime. In some way that contraption had been used to circumvent the barrier of locked doors and windows. How? Had the automatic been fixed into the brass groove and fired by the release of the coil-spring and plunger? To what advantage? Simply this; the Colt could have been discharged at a distance of some three feet from the person holding the catapult. But, again, to what advantage? On the other hand, Boddy realized that the automatic *would* fit into that groove and fit into it rather neatly. But not by any exercise of his imagination could he fathom how the release of the coil-spring could have pulled the trigger. In fact, the natural result of pulling on the wire attachment would be the immediate catapulting of the whole gun into space. A damned ridiculous idea! What the devil was to be gained by—?

His *Times* slipped unnoticed to the floor and he gripped the wheel with a sudden influx of new interest. Hold on! Steady there! *Was* the idea so damned ridiculous? Suppose the murderer had in some way managed to shoot Lydia from outside the studio. What then? To suggest suicide he had to project the Colt and the empty shell-case to a point near the body. Had this been done by means of the catapult? Something in it, eh? Hadn't North commented on the fact that the automatic was lying some distance from the body? The suggestion was that it had skidded across the parquet as it fell from Lydia's nerveless hand. In precisely the same way it would have skidded across the polished floor if shot into the studio from the catapult. But devil take it, through what aperture had it been projected? Through what aperture had the shot been fired? The key-hole? Bah! Too small, quite apart from the fact that the key was in the lock. The window? Suppose the window had been partly open when the murderer arrived on the scene. Suppose Lydia had been shot through this gap and the Colt catapulted into the studio. Was there some method by which the murderer could have closed and locked the window from outside? He visualized the two big leaded casements with their patent locking device—a little handle was turned and a metal latch slid into a stout metal hasp. It was more of a bolt than a catch and, as such, surely impossible to push home from the wrong side of the casement? Besides, what of the curtains? They were drawn across on the inside of the window and would have completely obstructed the view of anybody trying to shoot. Yet, confound it, something of the kind must have happened. Only reasonable explanation. Was there some little factor he'd overlooked? Take another, more detailed look, eh? With this new theory in mind, it might—

He was aware of Gammon, waving a frantic arm, running up the lane from the main road.

"Start up, sir! Start up! Beg to report, sir, he's just turned out of 'is drive."

Boddy pressed the starter and before Gammon drew level the car was underway. Gammon made a grab at the door-handle, wrenched it open and flung himself, breathless, into the seat. As he did so, Boddy saw John Arundel's maroon-coloured car shoot across the head of the lane. The chase was on!

4

There was nothing in it. Arundel was a cautious driver and the two cars were of equal horse-power. Major Boddy had no difficulty in keeping his quarry in sight, though at no time approaching near enough to rouse his suspicions. Already there was traffic on the road and this served to make the Major's Popular Eight far less conspicuous. There were always dozens of Popular Eights turning out of by-lanes, careering through villages, drawn-up at kerbsides, spinning down the straight. They were ubiquitous little cars.

"SXT 1333," muttered the Major. "Do well to remember that, Gammon. Plenty of time to fix it in your mind, eh?"

They sped on through the homely Sussex villages—Frewenden, Wandhurst, Tyler's Green, High Otterton—through wooded vales and lush pastureland, up long winding ascents between copses of chestnut and hazel, out on to the great spinal ridge of windswept uplands that brought them at length to Hawkhurst.

"In Kent now," observed Boddy. "So far so good, Gammon."

So on, through the hop-fields and orchards, the dips and rises of Kent, until they reached the environs of Tunbridge Wells. So far Boddy had maintained excellent contact, admittedly losing the little maroon-coloured saloon round the major bends, but swiftly picking it up again and hanging doggedly on to its tail. But as they switchbacked over the hilly road which approached the town, he observed: "Brace ourselves for the real test now, Gammon. All damn fine in the open, but we'll have to keep our weather eye lifted in crowded streets. So watch out!"

The two cars careered down the long, slow-dropping hill. Fearing that Arundel might give him the slip at the first set of traffic-lights, Boddy accelerated and came right up behind the other car.

"Pull down your cap, Gammon. Grimace! Any damn thing! Mustn't be recognized."

At the first crossing where they were halted by the red, Boddy, by skilful manœuvring, shot into a gap beside Arundel's car and ordered Gammon to place his hand over his face. When the traffic broke at the signal, the two cars drew away, neck to neck, and for a short space raced side by side up the road. Then suddenly a baker's van, nosing out of a side-street, forced the Major to drop back for an instant and when his forward vision was clear again the saloon was no longer in sight.

"Blast it, Gammon! Bad show, eh?" said Boddy forcibly. "My own damn fault. Too thundering careful. Should have taken a risk there. Held our course!"

But an instant later Gammon uttered an excited cry of: "There he is, sir. Turn right here, sir! else he'll give us the air again. *Sharp* right, sir. Whew!"

The "whew" was more than justified by the sudden appearance of an elderly lady in black, seemingly dead ahead of the bonnet, who by a miracle of reflex action tottered back in reverse at the very moment when disaster seemed inevitable. They left her, a pathetic figure, groping in the gutter for her spectacles.

"Near shave, eh, Gammon?" said Boddy with a certain amount of pride.

"Very near, sir."

"Tickled you up, eh?"

"Come out 'ot all over, sir."

"But a justifiable risk, Gammon. Must admit it. There's our man dead ahead. Mustn't lose him again, eh?"

"We shan't, sir. Not with you at the wheel, sir."

Boddy looked sharply at his batman, then satisfied by his innocent expression that he had meant nothing derogatory, he went on: "So far so good, Gammon. He's still on the London road. Anticipate he *is* making for Ilford. Know Ilford, Gammon?"

"S'matter o' fact, sir, I've got a widdered uncle 'oo lives in Ilford, sir. Undertaker. Nice little business 'e's got too. Shows a real steady profit, sir."

"Relations all over the place, haven't you, Gammon? Maiden aunt at Frenshaw—undertaking uncle in Ilford. Come of prolific stock, eh, Gammon? Know Laburnum Crescent?"

"Laburn—! Sharp left 'ere, sir! No!—left, sir! *Left!* Gawd 'elp us—er—pardon me, sir. Phew!" Gammon mopped his brow; then with a tremulous calm: "Laburnum Crescent, sir? Do I know it? Like the back of my 'and, sir. Better slow up a bit, sir, we're pretty well up 'is exhaust. Yessir, Laburnum Crescent's only a stone's throw from—" Then with goggling dismay and a stare of incredulity, he added wildly: "'Arf a mo', sir. Take a look ahead, sir. We're sunk. Bin fooled fair an' dandy, sir. Take a dekko at that there number-plate!"

"ULK 64—" began Boddy, then with a choleric rush: "Good God, Gammon! You're right. Wrong car. Same colour. Same make, but *not* Mr. Arundel's! Foozled our drive when that damned van drew out in front of us, eh? Thundering bad show, Gammon. *Thundering* bad!"

5

But Boddy was taking no chances. He knew from his acquaintance with Big Shots in crime films and fiction that they had, when hunted, many cunning methods of eluding pursuit. One of these was a pedal which actuated a pair of interchangeable number-plates. It might be said that this refinement was as vital to the gangster's automobile as the choke, the carburettor and the armour-plating. He opened the throttle, therefore, and seizing his opportunity passed the car on a straight stretch of the London road. Lounging at the wheel, a cigarette dangling from geranium lips, was a young lady dressed in mustard-coloured tweeds with a bandeau about her sleek gold head.

"Well, that's that," grunted the Major, as he drew up on the roadside and allowed the maroon-coloured saloon to re-pass him. "No doubt about it, we've lost our quarry. Gammon. Must work out a new plan of campaign."

Five minutes later Boddy had made up his mind. Now that he was already *en route* for London, why not drive direct to Laburnum Crescent? He was highly suspicious of this address and anxious to find out precisely what sort of place it was. Moreover, John Arundel, now perhaps a mile or two ahead, might still be making for Ilford and Mrs. Peterson. It would go a long way towards establishing his *bona fides* if he were actually *staying* in Laburnum Crescent. Boddy had no proof that he had turned off the London road when he had given them the slip in Tunbridge Wells. Admittedly Ilford was a long way from the British Museum, but Arundel might have specific reasons for making this his London headquarters.

Now that all elements of the chase were absent, Boddy drove at a leisurely pace through the Kentish landscape and presently the first outlying bastions of London hove in sight—new brick-and-tile bastions, row upon row, pseudo-this and pseudo-that, filling-stations, tea-rooms, road-houses, chain-stores, utility plants and garish new public buildings faced with Portland stone—bastions rushed up overnight, as it were, to keep the legions of beauty from invading the Metropolis. Before these gradually advancing defences, however formless and flimsy, the countryside was slowly retreating. Soon, thought Boddy, the final phase of the battle would come, the last bastions of the perimeter would rise and the countryside would go down under the waters of the English Channel. His beloved Sussex would be no more, and London would stretch triumphantly from the cliffs of Dover to Beachy Head!

After a sandwich lunch in the snack-bar of one of the more pretentious of these mock-Tudor inns, a lunch which he democratically took with his batman, Boddy felt less depressed. Now that they were in the rabbit warren of streets, he handed over the wheel to Gammon, who knew the

South London district inside out. Restricted by the denseness of the traffic, Syd's driving was less inspired than usual and Boddy felt comparatively at ease. Lewisham, New Cross, the Old Kent Road, and soon they were rolling down to the river and across it. Then out the other side into more and more endless grimy streets, on and on through the squalor and noise and odours that formed the background to the lives of the crowds swarming over the pavements. By tradition the Major was a Conservative, yet the sordid atmosphere of these streets roused the humanitarian in him, the charitable, tolerant Boddy who so often over-rode the politician. There in the dingy murk, where a tree was something to remark upon, he had a sudden vision of the dew-wet lawns of Ladysmith, the flaming disks of the marigolds, the snapdragons, stocks and sweet-williams, the colour, scents and tranquillity of his little garden, and he wondered. He wondered and was uneasy. The fruits of the earth seemed strangely and unfairly apportioned, for here there was a premium upon sunlight and a rationing of natural beauty.

He was surprised and slightly bewildered when Gammon observed in a chirpy voice: "Does you good, sir, to get a whiff of ole Lunnon again. Nuffin' like it, sir. Livens a chap up no end. 'Ome to me, this is. I wouldn't swap it for 'alf the county of Sussex, sir; straight I wouldn't." Then with an air of excitement: "Jest coming into Ilford now, sir. Journey's end."

Boddy nodded but made no comment. He was thinking of John Arundel healing his sensitive soul in surroundings such as these. It seemed fantastic. He wondered what he was going to find at 224 Laburnum Crescent. Surely not Arundel in person? Somehow Ilford didn't seem to blend with those cream duck-suits, those white-and-tan shoes.

His perplexity deepened when Gammon swung the car off the tramlines of the highway and announced victoriously: "Beg to report, sir—'ere we are, sir. Laburnum Crescent."

"Right, Gammon. Draw into the side. Switch off. Got to work out a further plan of campaign."

He stared down the straight hard street in astonishment. Its name was a miracle of wishful thinking. For there was not, and obviously never had been, a single flowering laburnum within yards of this wretched alley-way. If there *had* been a crescent, then some astounding cataclysm must have bent back the houses overnight and left them in two ranks of impeccable alignment. More than ever Major Boddy felt that Arundel had no *personal* contact with No. 224; it was simply a forwarding address, a smoke-screen to cover some nefarious activity.

He turned to Gammon. "Going to send you out on patrol first, Gammon. Find out just where No. 224 is located. See what sort of place it is and report back here. Understand?"

"Very good, sir."

Five minutes later Gammon returned. "Beg to report, sir."

"Well, Gammon?"

"It's a greengrocer's, sir."

"Good God!" The thought that Mrs. Peterson might own a shop had never occurred to him.

"Living premises over'ead, sir. Notice up—Room to let. Mucky-looking sort o' place, sir. Shouldn't think that trade's too brisk round these parts."

"Well, what now, Gammon?"

"Beg pardon, sir, but might I suggest you sends me out as an advance party? With all doo respects, sir, but your presence might cause a bit of a stir in the dove-cot."

"Very well, Gammon. I'll wait here in the car. But go cautiously. Remember, if Mr. Arundel's there he might recognize you. Find out all you can without giving yourself away. See if Mr. Arundel is *known* there. Vital point, that. See if he arrived there this morning. If he's there now. If not, see if Mrs. Peterson knows where he is. A tall order, eh? But do your stoutest, Gammon. Fall in!"

"Very good, sir."

6

It was a job after Syd's own heart, and he tackled it with both fervour and good humour. Pulling his cap over one ear, he breezed into the shop, took a comprehensive glance at the meagre stock, and picking up an apple from a tray, sniffed it with suspicion.

"Na then, na then!" said the blowsy woman behind the counter. "Keep yer 'ands off the goods, carn't yer? If yer wants anyfink then ask for it proper. Good appils, they are, mate, nuffink wrong wiv *them*. Choice appils, *they* are."

"Orite, ma," said Gammon good-naturedly, dropping into the vernacular of his youth. "Keep yer 'air on—wot there is of it! Chap don't wanter buy a pig in a bloomin' poke, does 'e? 'Ow much?"

"Fivepence a pahnd."

"O.K." As the plump and wheezy proprietress was weighing out the apples, he went on casually: "See yer gotta room to let. Want a nice respectable lodger? Chap in a reg'lar job, eh?"

"'Oo, you?"

"Meaning me," nodded Syd. "Quiet 'omely chap, ma, no noosance abaht the 'ouse. Reg'lar muvver's 'elp."

"Might do worse. 'Ere's yer appils. 'Ow jer know I gotta room to let?"

"Saw yer notice, o' course. Mrs. Peterson, ain't it?"

"Wot, me? Na—yer wrong there. My monniker's Trusscott—Kate Trusscott—same as yer'd seen for yerself if yer'd tyken the trouble to read the sign over the burnt cinder. Mind yer, there *is* a Mrs. Peterson 'ere—first floor front—ole gal abaht eighty, she is, wot took my other spare room three years back. 'Ow jer git 'old of 'er name then?"

"Sorta distant relation o' my ole trouble-an'-strife. 'Adn't 'eard o' the ole lidy for years an' then sudden-like we gits noos of 'er. 'Course I ain't never seen 'er myself. An' knowing nothing abaht it, when I see you ahind the counter, ma—"

"Blimey! Do I *look* eighty?"

"Not 'arf you don't—'arf of eighty, I mean. But afore I asked abaht that room— See? I wanted to 'ave a dekko at the ole gal. So I bought these 'ere appils as a sorta excuse. An' then, blimey! If you ain't Mrs. Peterson arter all!"

"Jer wanta see the ole lidy?"

Syd nodded. "'Course I do. An' if I like the look of 'er dial as much as I like yer own, I'll tyke that there room, see? Got temporary work in the district. Three weeks. 'Od-carrier I am."

Mrs. Trusscott glanced out into the street, which was at that moment deserted and, putting the shop door on the latch, beckoned him to follow. "It's up these 'ere appils-an'-pears," she observed. "The ole gal'll 'av a surprise, eh?"

"'Ell of a shock more like," amended Syd feelingly, as Mrs. Trusscott stopped before a door on the first landing and thumped it vigorously with her clenched fist.

"Bit 'ard of 'earing," she explained.

A piping, quavery voice called out nervously: "Who's there?"

"It's me, granny. Brought a visiter to see yer."

There was a brief pause and the door was opened a few inches to reveal a crabbed, white-haired, exceedingly bent old lady in a black *moiré* silk dress of a style at least forty years out of date. On seeing Gammon, the old lady looked at him intently through her gold-rimmed spectacles and announced: "I don't know you. What do you want?"

Syd, now in a tight corner, fired a shot in the dark. "D'yer remember, Maggie, gran'ma? Maggie Peterson that was, afore she married me. One o' your ole pot-an'-pan's second cousins or sumfink, wasn't she?"

"Maggie? No, no. Clarence hadn't any cousins of that name. There was a Mary Peterson that he used to speak of—a dumpy, plain little girl, she was."

Syd laughed and slapped his thigh, at the same time edging cautiously into the room.

"That's 'er. To the life! My ole woman. Plain! Dumpy! But always bin Maggie in the family, she 'as, for years nah. Well, I'm 'er 'usband— Ted Smith." Then grasping the bewildered old lady's hand: "'Ow are yer, granny? Y'look wunnderful perky for yer age, straight yer do." He planted himself in a chair, his feet splayed, thumbs in the pocket of his waistcoat and beamed sunnily upon Mrs. Peterson. "Well, well, well, to fink I should really meet you arter all these years. Allus talkin' of yer is Maggie. Thinks the world of yer."

Mrs. Trusscott, who was standing in the doorway with a foolish smile on her face, now tactfully broke in: "Fink I 'ear somebody 'ammering on the shop door. Slip dahn an' see 'oo it is. S'long, mate. I'll show yer that room when you an' granny 'ave 'ad a nice long 'eart-to-'eart."

Alone with the doddering, short-sighted Mrs. Peterson, Syd took a brisk look round the room. The old lady, obviously bewildered by his visit, gazed at him as if trying to sort out the memories that time had so unkindly befuddled. She had a vague notion that Mary *had* married, but when and whom she was by no means certain. She tottered to a rocking-chair and, sitting down, spread out her voluminous skirts in a big black fan.

"I don't remember seeing you before. I don't remember ever seeing Mary's husband. Have you got any little ones?"

"Six," said Syd with gusto. "Youngest's two. Fine little nippers." Then off-hand: "Live 'ere all on yer own, do yer, granny?"

"I've been here ever since dear Clarence passed over," announced Mrs. Peterson in a querulous voice. "I'm a very lonely old woman now. Nobody ever comes to see me. Nobody remembers me now."

Syd clicked his tongue in commiseration. "Na, na, granny! Nice little place yer got 'ere." He jerked his thumb in the direction of the inner door. "Wot's through there, bedroom?" The old lady nodded. "Can I tyke a dekko? Maggie 'ud like ter know you was comfortable 'ere." But before she could make any answer, he had crossed over and peered into the second room. Then satisfied that it was empty, he added chirpily: "Fink of joinin' you 'ere for a week or two, if I like the room wot's ter let. Maggie 'ud like to fink as I was chappyroned, eh, granny? Yer see, I just gotta—" Then suddenly his roving eye was arrested by something on the mantelshelf and he broke off to add in astonishment: "Blimey! 'Oo's that? I seem ter reckernize the bloke in that there photo—damned if I don't!"

Following his outstretched finger, the old lady hesitated an instant and then said firmly: "No—you wouldn't know him. Mary never knew him either. It's just—just somebody I used to know when dear Clarence was alive. A long time ago now—yes—a long, long time—"

"Name o' Arundel, eh, granny?"

"No. No. That wasn't his name. Darby—Richard Darby. Mr. Richard Darby. He was a great friend of my dear husband's. A very great friend. A solicitor by profession. Mary never knew him."

"Funny," said Syd, running a hand round his chin. "I coulda sworn—"

He knew he wasn't mistaken. Although the photo was blurred and faded and the subject posed in one of those frozen-faced, stiff-necked attitudes dear to the Edwardian photographer, the features, above the absurdly high collar, were unmistakable. The bland, moon-like innocence, the vaguely unreliable eye, the broad mouth and dimpled baby-chin—these *were* the lineaments of John Arundel—not as he was, but as he must have been twenty years before. What the devil, thought Syd, was it doing on the old lady's mantelpiece? That photograph forged an unshatterable link between the owner of The Oasts and 224 Laburnum Crescent. The Major's instincts had served him well.

"Ever see this Darby bloke nah, granny?"

"Dearie me, no. I haven't seen him for a long, long time. Why it must be ten years or more. I don't even know where he lives these days. Perhaps he's no longer with us. Perhaps he has passed over, like poor dear Clarence. Nobody visits me now. They've all forgotten. All of them. I'm alone now, quite forgotten."

"Nah! Nah! Chirp up, chicken!" said Syd cheerily. "No good gettin' in the dumps. Doncher ever git any letters, granny? This Mr.—er—Darby; don't 'e ever write yer?"

The old lady shook her head and enlarged dolefully on her loneliness, and Syd, realizing that she had nothing more to give away, presently left her to seek out Mrs. Trusscott. As the latter was showing him over the gloomy little bed-sitter, he observed: "The ole lidy seems properly dahn in the mouf, eh? Real misery-me. 'Asn't she got any friends?"

"Not as I've ever seen. She don't 'ave any visiters, if that's wotcher mean."

"Nobody never writes the ole gal either, eh, ma?"

Mrs. Trusscott flashed him a quizzical look and said with a sniff: "Full o' curiosity, ain't yet, mate? If she got any letters I'd know abaht it, wouldn't I? Well, she *don't* git 'em—so there! Wotcher so nosey abaht 'er for?"

"Maggie 'ud be upset to think the ole gal was lonely—see?" Then lighting a cigarette and carefully breathing on the match, he added: "Funny abaht them letters though. Maggie an' I always thought as 'er nephew young Alfie Arundel 'ad 'is letters sent on from 'ere. A commercial is

Alfie—always on the move. No address of 'is own, see? Was only talkin'
to young Alfie last week." Then with genuine inspiration, joining two
bits of prevarication with a perfect link: "It was 'e 'oo put us on to the
ole lidy's address."

"Well, none of 'is letters 'as ever come 'ere," said Mrs. Trusscott tartly.
"Nah, wot abaht the room, mate? Yer like it?"

"Not so dusty. Not 'arf bad," said Syd with a final patronizing survey.
"Bit cramped. Pity there ain't no pianny. I'm a bit of a moosician in me
spare time. Rather wanted to 'ire a room wiv a pianny."

"Lah-di-dah!" exclaimed Mrs. Trusscott sarcastically.

"Tell yer wot I'll do," said Syd, as they went down again into the shop.
"I'll try another address wot I got, an' if they ain't got a pianny then I'll
come back 'ere. That soot yer?"

"'Obson's choice," sniffed Mrs. Trusscott, even more tartly. She had
been bitten this way before. "But I warn yer, there's one or two others
arter that room."

"Don't wonder," said Syd, pouring oil on troubled waters. "'S'nice
room, ma. 'S'very nice room an' I'd like to be near the ole lidy. Maggie
'ud like that too. But rather set me 'eart on that pianny, I 'ad. Well, cheero,
ma, an' thanks for showin' me arahnd."

"'Ere, don't forget yer appils."

"Blimey!" laughed Syd. "That won't do, eh? Not at fivepence a pahnd,
it won't!"

Still chuckling, he edged his way out into Laburnum Crescent and
made off in the opposite direction of the waiting car, which he noticed
was still parked at the far end of the street. It was a move prompted by
sound psychology, for he knew that his passage up the street would be
discreetly observed by Mrs. Trusscott from the shop-entrance. He had
been quick to realize that she had not taken him entirely at face value.
Neither had Mrs. Peterson. They had both been watchful, suspicious
of his questions, hiding something from him, and the temperature of
this suspicion had shot up alarmingly at the mention of Arundel. What
exactly did that name mean to these two sorry, downtrodden women at
No. 224? It was a long road from The Oasts to that grubby little greengrocer's shop.

7

The Major was taken off his guard when Gammon suddenly approached
the car from the wrong end of the street. He sidled up to the saloon
with all the slinky silence of a gunman who, at any instant, expects to
get the "woiks".

"Good God, Gammon!" snapped Boddy, irritated. "What the devil's
this? Hide and seek?"

"Beg to report, sir, patrol under enemy observation. Taken elusive
action, sir."

"All right, get in and tell me all about it. Been a damn long time, eh?
Have you obtained any information?"

Syd smiled, the quiet, rather superior smile of the cat that has swallowed the canary. "Beg to suggest, sir, that we turn into the main road
before I put in my report, sir. May arouse the enemy's suspicions, sir."

Once parked in a suitable place away from Laburnum Crescent, Boddy
lit his pipe and said impatiently, "Now, out with it, Gammon. Did you
discover anything? Anything important, eh?"

"Beg to report, sir"—and for the next ten minutes Syd talked without cessation, neatly outlining the results of his visit to the shop. As he
proceeded, Boddy grew more and more absorbed. His pipe went out
and he forgot, in the excitement of the moment, to relight it. For the
first time since he had come to the fateful decision to probe to the core
the mystery of Lydia's death, he felt that he had stumbled on real solid
evidence worth all his fancy theories lumped together. The full value of
Gammon's discoveries could not yet be appraised, but he was convinced
that in suspecting John Arundel's *bona fides* he was barking up the right
tree. Somehow this little greengrocery establishment in Ilford was connected with the tragic happenings at Beckwood. He was reaching out in
his investigations, but the little grains of truth were already beginning
to fall into his outstretched hand!

CHAPTER XIII

Gammon Picks a Lock

I

CERTAIN FACTS, THOUGHT BODDY, COULD BE TABULATED AT ONCE. They ran thus:

1. *Mrs. Peterson knew or had known John Arundel, though apparently under the name of Richard Darby, and was anxious to conceal the fact.*
2. *Arundel had not driven to Laburnum Crescent that morning—at least Gammon had picked up no clue to suggest that he was in the house. This seemed to indicate that No. 224 was merely a forwarding address.*
3. *Mrs. Trusscott appeared to be in league with Mrs. Peterson, and both, by their behaviour, had obviously been anxious to hoodwink Gammon about the letters.*

Apart from these three points, Gammon's sortie had proved once for all what Boddy had long suspected—John Arundel was engaged in some underhand business. He was, in brief, a fake; less an author than a swindler, less a swindler than a scheming little runt who, in all probability, had murdered his own wife. Boddy was ready to admit that this discovery at Ilford might have nothing to do with Lydia's death. He was not going to fall into *that* particular trap. John's shady activities might well have been something quite apart from his married life. It might be some financial ramp, a gambling racket, an illicit deal in diamonds, a peddling of drugs—some nasty bit of sculduggery of which Lydia had been unaware. Hence the pose of authorship, the faked necessity for historical research, enabling him to leave The Oasts for months at a time and carry on his nefarious business. In brief a Jekyll and Hyde affair, a dual rôle in which the ex-actor could well exercise his talents, however second-rate.

For all that, Major Boddy was not going to thrust Arundel lightly aside from the shadow of the hangman's noose. It was a psychological axiom that a man, perverse and anti-social in one direction, could be perverse and anti-social in another. If Arundel, for example, was a dope-pedlar, he might well be a murderer. The transition from one to the other would be facile, perhaps inevitable, for the cornered rat knows no restraint. What if Lydia, with her quick intelligence, had found John out in all his nastiness? What if she had held the threat of exposure over his head like the sword of Damocles? How would the rat react? Mightn't it invoke the blind courage of terror and seek to destroy with all its rodent cunning and skill? Well, there was a fresh problem tucked neatly away in a nutshell; was Arundel merely a rogue engaged in some underhand trafficking, or was he that and a great deal more—a cold-blooded murderer?

2

But before leaving Ilford, the Major was determined to make quite sure that Arundel was not in the vicinity. It was still possible that he had recognized Gammon's voice in the shop below and taken the opportunity to conceal himself in the attic or slip out through the back-yard of the house.

"That uncle of yours, Gammon? Where does he live?"

"Queen Victoria Street, sir. Only a stone's throw from here, sir."

"Does he know the district well?"

"Every lamp-post, sir."

"D'you think he'd give us a little information?"

"Well, sir," Syd grinned. "'E never was one to give much away, sir; but I don't think 'e'd jib much at that!"

As an undertaker, the Major found Uncle Jabez Gammon acutely disappointing. Instead of the gaunt long-faced spectre he had imagined, he found a jovial man of ox-like build and a temperament to match. He welcomed them into his show-parlour, a small cabinet lined with purple velvet, and offered the Major his tobacco-pouch. Then, slapping Syd heartily on the back, he inquired with broad humour if he were bringing him "a little bit o' business"? Under pressure of restraint, Syd managed to curb his natural wit and hand his uncle over to the Major.

"Can't explain fully my reasons for these questions, Mr. Gammon. Assure you they're all above board. D'you know Mrs. Trusscott of Laburnum Crescent?"

Uncle Jabez winked. "I oughter. I buried 'er 'usband, sir—four years back. Quiet respectable sorta woman. Bit dahn on 'er uppers since 'er ole pot-an'-pan's kicked the bucket. No business 'ead. The little shop's slid down'ill a lot of late."

"She's a local woman?"

"Lived 'ere all 'er life, sir."

"Did you know she had a lodger in the place?"

"Wot, ole Mrs. Peterson? Oh, yes, I knows 'er orite." Uncle Jabez winked again and ran his hand gently over a fine polished oak casket with brass handles, which was displayed on a pair of antique coffin-stools. "I got my eye on 'er, I 'ave. Gone eighty. Bin with Katie three years, nah. She's a quiet 'un too. Can't say where she come from, but I do know she's a widder."

"Any children, Mr. Gammon?"

"Not as I've 'eard of. Katie's never spoke of 'em an' she would 'ave done if they'd turned up to visit the ole gal. Lonely ole biddy, sir."

"One other thing, Mr. Gammon. Could you give me a list of the garages in the vicinity of Laburnum Crescent?"

"There's a tidy few, sir, but if you gives me a minute—"

A little later, armed with the necessary list, Syd and the Major left Uncle Jabez's funeral-parlour for the slightly less sombre atmosphere of the main street. Once in the car, Boddy said: "Got to make inquiries at every one of these garages, Gammon. We'll halve the list and proceed accordingly. Expect you to report back here as soon as possible. Be tactful. Looking for a friend of yours, understand? Believed to have garaged his car in the neighbourhood. Maroon-coloured Stanmobile saloon. Registration number—"

"SXT 1333, sir," broke in Syd promptly. "I rumble, sir."

"Right, Gammon. Dismiss!"

"Very good, sir."

3

It was a long and irritating task, but finally, when the Major had almost abandoned hope, he gleaned a meagre clue from the unpromising soil of Bert's Bonzer Garage, an establishment some three streets away from the Crescent. Bert recalled garaging a car of that description with a Sussex registration-plate for one night some three or four months previously. The reason for this astonishing feat of memory was simple—the gentleman in question had made an unusual request. He had asked Bert if he could refix the glass lens which had slipped from the rim of his monocle. Bert said it would be easy, had found it extremely difficult, but finally had succeeded and earned ten bob for his ingenuity. His description of the gentleman tallied exactly with that of John Arundel. But from that day to this he'd never set eyes on this particular client.

Major Boddy was satisfied. He had now established a really solid link between John Arundel and the borough of Ilford. If this link were to be incorporated in the chain of evidence that would lead to the murderer, well that was another pair of shoes. He was not sure whether he was now investigating some nefarious ramp or a murder case.

When Syd came back empty-handed to the car, Boddy put this point before him. Syd subsequently aired a lot of common sense.

"Beg to suggest, sir, it's like this. We know now that Mr. Arundel ain't all 'e appears to be, sir. Orite! This seems to suggest, sir, that 'e might well 'ave shot 'is wife, an' with all doo respect, sir, the thing we gotta do now is to find out by 'ook or by crook whether 'e *could* 'ave shot 'er. In brief, sir, we gotta get busy again in Beckwood. Beg to suggest, sir—we look upon this Ilford jaunt as a sorta side-line. We've picked up a bit of information about the enemy, that's all, sir. But we may as well be honest an' admit that we ain't found out another thing about the murder, sir."

The Major found this reasoning as sound as a bell. He was elated and disappointed at the same time. He wondered where Arundel had really been making for? What sort of hide-out he favoured when away from The Oasts? What sort of double-dealing he dabbled in, and whether Mesdames Trusscott and Peterson were inside members of the circle?

As it was nearly six o'clock when they reached the West End, Boddy compromised with Syd at a Corner House and ordered high tea. Then through the cooling air of the evening they drove in leisurely fashion out of London and back through the meadows and orchards of Kent until, once again, they crossed the county-border into Sussex. But on that journey, with Gammon preoccupied at the wheel, Major Boddy did a great deal of hard thinking.

For the time being he ignored the enigma of the catapult and the "sealed-box" aspect of the crime. He merely assumed that the murderer had made use of the contraption and had in some way managed to shoot Lydia from outside the studio. Accept all this, then how did John Arundel shape up as the possible murderer? The time-factor was undoubtedly the first thing to consider. If he had been ostensibly in the bath, could he have shot Lydia and regained the bathroom before Mrs. Willis started hammering on the door? Was it possible to get down into the garden from the bathroom window and climb back again? This second point could be settled once for all by a further survey of the house. Mrs. Willis's movements held the key to the first problem. And here Boddy broke into a silent chuckle of appreciation. Mrs. Willis, dammit! had not gone *direct* from the terrace to the bathroom. She had first gone through to the kitchen-quarters and called for her husband. It was not until she remembered that he was out that she had run upstairs. Surely, then, Arundel would have had time to dash up the garden and regain the bathroom before he was summoned by the agitated housekeeper? The final ruling on this assumption could be made when Boddy had seen the lay-out beneath the bathroom window.

There was, he admitted, just one other vital clue to take into consideration. After her abortive visit to Claydown Farm Honororia had seen a figure with a spade in the Studio Meadows. This would be about ten minutes after the shot had been fired. Accept Arundel as

the murderer and then what? This man with the spade must also have
been Arundel. But could he have slipped away from Mrs. Willis long
enough to have buried the "cattypault"? Boddy recalled the man's own
evidence: "The moment I had made sure that there was no hope, I left
Mrs. Willis, who had more or less collapsed, and 'phoned the constable
from the house."

Surely this was his opportunity? Mrs. Willis, shaken and weeping in
the studio, would be in no fit state to notice the passage of time. One,
two, five, ten minutes—it would all be the same to her. And Arundel's
excuse for slipping out of the studio was not only plausible but genuine.
He *had* rung Belling from the house. After that, only two or three minutes
would be needed in which to bury the "cattypault" since the hole could
have been dug previously and the spade left ready to hand. Perhaps hidden
under the conifers with the catapult itself. Yes, this part of the problem,
Boddy claimed, could be satisfactorily disposed of.

In the meantime, what was it safe to assume? That Arundel had actually soaked himself in the bath, flung a bathrobe round him when still
wet, rushed down to the studio, shot Lydia, regained the bathroom just in
time to open up the door to Mrs. Willis. The murder-method, whatever
it was, must have been patently simple to put into operation. He would
have had no time to carry out any elaborate plan of action. But confound
it! simple or not, how the devil had it been done?

Then Boddy, his mind now running sweetly, had another useful
thought. He had an idea how he could set the seal on his latest theory.

Just beyond Hawkhurst, he broke the prolonged silence. "When you
get near The Oasts, Gammon, want you to park the car in that by-lane.
We've still work to do."

"Very good, sir."

"Long and exhausting day, Gammon?"

"Yessir, but nice an' lively. Enjoyed myself no end, sir."

"Good!"

Presently they climbed the final rise and swung sharply round Church
Corner into the head of the long village street. The light was already
fading and the colour of things draining away into a soft monotone of
greys and blues and purples. Here and there an orange square glowed

with startling clarity from an early lamplit window. A few rooks were wheeling lazily over the elms in the churchyard and an old man came out of the lych-gate with a scythe over his shoulder. As the air cooled, the scents of the countryside grew more heady, wafting in through the open windows of the car. The harsh and littered streets of Ilford seemed a long way off, like the dusty memory of an old nightmare.

Boddy sighed with contentment as he got down stiffly from the car and stretched his cramped limbs. "Need to limber up a bit, eh, Gammon? Ready for our next sortie?"

"All present and correct, sir."

"Right! We're going down to The Oasts."

Once in the privacy of the Arundels' garden, the Major wasted no time. Crossing to the end of the terrace he gazed up at the south façade of the house and, from his long acquaintance with its interior, marked down the bathroom window. At once he realized that he'd drawn the first ace out of the pack. A small flat-roofed sun-loggia had been built on directly below the window and a child could have scaled this off-shoot and gained the window without a heart-flutter. He turned on Syd.

"Ever broken into a house, Gammon?"

"Yessir," said Syd smartly.

"Successfully?"

"Very, sir."

"When *was* this—er—Gammon?"

"End of '17, when you was on leave near Aldershot, sir. Question of smuggling a bunch of carnations into Mrs. Hambledon's bedroom, sir. Dessay you recall Mrs. Hambledon, sir? A widder you was interested in about that time. Well-built, rather matronly lady in my opinion, sir."

"Gammon!"

"Beg pardon, sir."

"Point is, what about those French windows? Can you open them?"

Syd examined the latch through the glass with a professional air. Then he observed, "Beg to report, sir—easy, sir, with my thin-bladed pen-knife."

Five minutes later Syd flipped back the catch and the door swung inwards.

"All opposition overcome, sir."

"Right, Gammon. Now listen carefully. I want you to stand down by the studio. When I clap my hands, run like the devil up the garden, climb this loggia and get into that window."

"Window's not open, sir."

"I know that, you blithering idiot! Run upstairs and open it now. At the double, Gammon!"

A few minutes later the scene was set and Syd reported from the gathering dusk that he had taken up his position by the studio door. Boddy, representing Mrs. Willis, stood in the open French windows almost on the terrace. Suddenly with an explosive clap of his hands, he set both Gammon and himself in motion. Crossing through the sitting-room, he gained the hall, went down a brief passage and entered the kitchen-quarters. There, in his imagination, he called hurriedly for Willis, paused for a moment to make sure that Willis was not there, then pounded back into the hall, breathlessly mounted the main staircase and, trotting along the landing, hammered violently on the bathroom door.

"'Ullo! 'Ullo, sir!" came Syd's cheery voice. "We win by a short 'ead, sir." He opened the door and poked his head into the corridor. "As you anticipated, eh, sir?"

Boddy was smiling broadly. "No difficulty in getting here first, Gammon? Devil of a scramble, perhaps?"

"So, so, sir. 'Ad time to draw breath before you knocked, sir."

"Splendid, Gammon! Splendid!"

By gad! it *was* splendid! The test left no room for doubt. John Arundel's alibi now held no more water than the empty bath. Provided he could in some way have shot Lydia from outside the studio, then all the facts were flocking round in a dark circle to accuse him of the murder. To set the seal on his test, Boddy now decided to put his second brainwave into operation. He believed that he might draw a second ace from the pack, for he noticed that when the bathroom light was on, the glow of it was clearly visible even through the drawn curtains. This was important.

Leaving his batman to relock the French windows and walk down to Ladysmith, he himself climbed into the car and drove direct to Phœbe Dell's cottage. As luck would have it, the girl was just taking a prolonged farewell of her intended under the lilac bushes of her parents' front garden. Twice already she had lifted the gate-latch and edged into the garden and twice her swain's power of persuasion had overridden the fear of her father's wrath. They were, in fact, just squaring up for the third round when the Major's car swished out of the gloom and caught them fair and square in its head-lamps. Jack Codley grinned sheepishly as Boddy stuck his head out of the window.

"'Evening, Codley."

"'Evening, Major."

"Can I have a word with your young lady? Shan't keep her a minute." Then as Phœbe emerged from the shadow of the lilacs, patting her hair, "Ah ha! m'dear, sorry to butt in like this, but important."

Codley with great tact fell back a pace as Phœbe approached the car.

"You recall that Wednesday night when Mrs. Arundel—er—shot herself, Phœbe?"

"Indeed I do, sir."

"Do you remember seeing a light in an upper room of The Oasts? Shining through closed curtains, eh?"

"Now I come to think on it, Major, I do. 'Twas along the right o' the house somewhere. An' after a bit, it went out sudden like."

"Gad! You're sure?"

"Oh, yes, sir. 'Tisn't all that long ago."

"And did it come on again?"

"Well, I noticed it a bit after we heard the bang, that I can say, Major."

"When did it go out precisely?"

"That was afore we heard the bang, sir—just afore. I can't recall exactly how soon afore. But only *just* afore."

"Good enough, young woman. Most useful. No need to say anything about these questions—understand? Well, well—won't keep you from your young fellah. When's the wedding, eh?"

Phœbe blushed. "Aw! it hasn't got that far yet, Major. Jack's saving up for the ring. But with harvest overtime he reckons to have it on my finger by Michaelmas."

"Start filling that bottom drawer, eh? Well, good night, m'dear. 'Night, Codley. And thundering good luck to you both!"

4

After a belated supper, Major Boddy lit a Henry Clay and inhaled its rare fragrance in the stillness of his garden. He needed this slow pacing with his thoughts, the cool exhalations of leaves and grass in his nostrils, this secluded perfect moment before closing an arduous day. He was tired, but pleasantly so, stiff rather than leggy, and in the abstract realm of his mind completely satisfied. This had been the longest, most diverse day since he had opened his investigation. He had learnt far more than he had even dared to expect. And from these scattered scraps of new evidence he was building up a fresh and entirely convincing picture of the *real* John Arundel.

He believed now, without any reservations, that Arundel had shot his wife! His alibi had been simple and clever, but not foolproof. This evening's work had torn the thing to shreds. As final proof that he was advancing along the right lines, there was Phœbe Dell's statement about the bathroom light. The girl's evidence was both clear and conclusive. The test he had carried out with Gammon proved the rest of his argument up to the hilt. All that remained now was to discover *how* Arundel had committed the crime and dished up his murder to look like suicide.

He gave an ironic snort. "All that remained"—it was an ill-chosen phrase. Rather like saying that he was nearing the end of a trip round the globe because he had successfully crossed the English Channel. Confound it, he was no nearer the solution of that "sealed-box" problem than he had been on the day he first convinced himself it was murder. How, how, how had John Arundel worked it all?

Standing stock-still in the very centre of the lawn, he screwed up his eyes and forced a picture of the studio to appear on the screen of darkness. An interior, hesitant view at first, gradually crystallizing; then the vision hardened and the details came sharply into focus—the window there, the door there, the easel, the model throne, the Récamier couch, the two small armchairs, the stove, the little tables, the rugs on the floor. In his mind's eye the smaller ornaments and embroideries settled on the larger objects and the picture was complete. But the loop-hole evaded him. The picture was too perfect. He was looking for a rent in the canvas and the canvas was flawless! Good God, Arundel's cunning was diabolical! Behind the jaunty, yet impassive face, a subtle perverted brain was working overtime. He was, Boddy claimed in his own defence, up against no ordinary criminal. This murder was of the malicious, soft-fingered, matchlessly executed variety. It was the work, not of a clumsy, hot-blooded layman, but of a deft and brilliant artist in crime. A murder *de luxe*, a masterpiece!

CHAPTER XIV

The Vanishing Car

I

IT WAS NOT UNTIL DUSK OF THE FOLLOWING EVENING THAT MAJOR
Boddy took up the threads where he had laid them down the previous
day. A long sitting of the Bench that morning had offered the perfect excuse
for an even longer doze in a hammock-chair that afternoon. Although the
Willises were on holiday, a gardener was working daily at The Oasts and
it was vital not to rouse this fellow's suspicions. But no sooner had the
shadows crept into the house, than Boddy and Gammon crept stealthily out
of it and, following the deserted bridle-path across the fields, approached
the studio. Once there, Syd examined the lock and declared that it was too
tough a nut to crack without a professional outfit. Boddy was prepared
for this. When interviewing Willis in the kitchen the night before the latter's departure, he had noticed a number of keys dangling from a row of
hooks. He suggested, therefore, that Gammon should again force the latch
of the French windows in the hope that the studio key would be among
those on the hooks. The Major's luck was in. The key was not only there
but clearly labelled. A few minutes later they were both in the studio.
Once there the Major said in a low voice, "Pull those curtains across the
window. Gammon. I'll attend to the blind over the skylight. Don't switch
on the light. Just use our pocket-lamps—understand?"

The moment the studio was more or less blacked-out, Syd asked def-
erentially: "Beg to ask, sir, what precisely 'ave we come 'ere to look for?"

"God knows, Gammon."

"Sort of general reconnaissance, sir?"

"That's it, Gammon. Tell you this much in confidence. I'm convinced
Mr. Arundel shot his wife!"

"Gawd above, sir!"

"But I don't know *how* he shot her, Gammon. *That's* the Gordian knot we've got to unloose, eh?"

"Exactly, sir."

"Know what a Gordian knot is. Gammon?"

"No, sir."

"Ha!" Then with a sudden frown of concentration: "We've got to go all over the walls and roof again, Gammon. Somewhere, confound it, there must be a bullet-hole!"

"Quite, sir, but 'ow the devil did that Colt .45 get into the stoodio through a bullet-'ole?"

The Major said something vehement under his breath. "Don't stand there asking damfool questions, Gammon! Hop round and find the answers to 'em. Actions not words."

For five, ten, twenty minutes the search continued in silence, the two circles of light moving this way and that over the furniture and hangings. Once, during that period, the rays of Syd's torch fell directly on to the Dingle portrait and he recoiled as if stung.

"Blimey, sir! Gave me a proper turn, sir, coming at me out of the dark like that. Turned me stomach over twice, sir, straight it did!"

"That's quite enough of that, Gammon. Won't have *lèse-majesté*, y'know."

"Very good, sir."

The search continued. Between them they moved every stick of furniture away from the walls, pried behind every hanging, peered behind every picture. It was all barren of result. Boddy, here in the very place where the tragedy had broken loose, felt the full weariness of defeat. So far he had driven home his investigation and now, well on the journey, the engine had seized up. Perhaps he had been foolish in thinking that he, a doddering, addle-pated amateur, could solve a major crime. It needed experience, a knowledge of routine, a whole mass of apparatus. He was trying to clean the Augean stables with a toothpick. Overburdened with this sense of defeat, he plumped himself down on the couch and buried his head in his hands.

Syd's exclamations of triumph did not at first penetrate the Major's numbed consciousness. Then suddenly, aware of the repressed excitement in his batman's voice, he rapped out:

"Good gad! Gammon, what the devil is it? What the deuce are you hopping around like that for?"

"Beg to report—er—beg to report, sir," gasped Syd wildly. "*I think I've got it, sir! We've* got it! Take a look there, sir."

Following the line of Syd's pointing finger, the Major sprang up and stared down the rays of the former's pocket-torch, and in an instant he knew that his batman was right! Framed in the silver circle of that torch was the answer to the problem that had confounded him! There could be no doubting it! Here was the only plausible explanation. And yet—? Catching the Major's eye, Syd was quick to note his change of expression.

"Beg to suggest, sir, the final proof lies outside. I've an idea, sir, that—"

"Right, Gammon! Come on! Don't waste time. But steady, flick out your light first. Mustn't take risks *now*, eh?"

Outside the studio their final doubts were set at rest. Here was the chink in the "sealed-box", and by gad! yes—here was the clue that would slip the hangman's noose about John Arundel's neck! Now the malevolent simplicity of the trick was apparent, the ease with which it could be worked, the almost foolproof nature of its design. As for the strange contraption they had unearthed in the meadow—

The Major was aware of Gammon's hand gripping his forearm.

"Sssh, sir! Somebody coming down the garden path. Take cover in these bushes, sir. Quick!"

Taking care not to rustle the foliage, the two figures drew back and merged into the shadows. There, with bated breath, they waited.

Although there was no moon, the sky was clear and glittering with stars. A faint wash of light lay over the garden and meadows. Through a gap in the conifers Boddy could distinctly see the outlines of a figure padding stealthily down the path. Skirting the outer edge of the conifers it came to the wicket-gate, where for a moment it paused as if listening, but in that instant both Boddy and Gammon were able to recognize the man's features. *It was John Arundel!*

"Well, I'll be—!"

"Steady, there, Gammon! Stand easy. No good acting yet. Watch and wait."

Opening the wicket-gate, Arundel crossed into the meadow beyond and, at a short distance from the studio, began to quarter the ground like a hound trying to pick up a lost scent. Cautiously Boddy and Gammon advanced to the screen of larches and, drawing aside the lower branches, peered through.

"Got the wind up, sir. Come to collect that cattypult, sir."

"Looks like it, Gammon." Then brisk with sudden inspiration, "See here, Gammon. I've got an idea. Slip down to Ladysmith and get the car. Park it without lights in that by-lane. Wait for me there. I'll keep in touch here. Understand?"

"Very good, sir."

Slippy and silent as a ferret, Gammon was gone. Boddy turned back to concentrate on Arundel. He was now kneeling on the grass, pulling up the loosened turf with his bare hands in a perfect frenzy of haste. Then there was a sudden cessation and a low muffled exclamation of surprise. For a moment Arundel knelt there as if bewildered, then once again his hands began scrabbling at the loose earth in a frantic attempt to deepen the hole. But at length he seemed to realize that he had been anticipated, for he got up abruptly and turned back towards the wicket-gate.

"Now!" thought Boddy. "Now!" adding a silent prayer that Gammon would get the car safely into the lane before Arundel left The Oasts. The Major was banking on the fact that he had driven into Beckwood and parked his car some distance from the house. But Boddy's luck held fast. Some doubt as to the wisdom of leaving that gaping hole must have assailed Arundel for he ran back and began to refill the cavity. This done, he capped it with the loose sods and stamped the place level. The next minute he was through the wicket-gate and creeping on tiptoe up the garden.

2

Everything that night dovetailed to perfection. Barely had Gammon raced by the drive-entrance and taken up his position in the by-lane, before

Arundel emerged into the main road followed at a safe distance by the Major. Once on the road Arundel turned to the left and, hugging the verge, began to slink up the rise towards Church Corner. This took him by the head of the lane where Gammon had already turned and parked the unlighted car, and when Boddy came opposite the turning he took the opportunity to issue further orders to his batman.

"Parked his car farther up the road, I imagine. Stand to, Gammon! Keep on your toes. I'll hoot like an owl when I want you—understand? Then start up and drive like the devil towards me."

The Major's surmise was correct. Some three hundred yards beyond Church Corner there was a cart-track that ambled down to a group of derelict oasts. Here Arundel had parked his Stanmobile and, in no time he had backed it out into the main road and headed it away from Beckwood. As the noise of the engine receded, Boddy cupped his hands over his mouth and produced an astonishingly life-like imitation of a barn owl. A minute later Syd came swishing round Church Corner, the car head-lamps blazing. For the second time, the chase was on!

On this occasion, despite the darkness, it was far easier to keep their quarry in sight. The roads were almost deserted and it was possible to see the flicker of Arundel's lamps for some considerable distance ahead.

"Beg to suggest, sir, enemy making for Tunbridge Wells as before, sir."

"Precisely, Gammon. And *this* time we'll hang on to his tail. No blunders, eh? Anticipate he'll turn off the London road somewhere in the town as he did before."

"Bit of orite, this, sir! Never thought the evening would end up so lively, sir."

"Confound it, Gammon, it hasn't ended yet. May be a damned sight livelier before we finish."

But in this he was wrong, for the first part of the chase ended in a distinct anti-climax. Reaching Tunbridge Wells a little after eleven o'clock, Arundel drove calmly up to the creeper-hung portals of the Royal Court Hotel and entered. Having parked the car a little up the road, Boddy and Gammon watched from the opposite pavement. In a few minutes Arundel came out again, followed by a hall-porter, who directed him to the hotel garages at the side of the block.

"Staying the night here, Gammon."

"Looks like it, sir. What's our strategy now, sir?"

The Major pondered the question in silence. It seemed improbable that Arundel would leave the Royal Court before six o'clock, however anxious he might be to proceed. Even to leave at six would arouse a certain amount of undesirable speculation. The best plan, therefore, would be to find accommodation near by, get a few hours' sleep and mount Gammon on guard outside the Royal Court early the next morning. He himself could then wait in the car some way up the road, ready to continue the chase.

The manager of the nearby Heathfield Hotel accepted the Major's glib reason for his lack of luggage and arranged for Gammon to sleep in the chauffeur's quarters over the garages. Before the latter left in the wake of a bell-hop, he asked in a husky whisper, "Er—what time's zero hour, sir?"

"Should be outside the Royal Court by six-thirty," replied the Major, *sotto voce*. "I'll spin some yarn about an early start. Order your breakfast for six o'clock. Park the car three hundred yards up the road from the Royal Court."

"Very good, sir."

"Have to sleep in your shirt to-night, eh, Gammon?"

Syd grinned. One eyelid quivered on the verge of a wink. "Wouldn't be the first time, sir. Boots, toonic, trousers, puttees—slept in the 'ole bloomin' issue, eh, sir, wiv mud near on up to our necks, *and* slept pretty, sir!"

"Ha! Good night, Gammon."

"Good night, sir."

3

It was not until nearly nine o'clock that John Arundel eventually pulled clear of the Royal Court and headed his Stanmobile up over the common. Sleepy, unshaven, bored with their long wait, Boddy and Gammon accepted his departure with relief. Once they had swung again into action their tiredness and boredom vanished, and with Syd at the wheel they

took up the chase with an edge on their excitement. Where exactly was
this tenuous thread going to lead them? What further clues did it promise to surrender? The Major's private vision was of a dark tumbledown
hovel buried in a thick wood, the H.Q. of some notorious gang of which
Arundel was the master-mind.

Clear of Tunbridge Wells, Boddy was on familiar ground for he had
often run over to Forest Row for a foursome on the Royal Ashdown, and
soon they had passed through that village on their way to East Grinstead.
There Arundel stopped at a filling-station and gave the Major the chance
to fill his own tank at a garage farther up the street. They drew away
together and swung on to the Horsham road barely four hundred yards
apart. When the road straightened or became more open, Syd slackened
off the pace and fell back, but when, presently, the red roofs of Horsham
rose on the horizon, his master urged him to close the gap.

"Vital here, Gammon. Any number of main roads run into Horsham.
So far so good. But we must keep right on his tail now."

Gammon did and in ten minutes they were clear of narrow busy
streets and out again into the open country.

"Guildford road," observed Boddy tensely.

Five, seven, ten miles and then, unexpectedly, Arundel swung left off
the highway and careered down a twisty lane bordered with high banks
and hedges. They passed through a sun-drowsy village, topped a brief
rise and dropped down again into a wide flat stretch of pasture, where
the lane straightened up. For a time Syd was forced to fall back until there
was nearly half a mile between the two cars. Then, in the distance they
saw the Stanmobile climbing a dead-straight gradient, saw it momentarily
silhouetted against the sky and finally drop away out of sight.

"Confound the fellah!" cried Boddy anxiously. "Proceed at the double,
Gammon! He may give us the slip beyond that ridge."

The little Popular Eight, now nicely warmed up, leapt forward with
the energy of a super-charged sports. Syd took the gradient with a flying
start and gained the crest without a gear-change. Then, with protruding
eyes, he turned blankly on the Major.

"Well I'll be—sir!"

"Good God, Gammon! What the devil—?"

They had sound cause for astonishment. Beyond the crest of the hill the road coasted down in a dead-straight line and scored an equally dead-straight course across the floor of the wide valley beyond. From the top of the hill it was obvious at a glance that no side turning ran into the lane. They could see down the whole length of the road to a point at least a mile off.

But, for all that, *Arundel and the Stanmobile had vanished completely!*

4

"Absolutely inexplicable, Gammon. Damn near impossible, eh? Of course, there must *be* an explanation. Got to approach the whole thing logically." They were seated in the car, now at the bottom of the hill, wrestling with their bewilderment. "We can assume that Arundel disappeared between the crest of that hill and a point half a mile ahead of it. Sound enough, eh? Seeing that we were just about half a mile behind him when he went over the ridge. Question remains, Gammon, how the devil has he done it?"

Syd pondered the problem for a moment, sucking at the cigarette which the Major had just offered him. Then he glanced up and said chirpily, "Beg to suggest, sir—might have had a super-charger fitted to his car. More under 'is bonnet, so to speak, than meets the eye. Twin carburettors, sir. Anything that might serve to 'ot up 'is engine. Then aware that 'e was being tailed, sir, waited 'is chance an' stepped on it good an' proper."

Boddy shook his head. "Quite a sound theory, Gammon, but I doubt if it's the right one. Even suppose he whacked his car up to eighty, I still claim we should have seen him when we reached the top of the hill. Farther off, admittedly, but still visible."

Syd nodded a doleful agreement and ran a hand through his carroty hair as if to comb an answer from the top of his head. "Then what the 'ell *as* 'e done, sir?"

"Can't say yet, Gammon. Must get out and reconnoitre. Get the lie of the land, eh?"

But even this sensible suggestion did little to relieve their perplexity. Along the right side of the whole half-mile of the road under survey ran a high grass bank, ridged with a scraggy hedge of blackthorn. No cuttings or culverts had been dug through this bank, nor was there a single gate. On the opposite side of the road the margin was varied. The hill itself was banked on both sides, then on the left, at the foot of the descent, the bank gave way to a low stone wall, beyond which was a corn-field. In this wall was a single gate, which naturally rivetted Boddy's attention. But the answer, he realized at once, was not to be found there.

"That wheat, Gammon, grows right up to the gate. If the car had been driven through the gate, it would have left a wide swathe of flattened corn in its wake."

They moved on with ever-increasing mystification. At the end of the wall, the corn-field gave way to a long copse of scrubby oak, thorn and hazel, fenced with split chestnut spiles, between which there was just about room to thrust a hand. This fence had a run of some two hundred yards and in it Boddy discovered no gate or breach of any description. The spiles had been driven in directly behind the low cement kerb which edged the road on either side. Beyond the copse was pastureland, where the fence ended and a twelve-foot quickset hedge took its place, obviously at one time a wind-row for a hop-field. In this was another gate. But once again Boddy rejected the possibility of the car having been driven through it. For one thing, it was stoutly padlocked and even if Arundel possessed a key he couldn't possibly have had time to unlock the gate, open it, close it and relock it. Further, the ground between the gate-posts was soft and soggy, due to the upwelling of a nearby surface spring, and any tyre-tracks would have been obvious. Finally, if Arundel *had* gone through the gate, where had he hidden the car? The three-acre meadow was as bare as a bone, offering no cover. From the crest of the hill it would have been clearly visible, and Boddy felt sure he would have spotted the Stanmobile if it *had* been driven across the field. Beyond this point he did not feel prepared to investigate, certain that Arundel could not have kept much more than half a mile ahead. Moreover, the high bank appeared again on the left-hand side and continued, more or less unbroken, to the horizon.

"Damn it all, Gammon! we solve one 'sealed-box' problem, now we're dished up with another. Where the devil has he got to? Spread wings and flown, eh? Gone through a hole in the ground? All thundering mysterious, y'know."

"'There is something in this more than natural', sir. Not mine, sir. Shakespeare's."

"Really, Gammon?"

"'*Amlet*, sir. Second act."

"Really, Gammon?"

"'Ad a neat way o' putting things, sir."

"Very, Gammon, very."

"And now what, sir?"

Boddy lifted his shoulders and shook his head. He was, once more, utterly bamfoozled!

CHAPTER XV

Deadlands Wood

I

THEY HUNG ABOUT FOR AN HOUR, POKING AND PRYING INTO EVERY conceivable spot where Arundel might have turned the car off the road. It was time wasted. There was no trace of either the car or its owner. Unfortunately the dry macadam had taken no imprint of the tyre-threads, so that it was impossible to solve the problem by stalking it up that particular avenue. In every direction the Major walked into a *cul-de-sac*. The high banks, the solid stone wall, the unbroken fence, the twelve-foot hedge—confound it! the Stanmobile might as well have been running on rails through a tunnel for all the opportunity it had for turning aside! Yet somewhere along that half-mile it *must* have left the road.

Sitting on the running-board of the car, he lit his pipe and began to analyse the mystery. At the end of ten minutes' cogitation, he had reached two conclusions. (1) The copse offered the only reasonable hiding-place for the car. (2) Arundel must, therefore, have in some way driven the car through a breach in the spile-fencing. He called across to Syd, who was sitting idly on the wall, drumming his heels against the stone. As they walked slowly down the road in the direction of the copse, the Major explained his new theory. "Save time, Gammon, if you start at one end of the fence and I, the other. Look for any fractures, loose stakes, anything, in fact, out of the ordinary. Damn it all! it *is* the only possibility."

They got down to work, laboriously testing every spile and wire and staple. Luckily the road was deserted, otherwise their peculiar behaviour might well have roused a lot of unwanted curiosity. One thing Boddy was swift to appreciate. If Arundel *had* driven the car into the copse, there would be no tell-tale tracks on the road-verge to betray the fact, since the fence was flush with the cement kerb. Beyond the fence was a tangle of undergrowth—bramble, thorn, ivy and wild clematis forming a perfect screen behind which a car would be quickly swallowed up. The fence, however, proved intractable. Every spile was stoutly wired to the next and, as the score mounted, Boddy began to lose heart. At the other end of the fence, Gammon appeared to be facing an equal disappointment. Gradually the distance between them was closing up. Eighty, seventy, sixty, fifty, forty yards and then, suddenly, Syd threw up an arm and let out a sharp cry. With a grunt of excitement Boddy broke into a trot and hastened to join his batman.

"Well, Gammon?"

"Beg to report, sir—there's something queer about this bit of fence 'ere, sir. It don't seem quite so firm as the rest of it, sir."

Boddy tested this theory for himself, spile by spile, and found that some twelve to fifteen stakes were definitely insecure. Not exactly loose, but shaky under the hand. The twisted wire between the heads of the spiles, however, appeared to be unbroken. It was not, in fact, until Syd, examining the base of the spiles, noticed the hair-line cuts in the wood, that they had found the true answer to the problem. The idea was neat and simple. About fifteen spiles had been sawn through just above the ground, the cuts made on the slant so that the fractures could not be easily discerned. The tension of the twisted wire kept the severed portions of each spile pressed tightly together. At one end of this "doctored" stretch the wire had been cut and the loose ends cleverly hooked together. Boddy appreciated at once the extreme simplicity of Arundel's arrangement. He pointed it out to Syd.

"Damned smart fellah, y'know, Gammon. Only had to unhook these two lengths of wire and roll back the severed length of fencing. Neat! Thundering neat! Drives the car through the gap beyond that riot of brambles, straightens up the fence and rejoins the wire. We'll try it ourselves, Gammon. Proof of the pudding, eh?"

A second or so later they were through the fence, pulling aside the festoons of bramble and wild clematis.

Then: "No doubt about it, sir," cried Syd. "Here's the marks of 'is tyres, sir."

"But, confound it, Gammon, why?"

"Beg pardon, sir?"

"I mean, why the devil did he do it? Did he suspect we were tailing him? Why this curious vanishing trick? Was he making for this place in any case?"

"Imagine so, sir. Don't think *we* entered into 'is calculations, sir. 'E was making for this wood because it's 'is reg'lar 'ide-out, sir."

"Agree there, Gammon. Well, we won't have to speculate on *that*, thank God! His car was driven in here. It hasn't been driven out. So *ergo*, Gammon, it must still be somewhere in the wood."

Only a few paces from the fence they made another discovery. At one time a rough cart-track must have joined the main road, probably before the chestnut fence had been erected. Just behind the tangled screen of undergrowth, this rutted, grass-grown track ran straight into the heart of the wood, and it was down this track that Arundel had unquestionably driven.

Boddy observed: "Damn sight more extensive than I thought, this copse. Must be several acres of it."

"Yessir, and there's another thing. Tisn't the first time 'e's driven the car in 'ere, sir. There's a number of tracks. See there, sir, where there's a sloppy bit of ground. 'E's been in an' out of this place dozens of times."

The Major was increasingly puzzled. Was his vision of that dark hovel about to materialize? Was this Arundel's hide-out when away from The Oasts? Was it to this lonely spot that he had retired to do his "historical research"? He was inclined to agree with Gammon that their quarry's swing off the road had little to do with them. He had slipped into the wood because it was the goal for which he had been making.

They had penetrated some three hundred yards into the copse when Boddy first glimpsed the outlines of a building through the brushwood. At this point the track rounded an abrupt curve, and once round the corner the whole of the building came into view. Expecting something far more in keeping with the image created by his imagination, he was acutely disappointed. They were confronted with nothing more than a simple rectangular box of corrugated iron, with crude double doors at the near end of it and a boarded window high up on the left-hand side. There was no sign of either Arundel or the car. Boddy glanced at his watch.

"Nearly an hour and a quarter since we lost sight of him. Time enough to give us the slip again, eh?"

"Beg to suggest, sir, tyre-tracks lead up to them doors, sir. Might assoome the car's inside, sir."

"We will, Gammon." He tried the doors and shook his head. "Padlocked. No chance to break in that way. Let's make a round of the building. May be playing possum inside, y'know."

But a circle of the building suggested no further means of entrance. Syd pointed to the little window.

"Might prise one of them boards loose, sir. That 'ud give us light enough to see inside, sir."

"Very well, Gammon. Up on to my shoulders!"

Syd snatched up a sharp-pointed stake, whilst Boddy, gripping his bent knee, took a firm stance under the window. With the agility of one whose reflex actions had been conditioned by a youth spent dodging the London traffic, Syd sprang lightly on to the Major's broad back, quickly gained his balance and began to work at the window. A few minutes later he had wrenched aside two of the boards and, half hanging on the narrow sill, was peering inside. Then he uttered an exclamation of triumph.

"Beg to report, sir—the Stanmobile! It's inside, sir. But no sign of Mr. Arundel, sir, unless 'e's 'id 'imself under the car."

2

Now what? Boddy was again facing a blank wall. Assuming that Arundel was not in the building—a safe bet since the doors had been padlocked on the outside—should they scour the vicinity in the hope of running him to earth, or wait patiently by this enigmatical garage until he returned? Neither course offered much profit. Major Boddy felt that he was not ready to confront Arundel as a murderer until the full scope of his underhand activities had been dragged into the daylight. In any case, once his dossier was complete, he'd be forced to provide Wilmott with his clues, since the police would have to engineer the fellow's arrest. This latest development had put a sharper edge on his curiosity and he was determined to satisfy it. He looked up to find Gammon no longer at his side.

"Hi! Gammon!"

"Here, sir. Round the far end of the shed, sir. I've got another clue, sir."

"The devil you have!" Boddy hurried round to join him and found him on his hands and knees examining the grassy track which, skirting the hut, drove yet deeper into the wood beyond. "Well, Gammon?"

"Funny, sir; there's tyre-tracks on this side too, sir. 'E's approached 'is garridge from two directions, sir."

"Wonder where the deuce this road leads to, Gammon? Better go out on *safari*. Follow the thing to its bitter end."

But the end was far more bitter than he had anticipated. After pounding through the woods for about half a mile they came suddenly on a second spile fence, this time breached with a five-barred gate, through which the cart-track debouched on to a fairly wide road.

"Back exit," observed Boddy. "Can approach his hide-out from either road. But I'm damned if I can fathom his idea, Gammon!"

As they moved back towards the hut, they stumbled on a further perplexing fact. At a point where the ground was exceptionally soft the tyre-tracks had made several deep and clearly defined indents. So clear, in fact, that Syd declared with absolute conviction: "Beg to report, sir, *this isn't the same car*! These are stud-markings—those on the Stanmobile were diamond-shaped, sir."

"Good God, Gammon. You're sure?"

"Certain, sir."

In a flash Boddy had grasped the implication of this latest clue. There was, he upheld, only one plausible explanation. Arundel had driven the Stanmobile *into* the wood and had driven *out* of it in a second car. In brief, he used this isolated copse as an *alfresco* dressing-room. He entered it with one identity. He emerged from it with another. Not only, perhaps, with a different car, but with a different face, in different attire, with a different personality. It was here that John Arundel, Esq., The Oasts, Beckwood, vanished and the real Arundel took his place.

"Next thing to do, Gammon," he said briskly, "is to find out who owns this wood. Confound it! the place *must* belong to Arundel. Admit that. But not the John Arundel we know. Same fellah, another hat, eh? Bound to have an alias. Probably any damn number of 'em. We'll drive to the nearest farmhouse. Make discreet inquiries, understand? Obvious the fellah isn't in hiding here. I'll wager he's miles off now in that second car!"

3

The interview at Bonder's Farm probably marked the turning-point in the solution of the new problem. Boddy, of course, did not realize it at the time. In fact, Mr. Harrington's information, freely given over a tankard of ale in the cool farmhouse kitchen, merely served to deepen the Major's perplexity. For the six-acre copse, graphically known in the locality as Deadlands Wood, was owned by a woman! Harrington had never seen this woman but he understood that she was an invalid and very wealthy. An agent had acted at the auction when this totally useless bit of property had been put up for sale. Opinion in the neighbourhood was that she had more money than sense, and that her sole reason for the purchase was some vague idea of clearing a site in the wood and building a house there. It was obvious, during the course of conversations, that Harrington was completely unaware of Arundel's mysterious comings and goings.

"Can you give me the landowner's name and address?" asked Boddy.

Mr. Harrington shook his head. "I've an idea that her name's Faulks, but I couldn't say where she bides. But I tell 'e what, sir—if you're going through Horsham way, you might ask at Hollis and Frant's, the estate agents in High Street. They handled the deal and I reckon they should have her name and address among their records."

Boddy followed Mr. Harrington's advice to the letter and left Horsham with the necessary information in his wallet. Deadlands Wood was the property of Mrs. Bateman-Faulks, Cranwood Manor, Sheepwick, Gloucestershire. The question remained—was Arundel using the copse without her knowledge? Or was there some link between him and this wealthy invalid? The Major knew that he would have to find the answer to these questions, the more so since a glance at the map revealed that Deadlands Wood was more or less on the direct route between Beckwood and Sheepwick. It certainly looked as if Arundel had gone ahead in that second car to Cranwood Manor!

4

Back that evening at Ladysmith, Major Boddy was the recipient of a pleasant surprise, for shortly after his return Allnutt, the verger, rang up to ask if the Major had heard the good news. The Rector had arrived that morning, without warning or luggage, at the Rectory.

"Like a pilgrim 'e set out, sir, an' like a pilgrim 'e 'as returned," said Allnutt in the pseudo-episcopal voice he adopted for this kind of announcement. "The Lord 'as guided 'is steps back into the ways of peace." Adding on a less visionary note: "But 'e's still got a nasty bruise on 'is right occiput, sir. Gave me a proper shock when I first see 'im. But I thought you'd like to know, sir."

Boddy was delighted. So Swale-Reid had taken his advice and, overriding all thought of the past, had decided to return to his post. Honororia and Stanley about to be married; Swale-Reid back in his familiar pulpit—after all, it *was* an ill wind—

The next morning Boddy bicycled up to the Rectory and found Swale-Reid bent studiously over his study-desk, coping with the arrears of work that had accumulated during his absence. Although pale and tremulous, there was a new light of battle in his eyes, a more self-assured tilt to his chin. He greeted the Major with considerable warmth and plunged without delay into a detailed review of all those little parish matters dear to the hearts of them both.

Presently he looked up and said in a quieter voice: "There's just one other little matter, Major. My return here yesterday was not entirely unshadowed by some very grievous news. Poor old Mrs. Willington of Yewdene Cottage passed away only two days ago. The funeral is to-morrow. A sad loss, Major, very sad. And as the mother of a much-respected son and ex-serviceman, I wondered if the Legion would care to—"

He left his sentence hanging, as it were, delicately in mid-air.

"Of course, of course," said Boddy gruffly, embarrassed as he always was by a charitable request. "And as Chairman of the Legion may I be allowed to make the—er—first contribution? I am sure the committee will endorse—"

He, too, mumbled his way into silence, as he dived jerkily into his breast-pocket and pulled out his wallet. As he extracted a ten-shilling note and handed it across to Swale-Reid, a visiting-card fluttered to the carpet. Inadvertently, as he stooped to pick it up, the Rector's eye took in the boldly written address on the reverse side of the card, and he gave a little start of surprise.

"Anything wrong, my dear fellah?" asked Boddy, accepting the card with a nod of thanks.

"No! No! Dear me, no! It was just that I happened to glimpse the name of Sheepwick on that card. Most unfortunate. I assure you I had no intention—"

"Of course not, dammit! D'you know Sheepwick?"

Swale-Reid smiled wanly. "Yes, rather well in fact. I was born there."

"The devil you were!"

"My eldest sister still lives in the parish. A delightful spot, idyllic. You know it well?"

"Never heard of it until yesterday." Then eagerly: "Good God, Swale-Reid, tell me this, d'you know Mrs. Bateman-Faulks?"

"Ah, dear me, yes—I've *heard* of her. She lives at the Manor there, Cranwood Manor. But, of course, Agatha would know her well. Poor soul! An incurable invalid. Totally bedridden, and still quite a young and attractive woman. Er—Mrs. Bateman-Faulks, I mean."

"Her husband's still living, eh?"

"Yes—er—I think so; but really, you see, I haven't visited Sheepwick for these last seven years or so. Agatha would know. Agatha knows everybody in the parish and everything about them. So alert for her years."

"Damn it then!" thought Boddy. "Agatha's the lass for me!"

What a curious coincidence, and yet how typical of life. Life had always been able to serve up more tasty coincidences than fiction, and here was a perfect one, piping hot, handed to him on a plate.

"Look here, Rector; could I have your sister's address? May be running up to Gloucestershire for a few days. Like to have one or two introductions. Always wanted to meet this Mrs. Bateman-Faulks."

"Of course, Major. By all means!"

The Rector wrote out the address. Boddy felt that Fate was standing behind his shoulder, whispering to him just how the cards should be played.

The next morning he and Gammon left in the car for Sheepwick. He promised to return within a week, because at the end of that time he was due to act as best man at the Preece-Hawkinge nuptials. Syd had already taken his morning-suit out of the oak-chest, unwrapped the tissue-paper and shaken out the camphor-balls. Murders and marriages! Life was something more than "a chequer-board of nights and days"!

CHAPTER XVI

The Bateman-Faulks

I

MAJOR BODDY BASED HIS OPERATIONS FOR THIS NEXT PHASE OF the attack on the Bowman's Arms, a mellow, lichenous, beautifully proportioned tavern in Cotswold stone, standing on the edge of the Sheepwick village green. From the moment he turned off the Cirencester road and coasted down into this sunlit valley, he knew that he had happened on one of those perfect corners of England, where the vulgar sneer about the lack of drains, and the æsthetic revel in the untouched beauty of a rural paradise. Every house and cottage in the village was a gem of quiet architecture, restful as the green and wooded wolds that held these gems in a velvet casket. Enormous fuchsia trees cascaded in the little garden before the inn, and his bedroom window was framed in a gnarled vine of wistaria. From this window, a practical vantage-point, he looked straight across to the burnished window-panes of Little Wells, the home of Miss Agatha Swale-Reid.

Major Boddy wasted no time. On the evening of his arrival he walked across the green and introduced himself to a small, stout, husky-voiced woman of dynamic energy. Agatha was the antithesis of her brother. Where the Rector was all tortured introspection, she evinced nothing but an unbounded optimism, an unabashed curiosity concerning her fellow-creatures. Her sitting-room was a reflection of her popularity, for it was crammed with all that useless bric-à-brac which silts up round a charitable and charming spinster. There was even a blear-eyed parrot in a cage and a pair of assagais crossed above the open fireplace.

"Very glad Peter had the good sense to mention me. So nice to see fresh faces. This is Clarence, a most intelligent bird. Make your bow,

Clarence, and say 'How-d'you-do'. There, there, isn't he clever? No, my brother, Major Boddy, doesn't really approve of me. He thinks I'm too flippant for a woman of sixty. That, to my mind, is the ideal age for ceasing to take life seriously. You're staying long?"

"A few days only. Unavoidable. Otherwise—" The Major implied a compliment to the charms of Sheepwick and gave a stiff little bow, a gesture which Clarence was swift to emulate. "I'm staying just across the green—er—at the Bowman's Arms."

"How convenient."

"Quite." Boddy was not sure how this remark was to be interpreted. "I'm really here on business. Some property I'm anxious to acquire in West Sussex. I discovered that it was owned by Mrs. Bateman-Faulks. The Rector imagined you knew her well. Thought perhaps you might be kind enough—"

"Nobody, Major Boddy, knows Kitty Faulks *well*," said Agatha flatly. "Oh, do look how Clarence is cocking an eye at you! The rascal! Kitty's been a recluse ever since she bought Cranwood Manor. I do visit her occasionally, but only for the briefest chats. It's her heart, poor child. Too much excitement is bad for her. I have to exercise the greatest restraint. And such a beautiful creature, like an angel—ethereal—"

"And her husband?"

"The strangest mortal. Not quite balanced, I feel. No! No! Clarence, we've no time to admire your pretty tricks now! He really is delicious, don't you think? Clarence, I mean. He's a peculiarly silent man. I'm referring now, of course, to Mr. Bateman-Faulks. He's a keen ornithologist, Major. He spends a great deal of his time stalking small birds with a very large camera. But wait!" Agatha moved briskly to the window and pulled Boddy unceremoniously after her. "Look! There he goes now! You must admit that he does look rather odd."

Boddy viewed the figure crossing the green with acute interest. Beneath a wide-brimmed black felt hat, he had the impression of a short, rather angular man with bowed shoulders and myopic eyes. He seemed to peer forward through his thick-lensed spectacles as if at every moment anticipating an obstacle in his path. A large camera formed a hump on his back and under one arm, like an umbrella, he portered a photographic tripod. He was dressed in a skintight Norfolk jacket, knee-breeches and stockings, which invested him with a kind of old-fashioned dignity. Although one or two yokels, seated on a bench under the village pump, touched their hats to him, he seemed too preoccupied with his thoughts to return their greeting.

"Eccentric sort of fellah, eh?" observed Boddy. "Much longer in the tooth than his wife, I take it?"

"Oh, yes, much. A most unusual romance. They met in London and were married quietly there before she was moved down to Cranwood Manor in an ambulance. That was about three years ago. His devotion to her is quite unique. We've never quite made up our minds in Sheepwick which of them has the money. I'm always trying to make Mr. Bateman-Faulks—such a mouthful, I feel!—take an active part in parish matters, but he won't. Most charitable in his contributions but—oh, Clarence, do behave yourself!—completely disinterested in his fellow-creatures."

"Umph, kind of you to tell me all. Anticipate a rough passage in getting down to brass-tacks. Don't sound very businesslike, eh? When would be the best time to introduce myself?"

"To-morrow morning, perhaps—*if* you're lucky! Be quiet, Clarence, and don't show off! He does so love showing off in front of visitors, the rascal. You see, he's often out on the wolds the whole day with his camera—Mr. Bateman-Faulks, that is. They say he sits inside a hollow cow for hours on end. It sounds appallingly stuffy, doesn't it? But really, Major, I should go up on the off-chance and then fix an appointment. He'll probably forget it, but persevere. Keep on! You'll get him in the end!"

"Keep on! Keep on!" echoed Clarence with an uncanny chuckle.

Those few casual remarks struck a prophetic note in Boddy's ears. Persevere! Keep on! In the long run, floundering in a net of fine-woven clues, he'd have John Arundel safely landed and ripe for the official gaff. As he walked slowly back across the green to the Bowman's Arms, his head was a whirl of new and startling speculations. He was wildly impatient now for that first visit to Cranwood Manor.

2

The next morning, after an early breakfast, Major Boddy set off on foot. He had decided against using the car, since the landlord of the Arms had assured him that the walk up through the woods to Cranwood was one of the prettiest in the district. Moreover, it was a perfect morning— windless, hazy, the shadows still wet with dew despite the promise of heat to come. For the first half-mile the path climbed out of the valley at a leisured gradient through the cool green shade of beeches, which later gave way to a forest of young spruce and fir. Bees were working in the early heather, a bourdon note to innumerable insect sounds. Then abruptly vegetation ceased and he climbed a stile over a dry-stone wall and found himself on the dead level of the wolds themselves. But of Cranwood Manor, which he had expected to see, once clear of the woods, there was no sign. The path, however, took him across two more big walled fields and then, unexpectedly, right at his feet he saw a roomy square stone mansion.

The Manor, like some secretive beast, crouched in a deep hollow, half-hidden by a cluster of massive pines. It was a dour, gloomy place, with heavy slatted shutters across many of its windows. Most of it lay in shadow, for the sun barely reached down into that dank hollow. On three sides the house was bordered by an unkempt garden, much of it sub-merged beneath a riot of yew and holly and laurel. From the outhouses, ranged behind the house, the paint was peeling and in many places the walls displayed their scars where the damp plaster had flaked away from the lathes. Over the whole place hung a pall of neglect.

Boddy was amazed as he looked down on the slate roofs of this mau-soleum. Agatha had not prepared him for this spectacle of dreariness and decay. For some reason the mansion looked ominous, as if the shadow of tragedy was already athwart the smokeless chimneys. The air which rose from the hollow was chill and sour with the smell of rotting leaves. Even as he made ready to descend the rough-hewn steps that led down into the little valley, he was aware of a white face in an upper window. There was no doubt that the person, whoever it may have been, was peering at him with a kind of watchful intensity.

At close quarters the house looked even more unwelcoming. Grass was sprouting thickly through the gravel of the drive and his footsteps as he approached the porch were unnaturally muffled. It was almost a relief to hear the far-away jangle of the bell breaking the deathly silence that reigned beneath the branches of the pines. After a time he heard the sound of feet shuffling down the hall and the next minute the studded oak door swung inwards to reveal a stolid pug-faced woman of about forty with a pallid complexion and tiny boot-button eyes. Boddy's first reactions were decidedly unfavourable. There was a shifty light in the woman's pupils, mingled with an air that was both hostile and suspicious.

"Ha! good morning," he said with over-emphatic heartiness, inwardly ranking the woman as a housekeeper. "I wanted to see Mr. Bateman-Faulks if convenient. Is he in?"

The woman shook her head. "Nod here. Gone out. I do nod know ven he vill be back. Vot you vish for him, *hein?*"

"German or Austrian," thought Boddy. Aloud he went on: "It's a matter of business. Must see him personally—understand? Can't leave a message."

"*Ach zo!* Business."

"Could I fix an appointment? Say to-morrow morning at ten. Or perhaps Mrs. Faulks—?"

"It is nod possible to see her. She is very ill. She can see zo few peoples. *Verstanden?*"

"Then Mr. Faulks at ten to-morrow? Arrange that, eh? Here's my card."

The woman took the card and glanced at it swiftly. It seemed that visitors were rare at Cranwood Manor.

"I vill tell him. It may be orite."

"I'm staying at the Bowman's Arms," he explained. "If it's convenient perhaps you'll ring me there. Don't want a wasted journey. If I don't hear—ten o'clock then."

As he turned from the door he was surprised to find the woman's hand on his arm.

"Herr Boddy."

"Well?"

"I like to varn you. Herr Faulks—he is very mean. He hate to spend. You vill nod do good business vith him, no? I varn you. This place—you see?—it is not fit for a peeg to live in. And she—ach!—zo very patient, zo very lovely. And he vill pay out noding to make her happy." For a moment the woman's expression softened and Boddy realized at once that all her sympathies were with the invalid wife. The husband she obviously hated. "It is nod right ven there is zo much money to spend. Zo much I vant to tell of this, but there is nod many peoples now vot come to Cranvood."

"But, confound it!" protested Boddy. "I thought Mr. Faulks was devoted to his wife. I hear he's most generous in his contributions to charity. Got the wrong end of the stick, surely?"

"Never, Herr Boddy!" said the woman forcibly. "That is vot he vish the oder folk to believe. But it is nod true! I haf his housekeeper been ever since they come here. For six weeks now he has paid me nodings. Clara and Karl—they too are Austrians—they haf nod been paid. Always Herr Faulks say 'Der-morrow'! Soon ve leave Cranvood. It is only for Frau Faulks that ve stay now. She is zo helpless, poor child!"

"But surely, she has a nurse to—?"

"Nein! Nein! Zomtime the doctor come, of course, but Herr Faulks say that it is nod necessary a nurse to haf." The woman glanced back over her shoulder and suddenly lowered her voice. "Herr Boddy, there is zomething wrong in this house. Ve all haf that feeling. It is Herr Faulks. Ve think he do nod care if poor Frau Faulks die! *Ve believe he vant her to die!*"

"But that's ridiculous!" He was perplexed. The woman's outburst, despite his first judgment of her, seemed genuine. It was the taut and brooding atmosphere of the house that had brought about her shifty expression. What did it portend? Had he trailed in the wake of one puzzle to be bogged in another? Or *was* there some dark link between Cranwood Manor and The Oasts? And then, with a blinding inrush of light, he heard himself saying: "Tell me, Herr Faulks—is he often away from the Manor? For months at a time, perhaps?"

"*Ach zo!* That is true!" cried the woman. "He leave her all alone. But vere he go and vat he go for I do nod know. There is zomething strange about him, Herr Boddy. Zomething strange and cruel. Zome day I think zomething terrible vill at Cranvood happen." Then anxiously: "But please, you vill say noding of all this to him. I am zo afraid. Nod for myself, but for *her*. She is zo innocent that she does nod anything suspect, no? Please, please, Herr Boddy, nod von vord of vot I say to you!"

"No! No! Of course not! Keep it all under the *punkah*—er—Fräulein—er—?"

"Frau Dierfeld. Leni Dierfeld."

"Well, thundering glad you've told me all this. Makes me want to see Mr. Faulks all the more, y'know. When I come to think of it, don't give him my card. Tell him Mr. Jones called to see him—Mr.—er—Jack Jones of—er—Cheltenham. Call to-morrow morning at ten—understand? Can't give my reasons for this alias, Frau Dierfeld. But rest assured, they're damned sound ones!"

After all, if this suspicion were correct he didn't want to forewarn the fellah. For he was convinced now, of what he had suspected from the start, *that Mr. Bateman-Faulks and John Arundel were one and the same man!*

3

Striding back to the Bowman's Arms down through the woods, his thoughts tumbled over each other. So much that had puzzled him went overboard with the adoption of this new theory. He felt competent now to place one finger on Arundel's particular "ramp" and another on the motive for the murder. First and foremost, this fact loomed on the horizon as big as a mountain—if Faulks and Arundel were two manifestations of the same personality, then Faulks-Arundel was a bigamist! He had been definitely married to Lydia, for Boddy, although in India at the time, knew several Beckwood celebrities who had attended the wedding. According to Agatha Swale-Reid he had married this other woman about three years ago. Admittedly this second wedding had been a quiet affair, but this gave even more reason to believe that he had scored a bull's-eye.

What followed? Simply this: for the last three years Arundel (or rather Faulks-Arundel as he must now think of him) had been leading a delicate and difficult double life. With consummate skill and masterly prevarication he had worked a kind of matrimonial shuttle-service between The Oasts and Cranwood Manor. Hence his pose of authorship, which gave him the excuse to leave Lydia for Kitty whenever he felt it was diplomatic to put in an appearance at Sheepwick. Doubtless bird-photography was the smoke-screen behind which he slipped away from Kitty to resume his life with Lydia. The former's inability to move about was of paramount importance to his deceit. Fettered to her bed by an incurable illness, Kitty had no chance of checking-up on her husband's movements.

As for the problem of Deadlands Wood; well, that, thank heaven, was no longer a problem! Within that copse Arundel changed his personality. He entered as the bland, rather dandyish, well-dressed *bon viveur* of Beckwood. He emerged as the eccentric, myopic naturalist of Sheepwick. Inside that corrugated-iron hut he changed his clothes, his facial expression and his car. The differences were subtle rather than marked. Arundel, the ex-actor, had not overplayed the part of Bateman-Faulks with a false beard, blue-tinted spectacles and a limp. He had cleverly disposed of his natural tendency to plumpness by wearing a tight-fitting, outmoded Norfolk jacket and knee-breeches. With this went a slight stoop, which not only sliced an inch or two off his height but suggested the decrepitude of increasing years. The jaunty monocle had given way to the thick-lensed spectacles; the cocky strut to the hesitant stumble. Above all, the loquacious easy charm of John Arundel had been usurped by the foolish, *distrait* mumblings of the bird-lover. It was a nice piece of dual characterization. Not precisely foolproof but highly misleading.

"So far so good," thought Boddy, as he passed through the flickering mosaic of leaf shadows. "But why the devil *two* wives? Dammit, most fellahs make a song about one! As I see it, there *can* only be one explanation. Money, eh? Both wealthy women. Both naturally drew up a will in Arundel's favour. In brief, that was his motive for murdering poor Lydia. If Frau Dierfeld is right, Kitty Faulks is being hounded the same way. Long incurable illness. No nurse. Casual medical attention. Refusal to spend a penny on the upkeep of the estate. One fine morning, confound it, they'll find that unfortunate young lady stiff in her bed. Death from natural causes, eh? Ha!"

He realized that it was high time to rope in Tubby Wilmott, if only to prevent the execution of a second cold-blooded murder at the Manor. After all, he had now collected enough circumstantial evidence to hang John Arundel three times over and, from the Law's point of view, to hang a felon *once* was considered perfectly adequate!

CHAPTER XVII

Tubby Takes the Rap

I

WHEN BODDY ARRIVED BACK AT THE BOWMAN'S ARMS, HE FOUND that Gammon, always anxious to make himself useful, had set off for a neighbouring village to deliver an urgent message for the landlord. The Major was in no way annoyed, for in spite of this new sudden twist in the case he was in no hurry to leave Sheepwick. Moreover, the trudge back through the woods had put an edge on his thirst. Finding a shady corner under an acacia-tree in the neat walled-garden behind the inn, he ordered a pint of shandy and settled down in a hammock-chair with his pipe and his reflections. Before leaving Sheepwick he was anxious, if possible, to set the seal on his Faulks-Arundel supposition. He was puzzled as to how it could best be done. To confront the fellow point-blank would be both stupid and dangerous. Once Arundel realized he was in the vicinity and that his disguise had been penetrated, he would be off like a shot into space. And this time it might be impossible to trace his whereabouts. No, this conclusive proof had to be collected in a more subtle manner, obliquely. But how?

Worrying round this problem he suddenly hit on a possible idea. Snatching out his diary, he first made sure of the date. He was thinking of Jed Willis. Jed and his wife had left for Hastings just a week ago, which meant that they would in all probability be returning to The Oasts that evening. Both Cranwood Manor and The Oasts were on the telephone, so here was a perfect chance to ram home the wad of his suspicions with the rod of proof.

Finishing his shandy, he strolled into the inn and discovered the whereabouts of the telephone. A few seconds later he was through to Frau Dierfeld at the Manor.

"Sorry to pester you again. But this is highly important, Frau Dierfeld. But first, tell me this—your master hasn't returned yet? No? Good! So you can talk to me without interruption. Now please think carefully. Can you recall the dates when Mr. Faulks has left and returned to the Manor during the last twelve months? No! No! Can't expect the *exact* dates, of course. A rough estimate. If you can't do it off your own bat—Eh, what's that? Yes, off your own bat. No—*bat*! B-A-T! Cricket-bat. Oh, confound it! of course you don't tumble to the idiom. Forgetting. If *you* can't remember, Frau Dierfeld, have a talk with the other members of the staff. Lay your heads together. Work it out—*verstanden*? Then ring me at the Bowman's Arms. Ha! that's the ticket! Splendid! Splendid!"

He did not have long to wait. He had just knocked out his pipe, after a stroll or two up the garden, when the 'phone bell rang. Frau Dierfeld's thick voice was rich with triumph. Between them the staff had come to a unanimous conclusion about those dates. They were not precise to a day but it was all that he had hoped for. Before ringing off, he made several careful notes.

Barely had he done so when Gammon's ferrety face, beneath its carroty nimbus of hair, peered out of the public bar. To judge from his lack of breath, he had been running. "Beg to report back to duty, sir. Didn't expect you to return so soon, sir."

"All right, Gammon, stand easy. Shan't want you at all to-day. Probably return to Beckwood to-morrow. In the meantime, better clean the car, eh?"

As the Major moved towards the garden, Syd detained him. "Er—beg pardon, sir."

"Well, Gammon?"

"Something vital to report, sir. Urgent, sir."

Boddy waved a hand toward the acacia-tree and they strolled down the lawn.

"Well, out with it!" snapped Boddy, dropping again into his hammock-chair.

"I've 'ad a bit of a fright, sir. Fair knocked the wind out of me, sir. Just taken a message for the landlord 'ere over to a little place called Windcombe. Good deed for the day, sir."

"You can cut the cackle, Gammon."

"Very good, sir." Syd clicked his heels through force of habit and went on urgently. "Path runs up and down and all over the blooming place, sir. Part of the way it runs through a tidy-sized wood. Lonely sort of place, sir, tucked away neat in the bottom of a valley. Well, sir, it was on my way back to H.Q. when it 'appened. Nearly trod on 'im! A queer sorta cove in a black 'at and breeches, squatting in a clump of bushes with a camera 'eld at the ready, sir."

"Good gad!"

"When 'e saw me 'e jumped up and started creating good and proper, sir. Seemed 'e was taking photos of birds in their natural 'aunts an' accused me of disturbing 'em. Then when 'e was at the top of 'is form, 'e suddenly shuts 'is mouth, gapes at me like I was a ghost and rushes off through the wood as if the devil 'imself were nibblin' at 'is 'eels, sir! Fair gave me the jitters! Looney, of course. Slipped out of 'is padded cell most like. Though where the dooce 'e 'alf-inched that camera—"

The Major uttered a single improper ejaculation, swallowed hard and shot out, "Damn and blast it, Gammon! Of all the thundering bad luck! He knows now that we're in the vicinity. Be on his guard. Beat a strategic retreat. May already be too late."

Syd gaped like a gaffed carp. "But 'oo—?" he began, bewildered.

"Arundel," said Boddy tersely.

Syd's eyes and mouth formed three ever-widening circles.

2

Tortured by indecision, Major Boddy toyed with an excellent lunch, refused coffee and slipped up to his bedroom. There he planted himself squarely on the side of the bed and cupped his face in his hands. What now? Should he and Gammon storm the citadel direct? How? Under what authority could they act? The police alone could apprehend the man on a murder charge, and even for that a warrant for arrest was vital. He could, of course, place all the details of his long investigation in the hands of the local constable, but that seemed to Boddy as sensible as placing a Sèvres vase between the pads of an elephant. Arundel was smart, intelligent and cunning as a weasel. The Sheepwick constable would be left standing, if it came to a battle of wits. As for a direct assault on Cranwood Manor, it was out of the question. Arundel might well anticipate such a move and the moment either he or Gammon showed up, the bird would spread its wings and migrate. No, there was only one thing to be done. He must get in touch with Tubby Wilmott and, in the meantime, send Gammon to keep the house under observation. Somehow he did not believe that Arundel would desert the Manor until it was absolutely necessary. After all, he had no idea that he was under suspicion as a murderer. He merely knew that Gammon was in the district and that his second personality was in peril of discovery. Surely his natural instinct would be to return post-haste to Cranwood and once there lie doggo until the danger had passed?

The moment the Major had evolved a scheme he acted upon it. Five minutes later Gammon was on his way up through the woods to the Manor and Boddy was dialling police headquarters at Cobbleden. Here he encountered an unexpected set-back. Wilmott was out and was not expected to return to his office until five that evening. The sergeant on duty had no idea where he had gone, but he assured Boddy that the Chief would be at his desk for at least an hour before returning to his home. A further call to his private address produced a housekeeper but no further information as to Tubby's whereabouts. Boddy realized that he would have to control his impatience and he rang off in a mood of repressed ill-temper.

In the meantime he decided to take a chance on Willis's return from Hastings and ring The Oasts. This time his luck ran more sweetly. It took Boddy some considerable time, however, to break through the crust of Willis's stupidity, but at length the house-boy realized what was wanted of him and, after consultation with his wife, his information came shunting back in jerks over the wire. For the second time the Major took a set of detailed notes and the moment he had hung up he hastened to compare them with those he had jotted down that morning.

It appeared that Arundel had operated the following shuttle service between Cranwood and Beckwood during the past twelve months.

(a) *According to Frau Dierfeld.*

 1. *A. had left Cranwood the previous August and not returned until mid-November.*
 2. *He had left again about a week before Christmas and returned to Cranwood towards the end of January.*
 3. *About the middle of April he had again left the Manor and not returned until a week ago.*

(b) *According to Jed Willis.*

 1. *A. had returned to The Oasts about the third week in August and left sometime in November.*
 2. *He had turned up again a few days before Christmas and stayed at The Oasts about a month.*
 3. *He had shown up again in April and had stayed at The Oasts until after the death of his wife.*

"And that," thought Boddy, "is conclusive! The two lists dovetail absolutely. Confound it! Arundel's dual-personality is no longer a theory. It's a fact. And now I've got to hand over to Tubby. Can't do less, eh? We do all the spadework. He reaps the crop."

3

About four o'clock the Major went up through the woods and made contact with Syd. He was stretched full-length on the lip of the hollow, camouflaged by a few leafy branches from which, unhappily, rose a thin spiral of cigarette-smoke. "Umph! the burning bush," commented the Major sardonically, dropping down beside him. "Anything to report?"

"'E's in the 'ouse, sir. I know that much. Saw 'im standing in one of them front lower windows about 'arf an hour ago. All quiet otherwise, sir. No sign of any of the skivvies or—" he broke off short and added in an excited undertone: "'Ullo! 'Ullo! Wot's all this about, sir?"

The French windows, which gave on to a little iron-railed balcony on the second storey, were suddenly opened and a small procession emerged into the patch of sunlight filtering through the pines. First there came

Frau Dierfeld with a bundle of rugs and cushions, then a maid pushing an invalid-chair in which reclined the unmistakable figure of Kitty Bateman-Faulks. Hovering in the background was her bespectacled "husband". Having arranged the rugs and cushions and made the patient comfortable, Frau Dierfeld and the girl retired. Arundel himself remained for a moment chatting with the invalid. Finally she opened a novel and began to read, whilst the man went back into the bedroom, closing the doors behind him. A few seconds later, for some incomprehensible reason, the curtains of the room were stealthily drawn and silence once more took possession of the hollow.

"Getting a whiff o' fresh air and sunshine, sir," commented Syd. "Poor girl looks like a ghost, don't she, sir?"

Boddy inclined his head but made no answer. There was something pathetic and defenceless about the still figure in the chair which roused the sentimentalist in him. He recalled Frau Dierfeld's ominous remarks and, despite the heat, he shivered. Presently he scrambled cautiously to his feet, keeping the low thorn bushes between himself and the girl on the balcony. "Better hang on here a bit longer, Gammon. If you notice anything unusual nip down and report to me at the inn. I'll be out here again later. Hope to have the Chief Constable with me. Dammit! I nearly forgot—this haversack. The landlord's put up some rations for you. And, Gammon."

"Yessir?"

"Not too heavy on the rum issue. Understand?"

4

Punctually at five o'clock Major Boddy rang police H.Q. at Cobbleden. No—the Chief had not yet shown up. Would the Major leave his number, then the Chief could ring back the moment he came into his office?

In the interim, racked with impatience, he ran over his collected and collated notes of the case. Later he made contact again with Gammon, but there was little to report. The invalid had remained on the balcony for about an hour and then Arundel himself had come out and wheeled her back into the bedroom. Beyond that there had been no further activity in the vicinity of the mansion.

And then, just before six, when he had almost abandoned hope, the potman came into the lounge-bar and told him he was wanted on the 'phone. The next minute Tubby's cheerful husky voice was seeping over the wires. The Major saved his breath to cool his porridge. In a few succinct sentences he had outlined the situation.

"In my opinion, must drive over to Sheepwick at the double. Can't explain everything now. Point is this, Tubby, he's in the Manor at the moment but we've no guarantee he'll *stay* there. Undoubtedly jumpy. That contact with Gammon was damned unfortunate. I suggest we go into conference to-night—we can fix you up at the Bowman's Arms—and arrange for his arrest early to-morrow morning."

Tubby's throaty chuckle held a hint of mockery.

"What I love about you amateur sleuths, my dear chap, is your beautiful presumption. It simply doesn't occur to you that all your suspicions may be no more than moonshine! You dig out a few plausible clues and, hey presto! you've got your man in the bag."

"But dammit all—!"

"Oh, I know. You've got the proof all nice and tight corked up in a bottle. Well, Boddy old man, I'll take a chance and come over. But heaven help you if it turns out to be a wild-goose chase!"

"It won't, you damned sceptic."

"And there's another thing, Boddy. I suppose it hasn't occurred to you that I have no jurisdiction in the county of Gloucestershire? Before we dare lift a finger, I'll have to get in touch with Redwing, the C.C. at Gloucester. As luck would have it, we happen to wear the same school tie, and with all due respect to the Western Brothers, it *does* still make a difference. A snobbish form of freemasonry, maybe, but still curiously effective. Now, how the devil do I get to this one-eyed hamlet?"

Boddy, now that he had gained his point, was elated and affable. He felt certain that once he had confronted Tubby with the facts of the case, he would be converted. He saw the landlord, booked an extra bedroom, had a quick snack and took a final stroll up through the woods to see Gammon. Dusk was already falling by the time he arrived at the

Manor and the sombre hollow was heavy with shadows. A few lights glimmered wanly in the house and an owl hooted in the pines. Beyond that the silence seemed even more oppressive, like the strange hush that precedes a thunderstorm. Gammon was no more than a slip of darkness against the ground.

"Well, Gammon, I've persuaded the Chief Constable to come over. He's on his way now. Nothing further to report, eh?"

"No, sir."

"I don't imagine he'll give us the slip during the night, Gammon. But if you're game I suggest we still keep our O.P. mounted. Brought the car rug in case it gets nippy. The C.C. and I will relieve you as soon as we can."

"Very good, sir. If he should make a dash for it, sir?"

"Well, you can't stop him, confound it. But report back at once. We may be able to follow up or intercept."

"Very good, sir."

"Good night, Gammon."

"Good night, sir."

5

It was just after nine-thirty when the Chief Constable's Alvis sports shattered the evening quietness of the village-green. Boddy was dozing on the settee in the Victorian sitting-room, but in a brace of shakes he was wide awake and ushering Wilmott into the hall. A bottle of whisky and some sandwiches stood ready on a tray, and after the exchange of a few pithy remarks, the two men got down to brass-tacks.

"Now first and foremost—" began Tubby in his official voice.

"Read this," broke in the Major, thrusting forward a sheet of closely written foolscap. "It explains everything. Read it and *then* talk." Then gleefully, "I've got you, Tubby! Fair and square this time! You're stymied, my dear fellah. Have to bend a knee, eh? Thundering well apologize."

Tubby took the sheet with ill-grace, threw a sardonic glance at Boddy but said nothing. Then he began to read. And as he read his expression altered. His sixteen stone seemed to grow rigid with ever-increasing interest. His pipe went out and his second whisky and soda remained untouched.

Reasons for suspecting that J.A. murdered his wife.

1. *He had motive. Lydia had drawn up a will in his favour, leaving him a not inconsiderable fortune and a handsome bit of property.*

2. *The garage incident. Only four people had access to the key of The Oasts' garage—Jed Willis and his wife, Lydia and Arundel himself. Willis was the one to investigate the incident. Mrs. W. was fast asleep in her bed. In view of the fact that the soldering job was undoubtedly connected with the crime, Lydia can be crossed off the list. This leaves Arundel. Have proved that he could have slipped into the front of the house and up the front stairs to his bedroom, the moment he saw Willis switch on the light. By the time Willis had raised the alarm, A. was to all intents and purposes asleep in his bed.*

3. *A. was one of the few people who knew that Lydia always locked the studio door when working on a picture. An essential factor in the murder method.*

4. *The Colt automatic and the .45 ammunition belonged to A. In other words, he could easily lay his hands on a lethal weapon.*

5. *Have proved that on the night of the murder he could have got out of the bathroom window, run down the garden, committed the crime and climbed back into the bathroom. This supposition fits in with the time-factor.*

6. *To prevent his silhouette from being seen outside the house, he would naturally have to switch off the bathroom light before climbing out of the window. Phœbe Dell remembers seeing the bathroom light go out just before the shot was fired. It came on again a few minutes later.*

7. *Parts of the catapult contraption unearthed in the Studio Meadows had been recently soldered together.*

For the first time Tubby Wilmott looked up and demanded: "Catapult? What the deuce—?"

Boddy smiled. "Ha! Anticipated your perplexity. Got the thing here, Tubby. Brought it along in the boot of the car. Vital piece of evidence at the trial, eh? Well, what d'you make of it?"

"For God's sake, my dear chap, don't look so darned sly. I can't make anything of it. You know that."

"Then I'll explain," said Boddy.

"Thanks. Only take that sadistic edge off your voice." When the explanation was complete, Wilmott's mood had again undergone a transformation. He rapped out, "To catapult the whole automatic into space, you say. But why, Boddy, why?"

"Come to that in due course," was Boddy's smug rejoinder. "I want you to finish reading those notes first. Confound it, Tubby, my first job is to convince you that John Arundel *is* the murderer."

"I'm more than half persuaded already. However—" He returned eagerly to the Major's notes.

8. *Two nights after A.'s departure from Beckwood, he returned to The Oasts with the intention of recovering the catapult which he had buried in the Studio Meadows. Both Gammon and I identified the man as he went through the wicket-gate into the field. This in itself presents the perfect incriminating clue.*

9. *Indirect evidence of Arundel's criminal nature. (a) He claimed to be writing a novel. The MS. does not exist. (b) He's a bigamist. (c) He is masquerading in Sheepwick under the name of Bateman-Faulks.*

As Tubby Wilmott neatly folded up the foolscap and handed it back to Boddy, there was a twinkle in his eye.

"All right, my dear chap. *You* win! I'm the insufferable bonehead this time—no doubt about it. I took too much for granted, Boddy—not enough professional curiosity about the case. I knew nothing, of course, of this dual-personality stunt. You'll have to bring me up to date with that, but on the other count I'm convinced he's guilty." He pointed to the Major's notes. "You've got enough evidence there to sway the toughest jury. I'll stake my reputation, for what it's worth, on *that*!" The Major beamed with pleasure. "Except for one rather important omission, my dear chap." The Major's smile vanished. "You fail in that little document to say *how* he committed the murder. Defending counsel could make the devil of a lot of that point, y'know."

The Major's smile returned. "Couldn't write out a full explanation. Too laborious. But if you must know how he did it, Tubby, I'll tell you."

"It might be as well," said Wilmott dryly.

"Well, it was like this," began the Major. "I knew he must have shot poor Lydia from *outside* the studio, but I'm damned if—"

There was a sudden commotion in the hall. The door of the sitting-room was flung violently open and Syd, breathless and dishevelled, burst into the room.

"Confound it, Gammon!" thundered the Major with a black look. "Confound it all!"

"Beg to report, sir."

"Well, Gammon?"

"He's gone, sir! Driven off 'ell for leather in 'is car, sir. Couldn't stop 'im. But made sure it was 'im, sir, by the light of the front door when 'e came out."

"Next round to friend Arundel," chuckled Tubby with irritating unconcern.

"—!" exclaimed Major Boddy, red about the gills.

CHAPTER XVIII

Conflagration at Cranwood

I

"NOW WHAT?" DEMANDED BODDY.

Through force of habit Tubby had already taken command of the situation.

"First and foremost, d'you know the make and registration number of his car?" Boddy shook his head. "A pity, however, a call to the Manor will soon give us a line on that."

"There's his housekeeper, an Austrian," explained Boddy. "Frau Dierfeld—an ally of ours, Tubby. She'll help."

"Good. Now where the deuce do they hide the 'phone in this one-horse hostelry?"

The Major led Tubby to it and in a few minutes the sleepy, guttural voice of the housekeeper was answering the Chief's questions. The car was a sixteen-horse Brenchley and its registration number was ULD 4419. Tubby made a note. No, Frau Dierfeld had no idea which road her master had taken. She only knew that shortly after nine o'clock, Mrs. Faulks had rung the bell in her bedroom and told her to pack the master's bag as he would be leaving the Manor that night. No reason had been given for this sudden departure, but Frau Dierfeld had overheard him say something about "an old friend in London". Yes, earlier in the evening he *had* received a 'phone call but, of course, she couldn't say if this were connected with his unexpected change of plans. No, Mrs. Faulks seemed to accept his departure without surprise. She was in no wise upset.

"So much for that," said Tubby briskly as he rang off. "It's little enough, I admit, but the probability is that he's taken the direct road

to London. Now, let's take a squint at this map—ah! here we are—
Chippenham, Northleach, Burford, Witney, Oxford, High Wycombe,
London. That seems to be his best route. We've just one slender hope,
Boddy, and only one as I see it. I'll ring county H.Q. at Gloucester and get
them to warn the police in the towns I've named. They can hold him for a
few hours on any damned pretext, that's their pigeon. Then, the moment
we hear he's in the pen, we'll sally forth with the warrant for arrest. The
C.C. at Gloucester can fix that for us. Agreed, Boddy?"

"Umph—yes. Unless his remark about 'an old friend in London' was
deliberately misleading. Might be making for Deadlands Wood."

"Deadlands Wood?" exclaimed Tubby, bewildered.

"Good gad! of course, I haven't told you about that part of our
investigation, Tubby. Put through your 'phone call, and then I'll post
you up to date."

When, some twenty minutes later, Boddy had given his explanation,
Tubby shook his head. "But, heavens above, my dear chap, why revert to
the personality he was using when he actually committed the murder?
Asking for the noose to be slipped round his neck, surely?"

"Not a bit of it," contradicted Boddy flatly. "He hasn't run away from
the Manor because of a possible murder charge. He thinks Gammon may
have recognized him—seen through his disguise. It's the bigamy aspect
of the case that is worrying him at present. He wants to give Sheepwick
a wide berth as long as he knows Gammon's in the vicinity. Sense, eh?"

"You're right, absolutely," agreed Tubby with typical generosity. "And
the chances are that to-morrow morning we shall find him seated quite
comfortably in that little bar of his at The Oasts. If we don't collect him
off the London road to-night then I swear that's the first place to look for
him to-morrow. In the meantime—"

"Bed!" grunted Boddy decisively.

"Oh, no, my dear chap!" Tubby had already lowered his sixteen stone
into an armchair. "For one thing I've got to wait up in case I get a police
call. For another, you were on the point of a great revelation when your
batman interrupted us. I still don't know *how* Arundel shot his wife. Well,
Boddy old man, are you going to satisfy my curiosity, here and now, or
are you going to force me to—?"

"All right," conceded Boddy. "Tell you now, eh? Then listen, my dear fellah—"

2

"—no question of a bullet-hole in walls, window, skylight, ceiling or door. Made exhaustive examinations. Nothing. Confess I was flummoxed, Tubby. Then there was the question, not only of the bullet, but of the automatic. Also had to be introduced into the 'sealed-box' if the murder were to look like suicide. Well, it was Gammon who spotted the chink in the armour. Stout fellah, my batman, Tubby. One in a thousand. Observant. It was he who suddenly realized that we'd overlooked the only possible answer to the problem. A breach, not only big enough to allow the passage of a bullet, but of that damned pistol. Quite simple, Tubby. That, confound it, was doubtless what commended it to Arundel. You see, *we'd completely overlooked the slow-combustion stove!*"

"But how the deuce—"

"Coming to that!" went on Boddy impatiently. "You know the usual type of stove? Burns coke. There's a flap at the top which lets down, so that you can shovel the stuff in. Well, when the murder was committed *that flap was hanging down!*"

"But even then, my dear chap—"

"All in good time, Tubby, all in good time! I'll deal with this side of the stove first. On the night of the murder the stove, of course, wasn't lit. Arundel had obviously been into the studio beforehand and opened this flap. Lydia, bless her heart, didn't notice it. She wouldn't. A naturally untidy woman, Tubby. After Arundel had broken into the studio with Mrs. Willis, he quietly closed this flap without the housekeeper noticing. Obvious, eh? That's just why *we* overlooked the damn thing."

"But look here, Boddy, I still don't—"

"I know just what's puzzling you. How was the breach effected *outside* the studio? Again it was all thundering simple. Lot of unpleasant fumes with coke. These have to be carried away. Admit that? Well, in this case there was an ordinary right-angled flue-pipe. One short arm went through an aperture in the studio wall. One tall arm ran parallel with the wall outside to just above the eaves."

"But, good heavens, I *still* don't—" broke out Tubby, exasperated.

"Steady there! Stand easy, my dear fellah! Now I come to the factor on which the whole idea pivoted. Just at the right-angled joint in the flue-pipe there's a small metal plate. It's screwed into position with two wing-nuts. Idea is this, Tubby—the flue-pipe, like any ordinary chimney, sometimes needs sweeping. To do this, the metal plate is removed, so that the sweep can push his brush either along the short arm or up the long one. But this is the vital point—when the flap of the stove is down and the metal plate detached outside, *one can see straight into the studio!* A clear view through an aperture of at least four inches diameter. Well, Tubby, there's the solution of the mystery. Arundel quietly removed the outside plate, took careful aim and fired. He then fitted the automatic and the spent cartridge-case into the groove of his fancy catapult and pushed the contraption through the short arm of the flue-pipe. Essential this. If he'd tried to project the Colt into the studio from the outside, it might have fetched up in the stove itself. Hit the inside, perhaps, and dropped down. But his method was foolproof. He didn't release the trigger of his catapult affair until the Colt was fair and square in the flap opening. Confound it, Tubby, he left nothing to chance! But for one or two lucky inspirations we should still be in a fog. But mark you—Gammon really discovered the rift in the lute. All the kudos belongs to him. Smart fellah, Gammon. Like most old soldiers he's observant. Like *his* part in the affair to be stressed in the official report, Tubby. Please him a lot that would. Grand fellah, Gammon!"

3

Tubby's vast face split into a yawn, which he smothered with a ham-like hand, and he glanced at his watch. It was nearly three o'clock. For the last four hours, heedless of time, they had been discussing every aspect of the case. The whisky bottle was empty, and their heads, under the stress of profound discussion, were going the same way. Wilmott came up out of his chair like a leviathan from the deep.

"No point in waiting up longer for that call," he grunted. "If they'd pulled him in we should have heard by now. He's probably tucked up at the Savoy and snoring his contempt or fast asleep in his bed at The Oasts. Better turn out these lights, eh, Boddy?"

The Major did so, and Wilmott, crossing to the big window, idly drew back the curtains to see what sort of a night it was. At once his voice, bereft of its former drowsiness, broke out of the darkness. "I say, Boddy, come here quickly, will you? What the deuce d'you make out of that?"

"Good God," breathed Boddy, after a brief survey. "There's trouble abroad for somebody!"

The Major was right. Hanging above the roof of Little Wells on the far side of the green, but obviously some distance off, was a sullen and lurid glow of light. The night sky had clouded over and it was the underside of this cloud-bank that trapped and magnified the red and leaping glare. Even as they stared through the window, the glare brightened and a flurry of sparks whirled up into the darkness. Somewhere up the village street, a bell began to clang, monotonous yet urgent, and the next minute they heard a violent thumping in the room above. As Wilmott and the Major stood in the hall, hustling into their coats, Willie Hogg, the landlord, came clattering down the stairs buttoning his braces.

"See the fire, sir? Can't stop now as I'm a member of the Sheepwick brigade, but to my way o' thinking it's the Manor, sir—Cranwood Manor! Flames have got a tidy hold on the place by the looks of it."

Pulling on his jacket, he rushed into the street.

"Know the way, Boddy?" The Major nodded. "Then come on! It may only be coincidence, but this *may* have some connection with Arundel's hasty departure. Hullo, here's your batman!"

"Beg to report, sir—"

"All right, confound you, Gammon! We're not blind. Better get dressed and come with us, eh? May be able to help."

4

The scene at the fire was phantasmagoric. The little hollow was like a bowl of liquid fire that seethed and boiled, a sheet of light against which pigmy figures were toiling heroically with bucket and hose. The village fire-engine was already in action, for above the roar and crackle of the flames, they heard the steady thud of its pump.

"Steps here," said Boddy.

The three men went down into the inferno, shielding their faces with their hands. As luck would have it the fire seemed to have started in a front room on the second storey, the very room, in fact, from which Mrs. Faulks had been wheeled in her invalid-chair. The light wind, blowing from behind the house, naturally drew the flames away and it seemed possible that at least three-quarters of the building might be saved. From a side door a long string of locals were handing out an endless chain of furniture and effects.

"That's where we can help," said Tubby. "We're none of us furniture removers, I admit, but I dare say we shall learn the gentle art in the hard school of necessity."

"I've got a cousin in Winchester, sir, 'oo's—"

"Ha! Your ubiquitous relations!" snorted Boddy. "Can't dodge 'em, eh, Gammon? Come on now. At the double!" One of the first people Boddy encountered in the crowd round the door was Frau Dierfeld.

"Mrs. Faulks," he snapped. "She's all right, eh?"

The housekeeper nodded. "The doctor gom and lift her into his car, Herr Boddy. He has taken her to his own house. It is zo terrible. It vas in her room that the fire begin. Ve heard her screams. Ve run to her, Karl and Clara and me, and ve carry her out just in time. She has zome burns but noding bad, zo the Herr Doktor tell us. It is just shog and her heart is nod good. *Ach Himmel!* something is nod right about all this. Did I nod tell you, Herr Boddy, that he *vant* her to die?"

Was there anything in it? he wondered. Yet how could Arundel be held responsible for this job? He had left the Manor just after ten o'clock and the fire had not broken out until nearly three. Five hours! Gad! it was too fanciful. Didn't hold water. Yet—had Arundel sneaked back in the small hours and set fire to his wife's room with the deliberate intention of murdering her? Once again there was motive. For the second time he would be the main beneficiary in the will of a wealthy woman. And wasn't it for this very reason that he'd married Kitty Bateman-Faulks?

All these thoughts were streaming through Boddy's mind as he worked like a beaver, with a score of others, to salvage the rooms immediately threatened by the blaze. The Sheepwick brigade had now been joined by two neighbouring ones and the core of the fire was already under control. About half-past five a portion of the roof caved in and a spiral of sparks, flame and steam shot into the sky. Gradually the air in the hollow cooled, the roar and crackle died away and only a few isolated flickers of light stabbed out of the debris. The unkempt lawns in the encroaching dawnlight seemed ready set for an *alfresco* jumble sale. The smell of charred wood was pungent in the nostrils.

Wilmott and the Major looked at each other's wan and grimy faces and were struck simultaneously by the incongruity of this diversion.

"You *would* let me in for this," chuckled Tubby as he lit a cigarette from a piece of smouldering wood. "I've lost a couple of stone, at least, but I think we're justified in calling it a day now, my dear chap. Can't do much more here by the look of it. And don't forget, we're booked for an immediate run to Beckwood. I still think we shall find our man knocking back a b-and-s in that little bar of his!"

5

But the Chief Constable was a trifle too optimistic. They did certainly find *somebody* in The Littel Bottel, but it wasn't John Arundel. It was Jed Willis and his wife, sitting comfortably at the bar over a bottle of Guinness. On seeing the Major, Jed slipped clumsily off his stool, stuffed the morning paper into his jacket, and stood there grinning sheepishly. Mrs. Willis, with far greater dignity, remained where she was, obstinately finishing her glass of stout.

"Well, well, Willis. What the devil does this mean?"

"The missus an' Oi, surr, be cleanin' up the bar."

"It looks like it," commented Tubby. "Mr. Arundel's not here, I take it?"

Willis shook his head. "'E went off early this marnin' in 'is car. To Lunnon, Oi reckon."

"Then he *has* been here?" broke in Boddy eagerly.

"Aye, surr. 'E come back late last night, 'e did—about midnight it were—'ad breakfast an' was on 'is way by nine. Rang last evening to say 'e was a-turnin' up unexpected."

"Sure he didn't slip away from the house in his car during the night, Willis?"

"No, Major. 'E couldn't 'ave done that without wakin' me an' the missus. Our bedroom, same as you recall, surr, is just opposite the garridge."

"Quite. Well, I don't approve of this behaviour, Willis. In a position of trust here. Not happy about finding you and Mrs. Willis in this room, y'know. Reprehensible. All right, that's all for the moment. Better finish the bottle. Go off otherwise." No sooner had the discomfited couple retired, than Boddy turned briskly on Wilmott. "So he *was* here, Tubby. Couldn't have been responsible for that other job. And yet—?"

"Exactly, my dear chap, you're as loath as I am to accept the fact that he *didn't* do it. Er—by the way, what's it going to be? He owes us this much, Boddy!"

"Whisky and soda, thanks."

"Good!" While pouring the drinks, Tubby went on: "Why don't we want to accept the fact? Because the whole affair was characteristic of his cold-blooded cunning. We both know that he had a great deal to gain by Mrs. Faulks's death and the Cranwood housekeeper felt certain that things were not all they appeared to be at the Manor. His sudden departure *was* fishy. Well, here's my theory for what it's worth. Arundel had planned this trap some time before and was only awaiting the perfect opportunity to spring it. Unfortunately he ran into Gammon and, thinking he might have been recognized, he got the wind up. He may even have suspected that Gammon's presence in Sheepwick was not entirely a coincidence. That where Gammon was, there was Major Boddy also, eh? At any rate, he had to push forward the date of his conspiracy to do away with his wife. Hence his sudden flit. The main problem still remains, however.

How could he have started that fire in Sheepwick when he was fast asleep in his bed at Beckwood?"

"I suppose—mind you this may be thundering silly—but I suppose it couldn't have been a delayed-action job? Sort of infernal machine. Set it like an alarm-clock and at the right moment the thing blows up and sets the place on fire."

"That's not so bad," admitted Tubby. "The only difficulty I see is this. That sort of gadget is usually worked by clockwork, and like a clock it has a tick. Since the fire started in Mrs. Faulks's bedroom, it suggests that it was there he placed your infernal machine. No wind to speak of last night, was there? Well, surely Mrs. Faulks would have heard the damned thing ticking?"

"Umph—there is that. Then, confound it, Tubby—how?"

"I can't say at the moment, my dear chap, but that fire reeks so powerfully of malice aforethought that I'm determined to find out. Even if it means returning to Sheepwick. We can cross-examine that housekeeper again and Mrs. Faulks herself. We might even have a rake round in the ashes for some sort of clue."

"And Arundel?"

Tubby shrugged his massive shoulders. "God knows! Willis thought he was making for London, but that was probably a blind. But here's my idea for consideration. Suppose we broadcast the news that Kitty Faulks has died. I don't mean over the radio but through the press. I can easily square the C.C. at Gloucester over this somewhat unethical suggestion. Arundel will, of course, see the news in the papers and, quite unsuspecting, turn up as Bateman-Faulks to clean up on the young lady's fortune. We can warn his solicitors to expect him. We mustn't lose sight of the fact, Boddy, that he knows nothing of your very—ahem!—admirable investigations, or your subsequent discoveries in Sheepwick. I feel, like you, that we can't just leave this Cranwood affair hanging in midair. It wants clearing up. I admit we could arrest him on a murder charge this very minute, *if* we could lay our hands on him, but to prove attempted murder as well would considerably strengthen our case in court. I say let's get back to Sheepwick—not to-morrow, but now, this very instant."

"But what if he clears out of the country?"

"He won't, not as long as he thinks he can collect that inheritance. In any case, a full description of him, his alias included, will go in to-morrow's issue of *Police Orders*. He'll have every member of the force on his tail. The moment they've run him to ground, they can shadow him in case he gets suspicious, as you suggest, and attempts a Channel crossing. We'll have the ports watched, too, and if in the meantime the police *can't* find him, then we'll simply walk into his solicitor's office and nab him there. In my opinion, we've got him either way."

"Just one suggestion, Tubby?"

"Well?"

"His forwarding address in Ilford. Just a chance he told Willis the truth. He may have gone straight from here to Laburnum Crescent this morning. That Mrs. Peterson—the old lady I was telling you about last night—I swear she knows more than is good for her, Tubby. We might drive to Sheepwick via London, eh? Look in at the greengrocer's. See if we can learn anything. Agree?"

"Right," said Tubby, finishing his drink at a gulp. "I'll ring H.Q. at Cobbleden first and see about having his description included in *Police Orders*. At the moment we can assume he's moving around as John Arundel—we might pick up his photo in the house, by the way—but I'll let them know all about his second personality. After that—onward to Ilford, my dear chap! And good luck to us!"

CHAPTER XIX

Chemical Climax

I

MRS. TRUSSCOTT EYED THE TWO MEN WITH UNDISGUISED SUSPICION as they marched into the shop. She had a feeling that their presence boded no good to *her*. Without haste she finished serving a couple of customers, wiped out the brass scoop of the scales with the tail of her apron and waited.

"Mrs. Trusscott?" inquired Tubby.

"That's me."

"Is old Mrs. Peterson in?"

"No, she ain't."

"When do you expect her back?"

"Carn't say."

"I see. Do you think we could go up and wait in her room?"

"No, I don't. 'Tain't 'er room no more, see? She's gorn. Leff the 'ouse."

"Good heavens!" broke in Boddy. "When?"

"Friends of 'ers?" demanded Mrs. Trusscott with a hostile eye.

"Yes, in a way," said Tubby easily. "When *did* she leave?"

"Well, if yer must know she leff this morning sudden like. Packed 'er things an' cleared aht soon arter eleven."

"Paid her rent?"

"She wouldn't 'ave got aht of 'ere wiv'aht paying it!" said Mrs. Trusscott emphatically. "But I'd like ter know wot business this is of your'n? You ain't busies by any charnce, are yer?"

Tubby nodded dolefully. "That is precisely what we *do* happen to be, Mrs. Trusscott. I'm sorry to confess to the fact, but we're rather anxious to trace the whereabouts of this Mrs. Peterson. I warn you, we have an infallible trick of finding out the truth. Now tell me, *why* did she leave?"

For a moment Mrs. Trusscott wavered, then she sniffed once or twice and said excusingly, "Well, I ain't one ter git mixed up in any monkey-business. Never 'ad no trouble wiv the pleece and I ain't going ter start nah! Truth is, a chap come 'ere in a car this morning an' took 'er an' 'er luggidge away—see? Didn't say as to where 'e was takin' 'er neither, so I carn't 'elp yer there!"

"Ever seen this man before?"

Again Mrs. Trusscott hesitated, then she nodded. "Once or twice 'e come 'ere before. Stoutish sorta chap. Wears a glass in 'is eye and speaks all la-di-dah."

"Exactly," broke in Tubby. "And his name's Arundel—John Arundel, eh, Mrs. Trusscott?"

"Blimey! 'ow jer know that?"

"A little bird told me."

"A ruddy *big* bird if you arsks me! But that ain't 'is real name. Assoomed, that is. Oh, well, I may as well be 'ung for a cow as a carf. You see, it were like this. Three years back this chap comes 'ere an' sets up the ole lidy in my best bed-and-sitter. Pays 'er rent reg'lar an' all. Only one thing 'e arsks special of me. 'Mrs. Trusscott,' 'e says, 'if letters come 'ere addressed to John Arundel, you don't know nuffink abaht it—see? The ole lidy will deal wiv 'em an' mum's the word. I'll make it wurf yer while, Mrs. Trusscott,' 'e says. An 'e did, too, to the toone of five pahnds. Mind yer, I don't know nuffink abaht 'is gime an' I don't arsk no questions. But I guess the ole lidy were put in 'ere jest to give 'im a forwardin' address. This much I *did* find aht. 'Is real monniker's Darby—Richard Darby, an' at one time 'e was on the boards. An' that ain't all!"

"Oh?"

"The ole lidy—she's bin married twice, she 'as."

"Well?"

"*She's 'is muvver!*"

2

When Wilmott and the Major left Kate Trusscott about twenty minutes later, they realized that for the second time they had missed their man by a mere couple of hours. There was no doubt that Arundel had driven direct from The Oasts to Laburnum Crescent, picked up his mother and vanished once more into the blue. Doubtless he was anxious to clean up, as it were, as he went along. No. 224 and the old lady were sign-posts pointing to his dual life, and now that this forwarding address was no longer a necessity, he was obliterating the clues. In due course he and his mother would probably reappear on the scene, living a blameless life on the proceeds of his two notorious inheritances. Faulks-Arundel, if otherwise without virtue, had flawless foresight!

"What next?" demanded Boddy, as they cleared the last suburbs on their way back to Sheepwick.

"Well," said Tubby. "First and foremost we've got to see Mrs. Faulks's doctor and arrange for him to keep her out of sight until Arundel walks into our trap. He's probably got her into a private nursing home by now, in which case it should be easy to put out the news of her 'death'. Then we must get hold of her solicitor and explain matters to him. He'll have to keep Arundel occupied with legal business until the police can get there to make the arrest. There's quite a bit to be done in Sheepwick itself, only I can't possibly stay away long from my desk at Cobbleden. I've 'phoned Redwing, the Chief at Gloucester, and told him that he can get in touch with us at the Bowman's Arms. He's in full accord, thank heaven, with my suggestion that Kitty Faulks should have a convenient relapse! The idea rather tickled his distorted sense of humour."

In point of fact, on arriving at Sheepwick about four o'clock, it was to find Redwing having tea in the garden at the Bowman's Arms. He was accompanied by an efficient-looking man, whom Boddy rightly suspected to be a policeman in plain clothes.

After Wilmott had introduced the Major, Redwing said, "And this is Inspector Jolly. He's accredited to your command, Wilmott, for as long as you need him. By the way, Mrs. Faulks seems none the worse for her ordeal. I've been in touch with Doctor Lester and he's placed her in the Highlands Private Nursing Home near Cirencester. I took the liberty of acquainting him with your idea and he's quite ready to work in with us. I think he's already squared the matron and staff at the nursing home. So, with any luck, the local press can get going to-morrow. We've got *them* in our pocket, thank heaven!"

"And her solicitor?"

"Yes, I've managed to find out about that. Cole and Cole, a reputable and well-known firm in Cheltenham. The Inspector here will give you the address and 'phone number. I'll leave that part of the affair to you, eh, Wilmott? Now tell me. How much more have you found out about Arundel's movements?"

Tubby explained fully what had taken place at Ilford and went on, "Both the Major and I feel convinced he fired the Manor, but we can't quite see how he did it. The trouble is, I daren't stay away from my desk a moment longer than is absolutely vital, particularly as this happens to be off my own beat. But I really don't see why Major Boddy and the Inspector couldn't take over here and keep us posted as to their progress. What do you say, Boddy?"

"If Redwing agrees."

"Of course. Jolly's presence will give you an official status."

"That's settled then," said Tubby, rising. "But before I get back to Sussex I'll drop in on Cole and Cole and explain exactly what we need of them. I'll make the run back *via* Cheltenham. It's not much off my route. I don't know how you're going to get along without a car, Boddy. What about ringing your man at Ladysmith and getting him to drive over at once?"

"Sensible. In the meantime, suppose the Inspector and I get a full statement from Frau Dierfeld? The landlord probably knows where she is. Then we'll visit Cranwood. Still hope to pick up a clue there, y'know."

After a little desultory chatter about various aspects of the case, the party broke up. Redwing returned to Gloucester. Wilmott set off to see the solicitors in Cheltenham and Boddy went through to 'phone Gammon and question the landlord about the housekeeper's present whereabouts.

3

Frau Dierfeld was still at Cranwood Manor. The domestic quarters at the back of the house were untouched and perfectly habitable. So Boddy and the Inspector took the now familiar path up through the beech woods and a little later arrived at the Manor. The housekeeper showed no astonishment at the Major's reappearance.

"I thought you vould gom back," she said. "I vant to help you to find out the truth, Herr Boddy. Please to ask all you vish."

Her statement was not only clear but extremely interesting. After Mrs. Faulks had been wheeled out on to the balcony, Herr Faulks had dismissed the servants and himself remained in the bedroom. About half an hour later a friend of Mrs. Faulks had rung up to confirm an appointment and Frau Dierfeld had naturally gone upstairs to deliver the message. Thinking the bedroom was by then unoccupied, she had opened the door, intending to walk through and out on to the balcony. To her astonishment she found the curtains drawn across the French windows and the room plunged into a semi-gloom. Herr Faulks was standing by the bedside and appeared to be fiddling with the telephone. On seeing Frau Dierfeld he grew violently angry and wanted to know why she hadn't knocked before entering. The housekeeper apologized, explained about the message and then hastily withdrew. *She noticed that there was a distinct smell of petrol fumes in the bedroom!* Later that evening she mentioned the fact to Herr Faulks. He explained rather shortly that he had been cleaning some photographic stains off a jacket. A little later Mrs. Faulks had rung from the bedroom (to which she had now returned) to say that the master was leaving that evening in the car.

"Well," said Inspector Jolly, as they strolled round to the front of the house from the domestic quarters. "I reckon you couldn't ask for a more incriminating statement. After all, sir, why did he pull those curtains unless he wanted to conceal his activities in the bedroom from Mrs. Faulks out on the balcony? As you were explaining, she couldn't see behind her propped up in that wheel-chair, but our man wasn't taking any chances! Petrol, too. That cries to heaven, eh, sir?"

"Quite, Inspector. Wonder what he was doing near that telephone?"

"Putting through a call on the sly, perhaps."

"Maybe. Maybe. Well, here we are. Pretty tidy blaze while it lasted, Inspector. See that for yourself. How about having a dig around in the debris?"

Five minutes later, from under a mass of charred beams and half-burnt furniture, they unearthed an object which at first glance did nothing to rouse their interest. It was in fact nothing more than an ordinary biscuit-tin, such as may be seen by the dozen in any grocer's shop. Admittedly the labels had been burnt off and the tin itself blackened by the fire, but otherwise it appeared to be perfectly innocuous. It was not until the Inspector picked it up that their attention was arrested. About two inches below the rim, a square of metal, obviously cut from the lid, had been carefully soldered to the sides of the tin. In this manner the whole of the lower part of the tin had at one time been sealed off. Now, however, an irregular-shaped hole seemed to have been eaten through this metal "shelf", whether due to the heat of the fire it was impossible to say, but large enough for a hand to be pushed through it. In the bottom of the tin, Inspector Jolly found more to puzzle him, a handful or two of broken glass and china, an ordinary brick, and a length of thin wire terminating in a small loop.

"Well, sir, what on earth do you think we've got here? Does it *mean* anything?"

"Can't say, Inspector. Certainly looks damned suspicious. Worth investigating, eh?"

The Inspector nodded and selecting a few bits of the broken glass, examined them closely on the palm of his hand. "May be I'm wrong, sir, but these look uncommonly like pieces of a broken test-tube."

"Really?"

"I tell you what I'm going to do, sir. There's a fellow called Stockton down at our police laboratory at H.Q. He's a wizard at creating order out of chaos. I reckon he could stick these bits and pieces together, make something of them and give us a definite line on the whole business. We'll wrap the thing up and send it down to Gloucester on the next Sheepwick bus. I'll ring Stockton from the Arms and let him know what it's all about."

"Good. And in the meantime?"

"What about interviewing Mrs. Faulks, sir? We've got to get her statement sometime; why not this evening?"

4

Syd Gammon, on receiving the Major's call at four o'clock, had driven all out for Sheepwick. He had made the journey in record time and, after a hasty meal, was ready to drive the others over to the Highlands Nursing Home. They arrived there shortly before eight-thirty and, after Boddy had explained to the matron, he and Inspector Jolly were ushered into the patient's private room. Kitty Faulks, more frail and ethereal than ever, was sitting in bed propped up by a pile of pillows. She listened patiently to the Major's quiet review of events, in which he stressed the police's suspicions that this was a case of arson, but carefully omitted to state upon whom these suspicions fell. Time enough for her to learn of her husband's duplicity when she had fully recovered from the shock of the fire itself.

"Now there are just one or two points we'd like to clear up, eh, Inspector? First point is this, Mrs. Faulks; did you notice a smell of petrol in the room that afternoon?"

"Yes—I did."

"When did you first notice it?"

"When I was wheeled in from the balcony."

"Hadn't noticed it before then, eh?"

"No."

"Did you mention the matter to—er—Mr. Faulks?"

"Oh, of course. He explained that he'd been cleaning some stains off a coat of his. So very like him to do it in my bedroom, Major Boddy."

"You were asleep when the fire started?"

She nodded. "And suddenly I was aware of smoke and flame. I woke up coughing. The room seemed dazzling with light. I cried out for help and—" She shuddered. "Please forgive me, but I still feel so weak and shaken by it all. I can't, can't imagine how it happened at that time of the morning when we were all fast asleep!"

"Where do you think the fire really started?" put in Jolly.

"That's the curious thing, Inspector, it's all such a nightmare, so confused in my mind, but I could have sworn that the flames were coming from the little cupboard beside my bed. That's how I managed to save myself in the first place. I rolled on to the floor on the far side of the bed and—"

"What do you keep in that cupboard?" broke in the Inspector. "Anything inflammable, Mrs. Faulks?"

"No, not exactly. It was full of illustrated weeklies and old newspapers. I use the cupboard really as a bedside table. The telephone stands on it. But it's strange you should ask about this."

"Why?"

"Because on the night of the fire we found the cupboard doors locked."

"Locked!" exclaimed Boddy.

"Yes. When Frau Dierfeld came to make me comfortable for the night about eleven o'clock, she found all the magazines and papers pushed into the bottom of my wardrobe. I told her to put them back at once in the cupboard. That's how we discovered it was locked."

"And the key?"

"It was missing. We imagined that my husband must have stored away some of his wretched photographic apparatus in it. He's very untidy and absent-minded—he's rather eccentric, you know."

"Did the smell of petrol seem to persist in the room?" asked the Inspector.

"Yes, it was very unpleasant, Inspector."

"You didn't notice by any chance if the fumes came from the cupboard?"

"Now you mention it, perhaps they did. But why do you ask, Inspector?"

"Because if your husband is absent-minded, Mrs. Faulks, he *may* have put the bottle of petrol back in the cupboard when he'd finished cleaning that coat."

"But even then, Inspector."

"Quite. How did the petrol ignite? Why was the cupboard locked? And why had all those papers been placed in the wardrobe? Tell me, Mrs. Faulks, after you'd settled down for the night, did you hear any strange noises in the house or outside in the garden?"

"No, nothing. I lay awake for some time as usual and I must have finally dropped off to sleep about two o'clock. The only interruption was a telephone call about midnight."

"A personal matter, Mrs. Faulks?" asked the Inspector tactfully.

"A wrong number, Inspector. Somebody wanted the West-dene Hospital. We're only one number away from them and people are always ringing up the Manor by mistake. It's rather annoying when it happens at night."

"The telephone is an extension?"

"Yes. Frau Dierfeld switches over direct to my bedroom when she goes to bed about eleven. During the day, of course, the servants deal with the calls downstairs."

The Inspector rose and glanced across at Boddy. "Anything more you wished to ask Mrs. Faulks, sir?"

"Yes, just one question. Did you recognize the voice on the telephone?"

"No, Major. It was a man's voice, rather a queer, high-pitched voice, but it was certainly nobody I knew."

"Thank you." Major Boddy extended a hand. "Most helpful, my dear lady. Thousand apologies for this intrusion. But feel we must get to the root of the mystery. The police are not satisfied that the fire was the result of natural causes. Possibly you feel the same, Mrs. Faulks?"

For a moment she hesitated, then looking straight at the Major, she said slowly, "Yes, I do, Major. Now that I've had time to think about it, and it's terribly disturbing!"

5

As Gammon drove them back to Sheepwick along the high, bleak Roman road, the two men discussed the interview with considerable animation.

"No doubt about it, sir, in my mind. The whole thing narrows down now to that bedside cupboard. If Arundel had fitted up some sort of mechanical fire-raiser, well, it's a penny to the Bank of England that he dumped it in that cupboard. He took the chance offered when Mrs. Faulks was out on the balcony to fit up the whole thing. I swear that biscuit-tin has something to do with it. When the floor collapsed, the cupboard was probably burnt to ashes and the tin fell through with the rest of the debris."

"Remember what stood on that cupboard, Inspector?"

"The telephone, sir."

"Exactly. Remember what Arundel appeared to be fiddling with when Frau Dierfeld broke into the room?"

"The telephone, sir."

"Precisely. At about midnight Mrs. Faulks answered a telephone call. Wrong number, I admit. She didn't even recognize the voice. But did you notice, Inspector, how the *queerness* of the voice impressed itself on her memory? High-pitched, eh? May be poppycock, but I suggest the voice sounded queer because it was *disguised!*"

"Good heavens, sir. Arundel!"

"I rather suspect it, Inspector."

"But why?"

"Just an idea. May be wrong. Hate making a fool of myself, y'know. Shall be better placed to advance my theory when your colleague at the laboratory has formed an opinion about that blasted biscuit-tin!"

And with this Inspector Jolly had to be content.

6

It was shortly after supper at the Bowman's Arms when the Inspector was called to the telephone. Stockton had examined the exhibit and could the Inspector come down at once to H.Q.

"Gammon shall drive us down now," said Boddy, when Jolly had handed on Stockton's request. "Anxious to hear what your expert's got to say."

Stockton, as a matter of fact, had a great deal to say and most of it was highly significant. He sat on his stool, elbows back on the bench, a hawk-eyed young man full of verve and colossal self-assurance.

"Well, Inspector, you've got something here and, as you outlined the facts of the case over the 'phone this afternoon, you've got what you were looking for! You suspect arson, don't you? Well, you're right all along the line. Your broken bits of china and glass made three different objects. Here they are, gentlemen, on the bench—reconstructed.

Exhibit A—an ordinary saucer. Exhibit B—a small test-tube. Exhibit C—a shallow porcelain crucible. By the way, Inspector, you failed to spot the porcelain among the china, but we'll let that pass. The fit-up of the contraption puzzled me a lot at first. Then I had a brain-wave. It struck me that before this bit of mechanism was put in motion, the whole of the lower part of the tin was sealed off tight by this metal sheet. Now the saucer and the brick were found in the bottom section of the tin. They must therefore have been placed in position there before the lower half was sealed up. They couldn't even have been introduced through this hole—it's not large enough. Don't forget the saucer wasn't broken when this affair was set up. Apart from that, I claim that this hole was not made until the explosive process—call it what you will—was put into operation. I'm ready to stake my reputation on this fact, gentlemen—*the tin shelf was eaten through by strong acid!* It was this part of the process which supplied the delayed-action factor essential to your man's alibi. Now this is how I see it. The lower section of the biscuit-tin was charged with petrol, at least to a level just below that of an upended brick. On top of the brick stood the saucer. So much for the lower part of the apparatus. Now *above* the sheet of tin we have to account for the crucible and the test-tube. Well, it's pretty obvious that the test-tube contained the acid. It was, in some way, supported on a pivot just above the tin sheet, so that this wire loop when pulled would tilt the tube and discharge the acid on to the metal. Now this, I confess, is where I fall down. *I can't see what jerked on the loop and tipped up the test-tube.* After all, it was obviously this action that set the whole thing into operation. Have you any ideas, Inspector?"

"None. What about you, Major?"

"I—er—well—perhaps," said Boddy diffidently. "Just an idea, y'know. May be tommy rot. But here's my theory for what it's worth. Remember that telephone-call, Inspector? It was put through about midnight, at a time when Arundel knew the line would be switched through direct to Mrs. Faulks's bedroom. Well, I suggest he deliberately dialled his own number, knowing people often rang the Manor in mistake for the Westdene Hospital. What he said on the 'phone was of no import. The vital thing was to get that call through direct to his wife."

"I'm afraid I don't quite—" began the Inspector, utterly bamfoozled.

"Ha, quite! But think what happens when you take a call. All the telephones in the Sheepwick area are of the old-fashioned upright type, remember. You lift the receiver, eh? Then what? *The receiver-arm jerks upward!* It's not depressed again until one hangs up. Now think where that telephone stood."

"On the top of the bedside cupboard."

"Exactly! *Directly above this infernal bit of sculduggery!*"

"And your suggestion, Major?" put in Stockton, now wildly interested.

"Simply this. Suppose a thread, which you uphold, was joined to that wire loop twisted round the test-tube. A hole could easily be drilled through the top of the cupboard. Fine enough not to be noticed, eh? Same with the thread. Well, confound it, there y'are! Arundel rings up from a point miles away from the Manor. Up jerks the receiver-arm, out pours the acid! And, dammit, the fellah's got his alibi. By the time the fire started he was asleep in his bed at Beckwood. Good God! it *should* have been foolproof."

"You're right!" cried Stockton, full of genuine admiration. "That's how it was done. That supplies the last link in the chain, or should I say, the first? The proof's in the bag, gentlemen."

"Here, not so fast, Stockton," said the Inspector. "How do you mean 'in the bag'? I still don't get the hang of all this. To begin with, what was in that saucer?"

"Water," said Stockton.

"Water!" exclaimed Jolly.

"Yes—plain H_2O. Adam's wine, Inspector."

"And the crucible? Where does that—?"

"Oh, that was placed on the tin sheet directly above the saucer. But in such a position that the acid did not fall on it when the test-tube was tilted by the lever-arm of the telephone. You can see that the sheet has been depressed in the centre so that the acid should collect directly beneath the crucible."

"But, heavens above, man, what the devil was in the crucible?"

"A small lump of sodium under a solution of naphtha."

"Sodium?"

"That's my story anyway," grinned Stockton. "And I'm sticking to it. This way, Inspector. The acid after a few hours eats through that metal shelf. With what result? The shallow crucible drops through into the saucer of water. Well, hang it all, you know what happens when a lump of sodium is dropped into water? Instantaneous combustion! Blue flames, sparks and miniature explosions! A regular firework display! Well, imagine this happening in the near vicinity of about half a gallon of petrol. The result's a foregone conclusion. The whole issue more or less blows up and everything in the neighbourhood catches alight. But look here, Inspector, I rather anticipated a difficulty in explaining the whole devilish process, so I've drawn a sketch of the reconstructed apparatus on the blackboard. Here you are!"

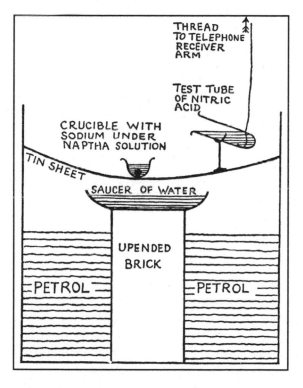

CHAPTER XX

Wedding Group

1

TWO SUBSEQUENT POINTS OF CONFIRMATION WERE OBTAINED TO prove Stockton's really brilliant piece of deduction, though one of these points had more bearing, perhaps, on the Major's part in the affair. The top of the cupboard, badly charred about the edges, was eventually found in the debris. *Through the centre of it a hair-fine hole had been drilled.*

The other "follow-up" was rather more prolonged but none the less convincing. By dint of inquiry the Inspector, keeping in mind Arundel's pose as an amateur photographer, succeeded in running to ground the chemist who supplied his plates and did his developing and printing. It was a well-known firm in Gloucester. Among his latest purchases were a small porcelain crucible, some test-tubes, a bottle of nitric acid and several grammes of sodium. He had made some glib reference to "a little chemical experiment". Until questioned by Inspector Jolly, the chemist had thought no more about the matter.

2

Now that his investigations were over, Boddy moved into a Cheltenham hotel and arranged nearby accommodation for Gammon. He wanted, above all things, to be in at the kill. The local press had already sprung the trap, but two days passed without a sign of the wanted man. Boddy had arranged for Cole and Cole to ring his hotel the moment he showed up. He was growing anxious about the time-factor, for in two days time he was due back in Beckwood as Stanley Hawkinge's best man. Then on the third day the long anticipated call came through. It was Cole himself speaking.

"He's just come into the office, Major Boddy. I've rung the police. My junior partner is keeping him occupied at the moment, but I trust, I sincerely trust they won't leave matters too long. If he suspects anything I fear he may—ah—prove intractable. I shouldn't like anything unseemly to happen on our—ah—premises."

It was strange that, having travelled so far along the road to this ultimate goal, John Arundel alias Bateman-Faulks should cheat Major Boddy of a really dramatic *finis* to his investigations. It all happened so suddenly that Boddy was some minutes before he could fully realize that Arundel had, after all, evaded the hangman's noose. The solicitors' discreet, old-fashioned offices occupied the ground floor of a Georgian building on Promenade. And it was from one of these open windows that a bespectacled figure in Norfolk jacket and knee-breeches suddenly sprang out and, pursued by two athletic young men in plain clothes, dashed madly across the road. It was eleven o'clock. Traffic up and down Promenade was at its height. The driver of the petrol-tanker had no chance to swerve and Arundel, in the chaos of that moment, was blind to its ponderous advance. It was all over in a second. A screech of brakes, topped by the even wilder screech of hysterical female voices, and Justice, lifted clean from the hands of the Law, was well and truly done. John Arundel was dead before Boddy was able to force his way through the ever-thickening crowd.

He might, thought Boddy later, have been granted a few more weeks to live. Lydia, with her dynamic, restless personality, seemed destined to cheat every trick and assault of time, to stalk resplendent into the tranquillity of a ripe old age. And Kitty Faulks, balanced on the rim of darkness, had emerged victorious from a dangerous brush with death and still clung tenaciously to her slender thread of vitality. Death Knows No Calendar. It was an old saying, but like most of the ancient laws it nursed the seeds of truth. Death indeed *had* known no calendar, and there was no gainsaying the fact that the Old Gentleman in Black would never learn to respect the man-made notches in the yard-stick of time. He was hopelessly, defiantly unteachable!

3

"Stanley!" came the high imperative whinny above the babel of excited voices.

"Yes, Auntie."

"Take off your topper and tuck it under your arm. You can't possibly be photographed in that appalling misfit. You look like a coachman. However Honororia came to—" Lady Dingle's eye swivelled on her niece and her shrill neighing broke out anew. "Honororia, my darling child, *do* set your veil straight. You look positively inebriate."

"Tho I am, Auntie Tharah," came the blissful rejoinder. "With happineth."

The bridal couple stood smiling and self-conscious in the church porch, facing a large old-fashioned camera on a tripod, behind which pranced and twittered a small old-fashioned photographer. At his side reared Lady Dingle marshalling her forces into the appropriate wedding-group. Behind this exclusive coterie milled the restless members of *hoi polloi*, clutching in their moist hands small bags of confetti and rolls of coloured streamers. There was a glint in their eyes, as of grenade-throwers in ambush awaiting an unsuspecting enemy. Their turn, they knew, was coming. In the meantime Lady Dingle held the stage.

"Close up a trifle, Milly dearest. You too, Laura darling. No! No! Don't crowd. You'll crush your posies. Oh, Stanley dear, do look a little more intelligent and hold her arm as if you *meant* it! No! No! Tom must go there between you and Hilary. Tom! Tom! Gracious me—where *has* the man got to? Ah, there you are hiding behind Mrs. Carstairs. Come along now, *do*—you're always far too modest. Ah, that's the way. I insist that you keep me a place next to you, Tom dear. I must insist on that! Lower your bouquet a few inches, Honororia darling, it hides the pearls I gave you. Now, now—smile, all you bridesmaids! You too, Stanley! Don't hold your hat like a collection-bag. It looks penurious. Ah! what about you, Rector? No wedding-group is complete without the real Master of Ceremonies. Against your principles? Oh, as you wish! Are we all ready, everybody? Now, how will that do, Mr. Piddington?"

Mr. Piddington glanced wearily at the double rank of grinning, frozen-limbed dummies and said with a little bow: "Delightful, delightful, Lady

Dingle. So natural. I think we shall get a really beautiful exposure with our final plate. If you'd have the kindness now to take your place—I think—yes—yes—"

With the air of a General about to complete his regimental group, Lady Dingle marched up the steps, performed a smart right-about turn and thrust her arm possessively through that of the Major. Then suddenly that weather-beaten, equine face broke into a smile of such alarming toothiness that Mr. Piddington could scarce credit his failing sight. He fluttered a handkerchief, prancing and pivoting behind his infernal machine. Lady Dingle's grip tightened on the Major's arm.

"Tom dear," she whispered, overcome by a sudden incomprehensible emotion. "My *dear* Tom!"

He patted her hand soothingly and faced the camera with soldierly unconcern, his back like a ramrod. "These dratted women," he thought. "Bless 'em!"

A sharp click and the ordeal was over. The dummies came to life. *Hoi polloi* cheered. Bags of confetti burst in the air and the sky was a whirl of coloured rain. With set face and cow-like eye, Stanley jerked his huge frame into motion, proudly conscious of the flimsy wisp of white floating from his arm. From somewhere behind the crowd Syd Gammon broke into a lively rendering of "They Are Jolly Good Fellows", and soon the hallowed air of the churchyard was rich with honest rural friendliness. There were tears in Lady Dingle's eyes as she marched down the path on Major Boddy's arm.

4

It was a curious fact that one year later, almost to the day, Lady Dingle again walked down the churchyard on the arm of Major Boddy. But this time her eyes were not filled with tears but with a quiet and smiling happiness. Her horse-like face, which had once been the despair of Lydia Arundel, had a strange beauty about it. It was a pity Lydia was not there to catch this expression and pin it down for ever in paint. Perhaps a double portrait of Major and Mrs. Tom Boddy on the auspicious occasion of their wedding-day!

ALSO BY JOHN BUDE

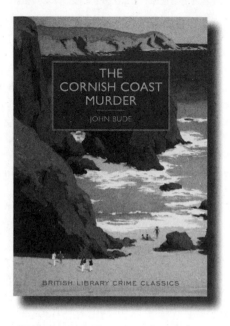

'Never, even in his most optimistic moments, had he visualised a scene of this nature – himself in one arm-chair, a police officer in another, and between them... a mystery.'

. . .

The Reverend Dodd, vicar of the quiet Cornish village of Boscawen, spends his evenings reading detective stories by the fireside – but heaven forbid that the shadow of any real crime should ever fall across his seaside parish. But the vicar's peace is shattered one stormy night when Julius Tregarthan, a secretive and ill-tempered magistrate, is found at his house in Boscawen with a bullet through his head.

This classic mystery novel of the golden age of British crime fiction is set against the vividly described backdrop of a fishing village on Cornwall's Atlantic coast. This British Library edition returns the classic story to print for the first time since the 1930s with an introduction by the award-winning crime writer Martin Edwards.

ALSO BY JOHN BUDE

'Luke flung the light of his torch full onto the face of the immobile figure. Then he had the shock of his life. The man had no face! Where his face should have been was a sort of inhuman, uniform blank!'

.   .   .

When a body is found at an isolated garage, Inspector Meredith is drawn into a complex investigation where every clue leads to another puzzle: was this a suicide, or something more sinister? Why was the dead man planning to flee the country? And how is this connected to the shady business dealings of the garage?

This classic mystery novel is set amidst the stunning scenery of a small village in the Lake District. It is now republished for the first time since the 1930s.

ALSO BY JOHN BUDE

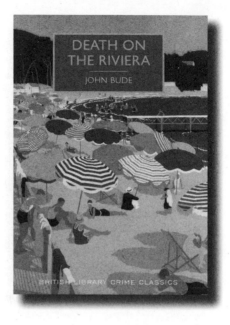

When a counterfeit currency racket comes to light on the French Riviera, Detective Inspector Meredith is sent speeding southwards – out of the London murk to the warmth and glitter of the Mediterranean. Along with Inspector Blampignon – an amiable policeman from Nice – Meredith must trace the whereabouts of Chalky Cobbett, crook and forger.

Soon their interest centres on the Villa Paloma, the residence of Nesta Hedderwick, an eccentric Englishwoman, and her bohemian house guests – among them her niece, an artist, and a playboy. Before long, it becomes evident that more than one of the occupants of the Villa Paloma has something to hide, and the stage is set for murder.

This classic crime novel from 1952 evokes all the sunlit glamour of life on the Riviera, and combines deft plotting with a dash of humour. This is the first edition to have been published in more than sixty years and follows the rediscovery of Bude's long-neglected detective writing by the British Library.

ALSO BY JOHN BUDE

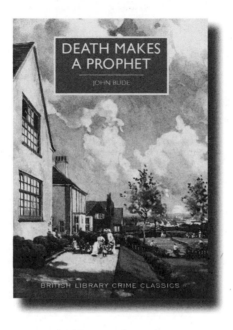

'Small hostilities were growing; vague jealousies were gaining strength; and far off, wasn't there a nebulous hint of approaching tragedy in the air?'

.   .   .

Welworth Garden City in the 1940s is a forward-thinking town where free spirits find a home – vegetarians, socialists, and an array of exotic religious groups. Chief among these are the Children of Osiris, led by the eccentric High Prophet, Eustace K. Mildmann. The cult is a seething hotbed of petty resentment, jealousy and dark secrets – which eventually lead to murder. The stage is set for one of Inspector Meredith's most bizarre and exacting cases.

This witty crime novel by a writer on top form is a neglected classic of British crime fiction.

BRITISH LIBRARY CRIME CLASSICS

ALSO AVAILABLE

Many of our titles are also available in eBook, large print and audio editions